SEER AND
THE SHIELD

Visit us at www.boldstrokesbooks.com

Praise for D. Jackson Leigh

In *Dragon Horse War: The Calling* "Leigh writes with an emotion that she in turn gives to the characters, allowing us insight into their personalities and their very souls. Filled with fantastic imagery and the down-to-earth flaws that are sometimes the characters' greatest strengths, this first Dragon Horse War is a story not to be missed. The writing is flawless, the story, breath-taking."—*Lambda Literary*

"*Call Me Softly* is a thrilling and enthralling novel of love, lies, intrigue, and Southern charm."—*Bibliophilic Book Blog*

"D. Jackson Leigh understands the value of branding, and delivers more of the familiar and welcome story elements that set her novels apart from other authors in the romance genre."—*The Rainbow Reader*

"Her prose is clean, lean, and mean—elegantly descriptive…"
—*Out in Print*

By the Author

Call Me Softly

Touch Me Gently

Hold Me Forever

Riding Passion

Swelter

Cherokee Falls series

Bareback

Longshot

Every Second Counts

Dragon Horse War Trilogy

The Calling

Tracker and the Spy

Seer and the Shield

SEER AND THE SHIELD

by

D. Jackson Leigh

2018

SEER AND THE SHIELD

ISBN 13: 978-1-63555-170-9

This Trade Paperback Original Is Published By
Bold Strokes Books, Inc.
P.O. Box 249
Valley Falls, NY 12185

First Edition: January 2018

Credits
Editor: Shelley Thrasher
Production Design: Stacia Seaman
Cover Illustration by Paige Braddock
Cover Design by Sheri (graphicartist2020@hotmail.com)

Acknowledgments

This trilogy has been a (very hard) labor of love initiated by some unusual dreams about dragons and my personal distress over the deterioration of civil discourse and lack of respect of our fellow humans.

When I decided in 2012 to write the trilogy, the first person I went to for advice was fellow author Jane Fletcher, who is a master at building and writing fantastic worlds. Jane shot a million holes in my initial outline and sent me back to the drawing table. Her advice made this trilogy a million times better.

There are thousands of details when you build your own world, but my wonderful editor, Dr. Shelley Thrasher, has been extremely patient and her sharp eye found every inconsistency. Best of all, Shelley always lets me feel like editing is teamwork rather than a bitter pill the writer has to just swallow. She's one of my she-roes.

A big thanks to my beta readers, VK Powell and Anita Kelly. Vic's honest, expert advice and willingness to read my manuscripts in a very short time to meet my contracted deadline makes Shelley's job easier, I'm sure. Anita's read of this manuscript was invaluable because she hadn't read the first two books and could tell me whether *Seer and the Shield* had enough backstory to make sense if someone reads only the final book of the trilogy.

I also offer sincere thanks to Bold Strokes Books for sticking with my project. Because fantasy has a smaller audience, my romance novels sell better and make more money for them and me than my fantasy titles. This didn't dissuade BSB publisher Len Barot, who stands by her commitment to publish books for the limited LGBTQ audience. The entire Bold Strokes Books team is so supportive of their authors that writing for them truly feels like belonging to a very large family.

The concluding book of the Dragon Horse War Trilogy is dedicated to everyone who stands against racism, sexism, and the me-first, name-calling, divide-to-win mentality of our current society. You are my hope for the future, because we are all different pieces of the same puzzle and stronger when we work together.

The Dragon Horse War

More than a hundred years ago, the great religions became so twisted by human interpretation that a great war pitting Christianity against Islam ultimately wiped all faiths and nationalism from the earth.

Born from that war's ashes was a world government and The Collective thought that valued diversity and championed worldwide sharing of food and educational resources. While some elements of human nature remained unchanged, the people worked in harmony to restore their environment and provide for all. Their minds unshackled from superstitions, the people discovered that some were genetically gifted empaths, telepaths, pyros, and more.

Peace reigned for more than a hundred years until a series of weather disasters threatened the world's food supplies and gave rise to a cult that believed only the strongest should survive and prosper. The Natural Order, led by a madman, grew in number as it preyed on the people's fears to take control of the world's diminished food and medical supplies. In response, an elite army of pyro-gifted warriors mounted on winged dragon horses was activated to hunt and destroy the cult's leaders.

The dragon-horse army's cause is righteous, but even they have lessons to learn from the mantra they defend:

We are stronger together.

Prologue

The transport sped down a long dark road to a remote airstrip and stopped next to a sleek silver jet. After a moment, Xavier stepped out, clutching the empath Nicole against his chest, and pressing his gun against her ribs.

Azar, red dragon eyes pulsing and blue flame spurting from his nostrils, swooped down from the night sky, abruptly landed, and rattled his huge bat-like wings in warning as Apollo, Phyrrhos, Potawatomi, and Bero—more dragon horses of The Guard—touched down behind him. Kyle slid from her perch on Phyrrhos, immediately missing the warmth of pressing against Tan's back. She joined Third Warrior Furcho as he dismounted from Azar and stalked toward Xavier.

Furcho's face was a mask of fury. "If you do anything to hurt her or my child that she carries, I will burn you so slowly you will feel every layer of your skin blister and char black."

"Protective, are we?" The headlights of the transport switched off, and Xavier's mocking smile was a flash of white teeth in the night's pitch black.

Darkest before dawn, Kyle noted. They didn't have much time before the dragon horses would transform to their daytime forms as regular horses. The hatch to the plane opened, and automated stairs hummed down, activating the plane's ground lights and illuminating their confrontation.

"We have you surrounded," Furcho said. "It will be simple for us to disable your plane. Let your hostages go and meet your judgment like a trueborn."

"That's where you're wrong, dragon boy. The way I see it, I hold all the cards." He turned his head and raised his voice without taking his gaze from Furcho. "Juan." Another man stepped out of the transport, holding a gun to the temple of a petite young woman and dragging her by the arm when she stumbled. Maya cried as the hard tarmac scraped the skin from her knees.

Kyle surged forward at the sight of her younger sister. "You bastard."

Furcho's upraised hand stopped Kyle's charge. A second guard appeared in the doorway of the plane, roughly holding Toni, Nicole's shield, by her collar. Xavier smiled again and gestured to Toni. "If you touch my plane, I'll shoot that girl." He shrugged and pointed at Maya. "Next will be Cyrus's daughter. We still have the wife to keep him in line." He narrowed his eyes, and Nicole flinched as he grabbed her hand and shoved the gun's barrel against her knuckles. "Then for every minute you continue to delay our departure, I will shoot off a piece of your girlfriend, starting with her pretty hand."

Nicole's eyes were wide with fear, and Furcho cursed.

Maya swayed, her eyes blank and unseeing. Her guard grabbed her around the waist to hold her up. "What the dung is this?"

"Maya?" Not now. Kyle had to think fast. "It's a medical condition, probably all the excitement."

Maya straightened, her pupils pinpoints in pools of iridescent green. Her voice was high and wispy as she spoke. "Moon's magic, sun's fire, Gandhi's heart, and Odin's sword. But first a trade, same heart, two souls will pay a debt long owed." Maya's pupils expanded, and she seemed to return to awareness. She looked directly at Furcho. "Do not be afraid. The shield will protect. Everything is as it should be for now." Furcho held her gaze for a long moment, then touched his ear to activate his communicator. He murmured instructions for the army to withdraw.

"Furcho, no." Kyle was stunned. "Maya." But Maya's eyes were closed now, and she slumped against the guard as he half carried, half dragged her toward the plane. Others departed the transport to board the plane. Several men carried Kyle's mother, still bound, while her father followed meekly. Cyrus seemed to be a confused shadow of the man who'd started this uprising.

"Take me instead of Maya," Kyle said desperately. "She'll be more trouble than you want for a hostage."

Xavier eyed her. "How gallant. But no."

Furcho's hand closed around her forearm, his fingers digging into her skin to silence her. He held Nicole's tearful gaze. "Trust Maya, Nic. Keep her and Toni close."

Nicole nodded, offering a small smile. "We'll be fine. I love you."

Xavier backed away from them, feeling his way up the boarding steps so Nicole was always between him and The Guard.

Kyle had never felt so helpless. Where were they taking Nicole, Toni, Maya, and her mother? Simon, her father's sinister second-in-command, had to be behind all this. She should have roasted all of him, not just his weapon hand, when she had the chance earlier. Kyle shook off Furcho's grip and stepped forward. She had to try again. "Don't you know who I am?" Her shout rang out above the hum of the plane's engine gearing up.

Xavier stopped in the doorway of the plane. "Should I know you?"

A calm filled her, so deadly she felt as if she could shoot lasers from her eyes to his. "I am the eldest born to Cyrus, the man you call The Prophet."

Xavier curled his lip and shook his head. "It seems I don't have a big enough plane for all his whelps." He pushed Nicole inside and reached for the door to close.

"Simon knows me," Kyle shouted.

Xavier hesitated.

"I am Kyle." She raised her hands and palmed two blue-white-hot spheres of flame. "You tell Simon that Kyle is coming for him."

Chapter One

Toni sat next to Nicole, who curled into a window seat and sniffled as she held Furcho's gaze through the portal until the last possible moment. When the plane lifted off, tears began to roll down Nicole's cheeks, and her shoulders shook with choked sobs. Toni was at a loss. Should she hold her hand? Rub her back? She didn't have a great deal of experience with women, especially opposite-oriented women. Nicole wiped at her tears with her sleeve. Stars. She didn't even have a tissue to offer.

"There's a clean handkerchief in the pocket of my skirt. I can't reach it, but you can get it for her."

Toni turned toward the low, soothing voice and stared into blue eyes.

Laine smiled from the seat across from Toni. "I got in the habit of carrying one when Kyle was young. She had a lot of childhood allergies and was always wiping her nose on her sleeve."

Toni hesitated. "You're Kyle's mom?" It made sense. They had the same dark hair, blue eyes, and angular profile. But Kyle's eyes were an intense cobalt laser blue. Laine's were a soft summer sky.

"Yes." Laine inclined her head toward the young woman who slumped in the seat next to her. "That's my other daughter, Kyle's younger sister, Maya. Their father, Cyrus, is in the seat behind us."

Unlike her tall, dark-haired mother and sister, Maya's hair was a rich brown and fell in waves past her shoulders. The resemblance to Kyle's sculpted features was obvious, but Toni found Maya's more rounded features softer, decidedly beautiful, and, well, angelic.

Toni peeked around the back of her seat to stare at Cyrus. He bent forward to rest his forearms on his thighs and clasped his hands together as he rocked slightly and mumbled to himself. Was he praying? She didn't think so. She couldn't make out all the words, but she could discern an occasional "I am The One." This was the man they called The Prophet? The man who started this misguided uprising? He didn't look that imposing, but they said he'd cut off a young boy's hand as a message to the First Warrior. He glanced up, and Toni was startled by the glazed, scary, wild look in his eyes. He was clearly delusional. Laine seemed to read her thoughts.

"He's ill and needs medical care. I feel responsible for not making sure he was properly monitored," Laine said. She shifted in her seat and nodded toward her hip. "The handkerchief's in that pocket."

"Oh, right." Toni glanced back at Nicole, who was now hunched over and covering her face with her hands as she cried.

Toni mentally shook herself. She needed to organize a plan. She was the only soldier here and the only shield available to protect these three innocents. Nicole, who was usually calm, was coming apart. Must be baby hormones. Toni had heard lots of stories about how they affected women. Maya's petite frame and feminine dress didn't scream warrior, so Toni doubted she could expect help from her. And, though Laine had Kyle's athletic body, she looked a bit beat up after her tussle with the guards that had prompted them to tie her hands and feet while they left the rest of them loose. She'd have to get them all out of the clutches of their kidnapper. Cyrus, she decided, could fend for himself.

The plane was an old fuel-based commercial commuter model that had been converted to solar power. The front of the plane had been gutted and refurbished with comfortable lounges, but the hostages had been herded to the rear, where the original seating was close and the aisle between them narrow.

A row of empty seats separated them from their burly guard. But all Toni could see of him were his legs stretched across the aisle, which meant he couldn't see her either. She reached across and retrieved the handkerchief from Laine's pocket. "Thanks."

Nicole didn't speak or look up when Toni gently tugged on her forearm to lay the handkerchief in her hand. She simply unfolded it and buried her face in the cloth as she sobbed.

Toni put her hand on Nicole's back. "Furcho and Captain Tan will get us out of this. And, until they come, I promise to keep you and the baby safe." But her reassurance only seemed to make Nicole cry harder. "Nicole..." Toni twisted in her seat when sudden thumping sounded behind them.

Cyrus was trying to stand but didn't seem to comprehend that he must release his seat restraint first. The more he tried, the harder he struggled, banging his arms and head against the back of Laine's seat. The guard stood and looked back at them, frowning.

"Release me." Cyrus's mumbling was evolving into angry words. "Infidels. You will regret this. I am The Prophet. Have you not yet seen the consequence of your sins?"

The guard walked back to glare at Cyrus. "I'd shut up and sit quietly before Xavier tells me to slit your trouble-making throat."

Cyrus flushed, and he sprang from his seat as his fingers finally found the release on the seat restraint. "I am anointed. The One and I are the same." He slammed his palms repeatedly against the chest of the guard, pushing him backward down the aisle to the front of the plane, where Xavier and four other men lounged in the more-comfortable seating. They stood as Cyrus pushed his startled guard to the floor. "Where is Simon?"

Xavier eyed him. "You'll see him soon enough."

"That is not an answer." Cyrus's roar filled the plane. He began to pace. "Why are we running from the infidels? The One would have given us protection. We should have stood and fought. We had more than a thousand Believers, most of them armed, and the unnatural army numbered fewer than a hundred." Spittle ran down his chin. "I am surrounded by cowards."

Xavier flicked his hand toward Cyrus and spoke to the two men flanking him. "Tie him in his seat if necessary."

Two of the guards grabbed Cyrus and manhandled him to the rear of the plane. Toni ducked to avoid catching an elbow in the ear as they struggled past her.

"Your souls will perish in hellfire. I am The One." Cyrus's screams filled the plane. "I am The One."

His loud rant seemed too much for Nicole. Her sobs became desperate wails. Toni wanted to cover her ears, but she tried to console Nicole. "Nic, you've got to shield him out. He's mentally unstable and you're absorbing his distress." She could put up a physical shield but not a mental one. Nicole would have to do that for herself. Toni cupped Nicole's face in her hands and forced her to look up. "Nic, please. You have to calm down." Nicole froze for a second, her eyes holding Toni's like a lifeline. Then she doubled over and wailed again.

Xavier stomped to the back of the plane. "Knock him out if necessary. Just shut him up."

"Wait. Don't hurt him. I can calm him if you just untie me," Laine said.

Toni turned back to them. If Laine could calm Cyrus, then maybe Nicole would settle. This couldn't be good for the baby. It was worth a try.

Xavier made a dismissive sound. "You've already assaulted my men in an attempt to escape."

"Where would we go?" Toni said. "We're in a plane, for star's sake, thousands of meters high in the sky. You think four women and a crazy man can overpower you and all your armed guards to hijack the plane? This Simon guy might not like it if you damage his mouthpiece."

One of the guards struggling with Cyrus crumpled as a knee connected with his crotch. Xavier grimaced and drew a switchblade from his pocket. He flicked it open. Sun and stars. Toni didn't like Cyrus, but her hands itched with the instinct to throw up a shield to protect him. She relaxed a bit when Xavier knelt instead and sliced through the bindings around Laine's feet, then yanked her forward to cut the twine tying her hands behind her back.

Laine shot out of her seat just as the second guard connected a bone-crunching right hook to Cyrus's jaw. The guard's angry expression dissolved into one of disbelief when the punch appeared to have no effect on Cyrus.

"I am The One." Cyrus's manic screech triggered another loud wail from Nicole.

Laine wrapped an arm around him from behind, placing one hand in the middle of his chest and the other along his temple. "Cyrus, stop. It's okay. Everything is okay. There's been a misunderstanding. These men are taking us to the City of Light." Though Laine matched him in height, she was much leaner in frame, and Toni marveled that she appeared to easily restrain him though two large men had not.

"I am The Prophet." His vehemence gone, he sounded more like an impudent child.

"Yes. And we're going to the City of Light. So, you must rest now." Laine guided him back to his row of seats, nudging him over so she could sit with him. Keeping one hand on his chest, she spoke in a soothing tone. "There will be much work for you when we arrive."

"I'm so tired," he said, quiet now.

Laine drew him down, cradling his head and shoulders in her lap. "Rest now. I'll keep watch and wake you when we arrive."

He closed his eyes.

The plane was silent except for Nicole's hitched breath and occasional sniffs. Toni slid her hand into Nicole's and sighed in relief. Sun and stars. She'd been ready to start screaming if the racket hadn't stopped.

"She's one of those degenerates. A witch," a guard said, eyeing Laine. "We should tie her and that idiot Cyrus up."

"I'm not a threat," Laine said. "My gift is simply a form of healing."

Xavier studied her. "No restraints, but I'm making you responsible for keeping everyone quiet back here. A guard will watch you at all times. If anyone makes the least bit of trouble, we will tie all of you."

"Understood," Laine said.

Toni watched the men as they returned to the lounges, their guard settling this time about five rows away.

"Oh." Nicole doubled over, and her hand tightened around Toni's. "Oh, no." Her tears started again as she gasped. "My baby."

"What? What's happening?" Toni's thoughts raced, tumbling, jumbling, tangling as she panicked. She worked in a hospital but didn't know anything about healing. She kept inventory and ordered supplies, for star's sake. "Nicole, no. You can't do this now." She had the same first-aid field training every soldier received, and it didn't include delivering babies. She didn't need to be a healer to know it was much too soon. Furcho, Alyssa, everybody was counting on her, and she was going to let Nicole lose this baby. Safe. She was supposed to keep— A hand on her arm stopped her mid-thought. She twisted to look down into warm green eyes.

"Maybe Mom and I can help." Weariness still etched Maya's soft features, but she'd left her seat and was kneeling in the aisle next to Toni.

"You're a healer, like your mother?"

Maya lowered her gaze, her smile fading. "No. I don't share my mother's gift, but I'm able to act as a conduit for her. She shouldn't leave my father right now, so I'll need to be her hands to help your friend."

Maya raised her eyes again, and Toni was suddenly lost in the swirl of green, flecks of gold and hint of blue. "Nicole's pregnant."

Maya's smile returned, soft but a bit patronizing.

Toni's ears heated with embarrassment. Duh. Nicole's baby bump, though not huge, was evident. Maya must think she was an idiot. She groped for something to redeem herself. Then she remembered that Kyle said Furcho was from her hometown. "Furcho is the baby's father."

Maya's face lit up, and Toni had never seen a more beautiful woman...ever...anywhere. "Furcho! He's a close family friend. Mom, did you hear? We must help."

Laine smiled from her seat, where Cyrus still slept with his head in her lap. "Yes." She cocked her head. "But she is gifted, isn't she?"

Toni nodded. "Nicole's an empath. She's usually strong, but..."

"Being pregnant, kidnapped, and absorbing Cyrus's strong emotions must have been too much for her," Laine said softly. "Maya, can you reach my hand if you sit next to Nicole?"

Maya stood and gestured to where Toni was sitting. "May I sit there?"

Toni squeezed Nicole's hand again. "I'll be two steps away, okay?" Nicole didn't seem to hear, grasping her belly and gasping as another spasm gripped her, so Toni quickly slipped from her seat and let Maya settle in her place. "You need to hurry."

Maya reached back to grasp Laine's hand, then laid her other hand on Nicole's belly and closed her eyes. When Laine closed her eyes, too, the air warmed around them. Nicole's spasm seemed to lessen. Then she cried out, and Maya jerked her hand away, her eyes wide.

"Maya?" Laine's puzzled expression worried Toni. Maybe these people didn't really know what they were doing. She was supposed to be shielding Nicole from danger. Was she opening the door and inviting it instead?

Maya opened and closed her mouth a few times before she finally spoke. "The baby is strong. Very strong. She's refusing my unfamiliar touch."

Nicole began to sob softly, and Maya rose to let Toni retake the seat. Toni didn't hesitate as she settled next to Nicole and stroked her back. "I told Furcho I'd make sure nothing happened to you and his baby, and I swear to the stars I won't let you down."

Nicole nodded and reached for Toni's hand. She spoke, her voice choked with pain and tears, for the first time since their captors had dragged them onto the plane. "You've always been dependable."

"Toni, would you lay your hand on Nicole's stomach? Perhaps the baby would accept your touch." Maya squatted next to Toni's seat and held out her hand. "Then hold mine and try to clear your thoughts. We need to convince her to stay where she is for at least another few months."

"Me?" Toni coughed to cover the embarrassing squeak in her voice. "I've never done anything like this. I'm not gifted like you guys—"

"Please, Toni. Try?" Nicole grimaced and rubbed at her side. "I'm still trying to master handling my emotions and hers, and shielding feelings from other people." She grabbed Toni's hand and pressed it to the bulge of her belly.

Toni jumped. "She moved!"

Laine chuckled. "It was more likely gas. It's too early in Nicole's pregnancy to be the baby."

Toni nodded. How would Laine know details like that since they'd just met when they were all kidnapped together? But she'd worry about that later. She tightened her hold on Maya's hand and closed her eyes. "Okay. Let's do this." She tried to clear her mind, but her genetic need to protect kicked in when heat spread up her arm from the hand Maya held.

Again, Maya opened her eyes wide, this time focused on Toni. "You *are* gifted. You're shielding her."

Toni glanced nervously toward the front of the plane. Maya had spoken softly, but she didn't know how well the guard could hear from his seat. "I don't know what you're talking about."

"Maya." Laine's voice was soft, too.

Maya glanced back at her mother. Great. Now they apparently both knew.

"We won't hurt her, Toni. You have our word." Maya's eyes were a sun-warmed meadow dotted with wildflowers.

Toni wanted to trust her. She really did. "How do I know that? How do *you* know you won't hurt her?" Toni asked.

Maya searched Toni's eyes, until Nicole's whimper of pain broke through their standoff. "Because I have a gift, too, that I don't let a lot of people know about." She sighed. "I'm a seer. Everything I see doesn't come to pass, because the future is not as set in stone as people would like to believe. But in my brief touch with the baby a moment ago, I saw a future for her. It was only a flash, so I can't recall specifics, but I can tell you she has a future if we help her now."

"She's being truthful, Toni. I can feel it."

Toni winced at the pain in Nicole's voice. She didn't need an empath to decipher the honesty in Maya's gaze. She took Maya's hand again and closed her eyes. This time, she welcomed the warmth that spread up her arm and drifted in the wondrous river of calm that flowed through her to the hand she pressed against Nicole's belly. She blinked when something seemed to press back. Why did she think it was a tiny hand? The image of a young dark-haired, golden-skinned warrior formed in her mind. Stars. She must be delirious from stress. Or maybe she was glimpsing the future because she was acting as a conduit for Maya. Nicole's sobs quieted. She began to draw deep breaths and finally sighed.

When Maya withdrew and broke their connection, Toni felt hollow. She had to remind herself that what had filled her came entirely from Laine. Or did it? The connection had felt unsettlingly intimate. She'd met these people little more than an hour ago. But this wasn't about her. It was to help Nicole.

"Thank you." Nicole sat back and rolled her shoulders. "I'm having a little trouble handling both my emotions and the baby's. So, I wasn't prepared to shield out what Cyrus was broadcasting. Being an empath sucks sometimes."

"Mom has him under control for now."

Nicole turned in her seat to study Maya kneeling in the aisle. "Is she an empath or a psychic healer?"

Maya shrugged. "I'm not sure. None of our labels fit her gifts."

"But you are a seer?"

Maya bowed her head and dropped her gaze to her lap, where she nervously traced the pattern on her skirt. Her next words were so soft Toni and Nicole leaned closer to hear. "Yes. But please don't tell anybody. What I see doesn't always come true. The choices we make can change the future, and most of the time, it's dangerous for people to know what might happen."

The tortured vulnerability in Maya's huge green eyes when she looked up made Toni's heart clench. She laid her hand on Maya's cheek. So soft. "Your secret is safe with us." She savored the brush of fingers against the hand she rested on Maya's face. "And I would ask that you keep my gift secret, too. I was assigned to guard Nicole, and now all three of you, if possible. If they know I can shield you from weapons, they'll try to separate me from you. I'd rather wait until we're on the ground and have escape options."

"I will," Maya said, squeezing Toni's hand before standing and sliding into the seat across the aisle.

"I like your strategy, Lieutenant Toni," Laine said from one row back, keeping her voice low.

Toni twisted, her eyes falling on the man sleeping in Laine's lap. She frowned.

"Don't worry," Laine said. "He's out cold. I'd be able to tell if he was pretending to sleep."

"You are Kyle's mother." Not a question this time, but an accusation. Hadn't Kyle told Laine what Cyrus had done to her before she escaped and found her way to join The Collective's warriors? They'd been together for at least a week after Kyle returned to the cult as a Collective spy.

Laine nodded, clearly understanding Toni's implication. She moved her hand from Cyrus's chest to caress the strong line of his jaw. "And this is her father. He suffers from a chemical imbalance that causes mental instability. The disease has grown as he's aged. But I have medication that will bring him back into balance if I'm allowed to give it to him."

"So, he doesn't really believe the dung he's been spreading that started all this mess?" That was a bitter pill to swallow. She had lost people she valued to this war—Jael and Uri. And though she had few friends in their camp, the many pyres of the recruits who were killed when attempting to bond with a wild dragon horse still affected her, as had the death of the warriors at the horrible battle in Brasília. She—and everybody else—needed someone to blame.

"The old religions have always fascinated Cyrus, so I can't say he doesn't believe some part of what he's saying. But I respect his right to believe whatever he wants as long as those convictions don't harm others who don't share them."

"Yet The Natural Order has harmed others," Nicole said quietly. "They are hoarding food and medicine, while others are starving and dying from disease that the medicine could treat or cure. The First Warrior was killed, and it has devastated her bond mate, who is one of my closest friends. Another Advocate, a gentle giant of a man and a colleague of mine, was murdered in the street by a sniper as he protected my fiancé from The Natural Order."

Laine closed her eyes and swallowed hard as she stroked her husband's hair. "Oh, Cyrus. I feel so responsible. I should have paid more attention to you." Tears dripped from the corners of her eyes, and she swallowed again. Maya stood and stepped close to lay a hand on her mother's shoulder. Laine opened her eyes and looked up at her daughter. "You tried to warn me. I should have listened."

"You've never sought what's about to be thrust upon you, but our world will fall into chaos if you continue to refuse to use your gifts," Maya said. "I saw this three times in three moons, then every seventh full moon since I was a child. It's the one vision of which I'm certain."

Laine held out her hand and Maya took it, lacing their fingers together. Laine appeared physically strong like Kyle, but she seemed to draw on her younger daughter's emotional strength. After a moment, Laine nodded. "I don't know how I can face the First Warrior's bond mate or the rest of The Collective's army and see, hear the loved ones they sacrificed," she said, resting her head against the back of her seat and looking from Maya to Toni and Nicole.

Was Laine also a necromancer? Did she see souls not attached to a physical body?

"We've all made mistakes we'd like to erase," Nicole said.

Sadness flickered over Laine's features. She appeared to know and understand the guilt Nicole carried like a heavy yoke. The young Advocate felt responsible because she'd asked Uri to bring her beloved Furcho home safe, and Uri had thrown himself between Furcho and the sniper's deadly bullet to keep his promise to her. Cyrus stirred, and Laine stroked her hand down his chest, then rested her palm over his heart. He quieted again into a sound slumber. The lights dimmed to conserve the plane's batteries, and the shadowed interior accentuated the fine lines of weariness etched into Laine's classic features. "Maya had warned me of the consequences. You had no idea the result of your request."

"If not Father, some other catalyst would bring what is to come. I feel sure of it. Everything is as it should be."

Laine didn't appear convinced by Maya's assurance, and lamenting what couldn't be changed wasn't an efficient way to use their time. Toni hated inefficiency.

"We can't erase our mistakes, but we can stop the rest of the dominos from falling," she said. "First we need to figure out a way to get out of this mess and back to safety."

Laine smiled slightly. "Kyle told me a little about her new friends. She said you were an organizer."

Toni stood but raised her arms and twisted back and forth as if stretching when the guard sat straighter and stared. She smiled at him and made a show of rubbing her lower back and executing a couple of standing lunges before she refocused on Laine. "I realize that, except for Maya, I'm probably the youngest person here. But I'm the only soldier, and all of you are my responsibility."

With a serious expression, Laine quickly bowed her head to acknowledge Toni as their leader. "What would you recommend?"

Toni bent forward over one leg as if she was stretching a cramp out of her hamstring. "We lifted off near dawn, so the dragon horses can't immediately follow us. We need to find a way to stall this plane to give them time to catch up. Can you or Maya drain their electric cells or shatter their solar screens?"

"Of course not." Maya's sweet face transformed into a dark cloud Toni would have never thought possible. "Maybe your gifts are suited for war, but our talents are only positive. We never use them to harm anyone."

Toni scowled. "Our warriors, and your sister, use their gifts to protect The Collective. I was talking about causing enough of a problem that they'd have to land to do repairs or wait until the batteries recharge. You think I want to crash and kill us all?"

"Isn't that what warrior-types want? To go out in a blaze of glory?"

Anger crawled up Toni's spine and heated her neck. She leaned close, nose to nose with Maya, and spoke through clenched teeth to keep her voice low. "You obviously know nothing about warriors. It would be a coward's way out to kill yourself and everyone else because you let the person you're supposed to be guarding get captured."

Maya didn't reply. Her gaze dropped to Toni's mouth, and Toni self-consciously swiped her tongue over her teeth and lips. Dung. Did she have something stuck in her teeth? Maybe Maya was about to fall out again with another vision of the future. But Maya blinked, her cheeks flushing an attractive shade of dark pink, and then her lashes fluttered as the spell seemed to recede and her gaze found Toni's again.

"Maya?" Laine appeared puzzled by her daughter's response.

"I'm so sorry." Maya backed away, dropping her chin and covering her eyes with one hand. She looked up, her gaze meeting Toni's and flicking away, her cheeks flaring from pink to a deep rose. Had she seen something in Toni's future? Her next words were so soft, Toni strained to hear. "The stress of our situation has me on edge. Please forgive my rudeness."

Toni took Maya's hand in both of hers. She'd never had the confidence to initiate physical contact with another person, unless it was to push them away or slug them for ridiculing her relatively short stature among an army of tall warriors. Her hand always felt too small for the tools in the stable's smithy or child-like any time she greeted another adult with a handshake. But Maya's hand—not smaller, just more finely boned—fit hers perfectly. "Nothing to forgive. We're all a bit tense, but we need to pull together." She couldn't lie to herself. The fiery side of Maya was beyond enticing. She didn't have Alyssa's red hair, but Maya's eyes held the same flame of temper as the First Advocate's, Toni's mentor and friend. Maybe that's why she was letting Maya off the hook so easily. She felt drawn to Maya, probably because she was a lot like Alyssa. Her body wasn't convinced. She flushed with a new heat, and something fluttered low in her belly. That never happened around Alyssa. She gently withdrew her hands from Maya's.

"How far can you project your shield?" Laine asked, dissolving the moment between Toni and Maya.

Toni glanced over her shoulder to make sure the guard wasn't listening. Since they'd dimmed the lights, most of the men had stretched out on the lounges up front to nap. The door to the cockpit was closed. Even their guard was nodding off. Toni turned back to Laine and shrugged. "I've never tested it."

Laine looked out of the window next to their seats. "The sky has turned overcast. That's why they dimmed the lights. They're probably supplementing the solar power with batteries. If you can block all the sunlight from reaching the solar panels, then the plane will drain its batteries and have to land. That will buy us some time for our rescuers to catch up."

"Holy dung. It probably has panels from nose to tail. I'd have to shield the entire plane."

"From weak sunbeams. You can do that, can't you?" Maya asked. Ouch. The sarcastic Maya was back. What was it with women? One minute they're going all googly eyed over you, and the next they're cutting your legs out from under you.

"The panels start at the wings, extend along each, then part of the way toward the tail," Laine said. "Kyle and I share a fascination with flying, and when we went to an airshow once, we saw one of these models that had just been converted from fuel to solar." She drew a T-figure in the air with her finger. "So, not the entire plane."

Toni eyed her skeptically. She'd never purposefully shielded anybody. It would just happen when she was in a tight spot. She'd throw up her hands, adrenaline would kick in, and the shield happen.

What if she couldn't generate a shield without imminent danger? She gestured toward the front of the plane. "I can't just stand in the aisle with my arms over my head, looking like a fool without one of those guys noticing."

"Are you refusing to even try?" Maya's hard stare was challenging, and her words felt like an accusation.

Son of a dung eater. Why didn't Maya just check in with the future and see if they got out of this mess and how they did it? A hand on her back stopped the childish retort before it left her mouth.

"Sometimes Toni thinks aloud when she's planning details," Nicole said. "Let's give her a few minutes to work it out. She's always resourceful. That's why she's been promoted so fast." Nicole slid her hand up Toni's back to clasp her shoulder and squeeze. "That's why Furcho trusts her to keep me safe."

The confidence in Nicole's eyes reminded Toni that her early planning and record-keeping had prevented an epidemic of influenza from destroying the dragon-horse army. Reminded her that the First Warrior had personally promoted her to be the First Advocate's top admin officer in the camp clinic. She pushed back old childhood feelings of inadequacy and being the odd duck.

She looked up at the ceiling. She could do this. Sun rays are just another form of energy. If she could block flame, she could easily block sunlight. Could she push a shield outside of the plane's shell? Well, she'd stood behind Kyle when she deflected flame directed at her. What would the guards think when she raised her hands above her head? Wait. She'd already done that before, when she pretended to stretch. But this would take much longer.

CHAPTER TWO

Toni stared at the floor for a minute, then looked up to scan the faces of the three women watching her. Nicole looked hopeful, Laine curious, and Maya skeptical. The last expression made her decide what to do. She straightened her shoulders and crossed her arms over her chest. "I'm not guaranteeing this will work, but it's better than doing nothing." She glanced over her shoulder. "I have this, uh, thing I can do with my back. Even if it sounds awful, don't panic. Just go with however I act, okay?"

Nicole smiled and nodded. Toni didn't doubt she would play her part well. Nicole had conspired with several of Toni's infamous pranks around camp—some good-natured, others with a touch of revenge for those who thought she was an easy target for teasing.

Laine watched Nicole's reaction, then added her pledge. "I'm in."

Maya's expression turned from skeptical to concerned. "You won't do anything to hurt yourself, will you? We can find another way."

Toni blinked. Not even a bipolar person could ping back and forth like this woman. Every time Maya spoke to her was like picking off another petal of a daisy. I like you. I like you not. I like you. I like you not.

"I can pop a vertebra in my back in and out with an awful crunching sound. It's painful if it gets stuck, but that's only happened once, and I've done it a hundred times to fool people. So, just trust me, okay?"

"I've seen her do it," Nicole said. "It's creepy, but really okay."

Maya chewed on her lip.

"I need everybody behind me on this," Toni said, realizing she could stare into Maya's beautiful eyes for hours if that's how long it took for her to answer. She didn't know why, but it was important that Maya agree.

"Okay."

Maya's consent was tentative, but Toni held her gaze and smiled. "Thank you," she said softly. "Having you on my team makes all the difference."

Maya blushed and ducked her head to hide the smile that transformed her lovely face to radiant. Toni's own face heated when Nicole playfully nudged her. But Toni had no idea where this new brazen-warrior-like flirting was coming from, other than Maya seemed to draw it out of her. She shook herself mentally. "Anybody have bottled water?"

They all shook their heads.

"Good." She sat in the aisle seat and coughed. After a few seconds, she coughed again, accompanied by a strangling noise, then furious coughing.

Cyrus mumbled loudly in his sleep, and Laine laid her hands on his forehead and chest and sang quietly, drawing the guard's attention to her measures to quiet him. She couldn't have played it better.

Toni took the cue and stood. She coughed loudly as she stumbled toward the front of the plane. Their guard rose from his seat to block her path. "Where do you think you're going?"

Toni put her hand to her throat. "Water. Do you have some water?" She choked out her words between coughs. She took a few more steps.

"Stop." Only a few rows of seats away now, he raised his gun and pointed it at her chest. "I've seen you pyros melt a gun, so you're not getting close enough to grab mine."

Toni wanted to roll her eyes. If she'd been a pyro, he and the rest of their abductors would be ashes by now. But at least he was playing right into her hands. She did her best to look terrified and shot her hands upward, coughing at the same instant she twisted her shoulders in the way she knew would pop that vertebra in and out. The crack of bone shifting was loud in the confined space of the solar plane, and she screamed. She scrunched her eyes closed and whimpered through a suppressed cough.

"What's going on?" The man Xavier had called Juan approached and peered at Toni over the guard's shoulder.

"She was coughing and asked for some water. But she was coming too close, and I don't trust these deviants. I pointed my gun to keep her back, and when she raised her hands like an idiot, there was a popping noise. I didn't touch her, but I think she maybe hurt herself."

Juan shook his head in disgust. "We don't even need this one. If we weren't flying so high, I'd open a door and push her out." He jerked his chin toward where the other hostages sat. "Take her back to her seat. I'll get some bottles of water for them."

"Please. Can I just stand here for a few minutes? A vertebra in my back misaligns sometimes. As soon as the spasm relaxes, I can pop it back in place."

The guard scowled. "How long will that take?"

Toni closed her eyes. She couldn't concentrate on forming a shield while she talked to this buffoon. "Sometimes a minute or two. Sometimes an hour or more. It depends on how tense I am, and you staring at me isn't helping me relax."

Juan returned with the water. "Why is she still here?"

"She wants to stand still until…" He waved his hand in front of her. "Until things go back into place."

Toni glanced sideways without moving her head. Actually, she was a few seats forward of where she should ideally stand. It was already getting hard to hold her arms up.

"Enough. Put your arms down and go back to your seat." Juan grabbed one of Toni's arms and tugged. She screamed, and he jerked his hand back.

"Punta. You do not want to wake Xavier." Juan snatched the guard's gun from him and pressed the tip of the barrel to Toni's forehead. "Maybe I should just put you out of your misery, and I'll be rid of this noisy problem."

"Imbecile."

Juan and the guard froze at the sound of Xavier behind them.

"You can't fire a projectile weapon in a pressurized cabin. You'll crash the plane and kill us all." Xavier glared at them. "Stuff something in her mouth so we don't have to listen to her scream and haul her back to her seat."

"Wait."

Toni closed her eyes against the sweat dripping into them. Dung. Maya was standing behind her.

"Give me the bottles of water, and I'll help her walk slowly back to where Mother can help her. If you get her screaming, the noise will rile Father again. You don't want that, do you?" Maya raised an eyebrow at the men when they hesitated.

Xavier's teeth flashed white in the dim light. "I like her." He gestured to the guard. "Give her the water." He watched as the bottles were passed around Toni, and Maya dropped one into each pocket of her skirt, then tucked one in the pocket of Toni's pants. He cocked his head, eyes gleaming in the dim light as he stared at Maya. "Maybe I'll see more of you after we settle in at our destination." Without waiting for a response, he returned to the front of the plane with Juan on his heels.

The guard frowned at them uncertainly, then went back to his post, sitting so he could keep an eye on them.

"Okay. How do we do this?" Maya's voice was soft, her breath warm on Toni's neck.

"Could you support my arms for me a few minutes before we move. I'm really tired of holding them up, but I can't lower them with that bone out of place."

Maya's hands were gentle but strong. She propped her elbows on the seat backs next to them, then braced Toni's arms with hers. Toni gradually relaxed, transferring the weight of her arms to Maya's support. It was a short but welcome relief.

"Either you're an incredible actress or you've actually hurt yourself. You're as white as new snow and perspiring like we're in a sauna."

Toni closed her eyes, drew in a shallow breath, and carefully dropped her chin to her chest. Lying in a bed of soft icy snow to numb the searing pain at the base of her shoulders appealed to her. "It was bad timing to cough just as I raised my arms. It didn't go like it usually does."

"When you're ready, can you turn around to walk back?"

Toni raised her head. "I'm ready." She turned carefully and stepped back against the seats to her right after Maya slowly dropped her supporting hands. Toni realized her mistake as Maya, a bare five centimeters shorter, faced her to squeeze past. Their eyes met, and Maya hesitated as her full breasts brushed Toni's smaller ones. For a few fleeting seconds, Toni forgot about their captors, shielding the solar panels, and even the pain that was sending rivulets of sweat down her neck.

"Sorry," Maya said, but her small smile contradicted her apology as she broke their gaze and stepped past.

Toni's impulse to drop her arms and pull Maya back sent a spear of pain up her spine, and she groaned. "Tease," she said under her breath as she turned toward the back of the plane.

"What's that?" Maya asked, again helping support Toni's arms from behind.

"Nothing." Toni swore she felt heat radiating from Maya standing close behind her. "Small steps. Right foot first."

Though they shuffled carefully down the aisle, Toni was awash with sweat and pain when she halted where the wings were visible through the plane's windows. They turned again, but with Maya at her back this time.

"Mother can't reach you from here," Maya said. "I can't even reach her to be a conduit for her."

"I need to be here to shield all the solar panels."

"Toni, let her help you first."

"No. We might be running out of time. Just support my arms."

"I can help, too."

Toni tried to turn her head to see Nicole, but her back muscles instantly spasmed.

"Are you a healer?" Maya asked. Many empaths were trained in the medical arts.

"Not by gift like your mother, but by training," Nicole said. She rubbed her protruding belly. "This little one makes it hard for me to kneel, but I can tell you what to do while I support Toni's arms."

Maya nodded. "What should I do?"

"Most likely the tense muscles around her spine are preventing the bone from slipping back into place as it usually would. Since I'm tall and my arms long, I can use the seat backs on either side for leverage and not only hold her arms up, but stretch her spine upward to space it out a bit. I need you to massage the muscles on either side of her spine to relax them, especially right at the base of her shoulder blades. I've seen her use this trick before, and that's where the bone is that she pops out and back."

"How can you dislocate a bone in your spine without damaging the spinal cord?" Skeptical Maya was back.

"It must be some type of birth deformity, but it doesn't seem to affect her in any adverse way." Nicole had returned to her normal chatty personality, all trace of her previous distress gone. "The first time I saw her do it, this bully pushed her into a fence. She popped it out, then pretended her legs were paralyzed. He nearly peed his pants, and I was in a panic. I could have killed her when she got off the stretcher at the clinic, stood, and raised her arms to pop it right back in. The First Advocate wanted to scan her to study the phenomenon, but Toni declined, and Alyssa said it was Toni's choice to preserve her privacy."

"Hello. Can you two gossip about me later?" Toni needed to focus and stop thinking about Maya's huge green eyes and pouty, kissable lips. "We're wasting time."

"Oh, right. Sorry." Nicole's hands replaced Maya's and tightened around Toni's biceps. Toni felt herself being lifted a bit, then lowered so that her heels touched the floor but didn't bear her full weight as Nicole braced her elbows on the seat backs. The stretching of her spine helped, but the real relief came from Maya's surprisingly strong hands kneading her tense back muscles.

Toni closed her eyes and moaned. "That feels so good."

They'd been speaking so quietly among themselves that they all jerked at the loud male voices coming from the front of the plane. "How much longer? Will we reach the City of Light before dark?"

"Not long after sunset." The door to the cockpit was open, and a man wearing a pilot's uniform stood there, speaking to Xavier. "We should escape this cloud cover soon so our batteries can fully charge. We'll be fine to fly the full distance without stopping."

"Excellent." Xavier waved a hand to dismiss the man, who returned the cockpit but left the door open.

It was now or never. Toni sucked in a breath and concentrated on projecting a shield past the roof of the plane. The feel of Nicole's hands on her arms and Maya's on her back melted away as her own hands warmed. It was working. She pictured the shield spreading the length of the wings and back to the tail of the plane. She'd leave the few solar panels positioned forward of the wings open so the plane didn't completely lose power. She smiled to herself. "Done. Now we'll see if it works."

Maya's hands paused at Toni's whispered words, and Toni realized that while she'd concentrated on the shield, her back muscles had relaxed. She twisted her hips slightly, and a soft pop confirmed that her spine had realigned. She drew in a deep breath, elated that the pain was gone. Maybe it was time to retire that trick from her repertoire of pranks. "I'm fine now, but pretend you're helping me sit down in one of these seats here. I can at least rest my arms against the back of the seat, but I have to keep them up to maintain the shield." Toni glanced toward the front of the plane. A glow of red flashed in short intervals through the open cockpit door. She could hear the rumbling of the pilots' voices. "Hurry. Both of you sit in the seats behind me."

"No. I'll sit next to you." Maya watched the cockpit as she and

Nicole pretended to help Toni shuffle sideways and sit without lowering her arms.

"I need you behind me if they figure this out and come for us. Please stay close to Nicole so I can shield you together."

Maya hesitated, glancing from Toni back to the cockpit. Then before Toni had time to react, Maya bent and pressed soft lips against her cheek. "Please be sensible. Don't sacrifice yourself for us."

Her quiet words made Toni shiver. She would be sensible because she wanted a chance to feel those lips against hers rather than merely grazing her cheek. But if the situation left no options, she *would* sacrifice herself for this young woman who had both exasperated and mesmerized her in less than a day's time. And for Nicole, too, of course.

Xavier frowned when alarms sounded from the cockpit. Were they crashing? Where would parachutes, if there were any, be stashed? Except for being full of fuel and flight ready, the plane had no attendants to point out safety features. The two pilots Juan had hired swore they'd flown this type of plane many times.

Xavier stumbled on his way to the cockpit when the plane bumped through a pocket of air turbulence. Juan, struggling to regain his balance, swayed into his path, and Xavier roughly pushed him to the side. Bracing himself in the cockpit's open doorway, Xavier shouted at the pilots. "Turn that dung-eating alarm off and tell me what's going on."

"The solar panels are malfunctioning, and we're losing power," the co-pilot explained as he punched several controls to silence the alarms.

The pilot frantically flipped switches with one hand and white-knuckled the control yoke with the other. "We're not going to make it out of these mountains to a straight piece of roadway, much less an airport. Get on the radio and send our coordinates to anyone who can hear, and help me put eyes on some place flat and clear enough for us to land."

"Find a place to land, but do not give out our location." Xavier yelled over his shoulder, "Juan, have everyone watch out the windows for a field where we can land."

"Do what I said," the pilot ordered his co-pilot.

Xavier pressed the tip of his handgun against the co-pilot's temple. "I give the orders. No communications." He yanked the man's headset off, unplugged it from the console, and tossed it into the main cabin before returning the weapon to his waistband.

The pilot's head moved back and forth, scanning the darkening landscape. "We're in the middle of government-mandated wilderness at least eighty kilometers wide. After we crash-land—and there will be injuries—we might have to hike thirty to forty kilometers to reach civilization."

"What about parachutes?" Xavier asked.

"You have a better chance of surviving an unplanned landing than parachuting from a plane like this into a dark forest."

"There!" The co-pilot pointed to a strip of land with a downward slope. The blackened, decaying remains of a few large trees lay like soldiers felled by a lightning fire, but thin saplings daring to reclaim the torched earth dotted most of the long strip.

"It'll be tricky, but it's our best chance." The pilot guided the plane in a wide arc, then switched on the landing lights.

❖

Toni's arms and head ached. She'd never had to maintain a shield this long and breathed a sigh of relief as the plane dipped toward the dark side of the mountain. The batteries were too drained to recover in the dim light of the mountain's shadow. She lowered her arms with a groan, and cool hands reached around her seat to massage her stiff shoulders. Stars, that felt good.

"We're landing," Laine said from behind them. "Check the overhead compartments for pillows or blankets or anything to cushion yourselves. If you find life jackets under the seats, use those, too."

Their guard was busy buckling himself as he stared out a window, so Toni ignored her stiff muscles and sprang from her seat. "Nicole, check overhead since you're tall. Maya and I will look under the seats."

They located old inflatable life vests under each seat, and nearly all expanded when Toni pulled their activation cords. Nicole found a cache of pillows and blankets, but the pillows were small and thin. Maya took four of the inflated vests and began packing them around her parents.

Toni glanced at one window. The mountain seemed to be rising to grab them. They had only minutes, and she needed to get everyone in place. "Maya, you need to get buckled in. We don't have much time."

Laine let Maya stuff one inflated vest around her feet, then shooed her away. "Go. I can position the rest."

Toni directed her to their row of three seats. "Let me sit by the window, then Nicole in the middle, and Maya in the aisle seat."

Maya stopped Nicole's protest. "She's right. We have to protect the baby."

Toni climbed across the two seats and pulled the plastic shield down over the portal, as well as the ones in front and behind. Then she lifted the armrests between seats. "Nicole, you shouldn't belt in because the impact could harm the baby. We'll both hold on to you."

"Good idea," Maya said, but she frowned. "But maybe I should take the window seat."

Toni wanted to roll her eyes. Was this woman going to question everything she did? "No. I'm going to throw up a shield to reinforce the bulkhead as well as protect us from flying debris or from fire if the solar panels short out and burst into flame."

Maya looked at Nicole. "She's quite handy to have around, isn't she?"

"You don't know the half of it." Nicole laughed, a ridiculous sound among the frantic shuffling and swearing of the men running for a last look out the windows, then fighting over the best places to weather the landing.

Two men snatched up cushions from one lounge and fled past them to the back of the plane. "They say the tail is the best place to be in a crash," one man said as he stumbled over Maya's outstretched foot.

"Oh, so sorry," Maya said. But the man barely paused, and Maya's smirk indicated the trip had been intentional. Her expression instantly went blank as Xavier and Juan approached.

Toni cursed but recanted with a "thank the stars" when the two men stopped several rows before them. They'd obviously observed their hostages inflating the life vests to use as cushions and retrieved several from the seats around them before settling to brace for impact.

Nicole muttered an Advocate's chant under her breath, imploring the universe to protect her unborn child as Toni and Maya packed vests around the three of them, then entwined their arms with hers.

"She will be fine. We will be fine," Maya said. "I have seen it."

CHAPTER THREE

Alyssa jerked up, a terrible scream tearing her from her dream. Pain shot up her back. The scream might have been her own, but another rattled the windows of the hospital ward. Dragon horse, not human. Night again. Commander Danielle, Second Warrior and clone to Alyssa's dead bond mate Jael, remained unmoving on the bed next to Alyssa's chair. They'd brought her back, unconscious from head and shoulder wounds, after the dragon-horse warriors' most recent clash with The Natural Order. Her wounds should heal though she'd lost a great deal of blood, but Danielle had not roused as expected. Alyssa stared at the smooth lines of her handsome face, willing her to wake. Another agonized shriek sounded, more terrible and closer than the previous. What was going on out there? She groaned as she stood and stretched. Running footsteps pounded down the hallway outside the ward.

Will, the clinic pharmacist, skidded through the doorway, breathless. "It's Titan. I think he's looking for the Commander. Maybe she's calling him. Is she waking up?"

Alyssa scanned the vitals monitor. No change. She shook her head. "I don't think so." The screams of Danielle's dragon horse were growing more frequent, and other dragon horses joined in a tortured chorus. Alyssa put her hands over her ears.

"I'll go see what's going on," Will said, shouting to be heard over the deafening clamor. Alyssa studied the monitors for any sign of change. Danielle's pulse and respirations were slowing and her blood pressure dropping. That couldn't be right.

Will returned and hugged her to him. "Michael said for us to stay inside."

"What? No. What's going on, Will?" She pushed him away. He was developing a relationship with Michael, but he obviously didn't understand yet how arrogant warriors could be when it came to dealing with non-warriors.

"Alyssa. Don't. He said you should stay with the Commander."

What didn't they want her to know? To see? She charged through the door and outside.

Danielle's buckskin dragon horse, Titan, nostrils flaring and spewing flame, paced the wide lane outside the hospital and beat his wings against the ground without taking flight. People peeked out of windows and from between buildings. Only the other members of The Guard and Kyle stood in a wide semicircle before the distraught animal. The dragon horses of The Guard hovered along the rooftops of the camp, still adding their voices to Titan's.

"What is it? Does he need to see Danielle?"

Titan breathed a long column of flame into the sky, then screeched out a wounded sound that slammed Alyssa so hard she nearly collapsed. Even as First Advocate and an extremely powerful empath, she didn't naturally sense animals. But she felt his despair as real as her own. Furcho bowed his head, unable to speak. Kyle grabbed Alyssa's arm to steady her but looked to Tan to give an explanation.

"Tan, what's happening?" Alyssa was surprised to feel the normally guarded warrior emotionally open, her feelings raw and easily read.

Tears trickled down Tan's face, but her voice was steady. "If a warrior passes this life and their bond is broken, the dragon horse usually goes mad from the pain. A lone horse will fling himself against cliffs until he dies. The lucky ones have a herd that will gather and end his pain quickly. That's why the others are here."

Titan slammed himself to the ground, got up, and charged the building to crash against it like a rabid animal.

"Stop him." Alyssa grabbed Furcho's arm. "Do something. He's hurting himself." Then Tan's words sank in. *If a warrior passes this life.* She ran into the hospital. The vitals monitor was silent and dark. "No, no. Not you, too. I can't make it without you." She hit the code button. No one came. Everybody was outside. She sprinted back to the street. "Tan, she's coding." She tried to drag Tan toward the door, but she wouldn't move. "You're a doctor. You have to come."

Tan turned to her, her eyes pools of pain. "She's gone, Alyssa. Their bond is broken. Danielle made me promise if this ever happened...her greatest wish has always been for her soul to be freed to rejoin her bond mate Saran."

Alyssa slammed her palms against Tan's chest, trying to force her to move. "You said her wounds weren't that serious."

Tan shook her head and grasped Alyssa's wrists to stop her. "They aren't. Still, she has to want to live."

"I don't understand what they're waiting for," Furcho muttered. "Azar just keeps showing me the wild stallion. I don't understand."

"There's your answer," Kyle said.

Dark Star's wings spanned the entire width of the lane as he coasted to a landing. Titan reared and cried out a pitiful sound. As he launched into the air, Dark Star bellowed a huge column of pure blue flame. Bero, Azar, Potawatomi, Apollo, and Phyrrhos joined their inferno to his, and within seconds, Titan was ash.

Alyssa could no longer hold back her sobs of grief and ran inside, closing the door to the ward and locking it. She wasn't ready to light another pyre. The hand she took in hers was still warm. She smoothed Danielle's blond hair as she cried and stroked the cheek so like her lover's. She wasn't Jael, but with Danielle's help, Alyssa was beginning to feel that she might find some purpose in this life until she could be with her love again. "I needed you, Danielle. I know you wanted to be with Saran, but without Jael, I needed you to stay with me."

She wished that people were as merciful as dragon horses and would send grieving souls to follow the ones to whom they were bonded. When they lit the pyre for Second Warrior Danielle, Alyssa would lose the last tiny piece of Jael, the other half of her soul.

❖

"The stars foretell it," Saran-Sung-Josh said.

"You expect too much!" First Warrior Jael threw arms up to shout at the seven ethereal figures gathered in a semicircle before her. She paced restlessly, her soul bond with Alyssa stretched agonizingly thin. They were The Collective Council, having ascended permanently to the spiritual realm after gaining the wisdom and experiences of multiple lives. Each presented in human form as genderless composites of their most recent lives. Newly ascended after many lives, she'd earned a place among them that would allow the life force of the most ancient of the Elders to divide and begin new soul journeys. But she wanted only to return to her lover—to feel Alyssa's heart beat in sync with hers, hold her as they slept, to love her with every cell of her being.

"From the wounds of The Chosen will come healing for all." An elder with a heart-shaped face and gray crew-cut, Morgaine-Viktor-Paola used a tone that implied no further explanation was required.

Jael whirled on them and, with supernatural strength, tore open the ragged rend in the silver battleskin where the laser had pierced her heart. "What about this heart?" The fatal wound still gaped between her breasts. "Who will heal my wound?"

The Ancient Elder, who stood at the center of their arc, held up a hand and raised white, sightless eyes as though listening in the silence. After a long quiet, the Ancient spoke in a voice like a chorus of many, in a language so old that another had to translate. "The First Advocate is not The Chosen who will rise to unite a new Collective."

Jael's anguished cry rang out, and the Elders turned to the Ancient, their human images flickering as the ethereal beings plumbed the universe for an explanation of this revelation. Still too tied to her human soul, Jael exploded. "I have served The Collective faithfully lifetime after lifetime as a solitary soul. I've given myself in battle over and over as your First Warrior, suffering grievous wounds and losses. When I am finally rewarded with the soul meant to bond with mine, I am torn away, and now you tell me our sacrifice was for nothing?" Her anger was a bolt of lightning, flashing, then gone. Deflated, she bowed her head and hugged her arms to her chest. "She is the other half of my heart."

The Ancient turned white pupil-less eyes to Jael. "Your sacrifice was but one path to the destination The Collective must reach. We underestimated the strength of your joining and only now feel the agony of your soul bond. For that, The Council offers its regrets."

Jael straightened as a new anger filled her, righteous and defiant. "Regret isn't enough. I'm invoking my right as First Warrior to demand justice."

The Elders' discussion of her petition was an indistinct hum until the Ancient raised his hand and all went silent. "What is done cannot be undone," the Ancient said.

Jael fell to her knees, eyes closed. The Ancient's words were like another stab into her shattered heart. Still, she could not let go of the bond that tethered her to earth, to her soul mate. How did Saran and Danielle survive their separation? Jael could feel that they also remained tethered. She raised her head and stared at Saran-Sung-Josh, silently imploring for help.

Saran-Sung-Josh nodded and turned to the Ancient. "Perhaps there is a path for restitution."

❖

Alyssa's sobs quieted, and her breath hitched as she rubbed her wet cheek against the solid chest. Maybe she was going mad like Titan. She could have sworn she heard the thu-thump of a heart. Madness might be better than waking each day with reality. Wait. She heard it again. She gasped as the chest under her cheek rose and fell. She sat up. Sun and stars. She *was* crazy. She couldn't be seeing this. The monitor over the bed lit up, and the readings climbed into normal ranges. Color flooded into Second Warrior Danielle's gray face. She ran to the door, unlocked and flung it open.

"Tan." She ran outside. No one was there. She turned to go back and collided with Tan in the hallway.

"Alyssa." Tan was followed by Michael and Raven. "I know you—"

"She's alive. Come quick." She ran back to the ward without waiting to see if they'd follow. The monitors still showed normal readings. Thank the stars. She wasn't hallucinating.

"This is impossible," Tan said, feeling for a pulse in the wrist and neck.

Eyelids rippled with movement, and the monitor showed heart rate, body temperature, and brain activity begin to elevate.

"She's waking up," Michael said.

Tan flicked on a penlight and had started to lift an eyelid when a clomping ruckus made them all turn toward the door.

"What the…get that animal out of here," Tan said.

Dark Star wedged himself through the doorway and stood at the foot of the bed, rattling his wings in warning when Raven moved toward him. He extended his arched neck, and his red, elliptical pupils pulsed as he touched his nose to the figure in the bed.

Alyssa stood very still until a groan drew her gaze back to the bed, and she touched the warm cheek as the eyelids fluttered. "Come on. You can do it. Open your eyes and look at me." The monitors quieted and the numbers dropped, and Alyssa held her breath. Her throat tightened with tears she didn't think she had left to cry. "Please don't leave me again."

"I'm here." The voice was hoarse but the inflection familiar. The numbers rose and steadied again. "It just took me a while to get back." The eyelids fluttered, and thick blond lashes lifted to reveal eyes as blue as the summer sky. First Warrior Jael swallowed and licked her dry lips. "We're growing old together. They promised."

CHAPTER FOUR

Maya was sure she'd see her next life soon when the plane touched down with a jolt, followed by the slap and pop of saplings against the fuselage as it pitched wildly over the rocky terrain. Then a second, much harder jolt jammed them against the row of seats in front of them—well, her and Toni. They managed to twist their bodies partially in front of Nicole and pad her lurch forward. But Maya wanted to let go of Nicole's arm and cover her ears when the terrible screech of tearing metal filled the plane. The left wing was ripped away, eviscerating the plane's fuselage. She watched in horror as several seats disappeared through the gaping hole, along with the two guards strapped into them.

Severed wires sparked and burst into flame, producing a black smoke that stung her nostrils and made her cough. Shards of glass and metal, anything left loose in the plane, and the rocks and dirt pouring in through the gaping hole filled the air but never touched them because Toni threw her arm up, and the debris bounced off the invisible barrier that surrounded them.

Maya thought that the screams of men tossed about the interior and the screech of twisting metal would never end, but the jarring ride suddenly halted, and the popping of new electrical fires was the only sound.

"Mom?" Maya's tentative query seemed to reboot the scene. A few small lights along the plane's ceiling, powered by individual batteries, flickered to life. Groans emanated from the men who had stupidly sought shelter under the upturned lounges rather than belting into a seat. They'd been tossed about like rag dolls along with the loose furniture and other debris.

"We're fine, Maya. Are you girls okay?" Laine's voice, firm

and alert, carried over the stirring of the others and Cyrus's irritated mumbling.

Maya let out a relieved breath and turned to Nicole. "How's the baby?"

Nicole rubbed her belly and nodded. "Good. Thanks to you guys." She squeezed Maya's hand and planted a kiss on Toni's cheek. "Other than being jostled around a bit, I think we fared better than anyone else."

"We're all good, Mom." Maya smiled at the flush darkening Toni's neck and ears in the dim light. Stars, she was cute. Maya had been attracted before to other girls—and some boys—but she couldn't seem to keep her eyes off this dark-haired young warrior with brooding brown eyes. Maya frowned. Her silly infatuation irritated her. She wasn't sure why. Maybe because the woman—like most warriors— was a bit bossy and self-important, or because she had always been sure her first real sense of chemistry would be with a scholar, craftsperson, or artist. Not a warrior type, for stars' sake. Maybe her lesson to learn in this life was humility. But wasn't she already learning that by being gifted as a seer, the most ridiculed of talents?

Maya glanced over, feeling suddenly shy when she discovered Toni watching her. As Toni's wary expression softened into a smile, Maya realized she'd been smiling at Toni. Sun and moon, could she be more obvious? She deliberately widened her smile to a sarcastic grin and mouthed, *my hero.* Toni shrugged, and her cheeks glowed brighter than the blush that Nicole's platonic kiss had elicited. Nicole raised a questioning brow at Maya. Oh, right. Jumping inconvenient having an empath around who could read her true emotions. It was Maya's turn to shrug, embarrassed at being caught trying to cover her true feelings. Toni deserved better from her. She *had* brought the plane down and kept them safe in the ensuing rough landing.

Xavier and Juan rose from their seats several rows ahead. Too bad they hadn't chosen seats on the other side and been sucked out with their two underlings. Maya immediately regretted the thought. Stars, she hoped her mother, who always seemed to hear her thoughts, wasn't listening.

Xavier straightened his suit jacket, then brushed dirt and bits of other debris from his clothes. He appeared otherwise unscathed. Juan held a bloody handkerchief to his rapidly swelling right brow, that side of his face marred by a multitude of small cuts from the window that had exploded next to him.

"Go check on the pilots and the rest of the men," Xavier said, ignoring Juan's injuries. "See who is able-bodied and who might be too injured to walk off this mountain."

Juan wordlessly turned and steadied himself by grasping the seat backs of each row as he headed toward the front of the plane.

Xavier eyed his hostages. "You seem to have fared well enough. Stay in your seats."

Toni shuffled past Nicole and Maya, then straightened to face Xavier in the aisle. He wasn't a tall man, besting Toni's height by only about eight centimeters. She pointed to a sparking electrical panel. "We need to get everyone off this plane. With the solar grid shorted out and sparking, the battery units could combust at any time."

"She's right, Boss. I've seen a plane smaller than this go up in flames when one battery exploded and set off a chain reaction that lit up the whole array." One of the two men who had taken refuge in seats at the tail of the plane was walking up the aisle behind Toni. The other man was trying to kick open an emergency door several rows behind Laine and Cyrus, but the odd tilt of the plane against the ground held it fast.

Xavier turned to survey the front of the plane and the ragged gap where the left wing had been. He gestured to the men, then the opening. "You two take our guests out through there. I'll check with Juan about getting the rest out."

Toni's group was already rising, eager to depart their treacherous transport. Maya reached for one of the battery-powered lights. "Hey, these are detachable. Let's grab the ones back here and take them out with us."

"I bet there's a first-aid kit either near the cockpit or in the rear steward's nook. If somebody can bring it along, I can help treat injuries," Nicole said. "I'm not a gifted healer like Laine, but I am a trained medical Advocate."

The man by the door didn't wait for Xavier's consent. After a quick search of the small nook where stewards prepared food and drinks, he held up a white metal box with a large red cross on it, then gathered two more lights as he moved forward to take up rear guard while they filed carefully through the tangle of severed wires that ringed the plane's jagged wound.

The new moon was a sliver, and their weak lights made tiny pools in the black night. Still, Maya could see green sprouting from the blackened landscape as they trudged uphill.

"Over there." Laine pointed her light toward a good-sized area mostly devoid of saplings, near the edge of the burn and about ten meters from the wreckage. "Looks like enough room for the injured to lie down, but we should have brought some seat cushions and blankets from the plane."

They all, even their guards, turned to look back at the downed aircraft, and Maya was suddenly aware of the raised voices and occasional screams as the injured were discovered and attempts were made to extract them or evaluate their wounds. Sparks from the exposed wires, however, had lessened. A man appeared in the gap where the wing had been and held up a light. His face was dark with blood on one side, his other arm belted against his torso. He stepped to the side so two more could exit—one apparently able-bodied who was supporting and half dragging a comrade with an obvious leg injury.

"I'll go back to get some blankets," the first guard said to the second. "You watch the prisoners."

"I thought Xavier said we were guests. I was just about to make my apologies for leaving early. It's been an exciting adventure, but I've had enough fun for the night." Toni's muttered sarcasm drew a frown from the second guard, who pointed his weapon at her.

"You think you're funny? Maybe I'll shoot your foot to make sure you stay put."

Maya didn't stop to evaluate whether precognition or something else made fear flash through her. She stepped between Toni and the guard. "None of us are stupid enough to go running off into the dark woods," she told the guard. She twisted to face Toni. "It's so dark, you could walk off a cliff without seeing it or run into a bear." Then she addressed the first guard, who had hesitated to make sure the second guard didn't need help. "I'll go with you. Two people can carry back more cushions and blankets."

"Maya, no!" Laine and Toni both protested.

"It's too dangerous. The battery array could still explode," Laine said.

"I'll go," Toni said.

"Mom, it looks like the wires aren't sparking so much anymore. And, Toni, you should stay with Nicole. We need her and Mom to help the wounded as they come out. So, that makes me the best person."

The guards shared an amused look, but Maya was used to people underestimating her strength and resolve because of her petite size.

"You will stay with your mother. I'll go help gather supplies from the plane. We'll need water and whatever food we can scavenge, too." All heads turned, their expressions shocked as eyes settled on the tall figure next to Laine. Cyrus's tone was firm and perfectly sane. He pointed to the second guard. "There'll be no shooting anyone in the foot, but keep an eye on these ladies to make sure nothing happens to them." He started down the hill, waving for the first guard to join him. "Come on. Let's do this quickly."

Maya stared after Cyrus, torn between hating the lunatic inside him and loving these increasingly rare glimpses of the father who'd raised her.

"That is the real Cyrus, the loving father who nurtured you, Thomas, and Kyle to adulthood."

Laine's soft voice caught her off guard, and Maya dropped her chin, sad. Lately, a lot of things made her that way. Maya stared at the small bit of greenery pushing up through the scorched dirt. She was even sad that winter would turn the vegetation brown within a month, perhaps weeks. If Kyle were here, she'd point out that the winter months were important for growing strong roots, rather than constantly expending energy to grow foliage or flower. Maya's eyes burned with tears, and her throat tightened with a desperate longing for simpler times when her older sister was her constant protector and mentor.

"Hey. Are you okay?"

Warm fingers gently grasped, then entwined with hers. Maya was surprised when she looked up into brown eyes instead of her mother's blue ones. She barely breathed as Toni raised her free hand slowly, as though Maya was a skittish filly. The touch of her fingers was soft against Maya's cheek, wiping away a tear that had escaped.

"Yeah." Maya cleared her throat and shrugged. "I was thinking about when times were less complicated." She stared into Toni's eyes, dark pools in the faint ring of light. "I miss the father I used to know, and I miss my sister and brother."

"I'm sorry about your brother."

"You know about Thomas?"

"Kyle told me. We were bunkmates for a few weeks when she first showed up at camp. Commander Danielle, Second Warrior, asked me to show her the ropes and help her keep Captain Tan's dragon horse from breeding."

Maya gasped. "So Kyle has a dragon horse now? She's a warrior?"

Toni cocked her head, her smile rueful. "Not exactly."

Maya frowned. She'd had dreams of Kyle with a glittering

reddish-gold dragon horse, accompanied by a dark warrior on a steed that was a deeper copper color. "Then my vision didn't come true. Tell me what did happen."

Toni chuckled. "It's a really long story that we don't have time for now. I don't know what you saw in your vision, but it could likely still happen." She looked past Maya. "Right now, the first of the supplies and more wounded are headed our way. If you can hang lights in some of these saplings, I'll try to organize things so Nicole and your mom can spend their time treating wounds."

"I can do that." Actually, Maya was relieved to have Toni take charge and for them all to be useful. She felt a little less like a helpless hostage.

Toni surveyed the bottles of water and single-serving bags of peanuts, pretzels, and biscotti. If they slit the life vests in strategic places, they could replace the air they held with water and their meager food supplies. They weren't ideal as hiking packs, but a water bottle slid into the collar behind the carrier's neck could provide a counterbalance to make wearing it more comfortable. She started to reach for the small razor-sharp knife she kept in her pocket for opening cartons of supplies in the clinic, then stopped. If they knew she had the knife, they'd take it. She couldn't believe her captors hadn't searched them for weapons. She showed Laine what cuts needed to be made in each vest, and Laine took the vests to Cyrus for help. Then Toni turned back to the water and snacks they'd scavenged. She began to divide the supplies into piles. Should she stuff a pack for each person? No, not everyone. She doubted Xavier would carry anything.

Toni tapped her chin as she calculated. Of the sixteen or so men traveling with Xavier, only five were unscathed. Well, six, if Toni counted Cyrus as one of them. He was ordering people around like he was in charge rather than a hostage. Xavier was ignoring him, too busy berating the pilot somewhere outside their circle of light. The remaining men suffered various degrees of wounds. Laine and Nicole had treated eight with head wounds and broken bones, including resetting one dislocated shoulder. Most could walk down the mountain if they took it slow, but three others were seriously injured and remained in the plane. Would someone stay behind with them? Or should she find something to use as poles and attach seat cushions or blankets to make stretchers?

Toni sighed and stared up at the stars, bright against the midnight sky, then closed her eyes. If she listened intently enough for the swish of dragon wings, maybe she could conjure a rescue force descending from the high air currents.

"Wishing upon a star?" Maya's fingers found and entwined with hers. They seemed to naturally do this anytime they were within touching distance. At least tonight, cloaked in darkness. Would they be different in the bright light of day?

"Just listening to the night sounds."

Maya edged closer, warm against Toni's side, and whispered, "Do you think they'll find us tonight? It's so dark."

"They don't need light. The dragon horses have clear night vision. But I don't know how they could have tracked us here. If the pilot filed a flight plan, it probably wasn't our actual route." Toni smiled when Maya's head dropped to rest against her shoulder. She wanted desperately to block everything else out and kiss her, but her responsibilities came first. "That's why I have to plan for all possibilities, one of them being that we might have to rescue ourselves." Maybe she should also consider future regrets for missed opportunities. Wouldn't want any of those. She twisted to palm Maya's cheek and brush a lingering kiss on her soft lips. "So, now I have to get some information from Xavier to finish my inventory planning."

CHAPTER FIVE

Jael?" Alyssa wavered between disbelief and elation. She pulled her hand back from the warm cheek. It couldn't really be Jael. Could it? No. She was officially cracking up.

"Hello, love." Jael reached for her hand and groaned when the wound in her shoulder stopped her. She tugged her other hand away from Tan, who was unnecessarily taking her pulse, and cautiously stretched toward Alyssa again. This time Alyssa eagerly took the upraised hand in hers and pressed it to her lips. She was so filled with joy that she had to blink away new but happy tears.

Tan frowned at the numbers flashing on the medical scanner she held near Jael's head. "How could this happen? It's medically impossible for a brain to rewire and eye color to instantly change."

Alyssa barely registered Tan's muttering or Raven and Michael's unsuccessful attempt to convince Dark Star to wedge himself back through the door to the outside. All she could see was the crystal blue of her bond mate's eyes, the soul she'd never thought she'd see, touch again in this life. She jumped onto the narrow clinic bed, straddling Jael's hips, and bent forward to pepper kisses onto the face that an hour ago had been the slack visage of the dying Second Warrior Danielle and somehow had transformed into the familiar lines of the warrior she loved with every fierce fiber. "I can't believe you're here." She wiped at tears wetting her cheeks.

"I refused to let them take me from you."

"But Danielle—"

Jael's smile contained a mixture of affection and sadness. She touched Alyssa's cheek and caught a tear with the tip of her finger. "It's okay. She's with Saran now. Her heart is whole again."

Alyssa nodded, her throat too tight for words to come. She completely understood. Half of her heart had been missing since the moment a laser gun burned through her lover's earthly body and twin missiles turned her and Specter into ash. The harder she tried to form the words, the more her throat closed around them. So, she simply captured the lips she'd only dreamed of during the past lonely weeks and fell into the warmth, the strength of their bond. Then she threw her arms out to catch herself before the rude push to her butt toppled her onto Jael, whose new body still bore the head and shoulder wounds of Danielle's last battle with The Natural Order. They all—except Jael, who just closed her eyes and grimaced—covered their ears with their hands as Dark Star unleashed a full-throated dragon scream that rattled the windows.

"Help me sit up," Jael said. "He's not going to leave until I talk to him."

Alyssa slid off the bed so she and Tan could gently assist Jael into a sitting position. Dark Star pressed close. As if understanding the First Warrior's injuries, he carefully touched his ridged forehead to hers and unfurled his massive wings to curl their tips around her back to hold her upright. Jael closed her eyes, and his dragon pupils pulsed and glowed with increasing intensity. The minutes seemed to crawl, but something was happening between them. Alyssa could *feel* Jael and Dark Star more and more. At last, Jael opened her eyes and sighed. Dark Star nickered softly and cautiously released her to Alyssa, who waited with outstretched arms to lower Jael to the bed. The dragon horse watched as Alyssa kissed Jael and stroked her cheek, then stretched to sniff Alyssa's neck, hair, and face thoroughly. He touched his nose to Jael's leg, and she nodded. This response seemed to satisfy him. The stallion folded his wings with a smoky snort, then wedged himself back through the door.

Alyssa watched him leave, then turned to Jael. "Really? Was he just checking me out?"

Jael smiled and reached with her uninjured arm to wipe a sooty nose print from Alyssa's cheek. "Don't worry. He approves of you, but he's still trying to understand why I'm the stallion over this army but service only one mare."

Alyssa caught and kissed the hand lingering against her cheek. Tears again filled her eyes. "I was so lost, so empty without you. Danielle was helping me survive, but when I knew I was losing her, too, I didn't know if I could bear it." She was unable to hold Jael's gaze because she knew her bonded would feel the shield she'd thrown around her emotions. She was ashamed of her weakness.

"Don't. The depth of our bond is not a weakness. It is our strength. My soul refused to let go of that earthly tether and transcend. Instead, I challenged The Collective Council. The Elders were not pleased. No one has ever challenged them, but Saran understood and stood by me. Saran's bond to Danielle still held, too. I could feel it. How Danielle has survived these years is beyond me. I couldn't have."

"I almost didn't. When I thought I'd lost her, too, I was sure I wouldn't. She was my only lifeline, like you were hers."

Jael understood. The deep joy of their soul bonds was worth the pain.

"This could only be possible because you are clones, even though a clone isn't a mirror image." Tan held her medical scanner next to Jael's head. "That's why you could feel Saran and Danielle's bond, and you were somehow able to take her place in the physical world."

Jael swatted the medical scanner away, then groaned when her stiff muscles protested. She was so focused on Dark Star and Alyssa that she'd forgotten Tan was still there. *Go away.* She scowled at Tan. Was she ignoring her telepathic order? "Why am I so sore, and why aren't these wounds healed already?"

Tan bristled. "They are nearly healed, but it takes a few days for the mended tissue to become pliable. She's been inexplicably unconscious and unmoving, so it's reasonable that your muscles would feel stiff and weak." She stared at the display on the handheld scanner. "This is different from just a few minutes ago. Your brain appears to still be transitioning...sort of recircuiting."

I need to get out of this bed. Again, Tan didn't respond to Jael's telepathed message. The transition from physical to spiritual and back to the physical had left her feeling off-kilter, and her irritation grew each time Tan ignored her. A direct verbal order from the First Warrior would constitute insubordination. "Didn't you hear me? Help me up."

Tan looked up in surprise at Jael's terse command. "Hear you?" She slid an arm under Jael's shoulders and helped her sit up and swing her legs over the side while Alyssa rounded the bed to stand beside her.

Jael realized for the first time that she couldn't hear her long-time friend's thoughts either. Had she lost her telepathic ability? Panic swept through her. It was like sudden deafness, even though she could hear audible words. "I can't hear you." She whispered the words she didn't want to believe.

Oh, love. I'm here.

Jael turned to Alyssa, gripping her hand desperately. *But I can hear you.*

Alyssa smiled and rewarded her with a quick kiss. "Perhaps you can hear me because of our bond, and you just can't hear Tan because your brain is still transitioning from Danielle to you." She turned to Tan. "Perhaps we should consult Master Han."

Tan nodded. "That might not be a bad idea. This is a bit out of my field of expertise. I'm a surgeon, not an expert on telepathy."

"I need to see what else might have changed," Jael said, cautiously sliding off the bed. Her legs felt weak, but strong enough to stand after a moment. Alyssa stepped around to her uninjured shoulder and took her arm as Jael tested a few steps. Good enough. She straightened, then rolled her shoulders, wincing when the healing injury throbbed. She rubbed it with her opposite hand. Alyssa looked up, and they both smiled when their eyes met. Jael had injured that shoulder repeatedly in previous lives, but never in this one. Still, she tended to rub it when she was deep in thought and had explained to Alyssa the unconscious gesture was a residual of her past lives. She kissed the sweet lips she'd thought she'd never taste again. "Let's get out of here."

Alyssa looked to Tan. "Is it okay? Will you find Han and send him to us?"

Tan studied Jael. "Sure. Where can he find you?"

"The training field."

"The cabin."

Alyssa and Jael spoke at the same time.

Jael frowned. "I need to know if my flame is still as strong."

You think so, huh? I've got other priorities. Alyssa held Jael in a challenging gaze. "First, you need a shower and something to eat, and then a nap. I'd prefer you don't test anything until we talk to Han and see what he thinks."

Jael kissed her again. *I love for you to be bossy.*

Alyssa smoothed a few strands of stray hair back from Jael's face and smiled. "I love you, too, but whatever medicine Tan has been pumping into you has left you with some serious dragon breath. We need to find you some mouth cleaner."

Tan chuckled. "Personal facility is over there. You might want to take care of that before you head out."

❖

Dark Star extended his huge leathery wings and surfed the brisk currents flowing among the already snow-capped Rocky Mountains until he came to a soft landing in the meadow of the First Warrior's mountain. The wildflowers had long given way to a dry winter forage, but the air was filled with the clean scent of spruce and pine. Jael's swell of joy at returning to her mountain and the cabin she called home was eclipsed only by the woman who shivered and pressed closer against her chest to absorb her pyro warmth. She chuckled and raised her body temperature a few more degrees. "Much more and Dark Star will start sweating and dump us before we can dismount." She kissed Alyssa's ear to soften the teasing remark.

"He might dump you, but he knows better than to let me fall. I'm the one who's been bringing him fire rocks since Toni left. He wouldn't dare anger his fuel source."

Jael kissed her cheek this time and tightened her arms around Alyssa's slight body. Slight but strong. She closed her eyes and savored the scent and feel of her. She'd thought she'd never feel this whole again. Alyssa's hand was cool against her jaw.

"We should go inside, love, so you can rest."

Jael buried her face in Alyssa's neck, unable to resist kissing the soft skin that met her lips. "I don't want to let go." While bed appealed to her, she didn't intend to rest right away. The anticipation of reconnecting with her soul bond was heating her in a different way.

Dark Star shook like a wet dog and clapped his wings against them as if to say "off."

Jael laughed and hopped down, then needlessly guided Alyssa to the ground. "Going. We're going." Clasping Alyssa's hand, she pressed her forehead carefully between the spiked ridges of Dark Star's forehead. The crude pictures that formed in her mind conveyed that he must return to the camp. He was needed there to reaffirm his rank among the other dragon horses. He was bonded to her now. First Dragon. The top stallion with the hottest flame and the greatest breeding potential. Jael smiled to herself. She needed to talk with Alyssa about part of her bargain with The Collective Council. But first things first.

Jael hesitated as they walked through the gathering room past the food-prep alcove. She felt a pang of loss as she was inundated with images of Second—the name Danielle preferred—standing over the chopping board. Second waving a chef's knife as she bemoaned Jael's monotone diet unless someone else cooked. Her cousin—no, her clone—had been her counterweight, her sounding board, the one who kept things moving as Jael led the way. She was more than Jael's second in command.

"She's with Saran now. That's where she most wants to be, isn't it?" Alyssa projected the emptiness of a half heart separated from her soul-bond, then the elation of their own rejoining. "You might have been ordained to come home to me, but your return is a priceless gift to Danielle as well."

Jael sighed. "It's selfish, but I'll still miss her."

"She was cloned from your DNA. Whenever you want to chat with her, just look in the mirror." Alyssa touched Jael's brow and smiled. "The scar where you stitched a cut for her is still here." She ran her finger down the slope of Jael's nose. "And there's the tiny bump where you broke her nose when you were sparring as teens."

"I knew I'd regret one day that I'd been so rough on her."

Alyssa's finger trailed from Jael's nose to touch the new, almost healed wound that Second had suffered in the recent battle against The Natural Order. Enough about the Second Warrior and wounds.

Jael pulled Alyssa to her and bent so that their faces were only inches apart. "I need more than rest to really heal. I need you to fill the places that went cold when I thought I'd never feel your heart beating against mine, in sync with mine, soaring with mine again." Her kiss held no gentleness, only fire, but Alyssa met it with a furious flood of longing and passion. She ignored Alyssa's protest and the dagger of pain in her shoulder as she swept Alyssa off her feet and carried her up the stairs to her bedroom. Their bedroom now.

Jael detoured past the bed to the personal facility. "Activate shower, setting Alyssa." She had noticed a few of Alyssa's belongings in the bedroom and the scent of Alyssa's favorite shampoo in the personal facility, so she concluded that she'd already programed her preferences into the house-management system. She gently released Alyssa to stand. She toed her moccasins off as she kissed along Alyssa's neck and ran her hands under Alyssa's tunic to release the tie holding her loose cotton pants at her waist. Alyssa captured Jael's wandering mouth with hers and mirrored Jael's action. They broke off their frantic kissing to step out of their pants and yank their shirts over their heads. Breathless, they stared. Jael savored the sight of her lover's naked body and the burn of Alyssa's eyes as they raked down hers. Silently, Jael offered her hand and led Alyssa to stand under the warm pelt of the rain-shower. Their kiss was a slow, languid reacquainting of taste and tongue.

Alyssa broke away and pushed Jael back with a hand to her chest. She held her other hand under the dispenser for soap granules, then used both hands to spread them across Jael's shoulders, chest, and arms, mindful of her injury. Jael also filled her hand with granules and began to lather Alyssa's hair, dark red and rich like a full-bodied wine. She soaped along Alyssa's shoulders and down her narrow back. Jael moaned and her nipples tightened when Alyssa's hands lingered on her breasts a few extra strokes.

"Turn." Alyssa's voice was soft as she reached for another handful of soap.

Jael obeyed the only woman who could command her, pressing her forehead and hands against the warmed tile of the shower wall and widening her stance before planting her feet. She closed her eyes and concentrated on the touch of Alyssa's hands soaping her hair, gliding over her shoulder blades, moving down to swirl over her buttocks with a slight scrape of nails that made her shudder. Then Alyssa was kneeling and soaping her legs. The shower began to fill with steam, and Jael had to consciously lower her body temperature. She'd lived so many lives as a pyro that control of her gift had been second nature before Alyssa came into her life. Her attention snapped back to Alyssa's hands working their way from her knees up the inside of her thighs. Her sex clenched and throbbed. The anticipation was both sweet and maddening.

"Turn."

Stars above. Bed now. Jael's control was sorely tested as she moved carefully in the small space her lover allowed and checked her temperature to ensure her hands weren't too hot when she grasped Alyssa's arms to urge her up.

Alyssa shook her head, gently moving Jael's hands from her arms to rest them on her shoulders as she remained kneeling. "Let me have you, love. Then I will give myself to you in any way you want as long as it doesn't injure you further."

Jael nearly drowned in the green pools of hunger that stared up at her. She could barely choke out the words. "I'm near my limit. I won't last."

"Don't even try. You said we'll grow old together. We'll have many more times."

Jael braced her back against the tile and widened her stance in invitation.

Alyssa smiled up at her. "Mist." The shower spray changed to a warm mist as Alyssa briefly stood to suck one of Jael's tight nipples into her mouth and tweak the other with her fingers.

Jael closed her eyes and hissed, her hips bucking at the shock that pulsed from her breasts straight to her sex. She bucked again when Alyssa's nails scraped across the very sensitive muscles below her navel and gasped at the next sensation of Alyssa's mouth between her legs and her fingers probing for entrance.

"Now. Won't last." Her moaned words were more request than command, but Alyssa thankfully complied, pushing into her, filling her and raking her teeth gently along the top of Jael's rock-hard clit as she sucked it. She barely had time to set a rhythm—one stroke, two, three—before Jael's orgasm gathered like a roiling ball in her belly and exploded in a burst of pleasure that flowed through her body like a tsunami. "Sun and moon!" Her shout reverberated against the shower walls.

"Are you all right, love?"

She opened her eyes at the gentle question and grinned at the cloud of steam engulfing them. "I should be asking you that. I didn't blister anything important on you, did I?"

Alyssa stuck out her tongue and held up her fingers, then grinned. "Don't worry. The parts you treasure most are fine."

"Sassy as ever." Jael laughed as she lifted Alyssa to sling her over her good shoulder. The hot shower had done wonders for her stiff muscles. She was relieved that most of her soreness was apparently from having lain in bed too long.

She paused under the air dryer before striding into the sleeping room and tossing her onto the bed. "My turn," she growled, then pounced onto the foot of the large bed.

Alyssa crab-crawled backward to the center of the bed. "You're not being careful." Her protest held little weight given the amusement, then arousal flickering in her eyes.

"I'm not as sore now that I've been up and moving." Jael stalked forward on her hands and knees. "Your therapy helped a lot, so I'm ready for another session."

Alyssa moved back another foot toward the top of the bed but allowed Jael to overtake her, spreading her bent knees to allow Jael between them. She sank onto the large pillow now at her back and cupped Jael's strong jaw. Her expression was serious. "I love you, my

First Warrior. First in my heart. First in my bed. There will always be only you."

Jael's throat closed on any words she would have spoken. She was a warrior, a woman of action, and her empathic mate could *feel* her proclamation of devotion. So, she touched her lips to those of the woman who held the other half of her soul. Their tongues danced in prelude, and then she paid homage to Alyssa's beautifully sculpted shoulders, her soft breasts and rosy nipples. Jael kissed her way down the soft, flat belly, dipping her tongue in the navel, then moved back up to stare into her emerald eyes as she guided Alyssa's legs to lock around her hips. She spread Alyssa's labia and pressed her own hard mons against Alyssa's swollen clit. She rocked gently against Alyssa's slick arousal, and Alyssa moaned.

"Yes, like that, love."

Jael began slowly, then increased her pace, thrusting faster and bearing down harder. Alyssa's lips parted as her breath quickened. Then her mouth dropped open in a small gasp.

"Don't stop. Don't stop."

Jael leveraged up from resting on her elbows to bracing with her arms fully extended to increase her point of contact.

Alyssa's eyes widened, her body stiffened, and her mouth opened in a long, loud groan as her nails dug into Jael's shoulders. When Alyssa closed her eyes and went limp, Jael stopped her thrusts and feathered light kisses along her shoulders. After a moment, Alyssa's eyes fluttered open, her gaze burned hot and hungry. Jael's own hunger—fierce and undeniable—rose to meet it.

In their time together, they had made love many ways, alternating control, each bowing to the other's need of the moment to dominate or submit. There was no control to take or concede as Alyssa flipped onto her stomach and parted her legs. This position was their mutual favorite, the one that never failed to arouse and satisfy them both.

Jael moved over her, sliding her hand between Alyssa's legs. She nipped her earlobe as she thrust her thumb into Alyssa's warm, wet center and felt for the rough spot of nerves that would again drive her lover to climax. Stars, she was so wet and slick from her orgasm.

Then Jael pressed her sex against Alyssa's firm butt cheek and grunted when Alyssa reached back to part her labia and slide her fingers along each side of her hardening clit. Jael returned the favor, her fingers stroking along Alyssa's clit each time she thrust her thumb in and out.

Their edge dulled by their first orgasms, they both closed their eyes and reveled in the pleasure of each thrust, each glide of skin against skin, each sound of pleasure without the strain of holding back. Jael opened her thoughts as well as her heart, and Alyssa flowed forth her affection and adoration as she absorbed the same from Jael.

Alyssa's fingers twitched and pressed firm against the spot along Jael's clit she knew was the most sensitive. But Jael had felt the swell of emotion before the physical signal. Alyssa's orgasm was gathering, and hers rose in answer. Jael thrust faster and bore down hard. The bed thumped against the wall with their motion, accenting Jael's grunts and Alyssa's shrill cries of "oh" and "yes." The chorus of sound filled Jael's ears as she bit down on the top of Alyssa's shoulder to anchor herself, and their shared orgasm exploded her into a million molecules of pleasure. When her scattered brain cells again coalesced in a return to awareness, she lay on her back staring at the ceiling. Alyssa was crawling on top of her, wiping tears from Jael's face and from her own.

In their beginning, the tears had shamed Jael. Warriors didn't cry. Now she fully understood their soul bond. As a rare prime telepath and the only known projecting empath, their sharing surpassed any that other couples could experience. Until death and beyond. Their bond had truly transcended their physical realm and held firm. She was lightning, and Alyssa was the rod that grounded her.

Alyssa's smaller body draped over Jael's. It was one of their favorite sleeping positions. Jael raised her body temperature a bit for her heat-seeking lover and stroked her hands down Alyssa's back. She sighed with contentment. If only she could wish this war away so they'd never have to leave their mountain.

"Yours. Always." Alyssa's mumbled assurance barely left her lips before her breathing evened out in sleep.

"And I yours. Always." Jael kissed the top of her head and drew a small fleece coverlet over Alyssa's back. A quilt would be too warm for Jael, but Alyssa would sleep soundly sandwiched between her warm body and the light fleece.

Jael reached out with her mind to find Dark Star. He showed her a picture of the moon. About four hours until sunrise, she estimated. All seemed well. Almost. Even when she wasn't consciously shielding, the world seemed too quiet. The absence of the millions of thoughts she'd grown used to shielding against worried her more than she wanted to admit. But she was tired. Very tired. She'd speak with Han tomorrow. And she needed to debrief with the remaining Guard.

"What are you thinking about so loud?" Alyssa's sleepy complaint brought Jael back to the present.

At least she had no trouble hearing or being heard telepathically when it came to Alyssa. "You know me. Just a to-do list. I didn't mean to wake you."

Alyssa kissed her. "Please try to rest."

"I will, love." Jael ran her fingers through her lover's hair. The short spikes stuck up in complete, adorable disarray. "Can we shift to our sides? I think this body has been on its back too much lately."

Alyssa rolled off next to Jael's uninjured shoulder so that Jael could spoon behind her. "Better?"

"Being with you is perfect no matter how we sleep." She closed her eyes, cleared her mind, and followed her love into unguarded rest.

Chapter Six

"Toni...Lieutenant Antonia."

Toni didn't open her eyes but smiled at the soft whisper and warm breath on her neck. She rolled onto her back, only to be jerked awake by a sharp stab of pain. Blinking into the morning haze, she realized why it felt like she was lying on a bed of rocks—she was sleeping on the ground, and the stab of pain was actually from a rock jabbing her back.

The night had been long and cold. Four of them had shared two blankets, laying one on the ground and then spooning Nicole up against Maya with Toni and Laine bookending them so one blanket could cover them all. Well, almost. Toni suspected that, like her, Laine was only partially covered. But Toni didn't complain. The cold kept her from enjoying the sensation of Maya's warmth against her back too much and prevented her from anything more than an occasional brief doze. She'd needed to stay vigilant in case a team swooped down during the night to rescue them. She scanned the sky and surrounding woods. The sun was just crowning the mountain peak to their right. The rustle of night creatures in the underbrush had gone quiet, and a few early birds were beginning to warble the new day's arrival. Toni was torn between disappointment that their warriors hadn't found them and relief that they hadn't swooped in and caught her napping. When exhaustion had finally won out, she'd slept deeply for almost two hours until Maya woke her.

Toni sat up and stretched. Nicole hadn't stirred, but Laine was already up and checking on patients. Most of the men, including Cyrus and the sentry serving his shift of guard duty sitting against a tree, were still snoring. Xavier and several of the men had gone into the plane to sleep on the comfortable lounges and seats, escaping the night's chill and the morning's dew. Toni had figured they paid for those comforts by enduring the constant moaning from the more seriously injured, the cursing from those with broken bones when they rolled over in their sleep, and the occasional startled exclamations of one seriously injured man when he temporarily regained consciousness and realized he couldn't feel his legs.

"Did you hear it last night?" Careful to leave the blanket tucked around Nicole, Maya sat up, too, and entwined her arm with Toni's as she pressed close. "The shots from a weapon." Maya's voice trembled, and Toni didn't think her shudder was from the cold. "I'd hoped that vision wouldn't come true. At least none of us are injured in any way."

Toni frowned. "What are you talking about?"

Maya's whisper turned from soft to irritated and fierce. "You couldn't have been asleep. I felt you tense." She tightened her arm around Toni's and gave her a small shake.

Toni sighed. Playing dumb wouldn't work with a seer. She'd been confused about what had jerked her from a doze a few hours after everyone had settled down to sleep. She'd listened intently for the swish of dragon-horse wings or a signal from the edge of the woods that maybe their rescuers had arrived. All she heard was the man in the plane wailing about his legs again, then the muffled pop of a projectile weapon inside the solar plane and the man went quiet. She'd remained still as someone in the plane barked orders, and the rest of the men, except Xavier and Juan, poured out of the plane while holding tight to their blankets and assisting less-able comrades. She was grateful they'd settled some distance away. They smelled of man sweat and blood, and she didn't need to be an empath to sense the fear in their sullen silence. "I heard it. I think the guy in charge, Xavier, decided to cull his team."

Maya bowed her head. "We have to build pyres. They'll be badly born into their next life if we don't properly release their spirits." She stared at the wreckage. "I'll go speak to him."

Toni shook her head, grabbing Maya's hand even though she hadn't yet made a move toward the plane. She was trying to keep them alive and didn't think it wise to argue with Xavier over last rites for the men she suspected he had executed. "Too late for that. I think they already had been badly born into this life. Besides, I'm sure The Guard will eventually track us tonight or the next night. They can make short work of setting their spirits free."

"She's right, Maya." Laine returned from checking the injured camped outside the plane and sidled close to join their quiet conversation. "We have to keep our focus on the larger mission."

Toni was glad Laine backed her up. Maya could be rather hard-headed. "Exactly. We need to stay focused on the four of us escaping."

Laine studied the ground for a few seconds, then looked up to meet Toni's eyes. "I know you want to return Nicole and her baby safely to Furcho, and I won't interfere. But my mission is different. I must reach the City of Light and take my rightful place."

"Mom—"

Toni stared, incredulous. "You can't mean that you buy into the crap your husband is spouting."

Laine shook her head, glancing over her shoulder at Juan exiting the plane and issuing orders to the men gathered a short distance away. "I don't have time to explain now, so you'll have to trust that I'm loyal to The Collective ideal of diversity and world responsibility."

This discussion wasn't over, and Toni's trust in Laine was precarious, ready to tip one way or the other with the slightest nudge. She'd be keeping a close eye on Laine, even though she was Kyle's mother. Even though Toni felt inexplicably drawn to Maya.

"Silence."

Nicole stirred as Toni, Maya, and Laine turned at Xavier's shouted command. He was standing next to three of the "walking wounded" who'd been arguing with Juan. They watched as the men shrank back when Xavier gestured angrily with his weapon. His voice was calm but too low for them to decipher what he was saying. Cyrus stood at Xavier's shoulder, his arms folded over his chest, but said nothing.

"What's going on?" Wrapped in their blanket, Nicole shuffled close and spoke quietly.

"Not sure," Toni said, watching Juan break off from the group and head toward them. "But I think we're about to find out."

"We will leave in a half hour." He surveyed the pile of life vests they'd converted into packs and stocked with their meager supplies. "Four of you and seven of us are fit to travel. Empty out those supplies and redistribute them into eleven packs." He hesitated. "No. Make eleven piles of supplies, but we'll take only ten packs. Divide Xavier's share between Cyrus's pack and mine. We'll carry his load."

"What about the other men, those too injured to hike down this mountain?" Laine's question was calm but tinged with accusation.

"We don't know how far we'll have to walk to find a town or a road leading to one. We don't have enough water to leave any." He looked down the hill at the injured men sprawled there, some already shivering with fever. "Our pilot has the coordinates of this location. We'll send help for them as soon as possible." When Toni started to speak, he sliced his hand through the air. "Twenty-seven minutes. If you aren't ready to leave, Xavier will shoot you like the men in the plane who were disturbing his sleep." He turned and headed back to the plane.

"He's lying," Nicole said. "They're leaving those men here to die."

"We can't think of that now. We don't have much time." His deadline had kicked Toni into organization mode. "Maya and Laine, empty these packs and start making piles while I go with Nicole for a nature call."

"Yes, please," Nicole said, shifting her feet in a tiny need-to-go dance. "This baby must be sitting right on my bladder."

"Go," Laine said. "I'll explain to the men if anyone notices."

Toni took the opportunity for a standing "field call" while her back was politely turned so Nicole could take care of her call to nature. She scanned the forest but mostly kept watch to make sure none of the men were coming after them.

"How do you do that standing up?"

Toni chuckled as Nicole shuffled around her while still pulling her pants up. "Learned it from one of the warriors who said she was a soldier in a previous life. I'll show you some time." She blushed at the thought of sharing something so personal with Nicole. Between soldiers, it was just necessary business. But Nicole wasn't a soldier. "Not now. We're running out of time."

Nicole lowered her voice as they neared the clearing. "I can feel your doubts about Laine, and I do feel something is unusual about her. But I don't sense anything dangerous. Her intentions feel genuine."

"Okay. But I still want you to be careful what you say around her, and please stick close to me. I can't shield you if too many people get between us."

Nicole grabbed Toni's hand and squeezed. "I will. I'm well aware that I'm responsible for more than myself now." She touched her stomach. "I have to keep this little one safe, too."

Laine and Maya stood over eleven neat piles with a makeshift pack next to nine of them.

Toni looked at Laine. How did she know?

Laine smiled at her. "I figured you and I could carry Nicole's share in our packs." Nicole started to protest, but Laine held up her hand. "You're already carrying extra weight. Even though you feel strong right now, I've been pregnant before—three times, to be exact—and I can promise that your energy won't hold up."

Toni was relieved when Nicole merely nodded, her protest derailed. "Okay, nine packs. You two take your turn in the woods, while Nicole and I stuff the packs. We don't have much time left."

They were nearly finished when one of the guards approached them, frowning. "Where are the other two?"

"Taking care of nature's call," Toni said, holding up a pack for him. "Each of the packs for you guys has two bottles of water and a share of the snacks we scavenged from the plane. Just wear the vest like it's intended." She helped him slip into it and snugged the back strap so it wouldn't flap against his chest. "They're not too bulky since we deflated them. If you send the other guys up, I'll help them with their packs. Do you want to take Juan's and Cyrus's packs to them? Their packs are a little heavier because they're carrying Xavier's share."

"Yes. I'll send the other three up." He hesitated, staring at her oddly before clearing his throat. "Thanks."

Toni smiled at him. "No problem. It's what I do…organize things." She wanted the guards to relax and see them as people, not just the enemy.

He glanced toward Laine and Maya emerging from the woods as he took the two packs Toni held out. "You should get your packs on, too, and be ready. You don't want to make Xavier angry by being slow."

"No worries. Send your other guys up, and we'll walk down with them."

Maya and Laine were watching the guard leave as they walked over to Toni.

"Everything okay?" Maya asked.

"Yeah, but get your packs on and be ready to move out." Toni turned to Laine. "We're missing some of three water bottles and five protein bars since I inventoried the supplies last night."

Laine looked over at the blanket they had lain on during the night. It was bunched in a haphazard pile that looked a bit too large for the thin covering. "They're hidden under the blanket over there. I wanted to leave the wounded men something."

"Here they come," Nicole whispered.

Toni grabbed her pack and spoke quickly. "I've folded some of the leftover vests and stuffed them in the collars of our packs. We might have need of their straps or water-tight material later."

Laine followed Nicole, who had stepped away to retrieve the packs for the three guards. She murmured something that Toni couldn't hear, and Nicole nodded, then reached up to adjust the collar and back strap of Laine's pack. They snagged the remaining three packs and brought them over just as the guards walked up.

"Does that feel okay?" Toni had rolled up their second blanket and twisted it around Maya's back strap, then adjusted the length so it fit snugly but comfortably around her waist. She straightened and was captured by Maya's gaze. Her smile was slow, like the burn spreading low and deep in Toni's belly.

"It's perfect."

"Not too heavy?"

Maya raised an eyebrow in challenge. "You're not the only strong one, Lieutenant."

Now a different heat spread up Toni's neck to her ears. "Yeah. I know."

"Where are our packs?" The cocky guard was the shortest of the three but, apparently, their self-appointed leader. His hard eyes raked over Maya, and his expression twisted into a leer. "I can adjust that for you," he said. "We wouldn't want to squash those lovely breasts."

Toni scowled and moved to step between them, but Maya put up her arm to hold her back. "I appreciate your offer, but it takes another woman to know what fits comfortably on a female body."

Laine swung a pack at the man's chest, and he let out a small "oof" as it slammed into him. "Oh, sorry," she said. "I thought you saw me tossing it to you."

The man glared at her, then turned and stalked away. The other two guards quietly accepted their packs, nodding their thanks, and turned to follow.

"That was risky, Laine." Toni grinned. "But you saved me from doing something worse if he put his hand on Maya."

❖

Laine looked to Nicole, who discreetly gestured to the largest of the guards—a barrel-chested man with a heavy beard stubble. "Emile." Laine called to him and held out a protein bar. "I think this fell out of your pack."

He glanced toward the other two guards, then walked quickly back to Laine. "Thanks," he said. "I'm starving."

Laine followed as he headed again for the plane. "You're welcome. We'll walk down with you if that's okay."

"Sure," he said, stuffing the snack into his pack, then lifting the vest over his head as Toni, Nicole, and Maya fell into step behind them.

"Hold on a second." Laine helped him adjust the strap that wound behind his back and snapped together at the front of the vest. He was tall and stocky enough that the vest looked like a child's size on his big body. She fiddled unnecessarily with the strap's clasp and nodded uphill. "The blanket still on the ground is hiding a few bottles of water and snacks for the men we're leaving behind. If one of them walks to the blanket from where they are now, then heads forty-five degrees to their left for about five minutes, he'll find a clear stream. I left six empty bottles under the blanket, too."

"Come on," Toni said, leading Nicole and Maya past them. She looked back over her shoulder but didn't stop walking. "Looks like Xavier is up. We need to get down there."

"That's the best I can do for them," Laine said. "I'll try to stall a few minutes more, but you need to find a way to get that message to one of the injured we're leaving behind. Can you do that?"

"Yes. Thank you."

She patted his chest, then spoke loudly. "I think that will hold. It shouldn't come loose again."

Toni frowned. "They'd probably have spotted the blanket sometime today and found the things you left for them."

"I needed to let them know where they can find more water."

Toni stopped walking and stared at Laine, her expression a mix of curiosity and suspicion.

"I can explain about Mom later, but not now," Maya said, shooting Laine a look of exasperation and tugging Toni into motion again.

When they reached the group, Xavier scanned them before settling his gaze on Laine. He stared at her for a long moment, then pointed to the pilot leaning against the plane. "We need him to go with us in case we find a town or community farm that has an airstrip and something that can fly some of us to our destination. But he's injured his ankle. Can you fix it enough so he can walk?"

This was her chance to stall their departure. "I'll do what I can. Then I can wrap it so it'll bear his weight."

He waved her impatiently forward. "Be quick. I'm ready to leave."

Laine turned to Nicole. "Can you get the first-aid kits we were using last night? Check if there's some tape left or an elastic bandage in one of them." Her eyes drifted to Emile, who gave an imperceptible nod, then moved among the injured. "If not, we'll have to take a bandage from one of the injured." She went to the pilot. His eyes were filled with fear as he slid to sit on the ground and she knelt to remove his sock.

"Do whatever you can. I'd rather stay here and chance starvation or hungry wolves than go with this maniac. But if I can't walk out of here, he'll likely shoot me like he did my co-pilot and two of his own injured men."

His ankle was swollen nearly twice its normal size. She laid her hands gently on either side and closed her eyes. She sensed swollen tissue and strained tendons, but no breaks in the bones of his ankle or foot. Her hands momentarily swelled as she transferred the damage to herself, then shrank as she slowly infused the ankle with a numbing cold that should last much of the day. She felt dizzy as she withdrew and released him. The damage had been worse than she first detected. Two of the tendons suffered small tears.

"I found a couple of rolls of adhesive gauze," Nicole said, placing a steadying hand on Laine's shoulder. "Let me finish up. We can put the sock back on and wrap the gauze over it so it won't stick to his skin."

"Wrap it tight, but not too tight. He needs to walk, but with minimum movement."

"Don't worry. I've done plenty of these. Those warriors in camp were constantly spraining an ankle or a wrist in training."

Laine smiled at the familiar feel of Maya's knees bumping gently against her back. She relaxed against her daughter. They'd done this many times—Laine healing and Maya quietly supporting her in the few moments of weakness that followed. But their time together was ending. She felt it and was sure Maya had seen it. Duty awaited, and Maya's star would fall as Laine's rose.

The pilot stood and smiled as he tested it, then frowned. "I can't get my shoe on over this bandage."

"What size do you wear?" Toni asked. He recited his size, then she ducked into the plane and emerged a few minutes later with a real backpack. She held up two lace-up boots like the ones most of the guards wore. "You're in luck. I found a pair of boots in your size and another boot two sizes larger for that swollen foot."

Laine knew where Toni had found them and reached up when she felt Maya about to voice the question in her head. "Help your old mother up, Maya."

Maya did as Laine asked, and they watched as Toni and Nicole helped the pilot slide on the boots and lace them tight. Laine heard the question rising again and shook her head to stop Maya from voicing it. Acknowledging that the boots had come off the feet of the dead men had no benefit.

Xavier slapped his hand against the plane. "Let's get moving. Is he good?"

"Yes. He can travel," Laine said.

Xavier narrowed his eyes. "Where'd you get that pack?"

Toni finished the double knot on the boot she was tying and straightened. "I found it in the plane when I was searching for some suitable footwear for this guy." Her tone was casual, as though she was reciting the weather forecast. "When the swelling goes down, he'll need a boot that matches the size of the one on his other foot, so I put the matching boot in that backpack, along with a few things from the first-aid kit. He can carry it. We didn't make a pack for him."

Xavier's lips contorted into a sneer, then suddenly relaxed into a smile. Wordlessly, he went into the plane and emerged several minutes later with a change of clothes and a shaving kit. "It is fortunate that I kept my bag in the plane. The baggage compartment isn't accessible from inside." He slapped the rolled-up clothes and the shaving kit against Toni's chest. "He can carry these in his pack, too. Throw his extra boot out if there isn't enough room."

Laine glimpsed a few other things in the backpack when Toni hurriedly added Xavier's things. She bent close to whisper. "Where did you find more water?"

Toni helped the pilot shoulder the pack. "It's only three, and they're partially full. I guess the guys who slept in the plane last night must have left them." She tapped the pilot on the shoulder. "They're for you. There's no food, though."

Tears welled in the pilot's eyes. "Thank you for all your help. If I ever get free of these men, I'll never hire out to those crazies again."

"Don't let Xavier or Juan hear you say that," Toni said, "or you'll be toast. Let's get moving."

CHAPTER SEVEN

Michael watched Diego shove the last of several heaping food platters onto the long table in the common room of the headquarters building where The Guard were assigned living quarters. He and Raven rose from their seats as heavy footfalls sounded on the porch outside, and they all stood expectantly as Third Warrior Furcho, his face grim, entered with Tan and Kyle on his heels. Furcho hesitated before walking past Jael's usual chair at the head of the table and standing next to the chair at the opposite end—the seat previously reserved for the late Second Warrior Danielle. He gestured for Lieutenant Kyle to sit in his former seat, across from her lover, Captain Tanisha. No one—not even Diego, who argued against everything—questioned the clear message. Kyle was Guard now. Her addition would restore their number to seven.

"Guard."

The group came to stiff attention and thumped their right fists against their left shoulders in response to Furcho's call to order.

He returned their salute. "Sit." He motioned to the platters. "Thank you, Diego, for preparing this meal. I'll see about having someone from support services bring our meals up from the dining facility so you don't have to in the future."

"It's no problem. I like to cook, but Second wouldn't let anyone else in her kitchen. I have someone in mind to assign to headquarters permanently." He passed a platter of plantains to Raven. "Someone who will step aside when I want the food prep to myself."

Furcho nodded. "Let me know when the paperwork is ready. I'll sign it." He stared down at his empty plate. "I need to reassign the quartermaster ranks to somebody." He looked around the table.

"Looks like you're stepping in to Second's role," Diego said. "She handled the quartermaster unit."

Furcho's jaw tightened, and his hands clenched into fists next to his plate. "I have to focus on our mission to retrieve those taken hostage and end The Natural Order. If he hurts her…" His growled words hung in the air. He didn't need to speak the last words because each of them silently completed his statement for him.

"We should wait for Jael before we begin making plans." Forks stilled, and all eyes warily studied Furcho as they awaited his response to Tan's declaration.

Michael blinked at the light tap against his shin under the table. Raven, seated across from him, met his eyes, then looked pointedly down at the two plates he'd been filling with food since he'd noticed Furcho passing but not taking anything from the platters of roasted pork, *arroz con pollo*, beans, and sweet plantains. He rose and swapped Furcho's empty plate with the extra one he'd filled.

"Actually, I've been working on an inventory program with Lieutenant Toni, who is an amazing organizer. I know she's Alyssa's assistant, but I think Commander Danielle saw Toni as more of her quartermaster protégé," he said as he returned to his seat. He casually took a bite of his food and chewed slowly, as though thinking something over. "I know the software, so I can handle those duties until Toni returns. The commander would have probably recommended Toni succeed her." He was careful to stop referring to Danielle as Second. He hoped the others would follow his lead. Jael would soon name a new Second Warrior to replace Danielle.

"I'd be fine with that." Raven offered him a slight smile and forked a chunk of roasted pork. "Anybody else volunteering for the job?"

A chorus of "nope" and "when pigs fly" mingled with forks clattering against plates as everyone else followed the redirection in conversation and the meal resumed. Even Tan seemed willing to let her challenge to Furcho drop—at least for now.

Michael kept a cautious eye on Furcho, who still sat straight in his chair. Maybe he wouldn't let it pass. This wasn't the calm, wise Third Warrior they'd known over several lifetimes. This was a pyro warrior holding on to his sanity by a thread, aching to burn a swath across the country to incinerate the men who dared take his fiancée and unborn child. And, if the reincarnated Jael wasn't up to the task of being First Warrior, Furcho was next in line to command the dragon-horse army. Stars. What if he challenged Tan right here, right now? Supposedly, after Jael, Kyle was the strongest pyro among them. Old friend or not, Kyle wouldn't stand by and let him hurt Tan. Sun and moon. If The Guard ended up in chaos, The Collective was doomed.

Diego tapped Furcho's hand with his fork. "Eat, my friend. You haven't even noticed that I made your favorites."

Furcho looked down at his plate, his posture relaxing a bit.

"You have to stay strong to go save your lady and child," Diego said, his gruff manner uncharacteristically gentle. "Eat to keep your strength up for them." Then he sat back and frowned, reverting to his usual rough tone. "Eat, or next time I'll slip in those peppers that make you run to the personal facility all night."

Michael chuckled, drawing glares from both Furcho and Diego. He grinned at them, and even Furcho managed to return a small smile before tucking into his food. Michael mouthed a silent "thank you" when Diego glanced his way. Furcho wasn't the only one this war had affected. The loss of Diego's friend Advocate Uri had changed the normally fractious member of their group.

"We'll figure it all out," Tan said. She waved her fork to indicate Furcho should continue eating. "When we're all done, I'll tell everyone what little I can explain about Jael's condition and maybe what we can do immediately."

Forks again hung in the air until Furcho nodded, and then everyone dug in to polish off the meal so they could get down to business. After the final plantain was consumed and the last dish cleared, they settled back into their seats and looked expectantly at Tan.

Michael was thankful that Tan, the group's rule-breaker, followed protocol for once and glanced first to Furcho for a nod to proceed.

"Some of you were present for some things, and others for different parts of Jael's unprecedented return. So, I'll start from the beginning and walk you through everything I know."

Michael realized for the first time that Kyle had changed seats while they were clearing the table so she sat at Tan's right, rather than across from her, and Tan subtly shifted toward her bond mate as she recounted the painful scene of Titan's demise, then the confusing reanimation of Second Warrior Danielle. Only Danielle hadn't come back to life; Jael had taken over the body of her cousin, the only existing clone of Jael.

"What little medical testing Jael would permit showed nothing abnormal. As you know, except for their eye color, Jael and Danielle had little physical difference except in their brains. Danielle did not share

Jael's telepathic abilities, and no one could match Jael's strength as a pyro. By the same token, Danielle had a superior mind for organization of details and a unique natural shield that barred even Jael from reading her thoughts unless Danielle consciously opened to them."

Tan glanced nervously at Kyle, who sat back in her chair and cocked her head as though listening for something.

Uh-oh. Michael sensed trouble. Kyle had been assigned to share Toni's quarters when she first joined their army—before Kyle bonded with Tan—and Toni had told him a lot about her tall warrior bunkmate. Besides being the daughter of The Natural Order's leader, she was a superior pyro and had an agile mind. If Michael was reading this right, Kyle was working something out that Tan might have failed to share with her. That appeared to worry Tan.

Raven straightened in her chair. "That's what's wrong, what's missing." She locked eyes with Kyle, who was nodding. They'd simultaneously realized what Tan wasn't saying.

Diego frowned. "Do you want to clue the rest of us in?"

Furcho shared Diego's look of consternation, but Michael held back his response until he was sure of Tan's revelation. He wasn't surprised that Furcho, who couldn't seem to think past rescuing Nicole, hadn't figured it out.

"Try contacting Jael telepathically," Kyle said.

Furcho was silent for a long moment, and then his eyebrows shot upward. "She's shielding us out? Why would she do this?"

Tan sighed. "I'm pretty sure it's not intentional. But before Jael and Alyssa left the clinic, Jael realized I couldn't hear the thoughts she was projecting to me." She paused before releasing the next information. "And she was unable to read my thoughts."

"Son of a dung-eater." Diego's soft swear was the only response as this news sank in. Jael had previously been the most powerful telepath to ever walk the earth.

"I've sent Han to evaluate her situation," Tan explained after letting the information settle. "It could be a variety of things. She can still communicate telepathically with Alyssa, and she's already established a bond with the wild stallion, Dark Star. Early readings indicate her brain is rewiring itself as it adjusts to her pattern of thought, her memories, and her mannerisms. Even when that's complete, Han might still have to help her recover her telepathic gift. Sort of like a stroke victim having to learn to speak again because of damaged brain cells."

"What good is that if she can't contact the hostages telepathically now, so we can locate them?" Furcho pushed his chair back and stood, his words growing louder and more insistent. "We can't wait while you run a battery of tests on her or Han retrains her to get past Danielle's hard skull. We have to move now if we want any chance at striking before they settle into that mountain fortress The Natural Order is building."

Tan stood, too, and matched his volume. "You can't just go barreling in there. They have a more defensible position and probably more weapons than they did in Brasília. Do you want to risk Nicole and your unborn child? An ill-planned offensive could sacrifice what remains of our army. Those brave warriors have families, too, you know."

Kyle stood, her voice quiet but strong enough to cut through the mounting debate. "I agree with Furcho that we need to act fast."

Tan wheeled on her lover, anger flaring in her eyes.

Kyle stopped her with an upraised hand. "But we can't charge in without forming a plan and meeting with Jael. She is First Warrior and still in charge of this unit of The Guard."

"I agree," Raven said. "What can we set in motion this very moment while Han is meeting with Jael?"

"We need to locate that plane," Diego said.

"Why? We'd never be able to catch up with them," Kyle pointed out. "Dragon horses can't move as fast as a plane and only fly at night. We should concentrate on locating this City of Light and get there as soon as possible the same way we got here—flying at night and transporting by solar rail during the day."

"If Jael's brain was working right, she could contact Toni or Nicole telepathically for some clue as to where they might be," Furcho growled.

Diego groaned. "We can't do this without Jael. Killeen was a cluster jump because it was impossible to hear any orders over those com sets once all those idiots started shooting those noisy projectile weapons. I never thought I'd wish for Jael's voice in my head, but we're like a dead network without her telepathic skills."

Tan slapped her forehead and turned to Kyle. "The network. Why didn't we think of them before?" She turned back to the group. "The people that helped us in San Pedro Sula are an underground network of gifted outcasts…techno-geeks that can hack any system and crack any encryption on the digital net. Every city has a group like them. I'm sure they can track a plane, even if it hasn't registered a flight plan." She showed them the small tattoo on her forearm. "I spent some time in my youth as one of them."

Furcho nodded. "While you contact them, Raven and I will review the army and get a head count of the battle-ready." He stood and started for the door.

Kyle spoke quietly. "Diego, could you check on possible travel arrangements? Michael, line up the provisions and support staff we'll need for the mission. Then we'll be ready if Tan's network can give us a destination."

Furcho whirled and stalked back to Kyle before they could answer her request. "Who put you in charge, Sparky?"

Kyle matched, even topped Furcho's height by a centimeter. She kept her voice even but didn't back down when Furcho thrust his face close to hers. "I have more at stake here than you, Furcho. That bastard Simon will have both my mother and my sister in his slimy hands as soon as that plane reaches the City of Light. And he has a personal vendetta against me." She narrowed her eyes and stared him down. "I'm not going to stand by while you let rage cloud your thinking about details that will slow us later."

Furcho's roar filled the room. "He has my child." Small flames ignited from his fingertips. Furcho was truly losing control, and Tan, Raven, and Diego all stepped toward him.

"Stand down." The barked command reverberated in the surprised silence.

All heads swiveled toward Michael, and he cleared his throat. He'd never yelled at anyone like that, not even at a thick-headed recruit. But he knew better than any the destructive road they were traveling. He sucked in a breath, letting his nostrils flair for effect, and drew himself up to his full height of a hundred and ninety centimeters. His time training troops in the past few months had added lean muscle to his frame and a healthy glow to his fair skin. His boyfriend Will said it contrasted nicely to his mismatched blue and green eyes and his short, blond mohawk. Will had given Michael the confidence to speak up now, rather than stay known as the silent member of group.

"Have you forgotten already the day we all stood outside Jael's office, waiting to hear whether Tan would be expelled from The Guard for drugging Jael and the rest of us when she was caught up in Phyrrhos's breeding frenzy?" Michael paused to meet the gaze of each—except

Tan, who stared at the floor as Kyle stepped away from Furcho to come to her side. "Danielle listened while we debated our opinions of Tan's transgressions, then reminded us of the oath we'd sworn as The Guard of The Collective. Are we dishonoring her leadership so soon?"

All, even Furcho, hung their heads.

Kyle was the first to lift her chin. She might be the newest member but was second only to Jael in pyro abilities. And she was a natural leader. Michael met her eyes and nodded.

Kyle thrust her closed fist into the center of the group. "Stronger together."

Michael immediately covered her fist with his hand, without taking his eyes from hers. "Stronger together."

Tan, Raven, then Diego followed, each repeating the oath as they added their hand to the group. Furcho hesitated, then laid his on top, his eyes full of remorse as he softly affirmed, "We are stronger together."

Michael smiled at Kyle. He was the youngest and she the newest of the group, but that didn't mean they had to run at the back of the herd.

Kyle returned Michael's smile. "Let's meet back here at zero-seven-hundred to share progress on our individual tasks."

Nods confirmed the plan, so Kyle raised her voice once again. "We're stronger together because we are…"

Furcho, his expression weary, hadn't objected. And, he joined the others in chorusing the familiar response to the dismissal Kyle had adopted from Danielle:

"…GUARD."

❖

Jael closed her eyes and savored the warm air current that lifted her over a mountain ridge before she rode it in a gentle swoop through a valley and back up again. The sun heated her huge black wings as she emerged from the shadow of the valley and topped the next ridge. She was part of the sun and the whispering wind. She was flying in daylight, rather than in the dark of night. Still, it felt natural rather than surprising.

Then wind whispered against her cheek and neck again. "Jael, honey."

She lifted her voice to the sky, and a dragon scream echoed among the peaks surrounding her as she glided in a wide spiral to the one who called her.

"Love, you need to wake up. Han is here. I can feel him." The wind kissed her neck and bare shoulder.

"Oof." Jael felt as though she'd been sucked back through a tunnel and abruptly dumped into her real body. She opened her eyes, then slammed them shut against the bright sunlight streaming in the window. She rolled onto her back and squinted up at the source of whispering wind in her dream—an adorably disheveled green-eyed woman whose short spikes of auburn hair looked as though she'd grabbed a live electrical conductor—and smiled.

"There you are," Alyssa said, stroking her hand down Jael's chest.

Jael rubbed her face. She'd never had that experience in this life, but she could remember the feeling from a previous one. She'd been a Skin Walker, someone who could mind-meld with her animal familiar and temporarily exist in its body. She'd forgotten the exhilaration of the experience. Was it her resurrection or the bond with Dark Star that had triggered it? Maybe it was just a very vivid dream, because the sun had been shining and dragon horses only flew at night.

Alyssa caressed Jael's bare arm. "I tried a couple of times to wake you."

The heavy throb in her sex might indicate what Alyssa had been doing to wake her, or it might be the residual arousal and need to assuage it that had always followed after she'd been skin-walking.

"I've never known you to sleep so deeply."

Was her body diverting energy to heal more quickly? Or maybe the unaccustomed silence in her head? But she'd sort that out later. Right now, she had one thing on her mind. She rolled over on top of Alyssa and stared down at her.

Alyssa's hips pressed into hers. "How's your shoulder this morning?"

Jael carefully rotated it, then smiled. "A little stiff, but it feels fully healed."

Alyssa kissed her lightly on the lips. "That must have been some dream you were having."

Jael laughed. "Was I talking in my sleep?"

Alyssa looked away, still absently trailing her fingertips up and down Jael's chest between her breasts. "Not exactly. You were broadcasting pretty strong, though." She looked back to shyly meet Jael's gaze. "It sort of jerked me awake."

Jael dropped a few soft kisses along Alyssa's shoulder. "I'm sorry. I guess the silence…not hearing the multitude of voices I usually have to block out…I was so relaxed I forgot to keep my shields up."

Alyssa opened her legs to fit them around Jael's hips. "You never have to shield from me, Jael. It just caught me by surprise. It seemed like you were Dark Star, not riding him. I don't mind being along for the ride, or flight. But if you start dreaming about bloody battles or other women, you might have something to answer for when you wake up."

"I can't control my dreams, love, so I won't promise no battle scenes." She cupped Alyssa's chin to capture her mouth in a long, sensuous kiss. "But you'll never have to worry that I'll dream about any other woman." She brushed her thumb across the flush coloring Alyssa's cheeks. "I have everything I want right here." Jael flexed her hips to rub against Alyssa's wet sex and dipped her head, intent on capturing Alyssa's tempting lips again, until a loud banging downstairs caused them to jerk apart.

They sat back and grinned. "Han," they said in unison.

Alyssa jumped from the bed and disappeared into the personal facility, but Jael detoured to stick her head out the door and shout down the stairs. "Don't get your bloomers in a twist, old man. We'll be down as soon as we wash up and dress."

When she stepped into the large shower, Alyssa stared at her.

"What?" Jael looked over her own shoulder. No one there. Then she looked down at her naked body. Nothing Alyssa hadn't seen plenty of in the past twelve hours. "You didn't want to share?"

"It's not that. It's just…I've only ever heard Danielle tease Master Han like that. I've never heard anything like that come out of your mouth."

Jael searched Alyssa's eyes for what she wasn't saying, then dropped her gaze to the shower's bare floor to turn her examination inward. She felt like a hundred percent Jael. But was she part Danielle, too? Last night…no. She snapped her eyes back up to Alyssa. "I might have a few brain cells left that function like Danielle, but only two people were in our bed last night." She took Alyssa's hands and tugged her close. She kissed her with every ounce of devotion she felt, which she knew Alyssa could feel. She slid her rough pyro hands down Alyssa's smooth back, resting them on her hips to press her even closer.

"You and me. If we ever share that bond, it will be with a child, our child."

"Or children," Alyssa said, her lips grazing Jael's.

Alyssa felt so good pressed alongside her, under her hands, against her mouth. Jael sucked at her neck and bent to nip her erect nipple, but Alyssa drew in a deep breath and pushed her away.

"You have to stop." Her face was flushed. The hot spray of the shower? Her breathless words seemed to indicate otherwise. "Han's downstairs."

"We'll be quick."

"Jael, no." The hand planted in the middle of her chest was firm. "I can't. My teacher, who has stars know what abilities, can probably hear or feel everything we're doing."

"Han comes from a culture that had paper stretched over bamboo frames for interior walls. He knows how to block out things."

But Alyssa was adamant. "Please. I…I can't. It's too weird."

Jael released her with a laugh. "You're modest?"

"Yes. I am about certain things." Alyssa took Jael's hand and turned it up to pour soap granules into her cupped palm. "Try using that wandering hand to get yourself cleaned up and smelling less like you've been having sex all night." She stepped out of the spray and into the drying chamber. "I'm already clean and ready to dress." She blew a kiss to Jael, then closed her eyes and raised her arms to fluff her hair as wind jets above and on three sides blew strong streams of heated air over her body.

Jael narrowed her eyes, then slowly soaped down her arms and across her chest. She poured more granules into her palm and massaged them into her breasts, down her belly, and moaned low when her soapy fingers slid between her legs. She watched Alyssa's eyes blink open at the moan, and Jael threw her head back while her fingers worked the melting granules over her sensitive flesh. She widened her stance and parted her sex, moaning again in satisfaction when Alyssa froze, her gaze fixed on Jael's hand. She wanted to laugh at how easy it was to reel in her rarely, but occasionally, prudish lover. Then the tip of Alyssa's pink tongue began to swipe back and forth across her lower lip. Was Alyssa even aware she was doing that? Jael's clit stiffened and swelled with that telltale gathering of pre-orgasmic pleasure, catching her so off guard that she was caught in her own trap. "Son of a goat herder!" Her voice echoed in the shower, and a drying cloth hit her in the face and draped over her head to leave her panting in darkness until she recovered. She laughed as she pulled it off and stepped into the now-empty drying chamber.

"Not fair," Alyssa shouted from the bedroom.

When Jael emerged from the personal facility, Alyssa was dressed and propped against the door frame as if prepared to make a quick getaway should Jael reach for her again. She pointed to the black T-shirt and dark-gray field pants that were Jael's usual wardrobe. "I laid out some clothes for you."

Jael began to dress, feeling more like herself in the familiar clothing.

Alyssa gestured toward the clothes storage. "Do you want your field boots or just the moccasins you prefer around the house?"

"The boots, I think. We'll need to meet with The Guard at headquarters tonight." She frowned at her clothes, which hung loosely on Danielle's less muscular frame. She'd need to eat a lot of protein and hit the resistance machine to achieve her previous body's level of conditioning. Jael sat in a chair when Alyssa brought the high-tech boots. "Thanks." Although the boots appeared rugged, the upper leather was surprisingly soft and flexible. A touch to the heel would transform the hard rubber sole—thick enough to withstand sharp rocks, an upturned nail, or shards of glass—to a razor-thin sole pliant enough to feel a slight toehold on a sheer rock face. She frowned, however, when she settled her foot into the first one. It felt tight. She closed her eyes and shook her head. She had three pairs, but she realized none of the specially crafted footwear would fit. Clones were not necessarily identical. And Danielle's foot was a half size larger. "I'll go without shoes until I have time to rummage through Danielle's things. Maybe she left a few pairs in her room across the hall."

Alyssa frowned. "Jael, it's nearly November. You can't go around barefoot. You'll catch your death of cold." Her hand flew to her mouth, and her eyes filled with tears as she realized what she'd said.

Would this worry that they'd be separated again always haunt them? While Alyssa had lived the horrible loneliness, Jael had felt the separation in the ethereal realm, too. The Ancient had said they would grow old together, but the Elders didn't know everything. They, too, had been surprised by Saran's early departure from the physical realm. Still, she and Alyssa had to free themselves of this anxiety, or it would taint their souls forever.

Jael propped her left ankle on top of her right knee. "Worried my feet will get cold?" She smiled as small blue flames ignited from each of her toes, and then she let the flame spread down to her heel.

Alyssa shook her head but smiled. "I don't know why you bother with shoes at all."

Jael extinguished her foot flame and intentionally raised what she hoped was interpreted as an indignant eyebrow. "Have you ever been around a bunch of dragon horses when they're eating fire rocks? They're sloppy eaters, dropping bits and pieces everywhere. Step on that mess with your bare foot, and you'll never forget it."

Alyssa laughed and swatted Jael's shoulder before bending to kiss her. Her eyes shone with affection. "Thank you. I'm trying to put it all behind us, but the memory of being without you is still so fresh."

Jael stood and hugged Alyssa to her chest, dropping her chin so they were cheek to cheek. "For me, too, love. But we'll get through this together."

Alyssa's arms tightened around her, then released. "I smell something delicious and we slept through breakfast. I don't know about you, but I'm starving."

Jael swept her arm toward the door. "Advocates before warriors."

Alyssa stepped toward the door but grabbed Jael's hand to make sure she was right behind her. "I thought you told me the warriors had to go first to make sure it was safe for the Advocate to follow." She looked back at Jael as they began to descend the staircase. It was wide enough for three to walk abreast, but Jael continued to trail behind her. "I think you just want to watch my ass, First Warrior."

"Guilty." Jael smiled. She *had* promised to never lie to her bond mate.

They both stopped at the bottom of the stairs. The person banging around in the food prep wasn't Han.

❖

Michael turned to Jael and Alyssa with a platter of arroz con pollo in his hands. "Oh, hi. When Han messaged for me to come over, Tan suggested I bring some of what we had for lunch in case you were still in bed." His fair features flushed bright red against his blond hair and sparse beard. "Sleeping, you know. So you can heal quicker. And because Alyssa has been at your bedside since we brought you from Killeen. She must have been exhausted."

"Nah." Jael sauntered over to the table and, without thinking, reached to pilfer a small piece of chicken. She hesitated before realizing that Danielle, who normally cooked for the two of them, wasn't there to swat her hand away. "Alyssa was insatiable. We haven't actually been sleeping very long."

Michael's bright-red face turned two shades darker.

Alyssa grabbed Jael's wrist as she reached for a second piece of chicken. "Wait until we sit down to eat." She glared at Jael. "I cannot believe you just said that. Of all the things you could have retained from Danielle, I wouldn't have chosen her bawdy sense of humor."

Jael blinked. Why did she say that? It wasn't fitting behavior for a First Warrior. And she never swiped food unless only she, Danielle, and Alyssa were present. It was a playful game between cousins. Jael tried to steal a bite or two when she thought Danielle wasn't watching, and Danielle would pretend to not watch so she could catch Jael at her petty theft. She cleared her throat. "Where's Han?"

Michael pointed to the front entrance of the huge cabin. "Outside. I'll put this back in the warmer if you want to speak to him first. I've already eaten, but I don't know if he has."

Jael nodded and headed for the door.

"Thank you, Michael. That would be a good idea if we're not back in the next few minutes," Alyssa said before following Jael.

Han was in the meadow beyond the porch, gracefully moving through an intricate kata of ancient hand-to-hand combat. Jael and Alyssa, both former students, walked to the edge of the meadow and knelt, bowing their heads as they waited to be acknowledged. Han finished his kata in a flourish of lightning-fast movements that belied his age, then held the final pose a handful of seconds before drawing himself to attention with his back still to them. He bowed to an unseen sensei and turned to face them.

They both silently bowed from their kneeling positions. "*Sensei, onegaishimas.*"

Han also bowed in acceptance of their respect. "Rise. I am humbled to be called Sensei by the First Warrior and the First Advocate, and you honor me by still asking that I teach you. However, you are two of four who wield the most powerful gifts on this planet. What you seek today is advice rather than instruction." He cupped Alyssa's cheek, his expression softening with affection. "It is good to see the light return to your eyes, Aly-san." Then he approached Jael with a curious expression. "When there is time, we will sit and talk at length." He extended his hand, and when Jael offered hers, they clasped forearms in a warriors' traditional greeting. "For now, we will discuss expedient matters only." Han gestured toward Jael's cabin. "Our meal and Michael await."

They followed him inside, and the three of them sat at the table. Michael brought the platters from the warmer. "Dig in," he said. "If I have to warm it one more time, I doubt it will be much good."

"Thank you, Michael-san," Han said with a slight bow of his head. "I know you've eaten, but please join us." He touched the chair next to his.

Flavors burst on Jael's tongue when she took her first bite. She tried the plantains that she usually transferred to Alyssa's plate because they were one of her mate's favorites. She closed her eyes as she rolled the sweetness over her tongue and then savored the next bite of her lunch and the next. Jael was surprised moments later that her formerly full plate was suddenly empty. "This is so good." Why hadn't food tasted this good before? She eyed the serving platter, and Han pushed it toward her.

"Eat. You need to put some muscle onto that body you've inherited," he said.

Alyssa discreetly moved the platter with a few plantains remaining out of Jael's reach, and Michael looked a bit amused at her speed eating.

Jael had never been one to rave over food. She would have lived off pro-chow protein pellets if Second, uh, Danielle hadn't cooked for both of them most of the time. Jael looked up at Michael. He was vegan, so she couldn't picture him preparing a chicken dish. "Did you cook this?"

Michael shook his head. "No. You know I won't touch meat. Diego was the chef. Pretty good?"

Jael frowned. "I've eaten his cooking before, and it wasn't this good." She felt Han studying her as she took another bite and chewed slowly, staring at the small amount remaining of her second plate of food. She snapped her eyes up to his, and he tilted his head.

"You've discovered something."

Jael swallowed and sat back in her chair. Alyssa gripped and squeezed Jael's thigh in a move to comfort rather than arouse. Jael dropped her fork and raised her glass to take a large swallow. "Everything tastes different."

"How does it taste different?" Han asked.

Jael stared at her plate a few long seconds as she considered his question, then looked up to hold Han's gaze. "I think I know why Danielle insisted on fresh vegetables and meat, and liked to cook elaborate meals." She took another bite and rolled the food over her tongue before chewing and swallowing. "She might have been cloned from my DNA, and I knew her feet were slightly bigger, her eyes a different color, but it never dawned on either of us that her taste buds were so much more developed than mine. I've never experienced such nuanced flavors before."

Alyssa chuckled. "That explains why you seemed to consider food a necessity rather than a delight."

Jael nodded as she scooped up the last bite on her plate. "I don't understand how she stayed so slim with a palate so developed. It'll take a long workout to burn off everything I've eaten." She aimed her fork at the last plantain Alyssa was guarding.

"Carbohydrates. You've just eaten a lot of carbohydrates," Michael explained, as Alyssa blocked Jael's advancing fork with her own utensil. "Danielle was an avid runner, which burned those carbs off before they converted into fat. That's how she stayed so slim. You ate a lot of protein, and your workout consisted of at least fifty percent strengthening exercises. That's why you were more muscular." He began to remove the empty platters and plates from the table.

Jael withdrew her fork and frowned at Alyssa nervously tugging on her earlobe—a sure sign her reflective mate was working through serious thoughts. She waited while Alyssa halved the last plantain and absently forked the slightly larger half onto Jael's plate. She shoved her half into her mouth and chewed, so Jael did the same and waited for her to speak.

"I don't know why these glimpses of Danielle keep surprising me." Alyssa put her fork down to touch Jael's chin. "The small scar on your chin is gone." She traced the brow over Jael's right eye. "Danielle's scar is still here." She ran her hand over Jael's shoulder and down her arm. "You have at least thirty pounds less muscle now." Then she cupped Jael's jaw. "Yet at some point in the scant day since you returned to me, I quit seeing Danielle when I look at you. I see my soul bond, my mate. So, it does surprise me when you make a sarcastic remark or comical gesture that is clearly Danielle, not my Jael."

Jael was unsure how to react. Was this transformation disturbing Alyssa? She certainly felt off-kilter now that she was confronted with what she'd been trying to ignore. She wasn't totally herself. Jael looked to Han, who had been quietly listening, and confessed her greatest fear. "I can't hear anyone but Alyssa, and no one except Alyssa hears me. The silence in my head feels like a prison."

Han studied her for a long moment before he spoke. "Your fear that you are no longer telepathic is unfounded."

"How can you know that?" Jael pushed her chair back and stood. She needed to move, to pace as she thought. Alyssa's hand touched hers, and a projected wave of calm stopped her. She sank back into her chair and enveloped Alyssa's hand in both of hers, entwining their fingers. *Thank you.* The brief tightening of Alyssa's fingers around hers confirmed the mental message had been received. She raised her eyes to Han again, and he signaled for Michael to sit with them and leave the cleanup for later.

"I know that your telepathic ability is intact and as strong as ever. Earlier, you were broadcasting so loudly even I was having difficulty shielding you out. The kata you witnessed was an exercise to focus my mind and deflect your private thoughts." He tilted his head as his gaze shifted to Alyssa. "The First Advocate's ardor for her soul bond as well."

"Oh, stars." Alyssa's face reddened as she ducked her head and covered her eyes with her free hand.

Han smiled at her obvious embarrassment. "Your gift of projection is growing very strong, Aly-san. We should discuss soon some exercises you should practice to ensure your control grows along with it."

Jael chuckled at her lover's mortification and the old man's endearment Alyssa had confided that Han used to comfort her at the unfamiliar temple after her parents left her, a terrified child, and never returned. She freed one of her hands to rub comforting circles between Alyssa's shoulder blades and glanced over at Michael. His mismatched blue and green eyes flicked between her and Han and back again. "What is it, Michael?"

His ears reddened, and he cleared his throat. "Forgive me, but I, too, could feel your projected emotions." He met and held Jael's gaze. "But if you were broadcasting, I didn't hear it."

Han nodded. "Now that Danielle has reunited with Saran in the ethereal, I am free to reveal something she asked me to hold in confidence until her physical death." He tapped his finger against his temple. "I was the only physical entity who could hear her thoughts without her intentionally opening to me."

Jael dropped her fork and released Alyssa's hand to shove back from the table. "You're telling me that I'm stuck with Danielle's thick skull? I'm not First Warrior just because I'm the strongest pyro and the best at battle strategy. My telepathic abilities make me the communications touchstone. I need to hear when one of The Guard is calling me. They need to hear me when we are in battle." She sprang to her feet, paced across the room, and threw her hands up as she turned to stalk back. "I need to be in contact with the hostages on that airplane right now so we can pinpoint their location and estimate their destination." She frowned when she realized they were smiling. "What?" She didn't even try to keep the irritation from her voice. Didn't they understand the seriousness of this situation?

Alyssa stood, and Jael crossed her arms over her chest in a useless attempt to block the flood of affection that preceded her approach. "Honey, we do understand. It's just…well—"

"Your impatient reaction was so Jael-like." Michael's smile broadened into a grin. "We're so very glad to have you back."

Jael opened her arms, and Alyssa stepped into her embrace. Michael's smile faded. The somewhat public show of affection was unusual for Jael but would have been normal for Danielle. Jael held his gaze but tightened her arms around Alyssa. "This is still me, Michael. If Saran hadn't helped me strike a deal with The Collective Council to return, I could have never been able to hold my bonded mate in my arms again. She has many more lives to live, yet I had lived my last. I don't plan to waste this second chance."

Michael nodded. He understood now why Han had requested that he join their meeting. He looked to the slight man who had been sensei to each of them early in this life or—in Jael's case—many lifetimes past. Han nodded for Michael to proceed.

"Tan is anxious to run some medical scans to compare to a previous scan of Danielle's physiology. She wants to see if anything has changed since your consciousness inhabited her body. Tan also wants a series of scans at timed intervals to see if your body is still changing."

Jael nodded. "The only time I feel like myself is when I'm with Alyssa. Otherwise, I feel like two people trying to inhabit one body." She paused and blinked at him. Her next words were soft and reverent. "You know something about that, don't you?"

Michael dipped his head in a slight bow to confirm her realization of the similarities of their conditions. Born third gender, he was literally two genders in one body with ambiguous genitalia. Even in this enlightened age of acceptance, the rarity of his kind made most people uncomfortable. He turned to the entrance of the cabin, easily recalling his nervousness as the tall, muscular, blond warrior woman had probed his mind, then asked him to identify himself.

"Do you remember the day I first came to you?" He looked back to Jael, who nodded. "You knew Han had sent me and had already probed my mind to review my thoughts and memories. Still, you asked me who I was."

Jael smiled. "I saw during my probe that your confusion was your biggest obstacle."

"Yes, it was. But you showed me a goal—the chance for a place among The Guard—and told me that dragon-horse warriors know who they are."

Jael let go of Alyssa and returned to the table. She sat across from him, turning her chair around to rest her forearms on the crown of its back. "My situation isn't the same. I know who I am."

"I'd always known, too, but no one before you had ever asked me to claim it. Becoming a warrior gave me a goal, but I still had to come to terms with my dual body." He pointed at her. "You have to come to terms with this body and make it yours."

Jael studied him, but he didn't look away. When she finally spoke, her words were measured and full of admiration. "You've come a long way since that timid young man slouched his way through my door a handful of years ago."

"I've had excellent teachers." He smiled as he remembered waking that morning with his boyfriend softly snoring against his back. He glanced over at Alyssa, who Michael knew had coached Will on how to win him over. "And letting Will into my life has let me finally accept that my existence is not a botched incarnation."

Jael stared at him for a few seconds, then stood again, her jaw set in grim determination as she turned to Han. "So, first order of business is how to get around Danielle's thick skull."

Alyssa interrupted. "Hold up before you get started. Michael, did you bring a med-scan with you?"

"I did." He rummaged in his backpack to find it.

"Honey, give us two minutes to record a scan. Then you and Han might want to go into your office or out on the porch for some place quiet to work while Michael and I clean up the lunch dishes."

Jael nodded and stood tall with arms held slightly out from her sides as Michael began the scan at her feet and traveled slowly upward.

❖

Jael shifted into the shade of the porch, while Han moved into a sunny spot. She mentally admonished herself. As a pyro, she often forgot that other people couldn't regulate their own body heat. She'd only experienced cold once when she and Danielle were children and had stood outside in a blizzard on a bet to see who could lower their body temperature most for the longest time. Han might seem spry for his age, but she was sure she heard a slight creak in his back and knees occasionally.

"I do have a bit of arthritis," Han admitted. "But the warm sun helps."

Jael slammed her shields up tight. "Sorry. The silence fools my mind so much that I unconsciously drop my shields because it seems like nothing coming in means nothing going out."

Han nodded. "But you haven't lost your ability to put up shields, because I felt you do it just now."

"You're right. I did."

"Now you must learn to tear down Danielle's shields when you wish to listen or speak with your mind."

"How can I lower them when I can't even feel them the way I feel my shields?"

Han turned his body into the sun and assumed the lotus position, his hands resting palms upon his knees. "Let us begin your first lesson."

CHAPTER EIGHT

Kyle absently scratched the top of Phyrrhos's withers and chuckled when the mare turned to thrust her butt under Kyle's hand. "Just like your warrior. Never subtle."

The dragon horse—currently in normal horse form under the afternoon sun—shook her head and backed another step to bump her rump against Kyle's chest.

"Okay, okay." Kyle scraped her blunt nails along the skin around the base of the mare's tail, and Phyrrhos lifted her nose in the air like a dog enjoying a good scratch.

"You've got to stop spoiling her because she's starting to expect the same treatment from me."

Pleasure flooded Kyle at the sound of her mate's voice. Still, she frowned.

"Not glad to see me?" Tan asked. Her tone was casual, not worried.

Kyle sighed. "How did you know I was here?"

"That is my dragon horse you're servicing. I called for her because I needed a ride to go look for you. But I got a clear picture back, indicating she was busy right now because you were scratching all her itchy spots."

"I came up to see Sunfire, but she's wandered off somewhere."

Tan turned in a semicircle to scan the high meadow carved into the side of the mountain. A cave on the mountain's face provided shelter during inclement weather, but only a thin line of scrubby trees ringed the other three sides before sloping sharply down from the meadow's edge. You'd practically have to be a mountain goat to reach the meadow on foot, so it made the perfect daytime pasture for the dragon horses while they were wingless. "Wasn't she here this morning? Doesn't she respond when you call her?"

"I think she was. But…" Kyle stared at her feet.

Tan's palm, rough and thick like those of all pyros, cupped Kyle's cheek. "What is it, babe? I thought we said no more secrets between us."

Kyle's frown deepened. "You didn't tell me about Jael's problem."

Tan kissed her gently, then drew back. Kyle stared at her feet as Tan's fingers tightened around the nape of Kyle's neck. "Look at me."

Kyle raised her eyes to meet Tan's gaze.

"I'm a physician, Kyle. That means I won't tell you things because of doctor-patient privacy. I hadn't checked my d-messages until this morning and found one from Alyssa giving me permission to share that information with The Guard. We didn't have a chance to talk before the lunch meeting. That's the only reason I hadn't told you before I informed the others."

Kyle gathered Tan in her arms and buried her face in Tan's neck. She inhaled Tan's unique scent of shea butter and musk. Stars, she loved this woman. Tan was her anchor, her strength. A niggling premonition told her she'd need that more than ever in the coming weeks. "Sorry. I'm just feeling a little…conflicted right now."

Tan kissed her again, lingering as their lips brushed together. "Let me help you think this through, then." She turned and drew Kyle's long arms around her. Tan wasn't short, but Kyle was about ten centimeters taller. They often assumed this emotionally and physically comfortable position for personal talks. Kyle liked to rub her cheek against the soft curls of Tan's mohawk, and Tan would absently trail her fingernails back and forth on Kyle's forearms. "Let's start with why you don't know where Sunfire has gone." Tan held on to the arms wrapped around her when Kyle started to pull away. "No secrets."

Kyle relaxed after a few seconds and confessed. "I'm not sure we're fully bonded."

"No? But you communicated with her while she was still in the womb."

Kyle tensed again at Tan's snapped response, then brushed her cheek along Tan's mohawk to calm herself. They hadn't had time to discuss her relationship to Sunfire while Phyrrhos still carried the unborn foal, but Kyle suspected some unresolved feelings remained from the pregnant Phyrrhos being partially drawn to Kyle rather than focusing solely on Tan, her bonded warrior.

Tan responded with an affectionate stroke along Kyle's arm. "Tell me why you aren't sure."

"Well, it's like she stalks me. She shows up here and there, following me. I see her flying around at night overhead and trotting behind me during the day, but she won't come close enough to touch. I still get mental pictures from her, but no indication that she hears what I try to send back."

"So, you haven't been able to catch her at dusk for a proper bonding?"

Kyle shivered as Tan grasped her hand and tickled her nails against the thick calluses of Kyle's palm. Only another pyro would know that would send a bolt of current straight to her clit. "No. Sunfire's never here. She must be part mountain goat." She dropped light kisses across Tan's newly shaved skull, behind her ear, and along the side of her neck. Two could play this game.

"Okay. It's hours until dusk, so I know that's not why you're here now. Let's talk about the other reason."

Kyle stopped her kisses, resting her forehead on Tan's shoulder. The jerk to reality was as effective as a cold shower. Tan not only was her confidante, but the very person who deserved a heads-up. "Furcho's falling apart. I've known him all my life, but I don't know the man he's becoming since Nicole was abducted."

"I agree." Tan gently extracted herself from Kyle's embrace and took her hand to lead her to the edge of the meadow. They sat in the grass, half facing each other and half looking out over the herd.

Kyle stared at her expectantly. Tan hadn't released her hand. Was she about to reveal something else she'd been withholding?

"Don't look at me like that." Tan smiled and entwined her fingers with Kyle's. "I happen to know that you come up here because watching the herd settles you." She squeezed Kyle's fingers. "That and rubbing your face in my hair."

Kyle chuckled and, in a rare flash of shyness, dropped her gaze to their joined hands. "You know all my secrets."

"Not all, I suspect, but I do know this. You were born to be Second Warrior."

Kyle jerked her eyes back to Tan's. Her mate's expression was completely serious. "I haven't actually been officially inducted into The Guard."

"There's no ceremony, Kyle, especially when we're in the middle of a war. The First Warrior declares it, and it's done. In this case, you were inducted by silent consent of The Guard. Did you see anyone object when you stepped up at lunch today?"

It was a bold move, Kyle knew, but it felt right, and she'd done it without a second thought—the same way she always seemed to end up leading whatever group she joined. Tan had been the only one to force her to follow until she proved herself.

"But if Furcho is unable to fill the job of Second Warrior, you are next in line. I'd never challenge you."

"And Jael knows I'd never accept the job. I'm the best scout in the group and the only physician. I love being a surgeon and won't give that up to spend my time pondering battle strategy."

"What about the others?"

"I ask again: did anyone challenge you today?"

Kyle shook her head and stared out at the horses. "Only Furcho." She kissed Tan's hand that she held in hers and rubbed her cheek against Tan's knuckles. "I'm not like Jael. I'm not sure I have the heart of a warrior. I love being a farmer in the same way you love being a surgeon."

Tan smiled. "Nobody is like Jael. Danielle was a chef at heart and a relentless organizer. It's our noble sense of right, our need to protect, and our dragon genes that compel us to answer the call of duty."

Kyle nodded. She felt so fortunate to have a mate who understood the complexity of living in two worlds. Her worries mostly assuaged, Kyle let her eyes drift to the graceful neck she'd been tasting only minutes before. Her thoughts moved lower, and she shifted slowly until she was straddling Tan's lap and pushing her back onto the grass while capturing those lush lips. Their couplings were sometimes playful battles for dominance, but Tan willingly acquiesced to Kyle's unspoken need after a brief war of tongues.

"Do we have time?" Kyle broke their kiss and sucked at the pulse visibly throbbing in Tan's neck as she worked the buttons open on her lover's sleeveless bush shirt.

Tan moaned her approval and thrust her hips upward. She wasn't as patient, grabbing the neck of Kyle's T-shirt and tearing it with her teeth so she would rip the shirt open. "I thought you wanted to find Sunfire."

Kyle pulled the Velcro closure on Tan's support band. She was careful since Tan would have to wear it while she wore Tan's shirt back to camp. She was familiar with Tan's T-shirt-tearing compulsion, having sneaked back into camp bare-chested more than once after other impromptu outdoor encounters.

They both fumbled with the closure on the other's field pants. Kyle stood and tugged Tan's boots off to yank her pants down her long legs and toss them aside. Tan stared up and pulled her knees up, opening her legs wide to expose herself. Kyle sucked in the scent of Tan's glistening sex as she shoved her own pants down to her ankles and fell to her knees between Tan's legs.

Tan reached up for her. They would make love later, slow and sweet. But Tan wouldn't fail to answer Kyle's more primal need now, just as Kyle would when Tan required it. Kyle rubbed her swollen clit through the silky evidence of Tan's arousal, bearing down and grunting as each thrust pushed her closer to relief.

"Like that, baby. Take what you need. Come on." Tan wrapped her legs around Kyle's hips and met each pump of her hips.

"Tan, Tan." Kyle's blood pounded loud in her ears, hard in her chest, and nearly to the point of pain in her clit. Thrust and rub, thrust and rub.

"Yeah, babe. Just like that. Stars, I'm going to come. I'm going to come. I'm…going…to…come." Tan's legs tightened, then released, tightened then released to urge Kyle faster and harder.

"Give it to me, Tanisha. Come for me." Kyle closed her eyes and focused on the glide of Tan's flesh against hers. She shortened her thrusts to meet the cadence of Tan's chant.

"I'm (stroke) going (stroke) to (stroke) come (stroke)."

Tan gasped, her strong legs tightening like a vise around Kyle's hips. Kyle threw her head back, Tan's climax coalescing in her own belly like a churning sphere, then bursting in her belly to stiffen her spine and slam against her sides. *Wait, what?*

Slam.

Kyle opened her eyes and stared down at Tan, whose eyes were wide and focused on something behind Kyle.

Slam.

Dragon wings were slapping Kyle on both sides. "Phyrrhos, what the jump?"

Slam.

"No…not…not dark yet. Duck." Tan's stuttered words and outstretched hands failed to hold back another assault of wings.

Kyle rolled away and to her feet, nearly stumbling because of her pants that trapped her ankles. She yanked her pants up. Three things clicked in her brain immediately. It was hours until sunset, yet a fully transformed dragon horse stood before them. The dragon horse was not

Phyrrhos. And the red-gold filly was inhaling to shoot a stream of fire at Tan, still naked on the ground. "Sunfire, no!"

The filly's fire was so pure, Tan would have never been able to block it if Kyle's powerful flame hadn't joined in. When the filly ran out of flame, they extinguished theirs as well. Her ears flicked back and forth, her red dragon eyes pulsing as her coppery hide glittered in the sun. Stars above, she was beautiful.

Kyle moved toward the young dragon horse, drawing her attention while Tan kept an eye on them and carefully gathered her pants, support band, and boots to dress. The filly snorted and took a tentative step back. "Easy, Sunfire. You know me, and it's time we had a head-to-head, get-to-know-each-other."

Sunfire stopped, raised her nose, and curled her upper lip to better open her olfactory sensors and take in Kyle's scent. Kyle stopped her approach and waited until Sunfire took a tentative step forward.

"That's right. You know me."

Sunfire's ears worked and her eyes pulsed.

"You know my voice, don't you? That's what you really recognize." Kyle resisted turning her head toward the movement in her peripheral vision but noted Phyrrhos was ambling their way. Tan smoothly intercepted her, pressing her forehead to her mare's. But the motion drew Sunfire's attention. No, no, no. This was the time. Kyle could feel it. No distractions. "So, what was all that wing-slapping about?"

Sunfire swung her head back to Kyle.

"Did you think I was hurting Tan? Or maybe that she was hurting me? Maybe you were jealous? Do I need to explain to you what she means to me and what we were doing?"

Sunfire snorted short blue flames and shook her entire body like a dog.

Kyle laughed at the dragon expression of "yuk." The sound seemed to amuse Sunfire. She bobbed her head, then stepped closer, her ears pricked forward to take in the sound. They were little more than thirty centimeters apart now.

"Maybe you just wanted my attention because you have something to tell me?" Kyle opened her hands, palms up, but didn't raise them. "Remember when you were still inside? I could hear you if I touched your mother's belly where you were growing."

Sunfire's double eyelids clicked shut as though she was closing her eyes to think.

"I need to touch you now to complete our bond so we'll be able to share thoughts even when we aren't touching." She didn't know how much language the dragon horses understood, but she did know they communicated in pictures, so she tried to concentrate on forming pictures in her mind of what they needed to do.

Sunfire stretched her long, elegant neck and snuffled along Kyle's face. Kyle exhaled to share her scent, and the filly lifted her nose and curled her lip to take it in. Seemingly satisfied, Sunfire dropped her head again to snuffle Kyle's neck, bare chest, armpits, crotch, and, finally, upturned palms. A hot tongue swiped across Kyle's fingers that moments before had been inside Tan, and Sunfire repeated the lip-curling move. This time she snorted and shook her head. Kyle laughed again, and Sunfire head-butted her in the chest in response.

In one swift move, Kyle grabbed Sunfire's ears and pressed her forehead between the V of ridges that ran from crown to nose on the dragon horse. She held tight when Sunfire jerked in surprise, then froze as heat rose where their heads touched and clear pictures—not just impressions—began to form in both their heads.

Kyle pictured them flying together, leading an army of dragon horses and their warriors through the night sky. In return, a picture formed in her mind of a solar plane making a crash landing in a meadow surrounded by tall mountains. Kyle pictured Sunfire as a regular horse during the day. The picture that returned was the dragon horse standing before her. Kyle pictured a night sky full of stars, and the return picture was Sunfire the dragon horse flying in the day sky, too? Kyle pictured Sunfire as a regular horse with no backdrop of either day or night. The filly stomped her foot and rattled her wings in irritation. *Sunfire is a dragon horse*, came the firm response. Kyle smiled and formed a beautiful picture of Sunfire glittering in the light, graceful wings outstretched and spitting perfect blue-white flame. This image seemed to please the filly, who broke their physical connection to nibble at Kyle's neck, then rub her head against Kyle's chest.

"Ow, ouch." Kyle pushed her head away. "Those ridges hurt when I don't have a shirt on."

Undaunted, Sunfire turned and extended her wings to prance in a showy circle. Kyle glanced over at Tan, who grinned and tossed her shirt to Kyle.

"Go ahead. Take some time to get acquainted. I'm going to check to see if my network has responded."

With a whoop, Kyle slipped into the shirt without bothering to close it, executed a running mount, clamped her long legs around Sunfire's lean frame, and grabbed a handful of mane as they launched skyward.

Chapter Nine

It's only a few hours until dusk. We can't wait for the rest to wander in whenever they want." Furcho paced the length of the long table, ignoring the platter of hot wraps prepared for quick, easy consumption. "As soon as Azar transforms, I'm aloft. The rest of you can sit here and plan until dawn, but I'm taking action."

That was her cue. Kyle swung the door open and strode in. "We are a team. We'll all go when we have a cohesive plan."

Furcho's eyes blazed. "You are not in charge here." Saliva dotted his unshaven chin as he spat the words at Kyle.

"You're wrong, Furcho. Second Warrior Kyle *is* in charge."

They all turned as Jael emerged from the darkened office at the opposite end of the large open room, with Alyssa following.

Kyle caught the silver battleskin that Jael tossed to her. She stared at the rank on the shoulder, then around the room. Tan gave her a thumbs-up. Michael, Raven, and even Diego nodded as she met each elite warrior's eyes. When she looked to Furcho, she realized that Alyssa had led him to a comfortable chair nearby and was rubbing his arm as she murmured something unintelligible in his ear. He was calm now and wiping the spittle from his beard stubble. He looked up, his eyes dark and wounded, to give Kyle a curt nod.

Kyle dropped her chin in a slight bow and thumped her fist against her shoulder. "The Guard honors me. It'll be difficult to fill Danielle's boots, but I'll do my best."

Jael strode over to clasp her shoulder. "I don't want you to be Danielle. I want you to be Kyle. You are the second-strongest pyro among us. Second to me, of course." Jael's wide grin eased Kyle's nervousness. "Effective immediately, you are promoted to commander. Lieutenant Antonia is now promoted in absentia to captain and will move up to commander when she returns to take over the quartermaster unit. When this war is over, I'll need you to oversee the rebuilding of those communities that these weather disasters have devastated. And, we need to come up with a plan to better protect our food sources from future disasters."

Kyle's heart beat faster as her mind instantly filled with the prospect. "I've got a million ideas."

Jael clapped her on the shoulder. "I was counting on that." She faced the group. "But first, we must restore peace to The Collective." She propped herself against the back of a long lounge that divided the eating area from the common room and extended her hand for Alyssa to join her. "Second Warrior, catch me up."

"The specific location of the City of Light is closely guarded. It wasn't even revealed to the believers that I infiltrated, even though it was to be our destination. So, earlier today we made plans for Tan to use the Network connections that proved useful in San Pedro Sula and distributed other duties among us to ready the army to mobilize as soon as we had reliable reports of the plane's route. However, I might have updated info—"

Furcho sprang to his feet. "We're wasting time." He whirled on Jael. "Are you still a telepath or not?"

Jael dropped the arm she had wrapped around Alyssa's waist and stood. Her eyes narrowed as she stepped into his personal space. "I am."

"Then why in blue blazes haven't you contacted Nicole to find out where they are?"

"If she's a prisoner on a plane, do you think they've let her in the cockpit to check their coordinates?"

Furcho's face reddened, and his eyes grew wild. "You could at least find out if my child is okay."

Alyssa stepped forward. "Your child, Furcho? Don't you mean Nicole and the child she carries?"

He grabbed Alyssa's forearm, his knuckles white as his grip tightened. "You don't understand—"

In an instant, Jael's long fingers gripped his forearm. "Release her, Third Warrior."

Furcho persisted, and Alyssa's face twisted in pain as his hand heated against her skin. "This child is special. Maya foretold it. The child is most important." He barely got the words out before he dropped his clench on Alyssa's arm and howled. The odor of burnt flesh permeated the room, and the imprint of Jael's palm and fingers blistered up on his forearm.

Tan shook her head and walked into the food-prep area, where a first-aid kit was kept. She returned with a canister of burn spray and a hypo-injector and walked to the three of them. "Give me your arm," she said.

Furcho glared at Jael but held out his blistered arm. But instead of the numbing spray, Tan wielded the injector in one swift move to administer a hypo of mild tranquilizer. Then she gently grasped Alyssa's hand and raised her arm to coat the pink skin on her forearm with the numbing spray.

Alyssa protested. "I could have calmed him. You didn't have to do that."

"It was only enough to help him control himself so he can still participate in the meeting." Tan gestured to Kyle. "As you were saying?"

Kyle eyed Furcho warily. She couldn't shake the feeling that something more was at play here. "Yes, well, I might have more updated information." She looked to Tan. "Did you tell them before I arrived?"

Tan shook her head. "Yours to share." She took a med-scan from her pocket and motioned for Alyssa to step back. It was time again for another comparative scan of Jael.

Kyle drew in a breath. "This is pretty incredible, but here it is. Sunfire, the filly out of Phyrrhos and sired by Specter, is now fully bonded with me." She held Jael's gaze and straightened her shoulders. "She doesn't transform."

Diego frowned. "What's that mean?"

Raven's whistle was low and followed by a First People phrase the rest couldn't interpret. "You're saying she doesn't lose her dragon during the daylight hours?"

Kyle shook her head. "She never loses her dragon. She flies night and day."

"She's been different from the start. Sunfire went from foal to yearling in a matter of days," Tan said. "I'm dying to get some medical scans of her."

"Back on subject." Kyle raised her voice to refocus the team. "Sunfire has informed me the kidnappers' plane has crashed in a wilderness area. From the aerial image she showed me, the plane is in two intact pieces, which means there's a high possibility of survivors."

"I would feel it if she has perished." Furcho's words were

mumbled, but everyone heard in the quiet as they absorbed the information about Sunfire and the plane.

"Location?" Jael asked.

Kyle shook her head. "I didn't recognize any landmarks she showed me, so I'll have to ask her to take us there."

"Can you tell us why you haven't contacted Toni or Nicole telepathically, Jael?" Raven's question held none of Furcho's accusing tone.

Kyle waited with the rest. Until now, everything had been speculation among The Guard.

Alyssa wrapped her arm around Jael's waist, lending emotional support. The First Warrior was not accustomed to confessing weakness.

"I'm still telepathic. Stronger than ever, according to Han. But I have a conflict. I trained several lifetimes ago to construct shields against the millions of thoughts that constantly bombard me or filter so only certain ones come through. Also, I learned to focus to transmit thoughts to a single person or a select group." She massaged her temples. "You all are familiar with Danielle's natural block against mind probes. She trained to do just the opposite, to dismantle her natural shield to allow my telepathic messages in." She twisted her head back and forth in a move to loosen tense neck and shoulder muscles. "I wasn't hiding in that dark office to surprise you. I was meditating away the headache that followed a session with Han, who's giving me a crash course in Danielle's training."

Tan looked up from the med-scan. "That might not be necessary. These scans we're running every three hours indicate that your brain synapses are rearranging themselves in a pattern more consistent with your previous medical records. And the process seems to be escalating."

Kyle straightened. "That's good news. Let's hear the rest of the reports. Diego?"

"I've reserved three engines, passenger and stock cars for fifty warriors and priority track passage for any time during the next week."

Kyle called for the next. "Raven?"

"We don't have fifty dragon-horse teams, and the number we do have changes from day to day, depending on whether the warrior or their dragon horse is healed or still recovering from injuries. Best guess is around twenty-five to thirty."

"Michael?"

"I can have a week of provisions for at least fifty packed and ready by dawn. We can use all able-bodied pyros, even if their dragon horses aren't fit for battle. And we'll need some support staff."

A blood-curdling dragon scream rattled the windows, and a loud bang preceded the cracking of two thick planks in the door. A second bang, and the door splintered into pieces as Dark Star pushed his way in.

"I'm afraid he missed puppy training class," Jael said, shaking her head. "Tan, grab your scout pack and meet Kyle and me outside. Let's see if Sunfire can show us where that plane landed."

"Already packed up and tucked in the corner over there. I included a med-pack in case I need to treat injuries."

"I'm coming, too," Furcho said, rising from the lounging chair where he'd sat when the tranquilizer kicked in.

Kyle still felt responsible for Furcho. She'd known him since childhood, and usurping his advance to Second Warrior surely was aggravating an already difficult situation. She tensed to intervene, then jerked in surprise when a soft whoosh preceded a tiny dart that embedded in Furcho's neck.

Tan lowered the blowgun from her lips as Furcho's eyes rolled upward. Michael caught him when Furcho's legs buckled and guided him into a lounging chair. Furcho was snoring before Michael hit the control to recline the chair. Tan grinned at Jael. "I've never been so glad to hear your meddling voice in my head."

Jael rubbed her temples again. "I'm just glad you had that dart handy and I managed to get the message past Danielle's thick skull."

❖

Kyle dashed to the second-floor quarters she shared with Tan and pulled on her new battleskin. When she turned to redress in her T-shirt and field pants, Tan was standing in the doorway with an odd expression.

"Wow." Tan walked forward and touched the red insignia on Kyle's upper arm. Only the First Warrior's battleskin was adorned with a red dragon horse on the chest and single red reversed chevron on her arm. While the Second Warrior's dragon horse image was black, like the rest of The Guard, the two reversed red chevrons on her shoulder indicated the succession of command in the event the First Warrior was disabled. Tan wiggled her eyebrows suggestively. "You're really hot in that uniform…in fact, sort of blazing," she said, grinning at her play on Kyle's nickname.

But Kyle didn't feel playful. "I don't want to leave you out there alone."

Tan's smile faded. "Your job is to advise the First Warrior when she asks your opinion, but you never question her decision or voice a doubt about her orders in front of anyone. If you feel she's made a risky decision, you speak to her only in private and always with respect."

"I know, but—"

Tan shook her head, sliding her hand behind Kyle's neck to grasp her nape and give her a small shake. "No exceptions. Not even when her decision is about me. I trust her with my life. But I do understand. I have to trust her with your life, too." She touched her lips to Kyle's in a soft caress. "And that's very hard for me, because I don't think I could finish this life without you."

Kyle captured Tan's mouth, plunging her tongue deep to capture her lover's unique taste. The kiss was too brief, but she withdrew at the polite throat-clearing coming from the doorway. Still, she pressed her forehead to Tan's. "And my world would be too dark to bear without you in it."

"Jael's waiting," Raven said quietly when they stepped back from each other.

"We're coming," Kyle said, tugging her clothes on over the battleskin, then grabbing her small tool kit.

Downstairs, Michael had gathered a bottle of water, a hot wrap for each, and a tubular pack filled with pro-chow and a handful of freeze-dried meals. "I made sandwiches since you're leaving before dinner," he said. "The pro-chow is in case the situation you find prevents you from flying back by dawn."

"Good," Jael said. "It always pays to be prepared."

They stuffed the water and sandwiches into the side pockets of their field pants, and Kyle claimed the pro-chow pack, lifting it over her head and settling it at an angle from her right shoulder to her left hip. Focusing on physical tasks kept her from thinking too much. She didn't want to be separated from Tan again. Jael had separated them before by sending Kyle to infiltrate The Natural Order. She watched as Jael drew Alyssa into her arms for a quick kiss. She flushed at her petty thoughts. They had paid an even higher price when that laser and missiles took out Jael and her first dragon horse. And, they too were newly reunited.

Kyle straightened her shoulders. She was Second Warrior. If the First Warrior and First Advocate could face separation and whatever dangers might be ahead after everything they'd already been through, she could buck up, too.

"Ready?" Tan asked.

Kyle reached for Tan's scout pack. "Ready."

Tan growled and swung her pack out of reach. "Watch it, Blaze. Don't get all macho and try to carry my pack just because you outrank me now."

Kyle laughed. That was the grumpy Tan she loved. "I wouldn't dare."

CHAPTER TEN

Toni twisted to catch Nicole, who stumbled over another tree root and pitched forward.

"Thanks again." Nicole's words were slurred and her eyes drooping with fatigue as Toni helped right her.

Toni glanced ahead. They were falling behind. "Is this guy going to march us through the night? We can hardly see where we're going."

"We must catch up with the rest. El Jefe will be angry if we slow them down." Emile's deep voice was urgent but gentle.

Nicole put an arm out to brace herself against the large tree that had tripped her with its root. "I can't. I can barely pick my feet up."

"You've got to, Nicole."

"Here. You carry this." Emile had unbuckled his vest pack and held it out to Toni. "I will carry her."

Nicole protested. "I don't want to get you into trouble."

"And I don't want to deliver a baby in the middle of the woods." His white teeth flashed in the gathering dusk before he turned his back and squatted in the path. "Hop up on my back. I've carried my brother many times like this," he said over his shoulder. "Hurry."

"Thanks," Toni said for both of them. She doubted she could have carried Nicole, who was a head taller, very far. She slung Emile's pack over her shoulder. "Can you jog a bit so we can catch up?"

"No problem," Emile said, rising to his feet and entwining his arms with Nicole's long legs to hold her up.

Only two guards were made responsible for the hostages, one walking in front of them and Emile bringing up the rear, and they hiked down the mountain in single file on a narrow wildlife path they'd located. The first guard glanced back and frowned at Emile as they caught up with the others. "Are you trying to anger Xavier?"

"She's pregnant, Robbie, and was slowing us down. It'll be okay."

"As long as you can keep up while you carry her, little brother."

"Don't worry about me."

Robbie didn't have to worry, because they stepped into a grassy clearing five minutes later, and the men at the front of their group stopped. Emile let Nicole slip down to stand before anyone noticed he was carrying her.

Juan and Xavier conferred, then turned to the group. "It's getting too dark to go on. We'll stop here for the night," Xavier said. He looked at Juan. "Get blankets for us." Then he turned and walked to the other side of the clearing and sat.

Juan eyed the men, then took blankets from two of them. The guards and Cyrus had observed Toni fitting their blanket onto Maya's pack, then did the same. The only ones without were the pilot, Juan, and Xavier.

"Hey, that's my blanket," one brave guard protested.

"You and…" he pointed to the owner of the other blanket he had confiscated, "and you. Stand guard first. The chill will keep you awake." He pointed again. "One of you there and the other on the opposite side of the clearing." He started to walk away, then turned back. "Four hours, then wake two others to replace you and sleep on their blankets." His eyes swept over the group. "No fires. We don't want give our location away if those cursed dragons are flying around."

The men grumbled as Juan strode away to join Xavier but silenced their complaints when Cyrus joined them. They eyed him, their expressions full of suspicion.

Cyrus ignored the looks and took Laine's hand. "You can share my blanket," he said to her. "That will leave more warmth for the other women."

Laine started to protest, then nodded and let him guide her to a grassy spot nearby.

Maya's whisper was harsh in Toni's ear. "You don't think he wants…you know…"

Toni looked at her in surprise. "Would your mom refuse if they were discreet? It seems to me that she still loves him."

Maya's expression was one of horror. "But right over there?"

Toni shrugged. "In the barracks, if two people hook up in a bunk, everybody else just turns politely away. Nobody complains unless they're too vocal and make it hard to sleep."

Maya scowled. "They're my parents. I don't want to witness them...them...you know...rutting."

Nicole smiled, catching the last part of their conversation. "Then we'll be sure and sleep looking the other way." She did a little dance. "I've got to pee again. Toni, can you come with me?"

Toni eyed the forest around them. The growing moon gave some illumination in the clearing, but the trees let nothing filter through their thick canopy. "We'll all go together, and not very far." She called Emile, who was happily consuming the protein bar Laine had given him earlier. "We need to take care of lady things before we bed down. I don't want to go too far into those dark woods, and I'd appreciate it if you'd stand here so we can call out if we bump into any local wildlife."

His head bobbed. "Sure, sure. Stay close enough for me to hear you."

Maya laid a hand on his thick forearm. "You're a good man, Emile." Her eyes grew hazy. Then she smiled and removed her hand. "You'll get through this fine and spend your last years of this life sitting in the sun and playing with your grandchildren."

His face lit up with a huge grin. "You see the future, yes."

Maya nodded. "Only some things, but I feel sure about this."

Toni grabbed Maya's hand. "Come on. I think the situation is getting dire." Nicole stood at the wood's edge, waving impatiently for them to hurry.

❖

The remnants of Jael's headache floated away on the chill mountain winds as she and Dark Star glided above Phyrrhos and Sunfire. The filly seemed to glitter in the night, as though she radiated the sunlight rather than simply reflecting it off her hide. Curious. They were flying fast and in an apparent direct route. Dragon horses could be a bit lazy and unconcerned about human matters unless it was a battle that allowed them to unleash fire. They liked to burn things. But when they flew, they preferred to glide along the wind currents, following them high or low to the next current, so they put out a minimal effort to keep their big bodies airborne. Sunfire, however, was flying with a purpose, working her young wings at a steady pace, unwilling to drift with the currents. This was no problem for Dark Star, with his huge wingspan. But the workout apparently didn't sit well with Phyrrhos, who snorted a cloud of hot breath periodically to show her displeasure.

Jael mentally walked through the steps to open her mind, then chuckled at the image in Tan's thoughts.

Quit complaining, you diva. The picture in Tan's head was of Phyrrhos daintily holding out her hoof for a stable boy to polish it, while others brought her samplings of hay to taste. Phyrrhos sneezed a cloud of soot that flew back into Tan's face. *Never tease a temperamental dragon horse. They'll always retaliate.*

Is Phyrrhos okay? She might not be fully recovered from the accelerated pregnancy and foaling.

She's fine. She's always been a bit of a drama queen.

Kyle glanced up at them. She barely had time to signal imminent descent before Sunfire dipped one wing and glided downward in a tight, smooth spiral. The only dragon horse Jael had seen come close to Sunfire's agile flight was Specter.

A shard of sadness pierced her as Specter's image formed unbidden in her head—that night he had landed on the ledge where Toni was introducing her to Dark Star. Curiously, Specter hadn't challenged the other stallion. They appeared to silently communicate, and then Specter flew away. Jael's breath caught in her chest. She'd always thought dragons having the ability to see the future was an eastern myth. Specter didn't challenge because he knew Dark Star would replace him.

Her sadness deepened. He'd known the Brasília battle would be his last, yet Specter had never faltered as they dove to intercept the two missiles that would have killed hundreds of innocents. Would have killed Alyssa. Tears began to fill her eyes, but she was shaken from her moroseness when Dark Star pushed a new image into her thoughts—a ghost-like Specter shadowing them as they followed Sunfire downward. It was so clear that she glanced over her shoulder and thought for a moment she detected a distortion in the sky. She leaned low over Dark Star's neck and affectionately scratched her nails along the ridge of bony spikes that replaced his mane when he transformed. "Thanks for that, buddy."

The tiny beacons of light below came into focus as they drew closer. Men huddled around two campfires that reflected off the metal skin of the crashed plane. Jael shook her head. Several were already pointing up at Sunfire. A couple of them stood and raised both hands, signaling surrender.

Land together uphill, at the edge of the clearing. Watch closely. This could be a trick. Jael's head was beginning to pound again with the effort to keep her telepathic connection open to Tan and Kyle. But she'd been a warrior in most of her lives and ignored much greater pain to join the charge into battle. So, she shoved the headache aside and focused.

Their mounts' hooves made little sound as they settled lightly on the soft ground. Kyle and Tan waited for Jael's orders, but she stood silent. The men with apparent leg injuries sat up and raised at least one hand skyward. Dark Star snorted a short blast of blue flame, and the men collectively flinched.

"We're unarmed," one man shouted. "The others took the women and are hiking down the mountain. We were too injured to travel with them."

Jael relaxed her shoulders and shook her head. "Damn. I wish we'd brought Alyssa with us. She could know for sure if they are lying." She started cautiously down the hill. "Come on, but stay sharp. Kyle, keep an eye on the hole in that plane in case someone's hiding in there."

"Phasers ready to fire," Kyle said quietly. Tan chuckled softly, despite the tension, at Kyle's nerdy reference to ancient fictional weapons.

As they drew closer, Jael realized that if this was a staged hoax, it was a pretty good one. Sweat beaded on the faces of several men moaning in delirium as their bodies jerked restlessly on blankets or cushions scavenged from the plane. The man who had shouted up to them stepped forward, one arm still held upward. He clasped his other arm close to his body.

They stopped in front of the pitiful sight. Dark Star moved close behind Jael, while Kyle flanked her on the right next to the plane and Tan on her left.

"That bastard Xavier left us to die. He said he'd send help back for us, but none here believe it." He took a step closer to Jael but stumbled back when Dark Star extended his impressive wings and rattled them in warning. The man straightened with a grimace. "Can I put my hand down? I think my collarbone is broken."

Jael nodded. "All of you can relax, but if anyone makes a quick or aggressive move, our mounts will incinerate the entire lot of you before you can draw your next breath."

Phyrrhos casually ambled to the left from behind Tan and stopped.

Her red pupils pulsed as she picked up a grapefruit-sized rock and pulverized it between her large teeth. The men closest to her edged away, their eyes wide.

Not to be outdone by her mother, Sunfire moved to the right of Kyle, directly across from Phyrrhos. Jael fought not to chuckle when the filly edged close to the men and raised her wings to rattle them like Dark Star. Her amusement vanished when Sunfire began to glow as though sunlight was pouring out of every pore of her skin. The light became so bright even the three of them had to shield their eyes. Sun and stars. Would the filly ever stop surprising them?

Kyle growled. "Enough, Sunfire." The blaze of light faded, and Sunfire stomped her hoof against the ground a few times as if to say "so don't mess with me."

Another of the wounded spoke. "Please. We want to surrender and beg for your help."

The first man stepped cautiously forward again. "My name is Esra. Xavier killed one of the pilots and two of our group last night because their moans of pain disturbed his sleep. That bastard has no soul. He got up from the lounge where he was trying to sleep and shot each in the head. Then he went back to his bed and was snoring minutes later. The rest of us sheltering in the plane crept out to get away. We were afraid we'd get a bullet, too, if we moaned or snored in our sleep."

A third man spat on the ground. "He would have left us without food or water if those women hadn't hidden some for us. The one who is with the crazy man told us where to find a stream nearby."

"You're not Believers of The Natural Order?" Tan's question dripped with disdain.

"We don't really know much about all that." Esra glanced away nervously, then sucked in a resigned breath and met Jael's gaze. "We tell people that we are, but Xavier doesn't care if we believe or not. He makes a lot of credits selling the supplies they take from the distribution warehouses, and he pays anyone who works for him very well." He shrugged. "Jobs are hard to come by in our region."

Jael knew this to be true. Everyone enjoyed basic food staples, an education, the d-net, and health care for free, but people still worked for luxury credits to pay for more than the essentials to live. Too many jobs had become automated, leaving too many people without work that gave them purpose. And not everyone wanted to explore their talent for art or literature or mechanics. Some just wanted a task to complete each day and family to go home to each night. But that problem wasn't hers to solve. She had a mission, and the next step in putting an end to The Natural Order uprising was to recover the members of her army who'd been kidnapped. "The women, were any of them injured?"

"Didn't appear to be. I don't know how they avoided at least getting a cut or two from the flying glass. Wasn't a mark visible on them," Esra said. "Then the pregnant one and the crazy man's lady helped bandage everybody up, while the other two gathered all the water and food they could find on the plane and turned those floatation vests they found under the seats into packs. The short, bossy one is smart."

"Why are you sleeping out here when you'd be warmer in the plane?" Kyle's gaze never left the gaping hole, as though she thought her question might flush out anyone waiting to spring.

Esra stared at the ground. "Nobody wants to sleep in there with the bodies, and none of us are able to drag them out."

Jael scanned the six men. Their injuries were real, but they didn't have the means or time to transport them back to the army's base "Tan, anything you can do to help here?"

Tan half turned so she could keep an eye on the group and dig through her pack still balanced across Phyrrhos's withers. "I've always got my field med kit, but we don't have the time, and I don't have what I need to fix all these guys." She pulled a smaller pack from the large one and went to a man moaning and shivering with fever.

"Kyle, send Sunfire to search this side of the mountain. Then take a look inside that plane."

"Yes, First Warrior."

"Elders forgive us." A man sitting on the ground stared at Jael. "It is you. We have died and are here to be judged."

"Don't light your funeral pyre yet," Jael said. "Your physical pain should convince you that you're still present in this life."

"But I saw you in Brasília. The laser, two missiles. One minute you were there on the ghost dragon and the next you were ash."

Jael had died violent but noble deaths in most of her lives as a warrior, but she felt no honor, no pride in this most recent death—only a sickening guilt she hadn't had time to examine. Her guilt, however, was instantly overtaken by a flame of anger. Dragon horses and the brave warriors bonded to them had been killed in Brasília as they defended The Collective. And these men had been there, working for The Natural Order.

"The Collective is in grave danger if this Natural Order takes control. The cult's values are selfish. It's divisive and oppressive. Its radical capitalism benefits only a few, while the rest follow like sheep." Jael's hands itched with the need to ignite. Her rant began low and firm, but her tone grew deadly, and her volume rose as she spit out the rest. "They would let old people starve and children die without the medical help they need. Are these the people you would work for? We are all merely souls scattered throughout the world. None are better than the rest. The Collective recognizes that we are stronger when we work for the good of every man, every woman, and every single child." She thumped her fist against her shoulder in an emphatic salute to The Collective. "My soul will not rest until we stand again on that solid foundation."

"Jael." Tan had paused in her examination of the wounded to stand at Jael's side. Her hand was firm on Jael's arm but her voice soft. "I think Xavier's betrayal has already opened their eyes."

Jael's anger cooled, but her frustration still simmered. Greed was an insidious plague, infiltrating and destroying souls like a flesh-eating virus. She longed for an enemy she could lay blade to or incinerate with her purifying flame. Tan gave Jael's arm a squeeze and returned to her medical triage, administering hypo-sprays of antibiotics and pain relievers. Jael knew Tan felt the same, but at least she could ease her feeling of uselessness by healing the sick and injured.

"Plane's clear," Kyle said, reappearing and extinguishing the small flame in her palm that had illuminated the dark interior. "Three bodies inside."

"We weren't able to move them," Esra needlessly repeated, staring at his feet. "And we have no pyres, no way to release their souls." He looked out at the dark woods. "We didn't want to drag them out where wild animals could get at them."

Jael glanced impatiently at the moon, estimating their time until sunrise. They certainly didn't want to get stuck here.

"Sunfire has found their camp." Kyle's eyes were unfocused but her words sure. "They appear to be sleeping but have guards posted."

Jael nodded, strategy instantly forming in her mind. "It's too late for the three of us to mount a rescue tonight."

Tan stood from treating the last of her patients. "So, what's the plan?"

"We have a little time, so let's clear the plane. With the fire power we have among us, we can release the three souls quickly and move the seriously wounded inside." She looked at Esra. "We'll send a medevac team for you as soon as possible, within a day or two." Then she turned back to Tan and Kyle. "I'll head back with Dark Star and Phyrrhos. It's too near dawn to risk their transformation here. Kyle, you and Sunfire can drop Tan close to Xavier's group so she can shadow them and keep me informed when they go on the move again in the morning. Then you and Sunfire should return to camp to help ready our warriors. Tomorrow night, we'll be back to get our people."

Chapter Eleven

Toni didn't move, but her brain went from sleep to instantly alert. Something had jolted her awake. She listened intently, scanning everything she could see without moving her head. The men were all sleeping. Even the chin of the man standing watch rested on his chest. The woods were still in the semi-dark. The only sound was persistent snoring. Maya was snuggled against her back, her soft exhalations warming Toni's nape. She sighed quietly and smiled to herself when Maya's arm tightened around her ribs. She could get used to this. Well, not sleeping on the ground every night, but Maya snuggling up to her back. Toni closed her eyes and let her body relax. She was drifting toward sleep again when a bird called from the edge of the woods.

She recognized that sound. At least she thought she did. Maybe she'd only wished it. The night was still too dark for birds to be stirring. Tentatively, she answered with her own low whistle. It was instantly followed by an answering variation of the call, soft and low.

"What is it?" Maya's question was a bare whisper.

"Listen." Toni's reply was little more than an exhaled breath. She answered again with another variation of the signal language they'd practiced in the barracks at the training camp. She was sure it was Captain Tanisha. She was the most skilled at the signals, and her whistle was distinctive. Toni scanned the woods. There. A slight movement between the trees behind the sentry. She squinted to make out Tan's hand signals. Dung. She should have paid more attention to learning those signals. She hadn't really bothered practicing them because she was a quartermaster. She counted bandages and other supplies at the camp clinic. And, well, she didn't have a warrior friend to practice the signals with. Except Kyle, and she'd been busy lately. She did recognize enough of the signals to get the gist of Tan's message. "It's Captain Tan. She's The Guard scout. She wants us to hang tight until dark."

"Thank the stars they've found us." Maya's whisper was giddy, and her arm tightened around Toni in a brief squeeze. "I knew they would if you could bring the plane down to give them time to catch up with us." A light kiss brushed the side of Toni's neck. "My hero."

Toni's entire body flushed with exhilaration. People had playfully said that when she found something nobody else could locate or planned ahead for things others routinely overlooked. But Maya's declaration held no tease. Toni's chest swelled. She liked being Maya's hero.

Some of the men began to stir, and Tan slipped back into the dark forest. Although the ground was hard and Toni was sure a rock had wedged between her ribs, she was reluctant to pull away from Maya and ready their packs. But it was her duty.

Nicole groaned and rolled onto her back. "Pregnant women should not have to sleep on the ground."

Toni squatted to roll up their blanket while Maya helped Nicole to her feet. "Could be worse. At least we had a blanket and it didn't rain on us. But I'll see if I can find a five-star hotel for you tonight, princess." She smiled to let Nicole know she was only kidding.

Nicole picked up the thread. "I'd like a room with a whirlpool tub and some foaming bath soap, Lieutenant."

Toni chuckled. "I will make it so, oh pregnant princess."

Nicole gave an aristocratic sniff and smoothed down her rumpled clothes. "See that you do, my humble servant." She scanned the woods. "But for now, I'm in need of the latrine. This little girl has been kicking my bladder for the past hour."

"She kicked me in the back most of the night." Maya's brow wrinkled, and her smile turned to a slight frown. "I thought Mom said it was too early to feel your baby move."

"I've never been pregnant before, so I don't know." Nicole rubbed her growing belly. "I think she might grow up to be an athlete. Sometimes it feels like she's practicing gymnastics in there."

Maya's expression grew serious, and she laid her hand on Nicole's stomach. She stared into the woods without actually seeing. "She is Furcho's destiny and his legacy. She will be the sky that holds everything—the sun, moon and stars—in place."

Chills ran down Toni's body as Maya's eyes refocused.

"Sorry. I—" Maya rubbed her eyes. "The visions—"

"Five minutes and we move out." Juan's loud mandate sent Emile their way.

"You must hurry. I'll stand guard for you," Emile said.

Toni tugged Maya and Nicole toward the trees. "Thanks. We'll only take a few minutes."

The three of them had no time for modesty. Nicole and Maya squatted behind a large tree, while Toni opened her pants while still standing and "field-peed" against another tree.

"She's got to show me how she does that," Nicole said to Maya. "It would be really helpful since I have to go about fifty times a day now."

Toni shook her head, fastening the closure on her pants. She was about to turn back to the others when a chittering noise drew her attention. A rustle in the underbrush let her know something or someone was very close.

"Don't turn yet. Don't speak. Act like you aren't finished. Blink twice for an affirmative answer to my questions."

Toni instantly recognized the whisper. She widened her stance as though she was still relieving herself and stared at the tree, even though every fiber in her wanted to turn to Tan, wanted to scan the woods to make sure no one else was close enough to hear.

"We'll strike after midnight. Until then, I'll tail you and relay our position to the strike force. Are all of you okay?"

Toni hesitated. Nicole was tired, but if she wasn't able to keep up, Tan would see that for herself as she followed them. She blinked twice to confirm they all were unharmed.

"Toni, we have to hurry. Oh. Look out!"

Toni whirled and slapped her hand over Maya's mouth to stop her startled cry. Before she could caution Maya to stay quiet, Tan stumbled from the brush, clutching her neck. She fell to her knees as she yanked a blow dart from her neck. "Son of a dung—" Her eyes rolled back in her head, and she fell face-first to the ground by their feet. They stared, stunned for a second, then jerked around to confront the man calmly approaching them.

Xavier moved silently with the grace of a panther. His feet were bare, and he held a blowgun casually at his side. He stared down at Tan when he reached them. "Ah. The fierce physician, who also is The Guard's scout." He nudged Tan's limp body with his bare foot. "Not so fierce when she's sleeping." He looked up and gave them a gloating smile, then combed his oily hair back with his fingers. "Yes, I know who she is. We have information on all of The Guard." He nudged Tan onto her back. Green body paint was streaked across her face and arms, effective camouflage when applied over her brown skin.

Toni stooped to pick up the dart Tan had pulled from her neck, then felt along Tan's neck. A strong pulse throbbed under her fingers, and there was little blood from the needle-like dart. She looked up at Xavier. "You drugged her? How did you—"

"I heard the bird call, too." He raised an eyebrow. "You are surprised?" He frowned, his tone turning harsh. "I grew up in the jungle, running messages for the cocaine lords." He leaned close, his face inches from Toni. "I am more dangerous in the forest than in the city. This is my natural habitat." He stood back and laughed as he called out. "Emile, come here." He lowered his voice to a normal volume. "Your pregnant advocate will have to walk today. Emile will carry your spy instead."

❖

The sun was peeking over the mountain tops when Sunfire glided gracefully to touch down next to Dark Star. The empty bucket at Jael's feet was evidence that he'd consumed his ration of fire rock before transforming from dragon horse to regular horse for the day. The gentle swoosh of Sunfire's wings in the wind had calmed but not extinguished Kyle's uneasy sense of foreboding at leaving Tan to shadow Xavier's group alone. So, for a brief moment, she turned her face to the soft sunlight and soaked up the morning bird song and the pleasant, steady sound of Dark Star's teeth tearing off the tender tops of meadow grass. Then she sighed at the mental picture that popped into her head of a full bucket of fire rock. Kyle muttered as she slid from Sunfire's back to retrieve the second, still-full bucket next to Jael. "Pig."

"She truly doesn't transform?" Jael's eyes never left the young filly as she held out the bucket of fire rock to Kyle.

Kyle shook her head and turned to watch Sunfire as she stretched her wings, then shook like a dog. She'd clearly enjoyed their nocturnal outing. "Apparently not. She's a bit arrogant about it, too." She held out the bucket and sent a mental picture of Sunfire coming to her to receive it, rather than Kyle fetching it for her. Sunfire stomped her foot and shook her head. "And stubborn." The youngster needed to learn their bond was a partnership, that Kyle wasn't her personal servant. She sent a new mental image of her setting the bucket on the ground, then igniting it into ash. She palmed a blue-white ball of fire to indicate her threat was real.

Jael chuckled when the filly hurried over to bury her nose in the bucket, then grimaced as the discordant crunch of rock drowned out the morning's more pleasant sounds. "You appear to have her in hand."

"Thanks. Our bond is still new." Kyle shifted her feet, her sense of foreboding suddenly blossoming in her chest. "First Warrior—"

"It's not necessary to address me formally unless I'm issuing orders, Kyle." Jael rested her hand on Kyle's shoulder. "As my second, you have to be my sounding board on a lot of issues. I need you to be at ease with me. I expect, no, I require that you voice your opinions honestly, especially when they conflict with my plans." Jael's gaze held hers. "When I say voice, I mean exactly that. I will never read your thoughts without permission, unless circumstances require it."

"I—" Kyle swallowed and stared at her feet. Would Jael dismiss her intuition? The dread that had begun to haunt her earlier tugged at her, and she looked up to meet Jael's gaze. What Jael thought of her suddenly didn't matter. This was about protecting Tan. "Something feels off about this. I felt it the moment I left Tan in the woods."

Jael cocked her head. "Are you a seer like your sister?"

"You know about Maya?"

Jael smiled. "We've never met in this life, but we've crossed paths in previous ones."

What must it be like to actually recognize people from your previous incarnations? Jael's expectant stare jerked Kyle back to their conversation. "Uh, no. I'm no seer. It's just…a gut feeling. An intuition."

"Never dismiss those," Jael said. Something washed across her face. Regret, guilt? Kyle wasn't sure. "To ease both our minds, I'll contact her." Jael gestured to the plush grass of the meadow. "Sit with me, and I'll include you in the conversation."

They sat in the grass, and Jael turned her face to the sun as she closed her eyes. Kyle took a moment to note the strong, smooth lines of her mentor's face. Though Danielle had been a clone of Jael, their personalities had always created a difference in their faces, their expressions. Already, the traces of Danielle were fading as Jael's emerged. Maybe it was the tense jaw, or the stiff set of her shoulders, or the tightening of her brow as she concentrated. But it was definitely Jael, not the easy-going Danielle who sat before her, systematically lowering her mental shields. Kyle closed her eyes and emptied her mind. Her eyes nearly popped open when she heard Tan in her head as clearly as she'd been standing next to her speaking. She could hear Jael, too.

They all appear okay. The rest of the camp, including their incompetent sentry, are still sleeping except Toni. She recognized my signal and knows I'm here.

Danielle was right to assign Lieutenant Antonia to Nicole, even though we were unaware that they'd know her connection to Furcho and snatch her.

The camp is waking up now.

Kyle smiled as Tan's mental chuckle fluttered through her brain. Stars, she missed Tan, even though they'd been separated only a few hours.

What?

Gotta love that girl. Nicole looks like she's doing the pee-pee dance.

What in blue blazes is a pee-pee dance?

She can't hear you, Kyle, because you're not a telepath and can't project your thoughts.

Kyle? Is Kyle with you?

Yes, and listening in.

What's she thinking that I can't hear?

She's wondering if pee-pee dance is a medical term, Doctor Tanisha.

Again, the flutter of Tan's mental laugh.

Yeah. I'll explain it to you later, babe—I mean, Commander Kyle.

Kyle's got a gut feeling that something's wrong, Tan.

She's just missing her morning orgasm.

Kyle frowned. She didn't like being dismissed by her lover, especially in front of the First Warrior. Her legs had barely tensed with her intent to rise and walk away, when Jael's hand on her knee stopped her.

I know you're joking, but—just as I couldn't dismiss your instincts—don't dismiss her intuition, Captain. Jael's tone had turned from friendly to command mode.

Sorry, Kyle. I'm sorry. I just tend to get sarcastic when...well, I feel it, too, and it's making me a little jumpy.

There was a pause, then a clear mental picture of Toni talking to a huge man and him nodding. It was as if they could see what Tan saw, except the picture was jumpy as Tan's brain sorted through a barrage of information, making instantaneous evaluations. The women heading for the edge of the forest, the man turning his back to them, Tan moving, skulking through underbrush to intercept them. Kyle saw brief flashes of Nicole and Maya beginning to squat to relieve themselves—thank the stars Tan didn't linger on that—and then of Toni standing next to a tree, taking field relief. Tan was speaking to Toni, but then a sudden wave of shock hit them, along with a quick, fuzzy image of a blow dart. The picture dimmed and Tan went silent.

Report, Captain.

Kyle's heartbeat quickened at the agitation in Jael's terse command.

Tan? What's happening?

Silence.

Kyle opened her eyes. "I can't hear her anymore."

Jael's brow furrowed and the muscle in her jaw jumped. After what felt like an eternity but was only a few seconds, she opened her eyes and met Kyle's. "Nothing. She's either been knocked out or drugged." Jael rubbed her temples. "Or maybe I just couldn't hold the connection through Danielle's iron skull." She rose to her feet and Kyle followed. Jael rubbed her temples again. "Son of a dung-eater, my head hurts. I can try contacting Toni after I rest a bit. If you aren't expecting telepathic communication, however, most people just dismiss it as their own random thoughts. Still, I should be able to listen in to her thoughts and figure out what's happening."

"Sunfire and I will go back and—"

"Negative." Jael started to shake her head, then stopped and pressed the heel of her hand to her forehead. "Jumping headache." She straightened her shoulders and stepped past Kyle before turning to her so that the sun was in Kyle's face rather than hers. "We're not going off half-cocked. Both Tan and Lieutenant Toni are resourceful. They'll be okay until we can launch an effective force at dusk."

"But—"

"That's an order, Commander." Jael snapped out the words, then squeezed her eyes shut and sucked in a deep breath. After a moment, she spoke again. "I won't need to rest long before checking in with Nicole or Toni." She opened her eyes, their ice-blue soft now. "My friendship with Tan goes back several lifetimes. Nothing's going to happen to her in this life, if I can help it."

Kyle gave Jael a terse nod and tried to swallow the churning of her gut.

"Get some rest, Commander, and allow your dragon horse to also rest." Jael gestured toward Sunfire and Dark Star. Both were lying in the thick grass, dozing after their morning meal. Sunfire slept with her wings spread, glittering even in the soft morning light, as though she were absorbing the sun's energy.

"I'll check in with the rest of The Guard to assure we'll be ready to mobilize as soon as the sun sets," Kyle said.

"Then—" Jael knew this would be a long day of worry for Kyle. She couldn't imagine how she would feel if Alyssa was in danger and she had to wait until that night to do something about it.

"Then I promise I'll try to nap so I'll be alert tonight."

Jael nodded. "Good enough. Tell the others that we'll convene for a debriefing and lunch at noon."

Kyle straightened to attention and saluted, thumping her right hand against her left shoulder. "Yes, First Warrior." She cast one last glance at Sunfire, who was still snoozing, then trotted down the path from the high meadow to the camp below.

Chapter Twelve

Toni couldn't take it a moment longer. Emile carried the unconscious Tan by shouldering one of her legs and one arm in a modified "rescue carry," but her weight wasn't enough to cause him to hunch over. He stood straight, which caused her body and other appendages to dangle and flop like a rag doll with every step he took. Toni was sure the bobbing of her head at that weird angle had to be tearing at her neck and shoulder muscles. "Emile, wait. Hold up for just a minute."

Emile turned to her, frowning, but continued to walk backward. "We can't fall behind. The boss man will get angry. Samuel, the man sleeping on guard duty when we all woke this morning, has no water or food now. The boss took them and says he will do the same to any of us who share ours with him. So, you must understand why I don't want to make him angry."

But Toni had already slowed to get behind Maya and remove the blanket from her pack as they continued behind the others. "Let me get this free, and I'll be really quick if you just stop for half a second."

"Um, could we make that two seconds so I can pee again?" Nicole asked.

Emile shook his head in disbelief. "Hurry."

Nicole stepped off the path, and Toni pulled her small whittling knife from her boot, then began to cut the blanket into wide strips.

"Hey. You shouldn't have that."

Toni didn't look up as she cut. "It's just a whittling knife, Emile. Do you think I could take on your whole group with one small knife? It's too small to stab anyone." She looked up at him. "But it's sharp and was my grandfather's, so don't even think about trying to take it from me. I really don't want to have to cut you with it."

Emile grinned. "A small knife for a small woman." He shifted his grasp on Tan's arm and leg. "But tell me why you are cutting up your blanket."

Toni put her knife away and motioned for Maya to help her. "I'm going to make it more comfortable for you to carry my friend. Turn around and let go of her so we can shift her around to carry piggyback like you did Nicole yesterday."

"She'll slide off if she can't wake up enough to hold on," he said.

"That's what the strips are for. We'll tie her against your back."

"My hands *were* getting tired of holding on to her." Emile turned so Toni and Maya could catch Tan as he released his grip. He was so trusting. Stars. She hoped he wouldn't be hurt when their rescuers arrived that night.

"Can you bend over? I just want to shift her around." Toni grunted as she and Maya struggled until Emile bent over and bore Tan's weight like a tabletop. "Excellent." She handed Maya a long blanket strip after they rotated Tan so that her arms flopped over Emile's shoulders. Tan moaned with the movement but didn't wake. "Quickly. Tie this one around her back and his chest. I'll use this wide one to secure her hips around his waist."

Nicole emerged from behind a tree as Toni was tying a third strip.

"These strips should bear most of her weight so you can let go and have your hands free if needed without dropping her." Toni glanced ahead. They'd taken too long and would have to jog to catch up with the others. "We better go."

Emile grinned broadly. "Thank you. This is much more comfortable."

Toni just hoped their quick knots would hold while they hurried to catch up, and that Xavier wouldn't question how they had managed to cut the blanket into neat strips.

They had to jog only a short distance to catch up because the others had stopped. Toni frowned. Had they missed them? She didn't want Emile to get into trouble.

Nicole must have sensed her apprehension. "It's okay. I don't sense any anger…just relief." They slowed to a walk, and as they took the last steps to rejoin the group, they emerged from the woods and found themselves standing next to a wide, smooth road.

Xavier didn't comment on their delay or their handiwork tying Tan to Emile's back. His eyes were fixed on a transport approaching from less than a kilometer away. He pointed to two of the men. "Get out onto the road and flag that transport down."

The men blocked the road, and the transport slowed to a stop a short distance from them. The driver was obviously wary.

Xavier smiled broadly and approached the vehicle. "Hello, friend," he said loudly. He held his hands out in welcome. "We are stranded, and I hope you can help us." After a short hesitation, the male driver lowered his window, and Xavier walked to the transport. Toni couldn't make out the rest of their conversation once Xavier began to speak in normal tones, but she watched him call out to Cyrus and wave him over. The driver got out of his transport and seemed happy to shake Cyrus's offered hand. The three talked together, Xavier staring down the road, past them, as the man explained something to them.

"Is your friend okay?" Laine had been with Cyrus near the front of their single-file hike, so Toni, Maya, and Nicole hadn't had the chance to speak to her since the night before.

"I hope so. I think he just drugged Captain Tan. She'll be mad as a hornet when she wakes up."

Laine looked up at Emile. "May I just touch her to check her pulse?"

"Yes, ma'am. I don't think he hurt her," the big man said.

Tan groaned and her eyes fluttered when Laine's fingers rested against her neck. After a moment, Tan seemed to relax and let out a soft snore.

"Her pulse is strong and steady, but she was waking up, and I don't think this would be a good time for it," Laine said. "I put her back to sleep, but it won't last long."

Toni wanted to tell Laine that Tan was a pyro and could probably single-handedly extinguish their captors. But, even though Emile had befriended them, she couldn't trust him enough to speak of it with him listening. Instead, she diverted their conversation. "How is Cyrus?"

"He's agitated. I'm doing what I can to keep him calm, but he needs his medicine." Laine shook her head. "I was sneaking it into his food but haven't been able to get it into him since we haven't had a real meal in several days."

"Any chance we can get him to side with us against Xavier?"

"Doubtful, unless he's had several days of medication."

"Mom, you're not planning to stay with him if we can find a way to escape, are you?"

Emile clapped his hands over his ears. "I can't be listening to this." He stepped away from them. "I'll see what's going on." Xavier had returned to the group of men, and Emile walked over to join them, Tan snoring softly against his back.

Laine brushed her fingers against Maya's cheek. "Trust your visions, Maya. All will be well in the end." She turned to rejoin the men because Xavier and Cyrus were walking back their way.

"Mom—"

Toni put a hand on Maya's arm. "Let her go." She was surprised when Maya turned and wrapped her arms around her, burying her face in Toni's shoulder.

"She does feel confident." Nicole tilted her head as if listening, considering something. "No. More like resigned, uh, resolved." She looked at Maya. "Your mom has very complex emotions."

"I'm just so scared she'll sacrifice herself for him."

Toni was more afraid that Laine's devotion to Cyrus had blinded her. She had an uneasy feeling that Laine was holding something back, and Maya hadn't shared it with them. Still, she was strangely drawn to this enigmatic woman clinging to her. Toni's endorphins hummed at the feel of Maya's slender body pressed against hers, and she instinctively stroked Maya's back. Dung. Maybe her hormones were blinding her. It wasn't like she had a lot of experience with women. Grasping Maya's shoulders, Toni gently disentangled them and held Maya at arm's length. "When we have a few minutes to ourselves, you're going to have to tell Nicole and me exactly how Laine is gifted."

Nicole nodded, glancing at Toni. "I have a feeling she can do more than just heal," she said absently, her attention focused elsewhere.

Toni followed her gaze to the knot of men. "What do you sense, Nic?"

"Xavier is happy. I suspect the people in the transport have agreed to help him."

Toni studied her friend. Nicole looked very tired, although they'd been walking only a few hours and most of the day was still ahead of them. "How are you doing?"

Nicole rubbed her belly. "This baby saps all my strength. She's resting on my bladder, but at least she's being still at the moment."

Toni scanned the roadside and saw nothing, not a big rock or a downed tree, that Nicole could sit on. Her survey was cut short as Xavier approached, Emile in tow.

"Our new friends are taking Cyrus, his wife, and myself to a town just down this road. We'll send a larger transport back for the rest of you within the hour." Xavier's dark eyes glinted in the sunlight. "Do not think my absence is your opportunity to escape. Juan has orders to shoot to kill—all of you, even if only one tries sneaking away."

Toni straightened her shoulders and glared back with defiance. "We're not stupid. Where would we go? Besides, we wouldn't leave the captain, who is still tied to Emile."

"Ah, yes. Your friend." He motioned for Emile to step closer, and he grasped one of Tan's arms that dangled over the big man's shoulder. Sliding his hand down to her wrist, he turned Tan's hand over to finger the thick skin of her palm. "A pyro, I see." He pulled something from his pocket. "I should just kill her, because she could be trouble if she wakes up."

"No." Toni's hands were already coming up to shield Tan, or at least knock Xavier back with her force field.

Maya was quicker, wrapping her in a hug from behind, effectively pinning Toni's arms. "Don't. He's not trying to hurt her...yet." Maya's fierce whisper stopped Toni's struggle. Or was it the nod Nicole added to confirm Maya's prediction? More likely, it was the hiss of a hypospray that reassured her Xavier didn't hold a small weapon—only another sedative.

He grinned at her, arching a single eyebrow. He seemed to enjoy toying with people.

CHAPTER THIRTEEN

The minute Jael walked into the headquarters, Furcho grabbed her shoulders. "Did you find them? Is she safe?" He gave her a shake when she didn't immediately answer.

Surprised by Furcho's deterioration, Jael wished Tan was with them and not scouting in the field. His normal impeccably neat appearance was a bit wild and disheveled. Exhaustion and desperation darkened his normally soft, intelligent eyes. She pried his hands from her battleskin but didn't release his wrists. "Stand down, Third Warrior." She eyed him. Was he going mad?

He didn't struggle against her grasp, but his eyes searched her face. "I have to know. Is my baby safe?"

"Jael?" Alyssa paused in the doorway of Jael's office, then walked cautiously toward them. Jael could feel the powerful calm flowing from the First Advocate and permeating the room. Furcho's shoulders dropped, his taut body relaxing. He glanced at Alyssa, then bowed his head. "She's important," he said. "So very important."

When Jael released him, Furcho dropped onto a lounge and buried his face in his hands. She looked to Alyssa, who frowned as she observed him. *Is he okay?*

Alyssa shrugged at Jael's telepathed query. *I can't decipher it. He's overwhelmed with an imperative to protect, and it seems to be focused on the baby Nicole carries. It's like a breeding frenzy, but different. His life force seems...I don't know...thin. Like he's fading away. That sounds ridiculous, but it's the only way I can describe it.*

The sound of boots on the porch signaled the rest had arrived, and Diego stepped out from the food prep, followed by another man carrying platters of food. The door opened and Kyle joined them, Raven and Michael in tow. Kyle sniffed the air, and Jael realized that she, too, was ravenous. They'd both given the sandwiches and pro-chow they'd taken with them last night to the men at the crash site.

"Let's eat while we talk," Jael said.

"Yes." Alyssa smoothed her hand down Jael's arm. "I'm sure everyone's hungry." She looked up at Jael. *And as much as I appreciate your new slim physique, I won't relax until you put back on the weight and muscle you had in your original body.*

Jael touched her lips to Alyssa's in a soft, lingering kiss as the others filled their plates. Then she pulled out a chair next to hers to seat Alyssa, though her proper place as First Advocate was at the other end of the table. Alyssa sat without questioning the change. They both still craved physical contact until the pain of their earlier separation had time to heal.

Jael filled her plate as food was passed around and made a weak swipe to block Alyssa's fork as she stole a few fried plantains from Jael's plate, even though she'd just passed off a platter laden with the sweet treats. They shared a smile at the familiar game between them, and Jael relaxed a bit despite the hurdles ahead of The Collective's dragon-horse army. She dug into her food, rolling the spicy forkful over her tongue. Stars, she hoped that as the cloned brain cells of her new body adapted to her neurological patterns they would retain Danielle's superior taste sensors. She stopped mid-chew, realizing she heard no clatter of forks against plate, no idle conversation. Jael looked up and found everyone—except Alyssa, whose eyes were closed as she savored the stolen sweet plantains—was watching her, more interested in her report than the food before them. She blinked. The old Jael would have already been calling on each to report their state of readiness. She sat back in her chair and met their eyes while she finished chewing and swallowed. She wiped a napkin across her mouth and cleared her throat, putting her fork down.

"Commander, has everyone been filled in on our mission last night?"

Kyle, who as Second Warrior sat in Danielle's usual chair at the other end of the table, shook her head. "I was waiting until we were all together."

"Can you summarize for everyone, then?" Jael forked the sole plantain on her plate and popped it into her mouth as Alyssa eyed it.

"In short, Sunfire led us to the mountain where Xavier's plane had crash-landed. It could have been worse. The plane was split, but into two intact parts. We encountered a small group of injured men whom Xavier had left behind to fend for themselves. There also were some casualties, but the injured men said our people were unharmed. Toni must have been able to shield them. Xavier, however, had left with the hostages and a handful of men who managed only minor or no injuries. Sunfire scouted and located the hostage party camped near the base of the mountain, and we dropped Tan nearby to tail them until tonight. We did what we could to help the injured, but Tan had only a field med kit, and our time was running short." Kyle paused and looked to Alyssa.

"As soon as Jael returned this morning and gave me the GPS coordinates of the crash, I instructed Will to organize a medical team and armed escort immediately. They departed three hours ago for a small airfield, where they'll meet two large helicopters provided and piloted by some nearby mountain rescue units."

"Armed escorts?" Furcho, who had been staring sullenly at his food, jerked his head up and spat out his objection. "We have few enough warriors left without sending them to rescue the people who kidnapped Nicole."

"You know that the dragon-horse units are not our only warriors," Raven said quietly. "Nearly a thousand answered the Calling and were trained to be soldiers. Their lack of sufficient DNA might have kept them from bonding with a dragon horse, but they are able soldiers nonetheless. Many stayed after they were screened out as potential dragon-bonding candidates to fill much-needed support positions and are anxious still to also serve as soldiers for The Collective."

"The Collective celebrates diversity in our population and talents." Alyssa smiled as she touched the Advocate tattoo that wound up the left side of her neck to her temple. "And our army celebrates the diversity of its soldiers."

Furcho tapped impatiently on the table. "Fine, but when are we going after Xavier?"

Jael took up the report. "I was able to contact Tan right after sunrise. She made discreet contact with Toni, so they know we've found them and are anticipating rescue. That's the good news."

Furcho's expression hardened. "And the bad news?"

"My communication with Tan was abruptly cut off. We have to assume she was discovered and incapacitated in some way."

All eyes turned to Kyle, who was absently rubbing her chest as if trying to ease a pain or calm an erratic heart. Her jaw flexed before she spoke. "We think she was drugged or knocked unconscious." She stared at them defiantly. "I'm sure I'd feel it if…if it was more serious." Kyle seemed relieved when Alyssa nodded.

Jael caught and held Kyle's gaze as she faltered in her report. "We're pretty sure she's drugged because her last thought before our connection went dark was the image of a blow dart that didn't have her markings."

All of The Guard knew of Tan's expertise with blow darts. They were silent for a moment as they considered the irony of Tan falling victim to her weapon of choice. Then Raven nodded for Diego to give their combined reports. "Of the original sixty-four dragon-horse warriors in our unit, thirty-two remain. A third of them or their mounts are still healing from injuries suffered in the Brasília battle but healthy enough to provide backup for the front line."

Jael shook her head. Brasília had cost them dearly. They'd have to rethink their strategy when they attacked the City of Light stronghold, but this mission at hand was different. Xavier was on the move and wouldn't have a brace of missiles to fire at them. She rubbed her chin. "So, thirty-two and seven Guard?"

Raven shook her head. "Those numbers include us—all seven members of The Guard."

Jael drummed her fingers on the table, her food forgotten for the moment. "Xavier's group is small and, from what we saw at the crash site, only as loyal as the credits Xavier pays them. The Guard will serve as the extraction team tonight. The army can stand down and give the ones still recovering another week or so to heal in anticipation of confronting Simon at the City of Light."

The door behind Jael swung open. In a lightning-smooth movement, she rose and faced it. A blue-white fireball swirled in her right hand.

"You might want to reconsider that plan." A lean young man with tousled dark hair and huge blue eyes sauntered in, followed by two young women and a boy. Another young man hung back, standing in the doorway and shifting his feet nervously.

Kyle stood, too. "Still short on manners, I see."

The dark-haired visitor shrugged. "What can I say? I grew up among social misfits."

Sun and moon. As if her pounding head wasn't torture enough, this pup was instantly getting on her last nerve. Jael stepped toward the impudent interloper, intent on impressing the protocol of knocking and waiting for permission to enter, but stopped when the boy moved to the front of the group, came to ramrod attention, and thumped his small hand against his left shoulder in salute.

"Private Pete reporting to Captain Tan," he said, scanning the room.

Jael raised an eyebrow at Kyle, who smothered a smile and shrugged. She looked down at the boy. "Well, Private Pete, Captain Tan is currently deployed on a mission, but you may report to Commander Kyle over there."

He grinned at Kyle but returned his attention to Jael, his expression serious. "Zack didn't mean nothing by barging in. We brought important news." His gaze swept the room again, then returned to her, his brow wrinkling. "Who are you?"

Jael squared her shoulders and schooled her face into a mock scowl. "I am Jael, First Warrior of The Collective."

The visitors stepped back and stared. Their rude young leader blinked. A flush of bright red crawled up his neck and colored his cheeks. Pete, however, was skeptical. "No way! I saw a vid on the d-net of those missiles hitting you, then POOF. You and the ghost dragon horse were gone."

Jael cleared her throat, casting a side glance at Alyssa.

The First Advocate pursed her lips together, her expression amused. *POOF. I can't wait to hear you explain that.*

Jael cleared her throat again. "Well, Pete. You can't believe everything you see on the d-net. Do I look like a pile of ashes?"

He cocked his head. "Not exactly."

The headache had taken a toll on her the past few days, but Jael didn't think she resembled a pile of ash. "Well, thank you for that assessment, Private Pete." She turned to Kyle. "Are these your troops, Commander Kyle?"

Kyle gestured for the red-faced young man to step forward. "Allow me to introduce Zack, leader of the San Pedro Sula Network." She smiled at the two young women. "And this is Haley and Oni." She eyed the man still standing nervously by the door. "Zack will have to introduce the last member of their group."

Zack's eyes shone now with new respect, and he held out his hand. "I've got so much to ask you. I was in on that mental chat you had with the Second Warrior and Tan. I'm good, but you..." Jael clasped his forearm, rather than hand, in a warrior's greeting. He mimicked Jael's greeting, then trailed his fingers down her forearm to the rough, thick skin of her palm and fingers. "A pyro and a telepath. Wow."

"I remember you."

Pete frowned up at them. "Zack, tell her about Sam and the d-message."

Jael mentally scolded herself for losing focus. "You feel I should reconsider our extraction plan?" she asked, remembering what he'd said when he burst into the room.

Zack relaxed into his casual slouch and shrugged, his awe of her apparently short-lived. "You're the tactician, so that's up to you. But the information we bring might cause you to change it."

Haley spoke for the first time, glowering at Zack's cocky attitude. "Just get to the point, Zack."

He sighed. "Tan reached out to us a few days ago and said you needed our help to locate that City of Light place where the bad dude is holed up. So, we hopped a solar train and—" He gestured to the other young man. "Sam sent out a series of search bots on general d-messaging pipes while we traveled. He's our best d-net spider. If the information is out there, Sam can work the web and find it. We were almost here when his searches snagged something interesting. That Xavier dude was reporting to his boss about their 'unfortunate' crash and requesting ground transport to their destination."

"Did they say when assistance would arrive?"

Zack nodded. "Around five o'clock this afternoon. Apparently, they had resources nearby that are headed his way."

"Dung." Furcho slammed his hand on the table. "They'll be long gone by the time we wait for sunset, then fly the distance to catch them."

"All the better," Jael said calmly. "You're right that we should change tactics, but the hostages will be easier to extract on the open road."

"There's the catch. The dude that talks like he has gravel in his throat told them to stay put for a few days. They're anticipating your attack. So, he's not just sending transportation. He's sending armed reinforcements. They're setting a trap for you."

"Jumping son of a dung-eater."

Alyssa backhanded Diego's shoulder. "Language. There's a child present."

"Diego is a child," Michael said, his tease momentarily easing the tension building in the room.

"Says you," Diego quipped back.

If nothing else, this mission to stop The Natural Order and restore unity had drawn The Guard together in an even tighter bond. Jael was surprised at the change in the prickly Diego, proud they'd stood by Tan during Phyrrhos's breeding frenzy, and relieved by their patience with Furcho's puzzling decline. They were, indeed, stronger together. Her decision was made.

"Then we'll answer their aggression. We leave one hour after sunset."

Alyssa stepped in. "Soldiers need nourishment, First Warrior. That includes you." She gestured to the long table where Diego's assistant had already placed warming pads under the many platters of food. "Zack, we would be honored if you and your friends would join us."

Jael offered a small smile to her mate, then noticed for the first time how Pete was staring hungrily at the table. "Yes. I'm afraid I'm the one lacking in manners now. This is First Advocate Alyssa, my soul-bonded. Please accept her invitation and dine with us. You can give me the details on the communications Sam intercepted."

"Star-tastic," Zack said as Pete scrambled toward the table.

More chairs were added as The Guard made room at the table and Diego's assistant brought plates and utensils for their guests. Pete grabbed a seat next to his friend Kyle, while Zack accepted the seat on Jael's left. Haley sat next to Zack, and Michael, The Guard's d-net nerd, invited Sam to sit next to him. Oni shyly declined the seat next to Haley, slipping instead next to Alyssa.

Jael studied the group as they interacted, sizing up their new visitors. Kyle had vouched for them as allies, but she liked to form her own opinions.

"Tell me about your Network," Jael said as Alyssa handed a platter of spiced rice to Oni and prompted the rest of the group to commence the meal. Haley, the apparent extrovert of the young couple, answered.

"All of us are gifted. Most of us were homeless or suppressed in our previous situations by people who still fear or don't understand or simply aren't equipped to deal with us as gifted children. The Network is a refuge where we found others like us, friends and mentors."

"It's our family," Pete said with a mouthful of food.

"Chew and swallow before you talk," Oni prompted him quietly.

"What are your talents?" Jael asked.

Haley nodded. "Oni and Pete are empaths. I'm a shield."

Jael logged that bit of information away. She'd never considered anyone but a pyro as a potential warrior, but meeting Alyssa had opened her eyes to other talents vital to an army. Empaths could be key to negotiations or evaluating an adversary's intent. Perhaps this shield gift could be useful, too. She looked to Zack, who was eating in huge bites, and methodically lowered her mental shields. *And you're a telepath.*

Everyone paused the meal and stared at Zack. He stopped chewing and swallowed. *I am.*

She nodded her approval when he also broadcast to the entire group. His range apparently was limited and his skills rough, but Zack's gift was strong. She made a mental note to have Han work with him. Aware that Alyssa was watching her, Jael resisted the impulse to rub her temple as the effort to hold down her shields threatened to ramp up her headache. "Tell us more about the communication you intercepted."

"We've pinpointed the origin of transmission," Zack said. "It's a small town at the base of a mountain, this continent. I can give you the GPS coordinates."

"Have you been able to contact any of our group yet?" Kyle's question was directed at Jael.

Alyssa answered for Jael in a tone that allowed no argument. "I insisted that she rest and eat before trying."

"Tan was tailing them," Kyle said to Zack. "But we lost contact with her this morning, so those coordinates will be helpful."

"Even better would be the coordinates of their intended destination, the City of Light," Jael said. That's where they'd find Simon. Cyrus might have started this cult, but it was becoming clear that Simon was running the show.

Sam shook his head. "They must have a master spider setting up their security. When I tried to follow the transmission back to its point of origin, thousands of false trails instantly appeared, and I barely intercepted a worm that shot back at me. It was a mean one, too. Would have fried my whole system."

Kyle dug around in one of the pockets of her field pants, then held up a small titanium-steel box. "Maybe you can crack this. It should contain their destination."

Jael stared at Kyle and felt a bit of the tension cramping her neck and shoulders loosen just a bit. "Is that what I think it is?"

Kyle nodded. "Yup. The plane's cockpit was smashed, but the tail section was in good shape, other than damage from what appeared to be a small electrical fire. It was easy to locate and extract the plane's recorder."

"Sure. These things are easy to break," Sam said as Kyle dropped the scorched box into his open palm. He grinned. "They now carry all kinds of information, right down to ownership records, maintenance, every flight plan since it first lifted off from the factory...everything."

"Well done, Second Warrior." If Jael had any niggling doubts, Kyle had immediately proved herself to be the right choice to step into Danielle's shoes. She scanned the people sitting around the table, then stood. Chairs scraped against the wood floor as they all stood and awaited her orders. Time to get this show on the road. "Michael, take Sam to the Advocates' cabin next door. He, Zack, and Pete can lodge there and set up a work space for Sam. Raven, show Haley and Oni to Danielle's old room upstairs. Diego, order the dragon-horse unit to their bunks for the next four hours. We'll assemble on the training field at eighteen hundred to brief them before dusk."

Michael, Raven, and Diego saluted, fist to shoulder, and chorused "as you command" before heading out to their tasks.

Jael held out her hand for Alyssa's. "Kyle, Furcho, and Zack, come with us. We'll try to contact Tan again." One last order. She methodically lowered her mental shields and reached out. *Han, can you come to my headquarters office?*

CHAPTER FOURTEEN

Toni and Maya both reached for Nicole's arms when she stumbled on the broken pavement of the neglected roadway. Even though Xavier had said he'd send a transport back for them, Juan and his men had decided they wanted hot food and showers sooner rather than later. They'd set off at a fast clip in the direction Xavier's transport had taken, and Nicole was having trouble keeping up.

"Are you okay?" Maya asked.

Nicole grimaced. "I'll be fine. I just need to focus on what's ahead—hopefully a full meal, hot bath, and a real bed. I could sleep—" She stumbled, then bent to grasp her right calf before sitting abruptly. Her face contorted. "Cramp, cramp. Dung."

Toni would have laughed at the uncharacteristic curse if it hadn't been obvious that Nicole was in pain. Pregnancy was bringing out a short-tempered side of the usually sweet, sunny Advocate who befriended everyone. She knelt and grabbed Nicole's foot with one hand to flex it gently. "Let me help, Nic." She rubbed Nicole's arch and Achilles tendon with her other hand.

Maya joined her ministrations, pushing Nicole's hands away to take over her frantic massage of the visibly knotted calf muscle. "Let Toni and me do this. You sit back and concentrate on breathing through the pain," she said to Nicole.

Emile stood over them, his expression anxious. "What's wrong?"

"She's dehydrated and her legs are cramping." Toni knew she shouldn't snap at Emile. He'd been kind and helpful. But she was tired and thirsty. They'd drunk the last swallows of their water when they rose that morning, and now she was kicking herself for not giving up her share to Nicole.

Emile dug—a bit awkwardly with Tan still tied to his back—into one of the deep cargo pockets of his pants and handed a quarter-full water bottle to Nicole. "Will this help?"

Maya looked up and beamed at him. "Thank you, Emile."

The big man blushed and scuffed his boot against the pavement. "I'm sorry I can't carry her, too." He glanced nervously at the other men, who had stopped some distance ahead. One of them was striding back toward them. "Maybe it won't be much farther, but I think we need to hurry."

The man, the same who had earlier suggested he should help fit her pack straps around her breasts, approached with a sneer. "Juan wants you up there," he said to Emile. Though the man had a slight build, Emile wilted under his mean stare and hurried back to the group, Tan's limbs flopping as he jogged. Then the man glared at the women. "Get up."

Toni stood to face him while Maya rose and held out a hand to Nicole, who failed in her first attempt when her weight pulled at her tender calf muscle. She plopped back down to the roadway.

"I said for you to get up, bitch." The man shoved Toni out of his path and drew his foot back to kick Nicole.

"No!" Toni charged into him, knocking him to the ground and going down with him. Their momentum rolled them several times before Toni ended up on top, her knife pressed to his throat. "Only a belly-crawling coward would kick a pregnant woman."

He tried to buck her off. Unsuccessful, he taunted Toni. "So, she's your girlfriend? I got the idea that you fancied the green-eyed tart. She's a tasty-looking morsel. Maybe I'll take a piece of her as payment to leave the Advocate alone."

Toni pushed the knife's point into his skin and a drop of blood leaked from the small prick. "Maybe I'll cut your manhood off, after I slit your jugular."

"Toni?" Maya's voice wavered.

Toni froze at the quiet click of a projectile weapon cocking next to her ear.

"I have to rescue you from this runt of a woman?" Juan spat on the ground next to the man's head and then pressed the gun to Toni's temple. "Drop the knife and get up."

Fury swirled in her gut. His remark tore at a life-long wound. She wasn't a runt. She was a warrior. She growled and pressed the knife deeper. The bead of blood was joined by more to form a tiny pool that filled and trickled down the man's neck. "Drop your weapon or I'll cut his throat." Maybe she'd kill him anyway. Then he'd never touch Maya. Ever.

Juan's cold laugh rang out. The gun no longer pressed against her head. "Drop your knife or I'll shoot the Advocate. Then we won't have to worry about her slowing us down."

"If you hurt her, Furcho will roast you slowly." The threat was a stall while she calculated whether she could slice her captive's throat and the tendons in Juan's ankle in one stroke...before he registered what was happening and shot one of them. It was a gamble.

"Toni. He's very serious." Nicole's soft words instantly dampened the fire driving her thoughts. Furcho and Alyssa trusted her to protect Nicole and her unborn baby, not gamble with their lives. And what if his bullet hit Maya instead? A sliver of panic shot through her. How had she even considered putting them in danger? Toni rose, and her captive scrambled backward before standing and dabbing at the blood on his neck, his sneer gone. She flipped the small knife and slowly offered the handle end to Juan. He took it from her, then backhanded her with the gun's grip. Pain exploded in her cheek. She staggered back but managed to stay on her feet. She touched her fingers to her throbbing face, and they came away bloody.

"Search her for more weapons."

She held Juan's stare as his man rifled through her pockets and ran his hands over her body. She willed herself not to react when he squeezed her breasts and crotch in his rough search.

"Nothing, unless she has something shoved up inside her. Want me to check that, too?"

Toni's stomach soured at the thought of his hand probing her. She'd hit him with her shield hard enough to crack his skull before she'd let that happen. She silently thanked the stars as a long hover bus appeared in the distance and the other men began to shout.

"No," Juan said. "Get in the transport."

The man hurried away. Toni didn't need Nicole's empathic powers to see his relief that Juan hadn't shot him for letting a woman best him.

Juan stood a moment longer, his eyes boring into each of the women in turn. "Don't test me again." He gestured for them to go before him as they walked to the waiting hover bus.

❖

Maya squeezed onto the bench seat with Toni and Nicole, then glanced nervously around the transport. Tan had been cut free from Emile and dumped unceremoniously onto the seats across from them. Juan sat up front, while the others settled around the bus. Nobody occupied the seats immediately in front and behind them. Not even Emile, who sat quietly in the very back of the bus. His kindness to them had earned him a cold shoulder from his comrades. Other than Juan chatting up the driver, the bus was sullenly silent.

A barrage of anxious questions swirled like a tornado in Maya's head. Was her mother safe? These men showed no respect for Cyrus as their leader but jumped to follow Xavier's orders. What about Nicole? She wasn't dealing well with pregnancy. And that baby. Maya had sensed something unusual when she'd touched Nicole's belly earlier. Would the rough conditions cause a miscarriage? Was the pregnancy advanced enough that a miscarriage would endanger Nicole's life, too? Toni could shield them from the men, but she couldn't stop a woman's labor. Could she?

Toni. Wow. A tingling sensation washed over Maya as she flashed back to the earlier scene. Toni was so brave and fierce. Maya itched to slide her hand into Toni's and entwine their fingers. Toni made her feel safe. And more. She glanced at Toni's serious profile. She was staring at her hands, full lips pursed in a contemplative pout. The swirling in Maya's head stopped, and a single vision pushed everything else away. Toni's pouty lips on hers, their tongues sliding together, hot and wet. Then Nicole's quiet words tore her from her pleasurable daydream.

"We should ask for a doctor to scan your cheek and make sure the bone isn't fractured." Nicole angled to sag against the window of the hover bus. "If they won't get one for you, maybe they'll give us some supplies so I can patch you up." Nicole's last words faded away as she closed her eyes and rested her head in the junction of the window and the back of their seat.

The memory of Juan's pistol cracking against Toni's cheek flashed through Maya, and she cursed her drift toward amorous thoughts. How had she gotten so off track? She cupped Toni's chin and gently turned her head so she could see more than Toni's profile. Maya covered her mouth as she choked back a shocked cry. An ugly bruise already swelled Toni's left eye nearly shut, and a dark trail of blood had dried along the ridge of her jaw and down her neck even as the cut on her cheekbone still wept a trickle of bright red. "Oh, Toni."

The right side of Toni's mouth curled in a tiny smile. "I want to say you should see the other guy, but I'm sure I look worse than him."

Maya raised her hand and Toni flinched, then held steady, her one visible eye holding Maya's gaze. She'd never seen such a rich shade of brown, framed by long, thick, dark lashes. Heat radiated from Toni's tortured flesh when Maya skimmed her fingertips over the bruise. She gently pried the enflamed eye lids open. "Your eye looks clear and undamaged," she said quietly. "What can you see?"

"Swirls of green and blue, like the deep part of the Third Region Gulf."

Maya blinked. Sun and stars. She'd fielded compliments before from would-be suitors, but Toni's murmured words fluttered the breath in her lungs and stuttered her heart. She dropped her eyes to Toni's mouth, and before she could analyze her intent, Maya closed the few centimeters between their faces and touched her lips to Toni's. The sudden scuffle of men moving around and past them jerked Maya back to reality.

"Perverts," one of the men muttered.

"Maybe they'd put on a show for us," another man said, louder. The group of them moving to exit the transport laughed.

Toni frowned, then turned in the seat to scan the bus as if she were counting heads. They were seriously outnumbered, and Maya feared what Toni might be plotting.

"Don't react. That's what they want you to do."

"I wasn't planning to give them the satisfaction," Toni said, frowning. "Something…I don't know what I'm looking for, but I just felt like I needed to look." She twisted around to wake Nicole but froze when the window reflected her image. She lifted her hand to her damaged cheek and carefully touched it. "Dung. I look like death warmed over."

"You should see the other guy," Maya said, drawing another tiny smile from Toni.

Emile was the last man to head for the exit. He said nothing, avoiding even a glance their way as he squatted to pull the still-unconscious Tan over his shoulder. Toni roused Nicole, and they followed him.

Juan was waiting beside the bus. "Come with me. Emile. Bring the pyro."

They rounded the bus and stared at a modest four-story hotel.

Toni paused in front of the sign next to the entrance, murmuring the hotel's name and the BELIEVERS ONLY sign attached to the wall below it. Her odd behavior made Maya wonder if more than her cheekbone was cracked. "Come on," she urged Toni, tugging her shirt.

After a brief conversation with the clerk behind the desk, Juan herded them into the lift and pressed his finger to the touchpad.

"Four," Toni whispered.

A man was working on the security plate of a door to their left and looked up as they exited the lift. "I've already taken care of the adjoining room, and I'll have this one done in just a second." He used narrow pliers to pull a wire loose and replaced the face of the lock. "All done. Did they give you the code at the front desk?"

Juan held up a card the desk clerk had given him.

"It should be good for both rooms. I disconnected the sensor that opens the door from the inside. The only way to exit is to tap your code into the security panel inside the room, same as you punch it in here to get in." He tucked the pliers into a tool belt at his waist. "If you lose or forget the code and get trapped inside, just buzz the front desk."

Maya glanced at Toni and Nicole. Toni was watching Juan and the hotel tech intently. Nicole was propped against the wall, staring into space. Maya edged toward the center of the hall, for a better view of the security plate. Toni didn't glance her way but gave a tiny nod to acknowledge Maya's move to make up for her blind side. Her eye was a thin slit now. They both waited.

"You're sure it can't be opened without the code?"

"We do it all the time for people with kids. Keeps them from sneaking out or constantly touching the door just to watch it retract and close over and over. But I'll wait while you test it." The tech stepped back to give Juan access.

Juan used his body to block even the tech's line of sight, but the tech wasn't watching Juan. He was staring at Toni's damaged face.

"You've got quite a shiner," he said to Toni. He pointed past them. "The ice machine is on this floor, last door on the left. Looks like you could use some."

"She's fine," Juan said, motioning for Emile to go into the room first.

The tech raised his eyebrows at the sight of Tan slung over Emile's shoulder, and his brow knitted as he glanced from Toni to Juan. Concern flickered in his eyes, then suspicion.

Juan apparently noticed and sighed dramatically. "These women came to The Natural Order for help with their addictions to mind-altering drugs and drinks. We thought they were doing well, but then these two showed up inebriated." He jerked his thumb to the doorway Emile had entered. "That one passed out and tripped this one as they were boarding the hover bus. That's when she hit her head."

Maya grabbed the opportunity. "Is there a doctor in the hotel?"

The tech started to answer, but Juan interrupted him. "We've already arranged for a doctor to come by later."

Movement in her peripheral vision caught Maya's attention. Nicole, alert again, mouthed *he's lying*. Emile emerged from the room, and Maya groped for a quick plan. She had to do something. She stepped forward and smiled. "Emile, could you please get some ice for Toni's eye?" She pointed down the hallway. "It's at the end of the hall, on the left."

Emile looked to Juan for permission. Juan gave a quick nod, then smiled at the tech. "So, you can see why I've asked for the security panel to be modified." He sighed again, his expression sorrowful. "It's regrettably necessary to save them from the temptation to seek out more drugs." He shook his head. "It's an illness, you know, and our duty to help them in their struggle."

While the ice was a small victory, Maya couldn't celebrate. Juan was a good actor and had outmaneuvered her with a lie plausible enough to relieve the tech's suspicions. Her hope that he might call the local peacekeepers to investigate died.

"Thank you for your help," Juan said, dismissing the tech as he ushered them into the room where Tan sprawled on the first of two beds, still out cold. The friendly expression Juan had maintained for the tech disappeared with the click of the door's lock. He went directly to the credenza and removed the receiver chip from the back of the large-screen digital viewer. They wouldn't be able to access anything outside the room—news and entertainment channels, the d-net, or even the front desk.

Toni disappeared into the personal facility, and the sound of retching quickly followed. Nicole shot a worried look in Toni's direction, then slid past Maya to check on Tan. Maya surveyed the room—sparsely furnished but clean. She eyed the door that connected them to the next room. Would guards be posted there? The thought of being trapped in these rooms with leering men made her want to retch, too.

When the musical tones of a code being entered into the outside security panel sounded and the door slid back, Juan's hand shot to the weapon strapped to his belt. He holstered his partially drawn gun as Xavier strode into the room, followed by Emile, holding a small waste can full of ice and another man carrying several large paper bags that he set on a table in the corner of the room. Maya nearly swooned at the aroma of food trailing him.

Xavier scanned the room. "Where's the other one?"

Toni emerged from the personal facility, chalk-white and wiping her mouth with a wet bath-cloth. Xavier stared at her face, then turned a questioning stare on Juan.

"She attacked one of the men." Juan shrugged as if it was nothing.

Xavier's expression darkened. "I told you to shoot all of them if even one tried to escape."

Juan ducked his head, his bravado disappearing at Xavier's cold, flat words, and Maya looked from one to the other. Nicole could confirm her suspicion, but she was already sure. Juan, Xavier's right hand, was afraid of his boss.

"Nobody tried to escape." Toni's battered face contorted in a half grimace. She swayed, then put a hand on the wall to steady herself. "One of your bastards tried to kick Nicole because she stopped to massage out a leg cramp." She pointed to her eye. "This was Juan's reward after I stopped his idiot." She glared at Xavier with her one visible eye. "Only a man with a little penis would kick a pregnant woman."

Maya wanted to slap a hand over Toni's mouth to stop her from saying more.

Xavier narrowed his eyes and stepped into Toni's personal space. Toni pushed off the wall and straightened. Hands open and held loosely at her sides, she didn't give an inch. No, no, no. This was not the time. Maya hadn't seen it in a vision, but she felt it in her core. If Toni revealed her shield now, their future would change.

Maya slid between them, gently forcing Toni to step back. "I want to see my father. *He* is the leader of The Natural Order, not you. *He* understands that women are to be protected." She gathered her courage and punctuated her next words with occasional pokes to Xavier's chest. "And, while we might require protection and guidance from men, women are the source of new life. The Natural Order needs children to spread our beliefs and our dominance in the world." She leaned forward to counter the tug at her shirt that threatened to force a step back. She was warming to her lecture and far from done. "Only one stallion is needed for the herd to grow, but a herd of stallions with few mares is doomed."

Xavier's mouth curled into a slow smile. "I like your fire. Maybe I should be your stallion, no?"

The tugging of her shirt switched to an arm wrapped around her waist. Toni pulled her away from Xavier as she whispered into Maya's ear. "Maya, no. I'm sorry I started this, but it's time to shut up."

His expression amused, Xavier shrugged and drew back, too.

His white teeth shone as his smile widened. "But the food we brought is growing cold while I rattle on." He drew something from his pocket and tossed it to Juan. "Put these on the pyro and make sure they're locked tight on her wrists." He turned to Emile and gestured to the connecting door. "Open this, please, so our other guest can join them."

Emile hurried to unlock the door and smiled when it slid back.

"Mom!" Maya threw herself at Laine when she stepped tentatively into the room.

"Enjoy the food I've brought you, ladies. We'll be leaving tomorrow for the City of Light." With that, the men filed out, and the door to the hall slid shut with a click and faint whir of the lock engaging.

Laine hugged her youngest child to her chest. "Are you okay?"

Maya disengaged from her mother's embrace but grabbed Laine's hand and led her to Toni, who sat on the end of the bed, her head bowed. "I am, but you have to help Toni. That dung-eater hit her."

Laine stopped, cocked her head, and raised an eyebrow—a gesture she'd used Maya's entire childhood to check her children's bad behavior or language.

Fists on her hips, Maya rounded on her mother. "Really, Mom? We've been kidnapped, survived a plane crash, then made to hike through the woods and sleep on the cold ground. I'm not a child. I am a woman who is out of patience, beyond hungry, and desperate for a bath."

"Please stop yelling." Toni's weak request was cold water on Maya's fit of temper.

"Sorry. I'm so sorry." Maya spoke quietly, kneeling to stroke the undamaged side of Toni's face. "Are you going to be sick again?" She spotted a small waste bin next to the credenza and scooted a few steps on her knees to retrieve and place it between Toni's knees. Toni bent low and dry-heaved over the bin.

"Let me help." Laine sat on the bed next to Toni, who open-mouth panted a few breaths before heaving again. She grasped Toni's wrist and dug her fingers in a pressure point. Still bent over the bin, Toni coughed a few times, but her breathing slowed, and she wiped at her mouth with the cloth still in her hand. Laine laid her other hand at the base of Toni's skull, applying pressure behind both ears with her thumb and fingers. "Maya, get another cloth and wrap a handful of ice in it, please. Then see if there's a liner in the facility bin that we can use to make a larger cold pack for her cheek."

Maya got another cloth from the personal facility, put a big handful of ice in the center, tied the corners to form a small pack, and held it out to her mother.

Laine raised the heel of her hand where it rested on the back of Toni's neck. "Slip it under my hand." Toni tried to raise up, but Laine held her down. "Not yet. Just a minute more."

Toni didn't argue. She swallowed hard and rested her forearms on her thighs, then closed her good eye and gave in to Laine's touch.

Maya wanted to wrap her arms around Toni and hug her hard. She wished for the first time that she'd inherited her mother's healing gift, that she could be the one relieving Toni's pain. But she didn't, so she wasn't.

She picked up the bin of ice and took it into the personal facility. An extra liner was tucked under the one lining the small bin in there. But before she filled it, she dipped her fingers into the chips of ice, then held them to the back of her neck. She felt a little queasy herself. Queasy with worry. What if Toni's concussion was serious? Her brain could be bleeding. The extensive swelling worried her. If the cheekbone was shattered close to her eye, her vision could be permanently impaired unless she was taken to a hospital for surgery to repair it.

Maya tipped the ice bin over the sink to drain off some of the melted water. She wished they had a way to keep it from melting since they couldn't get more. When she tipped the bin back upright, a flash of color showed under the ice. She dug out a couple of small cartons of juice. Emile, bless his heart. She hoped his kindness wouldn't buy him more trouble. The gentle man didn't belong with Xavier's group. She shivered. She sensed a very dark soul when she looked into Xavier's eyes. He must have been badly born several times over.

She stepped back into the room with the ice pack and juice cartons to find Toni in the middle of the second bed, propped against the bed's headboard and supported by a stack of pillows. Laine sat on the bed where Tan was sprawled, her hand covering Tan's forehead and her head bowed in concentration. Nicole was taking bites from a cheeseburger she held in one hand while she unpacked the food bags with her other.

"This stuff is still warm, you guys," Nicole said between mouthfuls.

Maya set the juice cartons next to the food. "I found these in the ice bin. There must be a snack vendor in the ice room, and our big friend smuggled a few for us."

Nicole picked one up and held it to her cheek. "Sun and stars. I've been craving some apple juice."

Maya took one juice carton, a water carton, and two burgers from the food stash, juggling them with the ice pack and towel she'd grabbed. Toni turned her head toward Maya when she sat carefully next to her. She wasn't as pale now and tried to smile before closing her eye again. Maya leaned down and brushed her lips over Toni's. She hadn't thought about why when she'd kissed Toni on the bus, but she was ready to admit she was inexplicably drawn to this brave woman. When she started to pull back, a small tug at her blouse was all the encouragement she needed to return for a firmer caress. She swiped her tongue against Toni's lips before retreating again—a promise of more when Toni was well again.

"So sweet," Toni said.

Her wistful whisper made Maya want to really kiss her. Instead, she brushed a lock of Toni's dark hair away from her forehead and studied the bruised eye. "I've got an ice pack for your cheek, but if your stomach has settled, you might want to try to eat something first."

Toni's tongue swiped over her lips, and she held up her wrist. "Your mom said this is an old sailor's remedy for seasickness. It must work because I'm feeling better, maybe even a little hungry."

Maya recognized her mother's braided leather bracelet. A stone bead was threaded into the thickest part like a stone in a ring. But the bracelet had been turned inward and pulled tight so the bead bore into the pressure point Laine earlier held with her fingers. Maya opened the juice carton and stuck a straw in it. Toni took it and sucked greedily.

"Slowly," Laine warned her from the other bed. She rose and went to the table for her own burger.

"How's Captain Tan?" Toni asked.

Maya couldn't wait any longer. She unwrapped a burger and took a large bite. Toni was watching her, so she put a hand over her mouth and mumbled around the food. "Sorry. I'm about to starve."

Laine sat on Tan's bed again and began to unwrap her burger. "I was able to dissipate the drugs in her system somewhat. She should be waking shortly." As if on cue, Tan groaned and twitched.

Toni raised a hand to carefully explore her jaw, then sipped on the juice again. "The food smells great, but I'm not sure I can chew much."

Maya wanted to laugh at the hunger in Toni's eyes as they followed the burger Maya picked up to bite into again. She broke off a small bite from her burger and held it to Toni's mouth. "Try this. It shouldn't require much chewing."

Toni opened her mouth for the food, then chewed just a few times before swallowing. "More?"

Maya smiled and broke off another small piece to plop in Toni's eager mouth. Nothing was wrong with Toni's hands, but Maya was happy to feed her. She was aware of Laine watching them, but she didn't care. She put the ice pack in Toni's hand and guided her to hold it against her eye as she ate. Maya chuckled at a sudden memory.

"What?" Toni asked as she sipped her juice in preparation for more burger.

"I was just remembering your insult to the kicker's manhood," she said, offering the last bite to Toni, then opening the second burger for them to share. "I can't believe you actually said that to Xavier."

Toni swallowed another bite. "Yeah, well, sometimes my mouth gets me into trouble. Thanks for jumping in, but you were pretty close to the edge, too. I loved your stallion analogy, even though Xavier seemed to miss the intent." The swelling made her smile crooked, but Maya thought it was sort of sexy.

Her stomach seemed to have shrunk over the past few days, so she fed the rest to Toni. She sipped from her water carton while Toni chewed. Tan groaned again, and they watched the restless movements of her legs and arms.

"Why did they put gloves on her hands?" Maya asked.

Laine frowned. "They're fire-retardant gloves, designed to restrain pyros in mental wards so they don't hurt themselves or others. She can't form a flame without burning herself." She frowned. "They put them on Kyle when she was with me, but hers weren't connected to form handcuffs like these. Kyle was able to pick the wrist locks on hers and throw them off when everything started happening in Killeen."

Toni suddenly sat forward, and Maya stood to dispose of the litter from their meal. Maya followed her gaze. The captain's restless movements had stilled, but the muscles in her neck and arms were visibly rigid. Was she about to have a seizure?

"Mom?"

Laine, her face etched with concern and question, turned back to her patient. She reached out to investigate this new turn, but a low, animalistic growl stopped her hand mid-air.

Showing no warning flutter or dazed confusion, Tan's eyes were dark and alert when they suddenly opened. Her voice, however, was low and hoarse. "I'm going to burn him slowly into ash. The mother-jumper son of a dung-eater who put these suffocating gloves on my hands is mine."

CHAPTER FIFTEEN

Despite her earlier promise to Kyle that she wouldn't let anything happen to Tan, Jael knew she couldn't always keep vows that she made with the best of intentions. As the group scattered to their individual assignments, the expectation on Kyle's face weighed heavily on Jael.

She took her customary seat at the head of the conference table. Alyssa sat on her right, holding tight to Jael's hand as Kyle and Zack sat across from her. They all waited as she relaxed against the tall back of the black leather chair and closed her eyes.

"Empty your minds, and I'll tie you into our conversation," Jael said without opening her eyes.

A legion of voices filled Jael's head until she was able to filter and focus her probe. *Tan.* No response. *Tan.* Silence. Shuffling noises came from Kyle's direction, and then Jael felt a swell of calm. Alyssa's projected emotion soothed Kyle's anxiety. A bead of sweat trickled past her ear as her head pounded. She'd never failed to contact Tan before. Their bond of friendship was tight. She opened her eyes and rubbed her temples. "Something's keeping her from responding."

"What about Toni?" Kyle's gaze was sharp, her posture tense. "You said you could maybe listen in on Toni's or Nicole's thoughts to get some information."

"There's probably too much distance. I can contact Tan and other members of The Guard because their signatures are familiar to me and our bond strong. I've spent very little time with Nicole or Toni. They work under Alyssa, not me. Filtering their unfamiliar thoughts from among millions is nearly impossible." She rubbed her forehead in the spot where the pain had moved from her temples and taken hold. "I might be able to do it if I didn't have to also concentrate on getting past Danielle's thick skull."

Kyle's chair skidded backward as she abruptly stood. "Then Sunfire and I will depart immediately."

"I need you here." Jael didn't have to voice what they all knew. Furcho would be of little help in his befuddled state.

"You have Raven, Diego, and Michael." She strode to the door.

Jael's temper flared with the pain that spiked in her head. She expected advice, even questions from her Guard. But when the First Warrior issued an order, not even Danielle had ever refused to comply. "Stop right there."

Kyle froze at Jael's low, deadly tone. Her hand on the door and back turned to them, Kyle lowered her head for a long moment. She didn't speak, but her eyes were anguished when she turned back to them.

Tan is her beloved, the other half of her heart. Alyssa wasn't telepathic, but Jael was always tuned into her thoughts. *How would you respond if I was in Tan's place?*

Sympathetic green eyes drew and held Jael's. She was sure she'd drown in them one day. Her anger instantly drained away. Dung if that woman wasn't making her soft. She sighed. "Sit down, Kyle. I didn't say I wouldn't try."

"Since you are bonded, is it possible for you to access Alyssa's familiarity with the other women and use it to find their thoughts?"

She'd almost forgotten Zack was in the room. So he wasn't just a nosy telepath. The young man had a sharp mind, too. She admonished herself for not thinking of the idea first. The jumping pain was slowing her mind. She looked at her mate. Alyssa's gift had grown tremendously since she first found her way up Jael's mountain.

"I was able to sense over a long distance Tan's bond with you when I touched the jackets you'd both left at the clinic," Alyssa said to Kyle. "Maybe if I had something from Nicole's and Toni's things in their quarters at the Advocate's cabin."

Furcho jumped up from his seat. "I'll go." He hesitated. "With your permission, First Warrior."

Relieved to see a hint of the warrior she'd known for years, Jael waved him toward the door. "Thank you. That could help."

He was gone before she lowered her hand. In his wake, Han stepped into the room and bowed slightly.

"How may I be of service?"

Jael and Alyssa stood and returned the slight bow of the man who had trained them both—Alyssa recently and Jael as they reincarnated together in several lives.

"Han, let me present your next student." Kyle nudged Zack's shin with her foot. He frowned at her but rose from his seat. "Zack, this is Han. He is the master of many gifts over countless lifetimes. Alyssa and I bow to him as both teacher and sensei. If you have the focus to learn, he can help you expand your gift."

Zack slouched with his arms crossed over his chest as he eyed Han, who appeared to simply be a small, wizened old man.

Han bowed to him in acknowledgment of their introduction. "I am pleased to meet you, young Zack."

When Zack didn't return the courtesy, Kyle cuffed the back of his head hard. "Ow."

"You can start by teaching him manners and how to show respect," she said to Han.

Zack glared at Kyle, mining her thoughts for something to embarrass her in return for her rebuke. He was surprised to find his probe suddenly blocked.

It is customary to return my bow, and probing another's thoughts without their permission will bring you no honor.

Zack startled at the old man's voice in his head. He locked eyes with Han's. He couldn't read Han's thoughts either. He looked at Alyssa, Jael, and Kyle again. For the first time in his young life, he couldn't hear anyone's thoughts. He began to panic. "You're blocking me."

Han smiled and nodded to confirm the accusation. *Learn to show respect, and I can teach you how to do this and much more. Your gift is considerable but unschooled.*

Zack hesitated, then straightened his posture and dropped his arms to his side and bowed deeply. He'd never had a mentor. He'd just found his way on his own, collected his band of misunderstood kids and connected with other underground networks. His mind spun with the possibilities of what Han might teach him. After all, he'd been Jael's teacher, and Zack had never met a telepath more powerful than her.

Eyes down, chin down, and a slight bend at the waist is the proper bow of a student to his teacher.

Zack glanced at Jael, who gave him a nod, then tested his bow to Han again. "I would like very much to learn what you can teach me."

They sat again, but Kyle still glared at Zack. Han, who had

remained standing, rounded the table in smooth strides that belied his frail appearance. He stopped next to Kyle and put a hand on her shoulder. "Don't judge him too harshly. Boys are generally more affected by their physiology than girls and find it harder to subjugate themselves to someone else. You will understand this very soon as you begin to recall some past lives in which you were male." He gave her shoulder a pat and stepped over to Jael. Before he could speak to her, Furcho burst into the room.

He was breathless. "I've got Nicole's sleep shirt and the shoulder pack that Toni's always carrying around. Will that work?"

"Those are perfect, but I don't know if this will help Jael," Alyssa said as she took the items from him.

Furcho looked to Jael. The desperate expectation in his eyes mirrored Kyle's. Jael closed her eyes and pressed the heel of her hand against her forehead when pain lanced through her skull. Blast this headache. She'd held her shields down too long already. Alyssa's delicate hands were on her shoulders, cool on her skin as they massaged their way up her neck. Jael bit back a groan as Alyssa dug her fingers in the rigid muscles. She had to try.

Jael opened her eyes to find Han and Alyssa staring down at her.

"If you please," Han said to Alyssa. "Permit me to assist."

Alyssa returned to her seat on Jael's right, and then Han took her place behind Jael and spoke to the group. "To be successful in our endeavor, I must beg your patience. This crisis is very physically taxing as the First Warrior's brain cells remap to better fit her life force." He pressed his fingers to points on both sides of her spine, just behind her ears, and began to instruct her. "Close your eyes, and let your shields go until the pain is much less."

Jael gave a mental smile as a familiar scene formed in her mind. She stood in her meadow of wildflowers, staring at her refuge, her mountain home...no, her and Alyssa's mountain home. She turned around slowly, breathing in the sun-warmed scent of spruce and earth. Now Han stood before her, and they bowed to each other. Han bowed again, and Jael realized Alyssa had joined them, standing at Jael's right. Then Han pivoted gracefully and, with his back to them, they began in unison a familiar, flowing eighty-eight step Tai Chi kata. A sense of overwhelming happiness swelled around them, and when the movements rotated them ninety degrees, her throat tightened. Danielle and her beloved Saran had joined them. Danielle stopped and faced her as the others continued the kata. Jael blinked away tears that blurred the ethereal image of her cousin, her closest friend, her confidant and advisor—the original Second Warrior who'd been cloned from her DNA.

Don't erase all of me, Jael.

I would never. You will always be part of me.

Then look deep inside for that part of me already practiced in lowering your shields.

I will. I'll try.

Danielle held out her hand to take Saran's, and their images began to fade.

Danielle, wait. Tell me we did the right thing. Tell me you're truly happy.

Danielle shared a smile with Saran, who answered for both of them. *You don't need our words. Feel our joy. Just as your bond with Alyssa will endure, the threads of our destinies will always be entwined, Jael. As it was in this life, so they will be in your next.*

Danielle touched her fist to her shoulder in a warrior's salute. *Your return reunited me with the lost half of my heart. Now, look within and let me help you find both your strength and your peace.*

Then they were gone.

❖

Well familiar with Han's healing expertise, Alyssa had given up Jael to his skilled hands. Still, she clutched her mate's hand as the fine lines of worry began to melt from her brow, her eyes, and her mouth. Jael's jaw relaxed, and her shoulders dropped as her neck muscles relaxed.

"Join us, my daughter." Han's invitation had been unexpected, but Alyssa closed her eyes and found herself in the meadow with Jael. She'd felt Jael's stress drain as their bond guided perfectly synchronized movements. She'd nearly cried out her joy when Saran and Danielle appeared. She wanted to say so much to Danielle, convey so much gratitude, but she kept pace with Han and Saran to finish the kata as Jael and Danielle spoke.

As the ethereal forms of their friends faded away, Alyssa was jerked back to the conference room by the sob that finally found its way out of her throat. Jael was watching her and smiled when their gazes locked.

"Was it really her? Really them?"

Jael nodded and blinked away the tears filling her eyes, an unprecedented public show of emotion. Alyssa felt Jael's relief and affection for Danielle and projected the same emotions back to her mate. They reveled in their feelings for a moment, ignoring the others silently watching them.

Han eased off the pressure points at the base of her skull, and Jael's smile widened. "All good." She sucked in a cautious breath. "The pain is gone for now."

"Are you ready to try?" Alyssa asked. She hated that this attempt might restart Jael's headache, but she also was aware of the barrage of anxiety emanating from both Kyle and Furcho.

"Nicole first. I've been around her more than I have Toni," Jael said.

"Then let us begin," Han said. "Focus on your search for their thoughts, First Warrior. When you find them, I will broadcast what you see to the others here with us."

Alyssa squeezed Jael's hand to convey her approval. It was a good idea. Han also was a highly skilled telepath, but even he didn't have Jael's power to listen and project over long distances.

"That should help," Jael said.

Alyssa was chagrined when Jael pulled her hand back and flexed her fingers. She hadn't realized how tightly she'd been gripping it. "Sorry."

"'S okay," Jael said. "But I might have to start calling you Crusher."

They shared another smile, and Alyssa relaxed. A little. She was nervous. She didn't know how Jael stood the pressure of everyone always counting on her to make the right things happen. She looked across the table to the man who'd gently helped her navigate her gift and her life path so many times. "How do we do this?"

Han spread his hands, palm up, and gestured as though he was handing over the sword of engagement to her. "Take the object in your hands and let it tell you what its owner is feeling. Jael will attempt to follow your connection and seek out their thoughts as you read their emotions."

Alyssa picked up the blouse Furcho had brought. She closed her eyes and touched it to her cheek, inhaled Nicole's scent. She ignored Jael's hand that settled on her forearm, concentrating instead on her memories of Nicole. Agitation and fatigue. Alyssa's lower back began to ache, and something felt as though it was pressing on her bladder. She felt hope, tinged with uncertainty.

"Found her," Jael said softly.

Alyssa's head filled with Nicole's thoughts intercepted by Jael and broadcast by Han. *Stars, how much farther? Would kill for a bath and a massage.* An image of swollen ankles and feet, then a hand smoothing over Nicole's slightly swollen belly. *This baby is going to be huge. I can't believe I have to pee again.* Alyssa felt Nicole's agitation turn to anger. *That dung-eater Xavier should have already sent someone back to pick us up. If I was a pyro, I'd light his toes afire and scorch his man-parts.*

Alyssa felt a collective wince from the others sitting at the table. Jael's hand left Alyssa's, and Nicole's thoughts vanished.

"Well, that confirms Nicole and baby are cranky but okay," Jael said. "But she's too focused on herself and wanting to torture Xavier to give us any helpful information."

Alyssa didn't point out that Nicole's symptoms didn't match the estimated timeline of a normal pregnancy. Furcho slumped back in his chair. She felt his relief and exhaustion. She frowned and made a mental note to get a med scanner from the clinic and check him over. His personality change and unusual fatigue were over the top for the calm, wise warrior she'd come to know. "Okay. Let's try again."

Alyssa picked up Toni's backpack, and Jael again grasped her forearm for a physical connection. Sharp pain instantly reverberated through her face. The image of a man holding a gun, his eyes cold, formed in her head. Despite the jarring pain and mental picture, part of Alyssa rejoiced. Jael's connection had been quick and felt less strained.

Lieutenant Antonia.

There was no response to Jael's call, but a wave of revulsion, of violation washed over Alyssa.

Don't react. Don't react. If you do, he'll hurt them. But when they're safe, I'm going to hunt this slimy weasel down. I'm going to cut his balls off and stuff them up his ass.

Toni. Focus on me.

A thread of sour fear rolled into red, hot anger. *I'll slam him with a shield that cracks his skull. Can I do that? Could Juan shoot one of them before I can shield them?*

Your mission, soldier, is to protect and defend. Not to attack.

The man with the gun was pointing to a hover bus.

Show me the others, Toni. Look at Nicole.

Toni's mental images flashed a man with blood on his neck, then the gunman, and then the bus again. Rapid-fire calculations of the probability of successful escape now compared to where the bus might take them.

Belay that, soldier! Look at Nicole.

Alyssa projected questioning concern to assist Jael's mental suggestion, and the image of two dirty, bedraggled women formed. Nicole was limping, supported by a smaller woman. The image narrowed to the other woman, rather than Nicole. She was staring back at Toni, her eyes filled with concern.

I'm fine, but I'll die before I let them touch you.

The next images were disjointed—glimpses of the ground, the bus, the ground, Nicole's leg, the surrounding forest interspersed with longer views of Tan apparently unconscious and tied to the back of a very large man, Nicole and the other woman shuffling past her, boarding the bus and pausing while the ties binding Tan were cut to dump her onto a long seat, and then crowding onto an adjacent seat with Nicole and the other woman.

Look at Tan. Is she wounded?

It had apparently worked before, so Alyssa projected urgent concern. Immediately an image of Tan, sprawled awkwardly with her leg and one arm dangling off the narrow seat, appeared.

Still sleeping. How much of that drug did they pump into her? Dung. I wish she'd wake up right now and roast them all.

Show me how many are on the bus with you.

The image that followed, however, was Toni's hands in her lap, then the young woman's face, brow furrowed and her eyes searching.

How many, Toni? Look around the bus.

A slow scan of the bus revealed only a handful of men. They were as dirty and bedraggled as the women.

Where's the leader? Where's Xavier?

The images coming from Toni went dark.

Stars, my face hurts. Will we see Xavier when we arrive? Need to rest. Need to be alert when night falls. Need to plan a possible distraction for when our warriors arrive. Rest just for a few minutes. Just until the bus stops.

Jael's hand left Alyssa's forearm, and she joined the withdrawal. Her empathic focus switched to her mate, and Alyssa was relieved that the painful throb that had lingered after Jael's other telepathic efforts was missing.

"Maya," Kyle said. "The woman with Nicole is my sister, Maya."

Furcho nodded confirmation. His eyes were still dull with exhaustion, but Alyssa felt his relief that Nicole's only injury appeared to be something minor, like a sprained ankle or strained muscle.

"Cyrus and your mother appear to have been separated from them," Jael said. She and Kyle stared at each other for a few seconds. "If Laine isn't reunited with Toni and Nicole, we'll have to focus our rescue on the primary group."

Kyle gave a stiff nod. "Understood."

Jael looked around the table at The Guard, Han, and Alyssa. "Here's our battle plan—"

CHAPTER SIXTEEN

Tan rolled to the side of the bed and swung her feet down to the floor. Her head swam at the sudden move to an upright position, but she paused only a moment before standing. She had to put her hands out to brace against the wall when she swayed. Dung. Her legs felt as weak as a newborn filly's. A metallic taste lingered in her mouth, and the memory of pulling a dart from her neck was enough to piece together what had knocked her out, but she needed to know what had happened while she was napping. She closed her eyes and drew in a few deep breaths, aware of the others watching her. "I need water." The words were like sandpaper on her desert-dry throat.

"I'll get it." Nicole jumped up and ran into the personal facility, then returned with a full glass. "Are you all right, Captain?" she asked as she put the glass in Tan's cuffed hands.

Tan propped her back against the wall and downed half the water. She took a quick head count and mentally catalogued information. Toni hadn't had that shiner when Tan had spoken to her in the woods. The others appeared uninjured. Cyrus must be back with his cronies.

"You should drink that slowly."

Tan recognized the woman who spoke and lifted her glass in acknowledgment. "You're Kyle's mother, Laine."

"Yes. And you are Captain Tan, my daughter's bonded."

"Guilty." Tan scanned again for the source of the aroma that filled the room. "You have food?" She was a bit queasy from the drugs, but as a physician, she knew that eating a little something would help soak up some of the acid churning in her stomach.

"We have several burgers left. There's a warmer in the cabinet." Nicole pointed to the credenza.

"Just one, please. I need to eat something, but not a lot."

Nicole smiled. "Coming up."

Tan studied Nicole. She worked with Nicole in the camp clinic, so they knew each other well. Nicole looked tired but otherwise okay. Her ankles didn't appear too swollen, but her belly was larger than Tan would have anticipated for her estimated delivery date. "After I eat and my head clears a bit, I want to take a look at you and Toni." Dung. Her pack—with the medical scanner—was probably still in the woods where she'd hid it to sneak up to where Xavier's group had camped for the night.

"I don't have a scanner," Laine said, "but the baby appears to be fine. She's very strong."

"Laine has a healing gift," Nicole said. "I was having pains on the plane, but she was able to stop them."

"I can't be sure, but I detected only tissue damage to Toni's cheek," Laine said. "I'd welcome your expertise. Kyle told me you are a physician."

"I am, but don't believe anything else she said." Tan's heart both warmed and ached at the mention of her lover.

Laine smiled. "When we were together for several weeks before Killeen, you were all Kyle talked about." Her smile slowly vanished. "She was worried about your reaction after what happened on that roof, when she blocked you from sending Cyrus to his next life."

Tan shrugged. "We worked it out." She took the warmed burger Nicole held out and sat on the bed again. "We're good now." She missed Kyle. She stared down at her burger and smiled. "I'm surprised she hasn't already stormed in and lit up Xavier's entire group." She rubbed her forehead as if the massage would sharpen her memory. "I think I was communicating with Jael when I got hit with the dart, so they have to know something's wrong. How long have I been out?"

"Just today," Laine said. "It's a little after midday now."

Toni dropped the ice pack she held to her face and surged forward. "Either I'm hallucinating or your brain is still scrambled from the drugs. I thought you said Jael."

Tan nodded. How could she explain without sounding crazy? She took a large bite of the burger to stall for time to think.

"First a trade, same heart, two souls will pay a debt long owed." Everyone turned to stare at the young woman Tan knew was Kyle's younger sister. What was her name? Mae, Mia? Maya. That's right. She'd said the same words during the airstrip standoff between Xavier and The Guard. Kyle had later explained that Maya was gifted—a seer.

"That's right," Tan said, swallowing her food. "Danielle was seriously wounded in Killeen."

Toni interrupted. "Danielle?"

"Commander Second."

"Oh, no!" Nicole pressed her hand to her mouth too late to stop her outburst.

"I'd never heard her real name before." Toni's expression transformed from confused to alarm. "Is she…is Commander Second okay?"

Tan silently cursed herself. She'd forgotten that Toni had been promoted to the quartermaster unit and Danielle had taken the young lieutenant under her wing. But, as a physician, she was no stranger to delivering bad news. "No. I mean yes." She sighed. "This is going to sound farfetched, but I'll give it a shot." She bit into the burger again, chewed, and swallowed while she ordered her thoughts. "I don't know if you were aware, but Jael and Danielle weren't actually cousins. Danielle was cloned from Jael."

Nicole nodded, but Toni gaped at her. "They were so different."

"There are still ethical questions about cloning humans," Tan said. "Jael's aunt raised Danielle to ensure she would develop as her own person, so more than their difference in eye color would distinguish them."

Laine rubbed her chin absently. "I'd love to read any records on their development as they grew to adulthood."

"So—" Nicole twirled her hand in an impatient gesture.

Tan chewed the last bite of her burger and tossed the wrapper into the nearby bin. "Danielle didn't show it to many, but she's been bereft since Saran, her mate, died in a mountain-climbing accident. Her greatest wish was to be reunited with Saran in the spiritual realm. Danielle's injuries shouldn't have been fatal, but about twelve hours after the army returned to camp, she inexplicably flatlined. She'd made me promise never to resuscitate her if that happened, so I did nothing. About ten minutes later, the monitors lit up again, and her vital signs grew stronger. But when she opened her eyes, they were blue, not Danielle's brown irises. And the voice that spoke was undeniably Jael's."

"Sun." Toni stared at her. "Alyssa must—" She seemed to choke on the words and dropped her chin to stare at the floor. Maya gently took Toni's clenched hand into hers and pried it open to entwine their fingers. Tan waited while Toni took a deep breath, then looked up again.

"Alyssa is over the moon," Tan said, holding Toni's gaze. She knew they were close.

Toni nodded, but her brow furrowed. "But isn't it, I don't know, sort of weird? You know, to look at Second but be speaking to Jael?"

Tan chuckled, despite their circumstances. "Yeah, at first. I don't know how to really explain it. You'll have to see her. The eyes and mannerisms are all Jael. After a few hours with her it's hard to even see Second. I mean Danielle." She sat on the bed again and yawned, still sluggish. "And Jael has named a new Second Warrior."

"Furcho?" Toni guessed.

"Uh, no." Tan glanced at Nicole. Now she'd have to explain this situation. She cleared her throat. "Furcho hasn't coped well with Nicole being kidnapped, so Jael named someone just as qualified but demonstrating more poise in this bad situation."

"Kyle."

Everyone turned to stare at Maya. "I didn't understand what I was seeing..." She touched two fingers to her shoulder. "...the silver suit and insignia on her shoulder, until I saw your uniforms in Killeen."

Toni frowned at Tan. "It's true Kyle is the strongest pyro after Jael, but you should have been in line behind Furcho."

"I prefer my scout duties, and the responsibilities of second-in-command would steal time from my work at the clinic." She shrugged. "Serving as a warrior is my duty. Being a physician is my calling." She'd never realized that fact until the words fell from her mouth. Kyle had changed everything in Tan's life. She'd helped free Tan from the guilt that had followed her through life after life. She could finally look forward rather than back, and she wanted desperately to heal more than to destroy.

Toni raised an eyebrow. "I report to Kyle now?" It was a simple question, not a judgment.

Tan smiled. "Nope. Well, technically we all report to Kyle since she's Second Warrior." She stood and saluted, fist to shoulder. "In your absence, you, Antonia, have been promoted to captain for the interim. When you return to camp, you'll be in charge of the quartermaster unit and promoted to the rank of commander. Congratulations."

Toni's mouth dropped open. "But I just made lieutenant."

"Are you questioning the First Warrior's judgment?"

"No." Toni blinked, then stood to return the salute. "Thank you, Captain Tan," she said softly.

Tan sucked in a breath, still trying to shake the fog out of her head. Every cell in her wanted to sink back onto the bed and sleep off the lingering effects of the drug. She'd barely had time to complete the thought when she whirled at the tones of a security code engaging. The gloves smothered and cuffed her hands. No matter. She couldn't throw a fireball in the close confines of this room without burning down the entire hotel and incinerating a lot of innocent people. Hopefully, whoever was about to enter would discount her as a danger because her hands were restrained. They couldn't know that she was more effective with her feet than her hands in close combat.

Two men entered, weapons ready. The man on the right gestured with his gun to the other end of the room. "All of you. Get over there."

These weren't the men who had been on the plane, the ones Tan had seen when she caught up with the group hiking down the mountain. These men looked like real soldiers. She narrowed her eyes. Their weapons were similar to the old Krinkov AK-74 military rifles, but something was different. They contained no ammunition magazine.

A third man entered the room. Xavier. He smiled broadly at Tan. "Good to see you awake, my friend. Did you like my weapon of choice? Since my spies reported you also are proficient with the blowgun, I thought you would appreciate my skill."

Tan didn't answer.

Xavier spread his hands. "Your silence wounds me. Perhaps you're still a bit sleepy." He moved farther into the room, taking in the discarded food wrappers. "I'm glad to see you've taken advantage of our hospitality." He checked the IC on his wrist. "Four hours until sunset, but I expect your friends won't appear until after midnight."

Tan was glad that Toni showed no reaction but wanted to roll her eyes when Maya sucked in a shocked breath. So much for pretending they weren't expecting a rescue tonight.

He cocked his head at Maya's response. "Did you think we wouldn't expect a rescue attempt? We know they've tracked our small group here." He pointed to Tan. "We intercepted their advance scout." He tapped his finger against his chin and drew out his next words as if just reasoning things out. "They're thinking it's to their advantage to attack now, before we reach our fortress, the City of Light. It's a good plan." His mouth widened in a big, toothy smile. "Except our reinforcements have arrived with a surprise for your dragon soldiers." His smile disappeared, and his dark eyes became a cold abyss. "Brasília was a warm-up. The only real general among you is ash. This will be your army's last battle."

CHAPTER SEVENTEEN

Dark Star emerged from the night, his great wings outstretched to gracefully touch down behind Jael. Phyrrhos circled overhead, screaming her impatience to be reunited with Tan, her bonded. A meager army of warriors stood next to their dragon horses, waiting. The Guard were all mounted—Diego leading a group of nine warriors, Michael commanding a group of eight. Furcho and Raven waited off to the side. Kyle, astride a glittering Sunfire, galloped around their formation in a brief inspection before wheeling to a stop in front of the eight warriors Jael would personally lead. She saluted Jael.

"The defenders of The Collective stand ready, First Warrior."

"Issue the orders, Second Warrior."

Kyle turned Sunfire to face the troops. "Warriors."

They saluted in unison, and Kyle returned the gesture. Jael was again reassured that she'd made the right appointment for Second Warrior when Kyle's voice, strong and sure, rang out. "Each of you has been assigned to one of three groups. First Warrior will lead group one, Lieutenant Commander Diego, group two, Lieutenant Commander Michael, group three. You are to provide a distraction and melt any projectiles or weapons they fire while Furcho, Raven, and I retrieve our colleagues that The Natural Order abducted." She paused to study their faces. How many would not return at dawn? "This is to be a show of force. Do not engage the enemy unless you must do so to protect yourself or a fellow warrior. Understood?"

"Yes, Second Warrior," they chorused.

"Group one, mount up." Kyle had barely finished her command before Diego and Michael shouted the same order to their groups.

When the last warrior mounted, they spread their ranks to allow for wingspan and awaited the command to launch. Kyle, Diego, and

Michael wheeled their mounts to again face Jael and saluted their readiness. Jael returned the salute. Dark Star, vibrating with anticipation, extended and rattled his great wings as he screamed into the night. Sun and stars, she wished he hadn't been so close to her ears when he did that. She leapt onto his back and was about to order her group aloft when a wave of fear washed through her. Alyssa. As if by instinct, her gaze was drawn to a ledge where sentries were posted day and night to watch over the camp. The young soldier in Diego's transportation unit stood well back, giving Alyssa the best viewing spot. The wind ruffled her fiery locks and flapped the white linen of the loose clothing she preferred. Jael had never seen a more beautiful woman.

Alyssa, you're projecting. My army needs confidence, love, not your fear. Her admonishment was filled with affection rather than reprimand.

I'm not projecting. You feel my every emotion because you are the other half of my heart.

And you are the other half of mine. Please don't worry. The Ancient One of the Collective Council promised, love. We'll grow old together. Still, I'll let someone else play hero if necessary. I won't leave you again.

I love you, Jael.

I love you, my mate, in this life and beyond. Now how about sending us off on our mission by projecting some confidence to my warriors?

Jael could almost see Alyssa's projection wash over her warriors as shoulders straightened and chins lifted. She touched her fingers to her lips, then the red dragon-horse insignia that covered her chest and her heart—a private message to her mate—before turning back to her warriors. "Group one, aloft."

❖

Toni dropped the watery pack onto the table next to her bed. Most of the ice had melted, and the pounding in her cheek had subsided to a dull ache. She rolled onto her back. The gray haze of dusk showed through the part in the curtains. They'd have to prepare soon for what the night might bring, but the door separating the adjoining rooms was still almost closed, and no stirring sounds came from beyond. The ice must have helped. She could even see out of her left eye enough that when she rolled onto her side again, she could still make out the angelic features of Maya, dozing on the bed across from hers.

They'd agreed they should try to rest before nightfall, and Laine had invited Tan to nap in the other bed of her adjoining room. Nicole was already asleep next to Toni, her back turned to them. Tan had glanced at Maya and quirked a small smile in Toni's direction, then accepted Laine's invitation without argument. Maya settled onto the bed where Tan had sprawled earlier, and Toni rolled onto her side and settled the ice pack over the left side of her face to hide the flush heating her cheeks at Tan's subtle innuendo.

"Did you sleep well?" Maya's voice was soft and quiet. Her long lashes fluttered, then opened, and her hazel eyes that met Toni's gaze were gray in the dim light.

"I dreamed about dragon horses and about you." Did she just say that? She'd never been brave enough to flirt, always expecting rejection. Until now. Her fascination with this woman made her bold. The world, their situation, was moving so fast Toni was afraid Maya would disappear from her life too quickly. She wanted to yell for everything to pause so she could explore her feelings. Explore Maya.

Maya smiled. "I dreamed about you, too."

Even in the low light, Toni could see Maya's cheeks darken. She wanted to know everything about this woman. "Are you scared about tonight?" Toni saw her eyes, the way her expression changed the instant her question registered, in that split second before Maya averted her gaze. Coldness filled Toni's chest. "You've seen something…about tonight?"

Maya shook her head. "No. I just feel this…this sense of dread."

Toni sat up, cautiously pausing to be sure of her steadiness, then slipped over to Maya's bed. They sat together, propped against the headboard, and Toni took Maya's hand. It was so soft, as large as hers but more delicate. "I won't let anything happen to you."

Maya entwined their fingers and pressed her shoulder against Toni's. "You can't promise that, just as I can't promise that any of the things I *see* will actually happen." She stared at their hands. "That's why I never tell people about my gift." She made a disgusted sound. "It's been more like a curse."

Toni drew her hand from Maya's and wrapped her arm around Maya's shoulders instead. Maya laid her head against Toni's neck and reached for Toni's other hand to again entwine their fingers. "Until recently, I hid my shielding gift, too. Even after I arrived in camp and was surrounded by gifted people, I didn't let anyone know about my shield. It seemed stupid in comparison to people who were pyros, who carried the dragon-horse gene, or were empaths. I had no idea why I was compelled to answer the Calling. I didn't have a shred of the DNA required to bond with a dragon horse." She drew their hands to her mouth and kissed the back of Maya's. "But in the midst of people with all those other gifts, mine seemed to grow stronger. Then in a moment of danger, I outed my gift to Kyle and Tan, then Alyssa." Maya instantly went still, her fingers tight around Toni's.

"You and Tan spoke about her earlier. Who is Alyssa?"

Toni pressed her lips to Maya's forehead before answering. "She's the First Advocate, mate to First Warrior Jael."

Maya drew back and looked in Toni's eyes. "But you care about her."

Toni touched Maya's cheek and smiled. "She is…or was my boss in the medical clinic." She looked away as an embarrassed flush crept up her neck to burn her ears. "More than that. She saved me."

"Saved you?"

Toni disengaged her hand to stroke Maya's forearm, to play with a soft strand of her hair that lay against her breast. Touching her helped calm the nerves that churned in her stomach. She'd never admitted her shortcomings to anyone, but she felt she could trust Maya with them. "I had a reputation in camp as a screw-up. The others teased me a lot about my height, and I laid into more than one of the warriors. They all grew closer during training, but I ended up on the outside. After we were all tested for the bonding gene and I had none, I was assigned to the stables to shovel manure." She paused, recalling the worst. "I liked working with the animals. They didn't judge.

"The teasing grew worse, though, when I went back to the barracks smelling of dung every night, and one of the warriors gave me quite a beating after I jumped him for just making a face at my aroma as he walked by me. The officer in charge of our barrack showed up to interrupt the fight and ran all the warriors extra hard at training the next day. They never spoke or touched me after that, but, a few days later, I was late to dinner. The serving line had closed, but a plate of food was waiting for me at the end of the counter. About an hour after I ate, I was vomiting and bent over with stomach cramps, and the barracks officer ordered me to the medical clinic."

When she paused again, Maya snuggled closer, and Toni drew courage from the warmth. "Captain Tan lifted my shirt to palpate my stomach and saw the bruises over my ribs. She ran a med-scan and determined that two of my ribs were cracked. When my lab tests diagnosed my current problem as food poisoning, she gave me a hypo-spray of anti-nausea medication and told me to stay put because someone else would come bind my ribs before I was dismissed to return to the barracks. I'd already decided, though, that I would sleep in the stables before I went back there for anything other than to grab my belongings. I was even thinking about hitting the road, except I had nowhere to go.

"Then Alyssa came into the exam room. I'd never been introduced, but I knew who she was. Everybody did. She's a very powerful empath, and I was terrified she could see right through me." Toni smiled at the memory. "She was really gentle when she wrapped my ribs, and so kind. She started with questions you'd expect from a healer. What type of work did I do in camp? Did I need an order for light duty for a few days? Did an animal kick me in the ribs? When I made up a story to cover the truth, she only smiled and said, 'Try again, soldier.' She could feel that I was lying. So I told her about the fight, and before I knew it, we'd been talking an hour or more. She'd coaxed me into telling her about my problems in the barracks, where I was from, and what type of work I did before coming to camp."

Emotion tightened Toni's throat. "After I answered her last questions, she looked at me for a long minute. She said she'd enjoyed our talk, because she'd been so bogged down with the clinic paperwork that she had little time to spend with patients. That was going to change, she said. She told me to get my belongings and move them to the Advocates' cabin because I'd be bunking there from now on. She said she'd speak to my...to my...my duty officer." She was finding it difficult to focus because of Maya's finger doodling an irregular pattern on her thigh. "She said I was to report to the clinic the next morning as her new assistant...um...in charge of paperwork and supply ordering."

"You're her assistant?"

Toni shook her head. "I got promoted and assigned to the quartermaster unit, under Commander Second...um...Danielle." She'd miss the friendly commander, whom everyone liked. "I guess I'm in charge of the unit now." Resolve washed away her sad thoughts. She'd make sure the quartermaster unit maintained Danielle's high standard.

"I'll still work out of the clinic, though. With Alyssa and Nicole. We've become…friends." The instant she voiced the statement, she realized it was true. "Kyle's my friend, too."

"I like Nicole." Maya's finger continued its wandering. "And I'd love to meet Alyssa."

"You will," Toni said, grabbing Maya's hand to still that maddening finger. She released it to cup Maya's chin and lift it so she could stare into the swirling green, blue, gray depths of Maya's eyes. Without a word, she touched her lips to Maya's in a caress, and when Maya opened to her, she plunged her tongue into Maya's sweet mouth. Their slow kiss, the dance of their tongues, grew heated and hungry. Toni wanted Maya more than she wanted to breathe, but this wasn't the time or place. She slowly withdrew, touching their lips together one last time before whispering a promise. "We're getting out of here tonight, and the second thing I want to do after our rescue is to introduce you to my friend."

Before Maya could reply, the sound of a throat clearing made them jerk in surprise. Toni cursed under her breath. She'd been so focused on Maya, she hadn't heard the connecting door swing open or noticed Tan standing in the doorway. Still, she held Maya's gaze for another long moment before moving back to acknowledge Tan's presence.

Tan tilted her head toward the other bed where Nicole still snored. "We should wake her up," she said. "It's time to prepare."

Laine stepped into the room. "I'll rouse her. Maya, we still have a few burgers. Can you pop them into the warmer, please?"

Tan held up her gloved hands. "I don't suppose you have a small magnet in your pocket," she said to Toni.

"Uh, no. Can't say that I do."

"Do you know how to pick locks?"

"I've seen Kyle do it so I have an idea what to use, but she didn't explain what she was doing when she inserted the tool into the lock."

"I can talk you through it if we can find something we can fashion into a tool."

The warmer chimed and Maya took out the burgers. There were only three, but everyone agreed that Nicole should have a whole one for her and the baby she was growing inside. The others split the remaining two. Tan wolfed down hers, then went to rummage in the personal facility for something they could use on the locks. Toni chewed more slowly and surveyed the room. If she dismantled the d-net monitor, she might be able to find some metal strips inside that would work. No.

Xavier might come in and find them hunched over the pieces and parts of it strewn all over one of the beds. And even if they hid it under the bed, he might notice that it was missing from the top of the credenza. She popped the last tasty bite of the burger into her mouth. On the other hand—

Toni jumped up and went into the other room, opening the cabinet door in that credenza, and yanked out the food warmer.

Tan stuck her head into the room. "You find something?"

"I probably will when I get the cover off this."

"Good thinking." Tan looked toward the window. It was full dark outside. "Take it into the facility. If you hear Xavier or his guards coming in, shut the door, wait a few seconds, flush, then come out. But close the door behind you so they won't see what you were doing."

"Gotcha."

Toni broke off two of her blunt fingernails prying open the back of the warmer. Yes! She silently fist-pumped into the air. Several flat metal clips held several bunches of wires together. She just hoped the wire was stiff enough to push lock tumblers around. She yanked a few wires and one clip free, then headed to the other room. When the others looked her way, she held up her bounty. "All I need is a way to strip the insulation from this wire. We might have to gnaw it off."

Tan jumped to her feet and began to carefully explore the tight curls of her mohawk. A second later, she held out a small, thin blade. "A surgeon is never without a backup scalpel. Let's go back to the other room."

Twenty minutes later, Toni threw her tools down on the bed in disgust. "This isn't going to work." She started to stand, but Tan's hand on her arm stopped her.

"Try once more. I know the tumblers are tiny, but close your eyes and visualize the inside of the lock, then keep them closed to focus on feeling each tumbler in it."

Toni ran her fingers through her hair. She wanted to pull out clumps of it in frustration. "You're the surgeon. You should be doing this, not me."

Tan held up her hands to point out they were encased in thick gloves that were coupled together, making it impossible for her to hold and maneuver the small tools. "You can do this, Toni."

Toni clenched her jaw and summoned her resolve. She would keep trying until someone showed up to drag them away. She inserted her tools into the lock, sucked in a deep breath, and closed her eyes. She used the flat metal clip to rotate the barrel of the lock as far as it would go, then carefully probed the tiny tumblers. Click. One down, but she'd managed that first one several times, only to have the barrel slip before she could find the second restricting tumbler. She pushed her probe deeper. Tumbler number two wasn't holding the lock. Deeper. There. The third tumbler resisted when she tried to push it. Toni held her breath. If the wire slipped or was too weak to move that last tumbler— Click. She and Tan stared at each other, motionless. Had it worked?

Tan carefully moved her other hand, and the lock pulled free. She grinned at Toni, then slid her hand from the glove. Toni watched as Tan's face lit up with relief. She rubbed her hand on the bedcover to dry the sweat from it, then raised it to eye level. Flames ignited from each of her fingertips as she growled. "I'm going to roast Xavier's nuts." She chuckled at her own comment, then held out the hand still locked in a glove. "Try this one, too."

Toni had barely slipped her tools into the second lock when the other room's security lock began to sound the tones that signaled someone was disengaging it and about to come in.

Maya appeared in the open doorway, her eyes wide. "Someone's coming."

Tan slipped her hand into the glove again, but the wrist gaped open without the lock holding it closed. Toni pulled the ends together and secured them with the clip. "It'll probably come loose if you pull too hard, so be careful."

Tan nodded and they stood. Xavier's guards, weapons raised again, came through the door just as Tan and Toni joined the others. This time, Cyrus entered on the guards' heels.

He went to Laine. "Wife, your place is with me." He looked over at Maya. "Both of you, until we reach the City of Light. Then you, daughter, will join the other single women until I match you with an appropriate mate."

Xavier strode into the room with Juan on his heels. "She's a beauty. She'll be inundated with suitors, but let me be the first to petition for her hand."

Maya paled, and Toni edged a few inches forward, ready to throw a shield hard enough to slam Xavier and his guards out the door. She steadied when Maya clutched the back of her shirt.

Cyrus eyed Xavier a few seconds, then nodded. "I will consider your petition. The pairing could be advantageous."

"I agree," Xavier said, dipping his head in a very slight bow. "But first, we must rid ourselves of these infernal flying pests." He stepped aside and swept his arm toward the door. "If you will allow my man to show you the way, Prophet, we'll watch their defeat from the roof."

Cyrus took Laine's hand and followed Juan into the hallway. When the rest of them hesitated, Xavier prompted them. "Don't you want to be there when we greet your friends?"

Tan guided Nicole to go before her but paused next to the guard at the doorway. "To the roof, eh?" She looked him over, from boots to crewcut, then thrust her face close to his. "Maybe I'll get a chance to push you off." She was out the door before he could reply.

Toni was careful to put herself between Maya and Xavier as they ascended the stairs to the door at the top. The roof was flat and black like the night. The moon had yet to rise. The nights were growing steadily colder as winter approached and they traveled farther north. When Maya shivered, Toni resisted the impulse to gather her close. It wouldn't be good to call attention to their growing bond. Not with Xavier and Cyrus present. So she was grateful when Laine, who didn't appear affected by the cold, wrapped her arm around her daughter's shoulders. Toni scanned the sky but could see nothing more than stars winking in and out as high, wispy clouds moved overhead.

She was aware of Tan's head turning right and left, her eyes scanning the roofs around them. The downtown area contained more flat-topped buildings, though none were taller than their four-story one. What was Tan searching for? Were the warriors already here? The roofs were black pits in contrast to the lighted streets below, and she had to squint to decipher what she thought was movement on one roof. A cold ball of dread formed in Toni's chest as her eyes adjusted. Groups of two and three men, all dressed in black and armed with the same weapons as Xavier's guards, squatted in the shadows on a half dozen roofs. A rifle barrel also jutted out from a maintenance port in a nearby temple steeple. Besides Juan and Xavier's guards, two more were positioned at the corners of their roof.

Xavier took a digital tablet one of the guards held out for him, and while they talked and tapped the selections on its screen, Tan edged next to her.

"Jael says they're close. I've let her know about the guys on the roof, waiting for them."

Toni stared at Tan, trying to sort out how she'd relayed this information.

"You know she's telepathic, right?"

Of course she knew. "Forgot." She glanced nervously at Cyrus, but he was shaking his head at something Laine was saying.

Tan's eyes gleamed with the hunger of a predator. "Just be ready. When the sky lights up, your priority is to protect Nicole."

"Nicole. Right." Not Maya. She edged close to Nicole, then looked over to find Maya, eyes smoky and troubled, watching her. Toni offered a small smile. *It'll be okay*, she silently mouthed. Maya broke their gaze and stared at her feet. What was that about? In the next instant, the sky and their roof were ablaze.

CHAPTER EIGHTEEN

Jael and Dark Star led their unit of ten in a high, wide circle around the small town. Michael's group followed hers, but Diego's cut a tighter, inner circle. Each unit flew in V formation so the distance and darkness would likely disguise them as migrating geese should they attract a casual glance from the ground.

Change of plans. Shooters are on six rooftops. Hostages held on the tallest building, three o'clock from the temple steeple. Sixteen to twenty that Tan can see. I want each group in and out so we don't give them easy targets. Warriors pair up, one to protect while the other attacks. They haven't had time to install big guns like at Brasília, but Tan advises that their guards are armed with weapons unfamiliar to her. Keep close to their perimeter in the initial sweep.

Jael relayed her orders telepathically to Diego and Michael, both attuned to her mental messages, then again verbally to her eight warriors via the short-range communicators they all wore in their ears. While longer-range communicators could prevent the necessity of Diego and Michael relaying orders to their units, the earpieces were deliberately short-range to reduce the chance anyone on the ground could intercept their chatter.

We'll attack their perimeter and leave the hostages to the extraction team. Kyle?

Standing by.

Diego, Michael?

At the ready.

Awaiting command. A veteran member of The Guard, Diego had requested that his team strike first, so his unit consisted of nine warriors—all volunteers to take the dangerous point position of their attack.

Warriors, engage.

❖

Kyle, Furcho, and Raven hovered in the airstream high above. They were too far away to see details of the rooftops, but their dragon horses' superior eyesight relayed constant mental images. Kyle glanced over at Furcho. His eyes were over-bright and focused on the town below. Raven also was watching him but shifted her gaze to Kyle and signaled a thumbs-up.

Kyle spoke through their communicators. "We'll wait until our warriors have the perimeter guards fully engaged. On my command, Raven will take a slow but direct descent from the west to draw their attention while Furcho flies in low between the buildings to come up from behind and take out the shooters on the east corners. My target is the gunman standing next to Xavier."

"Roger that," Raven said quietly.

"Furcho?"

"That bastard Xavier is mine."

"No. I want Xavier alive to take a message back to Simon."

"You're going to let him go?"

Kyle saw Raven wince when their earpieces vibrated with Furcho's shout. Kyle glared at the man she'd looked up to as a child. She and Jael had planned strategy past this engagement, but she didn't have the time or the duty to explain that fact to him. "You have your orders, Third Warrior."

Furcho's lip curled in a snarl, but before he could reply, the night lit up below them.

Diego's unit swooped in, working in pairs. One warrior laid down a bullet-melting wall of fire to protect them, while the other took aim to incinerate the shooter. Their strategy would have been successful if The Natural Order soldiers had been shooting their usual projectile weapons.

❖

Tan cursed in disbelief as blue beams of death took out half the first wave of warriors, while well-aimed flames ignited only five Natural Order soldiers. Xavier's laughter rang out as laser fire sliced along the torso of a dodging dragon horse, cleanly cutting through the thigh of its warrior before they both dropped to the street below.

The odor of burning hide and flesh filled Tan's sinuses and coated her tongue. Screams—human and dragon—rang in her ears. Her mind filled with furious, frantic images. Phyrrhos was near. "Hold above, Phyrrhos. Wait for my call." Tan muttered the words to help her focus on sending the image that should keep her dragon horse out of harm's way.

Another wave of warriors, only seconds behind the first, fared little better until Dark Star emerged from the night, breathing a huge column of flame that lit up an entire roof, while Jael and other warriors flung fire at individual shooters on other rooftops. Still, the blue beams cut down several of the darting third-team warriors. Tan slipped her hand from the unlocked glove.

Potawatomi descended like a falling gold-and-white star, and the African warrior in Tan rose at the sound of Raven's war cry and the sight of her fearsome Native People's war mask. Slashes of red and black—blood and death—marked her forehead, cheeks, and chin. With one hand still locked in a fire-retarding glove, she could hit only one of the gunmen squatting on the roof's west corners. She'd have to trust the other to Raven. The gunmen raised their lasers to take aim, and Tan ignited her palm. A spear of flame as hot as her fury shot out, straight and true, to engulf the man to her left. The second man fired, but Potawatomi folded her wings an instant before and dove like a bullet. Raven's fire joined her dragon's flame before the man could adjust his aim. His cry confirmed their aim had been true, because Tan was already whirling toward the dragon scream close behind her.

Her brain had barely registered the blank night sky before Azar surged up from below and emerged millimeters from the roof's edge. The dragon horse breathed a killing flame at the one gunman, but Furcho hesitated when the other ran, cutting across the roof at an angle that put the hostages in harm's way. Tan had a better angle and didn't hesitate. The gunman screamed as her flame engulfed and cooked him. His shriek, however, had barely sounded when three more blue beams cut through the night. Juan's laser sliced deep along Azar's flank and severed Furcho's leg as they flew overhead. A millisecond later, a thin column of intense flame amputated Juan's trigger hand, and another burned into his skull as the Third Warrior and his dragon horse dropped like a stone onto the roof, less than four meters from where the hostages stood. Juan lay at Xavier's feet, his eyes fixed and unblinking below the smoking hole in his forehead.

The mayhem and gore of battle stunned Toni. She was a quartermaster. How had she ended up in the middle of this?

"Furcho!" Nicole's scream rang out above the din of shouts, screams—both human and dragon—and constant swooshing flap of wings as Jael's warriors continued to bombard the other rooftops. Toni grabbed Nicole just in time to prevent her from stepping in front of an errant laser blast.

"Let me go." Nicole struggled out of Toni's restraining grasp and ran toward the heap of warrior and dragon horse.

His guards all dead, Xavier knelt to pick up the laser rifle at his feet, the weapon that'd taken down Azar and the Third Warrior. He shook loose Juan's severed hand that still grasped the trigger.

"Tan." Toni pointed to Xavier. A glance confirmed that Maya and her parents were huddled out of the way, next to the short wall that bordered the roof, so Toni took off in pursuit of Nicole, ignoring the laser beams crossing their roof as shooters on other roofs struggled to hit the dragon-horse warriors still darting between the buildings. Before she could catch up with the long-legged Nicole, a gale of wind knocked them all off their feet, and a flash of white light temporarily blinded her. Toni tried to blink the spots from her eyes as she crawled toward where she'd last seen Nicole.

"Shield!" Kyle's barked command wasn't even complete before Toni instinctively projected a wide shield. A laser blast reverberated down her arms and through her chest at the same time a new beam of blue shot across the roof.

Momentarily, Xavier stood stunned, blinking at the rifle and his severed left arm on the ground at his feet. His stump was nearly bloodless because Kyle's blue scalpel cauterized as it seared through flesh and bone.

Toni dropped her shield, and Maya ran to her. She opened her arms and hugged Maya tight as she whirled them around to put herself between Xavier and the two women she'd vowed to protect.

Kyle dismounted and stood like a gunslinger, hands open and ready at her sides. Her tall, broad-shouldered physique cast an imposing silhouette against the backdrop of Sunfire's glowing, glittering, unfurled wings. Her head turned toward Furcho, then back to Xavier, but she didn't speak.

Xavier raised his eyes to her. "You dung-eating bitch." He spat out the words as he fell to his knees. Still, he lifted his chin and sneered at her. "Go ahead. Finish me. The stain of taking an unarmed man's life will follow you to your next."

Kyle didn't respond, but Tan cupped her bared hand to instantly hurl a fireball if he reached for the weapon with his remaining hand. Everyone seemed to freeze for a few long, tense seconds. The air was so thick with tension, Toni could barely breathe. She followed Kyle's gaze past Xavier.

A magnificent black dragon horse coalesced out of the night sky and touched down across from Kyle. Toni sucked in a breath when she recognized Dark Star, the stallion from the wild herd, then gaped at the blond warrior who dismounted. The walk, the set of the jaw, the eyes as blue as the lasers still firing occasionally around them were all Jael. Toni couldn't see a trace of Danielle, her former mentor.

Her face a stoic mask, Jael strode to where Nicole knelt in a pool of blood, sobbing as she bent over her fiancé. Furcho's mouth moved, but he couldn't seem to form words as he labored to breathe. The lower half of his body was pinned under his dead dragon horse.

Jael knelt, too, and gently placed her fingers on his temples. "He has little time," she said quietly. "He thinks the fall has broken his spine because he can't move his arms. He wants you to press his hand to the baby you share."

Nicole's sobs deepened, but still she pressed a kiss to his unfeeling fingers that she clutched in hers, then placed them on her swollen abdomen. "I love you." Her tears dripped onto his cheeks as she choked out the words. Furcho's mouth worked, but his chest no longer heaved with the effort to breathe. His eyes, filled with desperation, shifted to Jael.

"Let me help." Laine knelt next to Nicole and placed her hands on Furcho's chest. A second later she gasped, but as she sucked air into her lungs, Furcho's chest rose, too. His eyes telegraphed a silent thanks to Laine as they gasped in unison—a second breath, then a third and another. His gaze found Nicole's again.

Jael closed her eyes. "I love you, too, but I've always known the truth."

Chills ran through Toni as Furcho's rich baritone came from Jael's mouth. She tightened her arm around Maya's shoulders as she trembled.

Tears leaked from the corners of Furcho's eyes, dripping onto Jael's fingers as they pressed into his temples and she continued to speak for him. "I was never destined to be your soul mate, only to sire the baby you carry for me, for us." His eyes went to his hand that Nicole held against her belly. "She will be the first of her kind—a warrior Advocate. I love you both, but your soul mate still awaits you. His destiny is to be your bond and Skyler's mentor."

"Skyler?"

"Yes," Jael intoned. "She is my legacy. She'll begin her life with all the knowledge I've gathered during all my lifetimes."

Furcho's hand glowed briefly as the light in his eyes faded and Laine gasped one last time. Jael withdrew her connection.

"He's gone," Laine said quietly.

Nicole's sobs began anew, and Toni hugged Maya tighter when she began to cry softly.

Jael stood and fixed her eyes on Cyrus. He'd crept closer, only a few meters away, to witness Furcho's death. Laine rose and stepped in front of Cyrus, her eyes imploring. Strangely quiet, Cyrus rested his hands on his wife's shoulders and made no move to step out from behind Laine as she and Jael stared at each other.

The night had gone quiet except for an occasional wail of loss when a warrior discovered a fallen friend or the thin cry of a dying dragon horse. Flames flickered from the curled and blackened remains of Natural Order soldiers on the rooftops around them, and the night was thick with the cloying smell of their charred flesh.

Toni glanced at Kyle, then Tan. Kyle had vowed to incinerate her father after he'd chained and nearly starved her to force her compliance in The Natural Order. Tan also had sworn to turn him to ash after she spent hours in surgery, reattaching the hand of a young boy that Cyrus had chopped off to send Jael a message. But they were Guard and bound to duty. The First Warrior would decide Cyrus's fate.

Maya clung to Toni. "Do something, Toni. Don't let them hurt my mom or my father."

Toni shook her head in answer to Maya's whispered plea. "Jael is the First Warrior. She is honor bound to enforce the will of The Collective Council. I can't…I won't stand against her." She held Maya firmly to prevent her from interfering.

One minute stretched into another as Jael and Laine stared into each other's eyes. Jael finally gave a curt nod, and her gaze moved to Cyrus.

"The reckoning for your acts against The Collective people will not come today, Cyrus. Although you have preyed on the people's fears to divide us, you have only served to remind us that we must be vigilant against the real evil. The embodiment of society's worst flaw—greed—awaits in your City of Light. Your reckoning is tied to Simon's, so I release you for now."

"I'm going with him," Laine said.

"Mom, no." Maya tried to struggle out of Toni's embrace.

Laine held up her hand, and Maya stilled. Laine held each daughter's gaze for a few seconds. "Just as Kyle has accepted the responsibility of her destiny, I must step up to shoulder mine. You have seen this, Maya, so you should understand. I have to go with your father now, but we *will* be reunited. You have to trust me like I've come to trust your visions."

Kyle gave a slow nod, then shifted her gaze, hard and sharp, to Xavier. "Take him with you."

Xavier, clutching at the stump that had been his arm, narrowed his eyes, then glanced down. The laser rifle, still lying next to his severed limb, was within his reach. Before he could snatch it up with his good hand, a fireball consumed both limb and weapon.

Toni shielded Maya's eyes from the grotesque sight of the melted gun and charred arm. She averted her eyes, too, when her stomach threatened to crawl up her throat at the awful smell.

"Sorry," Tan said. "I was aiming for the rifle." But her predatory smile showed no regret. "Too bad, eh? A good surgeon could have reattached that for you."

Kyle stepped closer, glaring at Xavier. "The Guard will not rest until the evil dividing The Collective people is extinguished. Take that message back to your master, the man who has dared to use my family to further his selfish cause. You tell Simon that Kyle, Second Warrior of The Guard, is personally coming for him."

Laine went to Xavier and helped him to his feet. She hesitated as they passed Tan, then stopped Xavier and searched his pockets. Laine tossed the key she found—the one to unlock the second glove—to Tan. Then she guided Xavier toward Cyrus, who held open the door to the stairway.

Kyle turned to Tan, who was trying to unlock the hated glove while fending off the worried snuffling of Phyrrhos. She took the key from Tan, unlocked it, then raised the freed hand to her lips. Phyrrhos butted Tan, causing her to stumble into Kyle.

Toni's insides tightened at Kyle's gesture and the smile the two women shared as Tan righted herself. She envied their obvious bond. Suddenly aware of Maya's body still pressed against hers, Toni wondered at how right it seemed. They'd met only a few days ago, but Maya felt like the glove that fit her hand, the sheath that cradled her knife. Could it be true that a genuine soul bond lasted over many incarnations? That soul mates, even if they hadn't evolved enough to recall past lives, were instinctively drawn by their familiar connection?

Kyle pointed to the rooftop door. "If your dragon can tolerate a few more minutes of separation, would you ensure they're provided a transport and leave this town immediately?"

Tan glanced toward Nicole, still hunched over Furcho.

Furcho shared many lives with me and much of Kyle's current life with her. Leave him to us. Toni and Maya will help Nicole. On your way out, tell them to evacuate the building if they haven't already. Send that group on their way as Kyle ordered, then start triaging any survivors on the street below. Kyle and I will join you there.

"As you command." Tan's verbal response was for Jael, but she stepped back from Kyle and saluted the Second Warrior. Their gaze held a moment longer as Phyrrhos launched skyward, then spiraled downward to meet Tan on the street below. After Kyle returned her salute, Tan disappeared down the stairwell.

Toni's thoughts buzzed with more than her connection to Maya. She puzzled at the familiarity of Jael's mental voice broadcast to her and Kyle as well as Tan. Then realization dawned. Her earlier impulses to survey her surroundings as they boarded the transport to the hotel were suggestions from the First Warrior. Awe, then confidence swelled in her chest. That meant she'd been a crucial factor in their rescue. Jael had used her eyes for advance surveillance. And she'd served as Tan's hands to unlock and free her of the first glove. Best of all, Jael trusted her to take over Danielle's unit of quartermasters. This noble group of elite warriors had quietly absorbed her into their circle. She was no longer a lone outsider. She belonged.

Toni took Maya's hand. "Let's go help Nicole."

They stood next to Nicole while Kyle knelt and placed her hand on Furcho's head. She recited the warrior's prayer, then gently thumbed his eyelids closed. "Safe journey, my friend." She bent to kiss his forehead before she rose and stepped back.

Jael spoke quietly. "Nicole, this will feel hard now, but Furcho requested immediate release. He said he could feel Danielle waiting to receive him."

Nicole nodded, but her hands trembled as she cupped Furcho's face and pressed her lips to his one last time.

"Nic, we need to move back," Toni said gently. She signaled for

Maya to help, and each of them entwined an arm with Nicole's. Her shoulders shook as she cried, but she allowed them to lift her to her feet and guide her a safe distance from Furcho and Azar.

In the past year, Toni had stood before many pyres. The field was ablaze with them after the new warriors swarmed the wild dragon-horse herd in a dangerous mass bonding. The entire camp had wept at the pyre of Uri, the universally loved Advocate who threw himself in front of a bullet meant for Furcho. And the warriors had despaired at the absence of First Advocate from the field of Brasília pyres that cut their number in half. Alyssa had been drowning in her own grief and refused a ceremonial pyre for Jael.

Toni had grieved each time. But this pyre tore deeper into her soul. She'd worked alongside Nicole in the medical clinic every day, and they'd shared the Advocates' cottage where Furcho had been a constant overnight visitor in recent months. They had been a genial match. Nicole's sunny personality was a comfortable contrast to Furcho's quiet, casual demeanor.

Nicole was a head taller, but Toni wrapped her arm around her friend's waist and pressed against her side to steady her. After a moment, Maya's arm joined hers from Nic's other side, and they waited in silence.

Potawatomi, Apollo, and Bero touched down beside them, and Raven, Michael, and Diego dismounted to stand at attention. Jael and Kyle took up position at opposite ends of the fallen. Sunfire and Dark Star raised their heads to the stars and screamed a dragon's tribute to Azar. The sound was still ringing in Toni's ears when Jael began to speak.

"Furcho, of the house of de Lara, second region of the Fourth Continent, has been my friend, my confidant, and valued advisor. He was exemplary in his bravery and loyalty as he served The Collective and The Guard. We will mourn his absence, yet celebrate the fulfillment of his journey in this life." She paused and looked to Kyle.

"Guard." At Kyle's call to attention, she, Raven, Diego, and Michael saluted Furcho's sacrifice. Jael thumped her fist against her shoulder in answer to their salute, then raised her arms to the sky and waited for Kyle.

You were like a daughter to him, Second Warrior. He was so proud of you and requested that you be the one to send him on his way.

When Maya began to sob along with Nicole, Toni knew that Jael must have broadcast that statement to everyone on the roof. She grasped and squeezed Maya's arm that rested against hers as they supported Nicole, and Maya squeezed her arm as well.

Kyle lifted her arms, her hands roiling with flame. "Glorious will be the day when all is as it should be and we are reunited, my friend." Her blue-white flame shot out first, closely followed by Jael's. Then Sunfire and Dark Star raised their wings and joined their warriors in pouring a purifying inferno onto the physical remains of their friend and his dragon horse.

"Glorious be the day," The Guard echoed.

The intense heat ignited the roof under Azar, and the flames began to spread. Toni felt Diego's hand on her shoulder as Kyle and Jael leapt onto their mounts. "I'm your ride back to camp," he said.

"Just one second," she said, releasing Nicole to Michael, who gently guided her to Apollo. Maya, her eyes wide, looked anxiously to Toni when Raven beckoned her to Potawatomi. "It's okay. Raven won't let you fall," Toni said, tamping down her own apprehension and giving Maya a little push toward Raven. "Diego and I will be flying right beside you."

Toni watched Raven carefully boost Maya onto Potawatomi's back, then leap easily to sit behind. When she turned to jog over to Bero, she tripped over something black. A laser rifle dropped by one of the slain guards. Toni grabbed the weapon and lifted its strap over her head to carry it across her back.

Alyssa will be waiting for Nicole.

Jael's words were as clear as if she'd been standing next to Toni, even though Sunfire and Dark Star were already gliding downward to join Tan and Phyrrhos among the dead and injured that littered the streets below. Toni nodded to herself. *Roger that.* Then she wondered if Jael could hear her reflexive response.

You don't have to be telepathic for me to hear your thoughts, Commander.

Toni's cheeks heated at the very idea that Jael might overhear some of her lascivious thoughts about Maya, but a sad chuckle rumbled through her brain.

I'll get Han to instruct you further when we aren't in the middle of a war. Until then, rest assured that I'll never pry into your private thoughts.

Roger that.

CHAPTER NINETEEN

Maya's teeth chattered in the frigid upper-air currents, and she clung desperately to Raven's arms that held her securely aboard Potawatomi, a beautiful pinto dragon horse. Then Raven's lean body heated against Maya's back, warming her like a snuggly blanket. Kyle had raised her body temperature to warm Maya when they were children. The familiar memory drained her apprehension, and she began to enjoy the amazing experience—snowy mountain peaks below and stars all around her. The muscles in Potawatomi's powerful shoulders had worked to pump her huge, bat-like wings as they ascended, but they were relaxed now against Maya's legs as the three dragon horses wove intertwining paths to catch and ride the upper airstreams.

When Bero glided close, and Toni, riding behind rather than in front of Diego, signaled a questioning thumbs-up, Maya grinned like a fool and nodded. Toni's answering smile warmed her even more and pushed aside, at least while they were airborne, the memory of their horrific past few days. Instead, Maya focused on this magical flight, on the feel of Toni's mouth against hers earlier, and on images of her brave young warrior organizing everything for the hike down the mountain, standing up to Juan, and concentrating as she worked to unlock the pyro-proof gloves that imprisoned Captain Tan's hands. Her warrior? When did she begin to think of Toni as belonging to her? Maya smiled to herself, glancing at the dark-haired young woman when Potawatomi glided close to Bero again.

She'd known from the beginning because she'd seen it—the repeating vision that showed her waking next to a still-sleeping, dark-haired lover. She'd seen only the woman's naked back and short, tousled hair because her face was turned away. Maya hadn't realized at first why Toni seemed familiar, but her subconscious had recognized her immediately. She only had to wait for Toni to realize their soul bond. Maya flushed with her next thoughts of making love with her warrior, bearing children for them. And for these few airborne hours, the stars seemed brighter, the night air fresher, and the awful battle scene they'd just left more distant.

Maya was growing sleepy when they finally began to descend. Soft moonlight illuminated the mountaintop meadow they were spiraling toward and the slender figure that awaited their arrival. She was surprised at how lightly Potawatomi landed and how cold the night felt when Raven released her to dismount. She warmed again when Raven stepped back to let Toni, who'd jumped down before Bero's feet were solidly planted, help Maya dismount.

Toni's hands were cold but her shoulders solid and strong when Maya gripped them so Toni could lower her safely to the ground. Maya's legs were a bit wobbly, and Toni wrapped an arm around her waist to steady her.

"Give yourself a minute to get your land legs back," Toni said, smiling when Maya pressed close against her side. "Flying is awesome, isn't it?"

"It is." Though the excitement of the flight filled her with an urgent desire to kiss Toni senseless, a sudden wave of shyness stopped her, and she instead laid her head against Toni's shoulder. "This is pretty nice, too."

Toni's arm tightened around her, and her lips touched Maya's forehead. "Let's check in."

Apollo was making one last spiral in preparation of being the last to land, and the woman who'd been waiting put her hand to her mouth, her horrified expression focused on Toni's face.

"Stars, Toni. What happened to you? How else are you hurt?"

Toni looked confused, but Maya understood. She stepped back from Toni but entwined their fingers because she couldn't bear to break their physical connection. "She was holding me up, not leaning on me. My legs were a little shaky after riding astride for nearly two hours."

The young woman nodded, but her face was filled with concern as she touched Toni's bruised cheek. "Jael said you were okay, but I know how tough you soldier types try to act."

"Really, I'm okay. Tan checked me out. It's just a shiner." Toni tugged Maya close again. "This is Maya, Kyle's sister. Maya, this is First Advocate Alyssa, bond mate to First Warrior Jael."

Alyssa looked from her to Toni and back to her. It was impossible to decipher their color in the moonlight, but her eyes visibly softened as she held out her hand. "It's so nice to meet you, Maya. And it's just Alyssa, please. We don't stand on titles around here." She glanced over to where Michael was helping Nicole slide down from Apollo's back. "We'll have a chance to talk later, but I need to tend to Nicole right now." Her brow drew together, and a wave of something...comfort?... washed over Maya. "We have other guests staying in Uri's old room, Toni, but Maya can share your quarters or stay in Nicole's room. I'm going keep her with me tonight." She began to walk away but stopped and pointed at Toni. "I want to see a med-scan of your cheek after you've rested."

"Okay," Toni said. "Send me a d-message if Nicole needs anything from her quarters. I'll bring it over to headquarters."

Alyssa gave a thumbs-up in acknowledgment, then trotted over and held out her arms for Nicole, who fell into the embrace of her friend and sobbed.

Chapter Twenty

When Jael finally extinguished her flame, Kyle, then Dark Star and Sunfire snuffed theirs, too. It'd been a long time since she'd expended the amount of flame she had this night, and the thick skin of her palm and fingertips felt tender. She stared at the ashes of the last warrior and dragon horse they'd incinerated and lifted her fist to her opposite shoulder in salute. "Soar free, my warrior. Your bravery and sacrifice for The Collective will be rewarded."

Jael turned to her surviving warriors. They'd started the night with twenty-five in addition to the seven Guard. Twelve warriors and six Guard remained. Their faces were streaked with sweat, soot, and—for some who had lost close friends or, in two cases, siblings—tears. One was propped against his dragon horse, who'd somehow escaped injury while a laser had lopped off the lower part of the warrior's leg. Two others had bandaged stumps where a hand had been. Most had blood drying where a laser had only grazed some part of their bodies. Their battleskin uniforms could withstand most flame but were no match for this new laser fire. Their natural pyro ability had cauterized these flesh wounds, but they'd still require treatment to heal properly.

Jael raised her fist above her head. "Glorious be the day when The Collective is reunited into one."

The warriors, including Kyle, responded. "Glorious be the day." She paused, surprised that a louder chorus had joined in, too. Beyond her unit of warriors, a large crowd of townspeople had gathered to form a semicircle just beyond the scorching heat.

This part of the town had been populated primarily by believers who had armed themselves as they intercepted and hoarded food and medicine shipments. But when live vids of the battle hit the d-net, those still loyal to The Collective—some who had been run out of their homes and businesses in this quadrant—had stormed the streets and began dragging the believers from homes. The streets had been clogged by people fighting with fists and anything they could use as a weapon— sporting equipment or long-handled agriculture tools. A few were wounded by projectile weapons before the guns were snatched away and thrown into the hotel fire that had become Furcho's and Azar's pyre. She'd instantly ordered her warriors to bring order to the chaos, stop the pilfering of homes and businesses, and corral any believers for later questioning and restitution for anything they'd stolen from The Collective citizens. The angry mob was defused and organized to water down adjacent buildings so that the entire town didn't burn.

Now, they all waited while Jael surveyed the aftermath of their battle. Only the crackle and sputter of the hotel fire broke the silence of the night.

"Tonight is a bittersweet victory for The Collective," Jael said. "We've lost many of our fellow warriors, just as some of you have lost family members—children, grandparents, mothers, and fathers— because The Natural Order believers have stolen and hoarded needed food and medicines. I lost a close, long-time friend." She stared pointedly at individual faces as she paced before the crowd. "But hear this. A fair court will judge those believers found to have actively participated in the theft of supplies or of committing violence against other citizens and sentence them to restitution of credits and community service. The town's peacekeepers will ensure each sentence is completed. No one is to be physically harmed. Only those who show no remorse and indicate they will repeat violence against other citizens will be imprisoned." She stopped her pacing and faced them, fists resting on her hips. "I am First Warrior of The Collective, and I so order this."

Her declaration was met with nods from the citizens and "as you command" from the uniformed peacekeepers scattered among the crowd.

"Be assured that we will restore order, so our citizens can again prosper and work together in peace. Why?" She stretched her arms out, palms opened to the sky. "Because we are—" A deafening chorus joined her, shouting at the sky as the sun crested the mountains to push away the night's darkness.

"STRONGER TOGETHER!"

Chapter Twenty-one

Toni shifted nervously in the hallway of the Advocates Cottage, unable to meet Maya's gaze. She stared at their hands, still entwined, and tilted her head toward the door on her left. "That's where I stay." She jerked her chin to indicate the opposite door. "That's Nicole's room, but she's at headquarters with Alyssa." Stupid. Maya was right there when Alyssa had said that earlier. She was babbling, so she opted for silence while Maya decided what she preferred. She thought her heart would stop beating in the seconds-long, seemed like hours-long, silence that followed.

"Toni, look at me and answer truthfully. Do you want, need to be alone for a few hours?"

Hope flared as Toni looked up and was caught in the swirling gray-blue-green of the eyes searching hers. "I'd like you to stay with me, unless you prefer to sleep alone."

Maya nodded. "We're both exhausted. I stink of smoke and... burnt things, but I'm afraid I'd fall asleep in the shower if I don't at least nap for a few hours first. If you don't mind the smell..." Maya ducked her head, hiding her small smile and the blush darkening her cheeks. "...I'd like to stay with you."

Toni drew Maya to her. She meant to only brush her lips against Maya's, but the temptation was too great. When Maya opened to her, she slid in for a taste of the softest, most wonderful mouth she'd ever explored. Not that she'd kissed many women, but this one felt so right. Her libido was alert and willing, but her brain was sluggish and her muscles barely able to move. She slowly ended the kiss and opened the door. The room had two beds, but both were large enough for two people, so she led Maya to the one where she slept and sat to remove her boots. "That's Kyle's bed over there, but she stays in Tan's quarters now."

Maya nodded but sat next to Toni and removed her shoes as well. Then she crawled onto the bed, her eyelids already drooping, and flopped onto the far side. Toni settled on her back next to Maya and glanced at the window. Daylight. Had Jael, Tan, and Kyle made it back before dawn? All thoughts of them, however, fled as Maya rolled to snuggle against her side. Toni instinctively raised her arm to offer her shoulder and, um, breast as a pillow. Their bodies fit perfectly together.

Alyssa silently descended the stairs, surprised to find Kyle reclining in a lounger. Her eyes were closed, and Oni was in the kitchen quietly heating water and filling an infuser with pinches of tea leaves from a variety of glass containers that had been Danielle's stash.

Though Jael had warned her that daylight might keep her at the battle site until Dark Star became dragon again that night, Alyssa was still disappointed that Kyle had returned alone.

Soon, love. Get some rest. I can feel your exhaustion.

Alyssa smiled at the familiar voice in her head. *I can feel yours as well. Will you rest today? Please? If not for me, then for your warriors? They need their leader to be a hundred percent.*

I'll do anything, everything for you, and nobody else. A bunk's waiting for me at the local firehouse. Our mounts are grazing in a nice field nearby. I'm on my way now. That's why my mental ear turned your way to check in.

Good. I'm going to have a glass of wine—Alyssa smiled wearily when Oni placed a cup of steaming tea before her—*or maybe a mug of tea to persuade my mind to shut down so I can sleep.*

Ah. Drink the tea. I told Oni what leaves to use from Danielle's collection. She and Haley both are receptive to mental messages. Probably because they've learned how with Zack.

I'll consider it over a glass of wine, but I haven't forgotten that you drugged me with tea that first night we met and I didn't wake up again until the next day. Alyssa closed her eyes and savored the low chuckle that rippled through her mind.

I needed to knock you out so I could respond to the message Han sent. The tea I asked Oni to make will only help you relax. I promise.

I'll drink it then. She lifted the cup and inhaled the sweet scent of apples and cinnamon. *My favorite flavor next to you.*

Don't raise my temperature any more than battle already has. It's hard enough not having you here to help me wind down.

I'm afraid I can't sympathize. You know that your emotions, and desires, are always transmitted to me. That's why I can't seem to sleep. So, go shut down and stop thinking about sex so I can rest, too.

Another chuckle. *Sleep well, love.*

You, too, my warrior.

When she looked up from her cup, Oni was watching her.

"Is the tea okay?" Oni met Alyssa's eyes for only a minute, then stared down into her own cup as her cheeks flushed. Her shy curiosity was easy for Alyssa to read.

"You can ask me anything you like, Oni," Alyssa said gently, projecting a sense of welcome to reassure the young woman.

Oni smiled and raised startled eyes to meet Alyssa's gaze. "I felt that. You aren't just an empath. So it's true that you can project emotions as well?"

That wasn't the question Alyssa expected, but she could feel that Oni was trustworthy. "Yes. Only The Guard and maybe a few others know that. Some people would be wary of such a gift, and it could make me the target of someone like the men we are tracking, who think they could force me to use the gift to their advantage."

Oni reached out—shock showing in her expressive eyes—but stopped short of touching Alyssa's hand. "I would never reveal your secret. Unless—" She shook her head. "Sometimes that meddling Zack sneaks into my head to listen to my thoughts. Haley says I'm just too open and trusting. She busted him in the nose once for doing it while we were making love."

Alyssa chuckled and clasped the hand Oni hadn't yet withdrawn. "Han will teach Zack the boundaries a telepath must respect. He's reined in more than a few brazen boy telepaths."

Oni looked relieved. "Good. Someone needs to teach him some manners." She seemed to reconsider her irritation with him. "I don't want to give you the wrong impression. He's actually a good guy. He started the San Pedro Sula network and rescued most of us from bad situations. He's very protective of our more vulnerable members, like Pete. But…well, he's a guy."

Alyssa shook her head. "Being male is no excuse for bad behavior.

But not to worry. It sounds like he's got a good heart. Han will help him mature to his full potential."

Oni nodded and studied her cup again.

"What else do you want to ask?"

She didn't raise her eyes and spoke softly. "You were communicating with the First Warrior just now?" She looked up quickly. "I mean, I wasn't listening. I'm not telepathic, but—"

Alyssa smiled. "You could feel my affection for her."

Oni nodded. "Yes. Exactly." Her cheeks reddened. "It's how I feel about Haley."

Alyssa realized that Oni was only about five years younger than she was. Had she been so innocently naive when she first met Jael? She patted Oni's hand before she pushed back from the table and yawned as she stood. The relaxer in the tea was kicking in, and her eyes felt heavy. "I think we'll have much to talk about after we get past this crisis, but I'm headed to bed after I wake Kyle and send her to her quarters upstairs."

"I'm not sleeping," Kyle said without opening her eyes. "I was just resting my eyes for a few minutes before I see Diego, Raven, and Michael to organize a mobilization. And I need to talk with Zack to see if Sam's any closer to pinpointing the location of the City of Light."

"Up." Alyssa's tone was firm. "They are all sleeping for a few hours, and you are going to do the same."

"Too much to do." Kyle rubbed her eyes and stood.

But Alyssa wasn't backing down. "And it will wait a few hours until you all have rested. You might be Second Warrior, but those orders come straight from Jael, and the last time I checked, she outranks you." She pointed to the stairs and glared at Kyle. "Upstairs now. Your arguing is keeping me from my bed."

Jael's chuckle rumbled through both their heads. *Better do as she says, Kyle. My sweet empath has a temper to match her fiery hair. You haven't had the pleasure of witnessing it yet, but I guarantee it'll scorch your eyebrows.*

Kyle threw her hands up. "I'm going. I'm going." She headed for the stairs.

You're supposed to be sleeping, too, First Warrior.

I'm in my bunk. Just waiting to feel you drift off. Then I'll be right behind you.

Alyssa didn't care that she was flooding the room with her affection. *You are my heart.*

And you are mine. Rest now, so I can.

Alyssa waved a good night to Oni, even though the sun was bright outside, and climbed the stairs. She looked in on Kyle, even though she'd felt her fall instantly to sleep. The newly promoted Second Warrior was lying across the bed she shared with Tan, boots still on and her mouth gaped open as she snored softly. She started to pull Kyle's boots off and throw a cover over her, but Kyle was a warrior and a pyro. Warriors didn't bother about dirty boots, and pyros never got chilled. Instead, she went to her own quarters and took a blanket from the closet. She'd need the blanket and the affection she felt coming from her personal pyro bunked several hundred miles away to keep her warm for now.

CHAPTER TWENTY-TWO

The few hours they'd slept that morning had been restless. Toni woke twice because Maya was twitching and whimpering as she slept, and Toni wished she could erase the previous bloody night and the tragic loss of Furcho from Maya's memory. When she finally fell into a deep sleep herself, she relived over and over the awful moment when she watched the blue laser beam slice across Azar's torso, eviscerating him and severing Furcho's leg. Each time after the first, she tried to save Furcho in a different way. She futilely willed that Kyle would arrive to unleash her killing flame seconds earlier and stop Juan before he could fire on Azar. In the next dream, she tried to charge at Juan as he began to raise his weapon to fire, but she was seconds too late. In the third dream, she began to run for Juan as Azar was rising behind them, but Xavier stepped into her path. The final time, she was so filled with desperation as she ran toward Juan that she instinctively projected a shield to knock Juan down before he could shoot and her aim was off. That last scene jolted her awake. She was sitting up, still in the bed, sweating and her heart beating wildly as Maya stroked her back to calm her.

"Toni, honey. It's okay. You're safe. We're both safe. This is your bedroom at the camp."

Toni sucked in a deep breath, then twisted to cup Maya's face and kiss her soundly before withdrawing to stare into Maya's eyes, their ever-changing color as green as new grass in the midday light. "I need your help to test something."

❖

Kyle shoved her empty bowl away. They'd all slept until noon, and now they'd eaten. She was about to call for the first report from her fellow Guard sitting around the table when Sam burst into the room with such force that the door, newly hung to replace the one Dark Star had splintered, banged loudly against the wall.

"I found it." He waved his d-tablet and grinned at Zack. "Their spider is good, but who is better?"

Returning Sam's grin, Zack jumped up and trapped him in a playful headlock. "You are." He rubbed his knuckles in Sam's hair before releasing him with a light punch to the arm. "You rock, man."

Kyle stood and indicated the empty chair next to Zack's. "Come sit down, Sam, and fill us in."

Zack and Sam noisily jostled like two children as they took their seats at the table, and the cook placed a bowl of stew and fresh bread in front of Sam. He shoved a spoonful into his mouth and took a big bite of bread, talking around the food as he chewed. "Okay. I knew he'd slip up, and when he did, I tracked him to his back door."

"Don't talk with your mouth full, Sam." Pete frowned as he repeated the admonishment often aimed at him. "It's bad manners."

Sam nodded, chewing and swallowing, while the others hid their smiles.

"How can you be sure he's at the City of Light?" Kyle asked. "He could be working from anywhere."

"True," Michael said. "That's why you follow their path and break through the security on their d-tablet to look for confirmation of their location."

Sam nodded. "Their spider keeps a tidy house. Almost every file was encrypted. But I had to unlock only a few before I found his banking records that showed where he'd been buying groceries lately. Then, focusing on that location, I pushed out bots to search for construction transactions and social chatter. I found delivery orders for some unusual amounts of glass and thin metal sheets of faux gold among big loads of regular building material…all going to the same mountaintop location. And there was a lot of chatter on social outlets about a huge fortress being built there." Sam tapped and swiped on his d-tablet. "I'm sending the coordinates to all of you."

"Excellent," Kyle said. She didn't have to ask how he knew the d-accounts of everyone at the table. "Can you throw up a holo-map to show us?"

A few more taps and a map hovered in the center of the table. A red dot appeared. "This is where we are." Another tap and a second red dot appeared. "This is the town where the battle was fought last night." Tap. A third dot appeared, then pulsed like a dragon-horse eye. Danger, danger, danger. "This is the City of Light," Sam said needlessly.

"Ah. They tried to throw us off by initially flying east, but judging from where they crash-landed, they'd already turned and were on a direct route toward their destination," Diego said, tracing his finger from the crash site to the town to the City of Light. He drummed his fingers on the table as he studied the map further. Mobilization and transportation were his bailiwick. "We're currently loading a good supply of fire rocks on the heli-transports that brought the crash survivors back here. They'll have room to take a handful of key personnel, too. Since our dragon-horse units are already halfway to our destination, we won't need to transport horses during the daylight hours by solar train. So, we can save significant time if we haul the rest of the support staff and supplies in the freight transports already in camp."

Kyle nodded and looked to the next. "Michael? How fast can we load up?"

"Thanks to your insistence that we go ahead and plan for mobilization even though we didn't have a destination, we're packed and can start loading immediately."

"Raven, how about personnel?"

"We can designate enough drivers to catch naps this afternoon while the others load. We can rig one transport with hammocks and rotate drivers to travel around the clock. We should be loaded and ready to pull out before nightfall."

"Aren't the transports equipped to auto-pilot?" Michael asked.

"They are," Diego answered. "But the legal speed on auto-drive is much lower on big transports than what's allowed for small transports or a human driver."

"Okay. Thank you." Kyle met the gaze of each of her fellow Guards. They knew the final hurdle they needed to clear but were waiting for her to address it. "We suffered heavy losses last night because of those laser weapons. Since we have no idea how many The Natural Order has available, we have to assume each of their soldiers will be armed with one. How will we protect the few warriors we have left?"

Gazes dropped to the table, but Sam tentatively raised his hand.

"Sam?"

"I've read about a new metal being tested for manufacturing processes that superheat. It's only in the experimental stage, but we could try to get our hands on it to fashion some type of armor."

Michael shook his head. "It would take weeks, but more probably months just to build one suit and test it."

Diego sprang from his seat. "Sun and stars. Those bastards could take control of the world in a few months."

"We already have the armor you need."

The room fell silent, and every head turned to the door where Toni stood, Maya's hand in hers and Haley at her side.

Haley stepped forward at Toni's nod and laid one of the dreaded laser rifles on the table.

"We've just come from testing shields that can withstand a blast from that laser rifle."

"Where are they?" Diego frowned, his doubt clear.

Kyle stood, her smile slow as realization dawned. Dung. Why hadn't she thought of this before? She swept her hand toward Toni and Haley. "We're looking at two of them."

CHAPTER TWENTY-THREE

Jael watched the heli-transports descend toward the sport field's neat turf and grimaced. She hated the noise of air transports. Over the years, the engines had gone from deafening to a thin whine, but Jael found the chop, chop, chop of the heli-transports' blades irritating. She much preferred the soft swoosh of dragon wings caressing the wind. Her agitation, though, didn't really have anything to do with the noise level. Alyssa was in one of those artificial birds, and even the remote possibility of mechanical failure had her nearly jumping out of her skin. So, when a thick column of blue flame licked at the lead heli, her first thought was of Alyssa's safety.

Jael! It's Dark Star. Stop him.

Her brain stuttered as Alyssa's thoughts rang in her head. But her warrior-quick reflexes were already forming and projecting an image of her mate riding in the heli-transport. The dark figure darted again toward the heli, emitting an angry scream, and Jael's head was filled again with the image of the strange bird swallowing Alyssa. No. She tried again. Bags of fire rocks in the birds' bellies. Fire rocks for the dragon horses. Dark Star swerved from his path to intercept and, instead, circled above them. Jael pictured Dark Star landing at her side, but he still hovered until all four transports settled on the ground.

She held her pace to long strides, despite her urge to run to Alyssa's heli, and realized her jitters were more than anxiety over Alyssa's mode of transportation. She needed desperately to see her and feel Alyssa's heart beating against her own. Alyssa, always in tune with Jael's emotions, showed none of her mate's control. The heli had barely touched down when the co-pilot's door sprang open. Alyssa leapt to the ground and ran into Jael's waiting embrace.

"We need some privacy before I can think about anything else," she whispered when Jael spun them around, her heart singing and the heavy weight of command temporarily easing from her shoulders.

"As you command, First Advocate," Jael said, holding Alyssa's hand firmly and already striding toward the ground transport she'd commandeered and the hotel room she'd arranged when Kyle had advised her of the change in their plans.

❖

Toni crept into her quarters, stripping down to her underwear and using the moonlight spilling through the window to find a clean undershirt. Maya was sleeping, her back turned to Toni and a blanket pulled only to her waist so that it draped over the curve of her hip. A small strip of tantalizing flesh showed where her T-shirt and blanket didn't quite meet. Toni's belly did a little flip. More than that, something new swelled in her chest. She recognized the T-shirt Maya had borrowed, and the thought of her clothes on Maya's body, caressing Maya's skin with every movement, felt like she'd laid claim to Maya or that Maya had claimed her. Toni shook her head at the silly notion. If she didn't look, she wouldn't be tempted. She slid under the shared sheet, then closed her eyes and tried to quiet her mind.

The day had been a whirlwind of ups and downs, beginning before dawn with the blood and pyres of battle, then the elation of soaring home among the stars, the perfect fit of Maya's body against hers when they napped that morning, only to have torturous nightmares invade it, which, in the end, had brought the revelation that might save their remaining warriors. In the dream that woke her, her shield had missed Juan but blocked the laser beam from hitting Furcho and Azar.

They'd dressed quickly and jogged to the side of the empty training field that ended at the rock face of a mountain. Toni showed Maya how to fire the laser rifle she'd brought back and, after some convincing, persuaded her to aim near Toni but not directly at her. Maya was reticent and, in the end, too fearful of hitting Toni to fire close enough for Toni to test the strength and breadth of her shield. She'd been about to give up when Haley appeared. They'd never met, but Toni was sure Haley—actually anybody—must have better aim than Maya, and, to Toni's surprise, after she explained what she was testing, Haley revealed that she, too, was a shield. Their experiments a success, they rushed to headquarters to share the news.

Sam's urgent request for volunteer shields that spread through the underground networks had delayed the plan to leave that night. After some debate that listing meet-up locations would reveal their route and destination, Kyle pointed out that The Natural Order already knew the dragon warriors were coming. She had ordered Xavier to deliver that very message to Simon. Still, they'd only stop to take on volunteer shields after dark, when the dragon-horse warriors could protect them.

Maya spent the afternoon with Kyle. It was the sisters' first chance to really talk since before their brother's death in the mudslide that had obliterated most of their hometown. Toni and Haley watched over Sam's shoulder as the news of his call for shields spread and the encrypted network lines began to buzz. More shields were identified, and those who weren't shields offered transportation to the pickup points. When they all met again for dinner, the response had buoyed Kyle, who had declared that the transports would leave at zero-eight hundred, in less than six hours. Toni stayed at Sam's side to answer any questions from respondents, but their nap that morning hadn't erased the exhaustion from Maya's face, and Toni insisted that she go on to bed.

Toni needed to sleep, too, but her body hummed with anticipation. She'd been assigned to be the First Warrior's shield. She was actually going into battle. No more waiting on the sidelines. She tried to clear her mind, but her body refused to ignore the woman lying next to her. Maya's legs—probably bare—were inches from her own. She concentrated on deep, measured breaths to slow her racing heart, but each inhalation filled her with Maya's scent.

She finally decided she should slip out of bed for a quiet trip to the personal facility down the hall. Maybe a little self-service would dull the sharp edge of her desire enough for her to rest. She tensed to slide carefully out of bed, but an unintelligible mutter from Maya stopped her. Was she awake? Maya's legs jerked, and the tone of her mumblings turned urgent.

Toni rolled to her side and propped up on her elbow so she could see Maya's face. Her brow was drawn and her lips a grim frown. Her eyelids rippled with rapid movement. "Maya, honey. Wake up." She stroked her hand down Maya's arm. "Everything's okay. You're safe." Maya's thrashing escalated, and her elbow connected with Toni's chin. Dung. That hurt. Ducking a second swing of the elbow, Toni wrapped an arm around Maya, pressing her body against Maya's back and pinning her arms. "Maya. It's Toni. I'm right here. You're dreaming."

She dropped soft kisses along Maya's cheek and neck. "Wake up, baby. You're safe." More kisses and a firmer tone. "Maya, it's just a dream. Wake up and show me those beautiful eyes."

Maya stiffened and gasped. Her eyes sprang open. "Toni?"

"That's right, baby." Toni loosened her hold and gently guided Maya onto her back. She smiled when Maya's eyes locked on hers. "See? It's just me. You were having a bad dream." She stroked Maya's cheek, then down her arm. "You're safe. It was just a dream."

Maya gave a small cry and flung herself back into Toni's arms. The movement rolled Toni onto her back, and Maya went with her. Toni nearly groaned. Maya was half lying on top of her, a bare leg pressed against the ache between her legs. She tried not to react as she stroked Maya's back to gentle her. But her fingers were becoming tangled in the soft cotton of the T-shirt, and, somehow, the shirt slid up and she was stroking bare, silky skin. Maya shifted so they were belly to belly, and she rose on her elbows. Her eyes darkened as she rubbed her leg against Toni's damp crotch. Toni grabbed her lower lip with her teeth, but her moan escaped anyway.

"Toni?" Maya stared down at her.

"You're going to kill me, Maya."

Maya's gaze softened. "No, sweetie. I'm going to love you." She slowly closed her eyes and skated her soaked crotch along Toni's thigh. Toni pressed upward to meet Maya's second stroke. Maya's face was a portrait of pleasure, and Toni had never seen a woman so beautiful.

"Take this off. I need to feel your skin," Toni said, tugging at the T-shirt.

Maya stopped mid-stroke and yanked the shirt over her head. "You, too. I want all of you."

Toni shucked her undershirt and briefs while Maya wiggled out of hers. They'd kicked the covers to the foot of the bed in their haste and paused now to explore each other with their eyes.

"I want you." Toni almost didn't recognize her own low, husky growl. "I want to taste you, to be inside you."

"Anything," Maya whispered. "Everything you want."

Toni rolled Maya onto her back and began to worship her. She traced Maya's fine brow and velvet cheek, then took gentle possession of her mouth. Maya tasted of mint, and her neck held the faint flavor of vanilla. Maya's hips bucked against Toni's leg when she tongued her pink nipples and pinched them lightly with her teeth. Toni certainly was no virgin, but this was the first time a woman had let her take the lead, the first time she'd wanted to know and taste every inch of someone's skin, the only time she'd wanted to please someone more than focus on her own pleasure. And she did so want to please Maya.

A strange sense of familiarity assured Toni that a careful bite to the earlobe would make Maya shudder, a tweak of her nipple would buck her hips, and the wider she spread Maya's legs, the more her erect clit would stand up and beg to be sucked. She somehow knew she should first bury at least two fingers deep inside Maya...like now...spreading them to stretch her, thrusting deep and hard as she licked and sucked Maya to a screaming climax. Yes, screaming...from under the pillow Maya grabbed so Zack and Sam in the adjacent room weren't witnesses to her surrender, to Toni's victory, to their intimate sharing.

Instinct told Toni to push Maya's knees to her chest and pump her own turgid flesh against Maya's soaked sex. Spurred by Maya's soft cries of pleasure, Toni thrust her hard clit along Maya's wet heat in smooth, even strokes. Toni's belly went rigid, and her own clit exploded with so much pleasure, her heart skipped and her vision dimmed.

Toni's groan was the alto harmony to Maya's "oh, stars, oh stars" soprano. Their duet ended like the clash of cymbals before their climax released them. Toni collapsed, her hips still wedged between Maya's thighs, jerking occasionally with lingering aftershocks. Their sweat and the sticky evidence of their coupling melded their bodies as their hearts beat wildly against their chests, against each other. After a moment, Toni rolled onto her back, pulling Maya with her so she could stroke her fingertips over the soft, drying skin of Maya's shoulders, down the elegant curve of her spine. Maya's fingers traced a soothing path along Toni's collarbone as she rested her head in the well of Toni's shoulder.

How could she find words to express utter fulfillment?

Maya's fingers slowed and stilled, her hand resting possessively over Toni's small breast. Her even breathing told Toni the events of the past twenty-four hours and two orgasms had finally taken their toll. Maya was asleep.

Sleep called Toni, too, but she wanted to savor this overwhelming happiness, this flood of wellbeing every minute, every second until dawn broke and duty called. Had their hearts been paired in previous lives? Was that why she instinctively knew what would please Maya most? It didn't matter. The past was of no consequence. Tonight convinced Toni that she'd found the mate to her soul, just as they would find each other again and again in future lives. She closed her eyes, finally drifting toward sleep with one last thought. Would they regret that they hadn't voiced what was surely in their hearts? No. They didn't need words to express what she was sure they both felt.

Chapter Twenty-four

How might I be of service, First Warrior?" Alyssa kissed the bare shoulder where she'd been resting her cheek while their hearts returned to a slower, normal rhythm. She fingered a strand of Jael's wheat-colored mane and looked up into summer-sky blue eyes. "Or did you ask me to come immediately just to satisfy our baser needs?" Alyssa's tease didn't draw the smile she'd expected.

"One of our warriors survived his wounds but lost his dragon horse to those blasted laser weapons. I can't describe how deeply that broken bond tears into a warrior's soul." Jael's brow drew together, and a flash of sadness clouded her eyes. "It drives most into madness. I'm hoping you can use your gift to help soothe his withdrawal from the dragon bond until he can hopefully bond with another."

"I'll do everything I can, love. I understand the emptiness of loss." She brushed her lips against Jael's to soften her last words. She knew Jael still carried the guilt of what Alyssa had suffered during their separation after the Brasília battle. "And what's on your agenda today?"

This question drew a surprising chuckle from Jael. "First, I intend to call that rogue Dark Star out of the sky and see if he can tell me how on earth he was winged in full daylight."

Alyssa sat up. Sun and stars. She'd been so focused on jumping into Jael's arms, she hadn't registered the fact that Dark Star was in dragon-horse form before sunset. "How is this possible? Has he done it before?"

"No. At least not to my knowledge. Only Kyle's bonded, Sunfire, has been dragon in daylight. I thought she couldn't transform to regular horse. Now, I'm wondering if she can but just doesn't want to."

Alyssa pondered this possibility. "Perhaps the dragon horses are evolving. Now that vids of them have gone viral on the d-net, they don't need to hide in daylight as regular horses."

"Maybe I can find out something from him, but there's no guarantee. Dragon horses don't generally understand the concept of explanation. In their minds, everything just is as it is." Jael rose from their bed and held out her hand to Alyssa. "Unfortunately, duty calls both of us. I'll find you at the clinic after I interrogate Dark Star. Will you join me in the shower now?"

"Always," Alyssa said. While each of them was powerfully gifted, they'd forever be stronger together.

❖

The ping of Toni's d-tablet alarm woke her from a deep sleep. She must have been dreaming because she was instantly aware that she was smiling. Oh, yeah. She had a lot to smile about. She rolled toward…an empty space where Maya had been sleeping. Toni willed her heart to stop pounding, her mind to stop jumping to unsubstantiated conclusions of abandonment. Maya was probably just using the personal facility. But her doubts, her instinctive sense that something was wrong refused to abate as her hand fell on the cool sheet. How long had Maya been gone?

She couldn't focus with the insistent ping of her d-tablet still sounding. "Silence alarm." She rose and stalked to the table to glare at the screen as if the tablet were at fault for waking her to an empty bed. Relief, uncertainty, and dread simultaneously gripped her when her eyes went to the red dot blinking in the upper right corner. She swallowed hard, then cleared her throat. "Open messages."

"You have two messages," the tablet recited. "First message, transmitted at zero-one hundred by Second Warrior Kyle, copied to all members of The Guard."

"Read message."

"Commander Toni, Sunfire and I will watch over the transports during the day and switch off with Diego, Raven, and Michael, who will fly over them at night. Since we'll be resting with our dragon horses in some safe meadow when we're off duty, I'm putting you in charge of the transport caravan. See you at zero-eight hundred."

"Delete first message. Next message."

"Message two, recorded at zero-four-thirty by Maya."

Apprehension constricted Toni's chest like an over-tight breast binder. "Read message."

"Toni, last night was…it was wonderful. But, since being with you, conflicting visions have tormented me every time I close my eyes. I can't bear it any longer. It devastates me to reveal the coward that I am by abandoning the mission to rescue my family and defend The Collective, but I'm going back to my aunt's home, where I can protect my sanity. I hope you'll one day find a woman worthy of you. Maya."

She must have heard wrong. "Repeat message." Toni listened again, her heart falling, then hardening. She gotten messages like this before. Maya's was polite but still a "thanks for the jump, kiddo." Maya regretted not helping rescue her family. But the message held no regret for deserting Toni, only blame for the onslaught of visions. And, unlike Kyle's voice message, Maya had typed hers so that it was delivered in the d-tablet's pleasant but impersonal voice.

"Would you like to delete or save this message?"

"Save." Why had she said that? She was about to reverse the command, but the tablet interrupted.

"Reminder: The time is zero-six hundred. You have two hours until departure at zero-eight hundred."

Toni sucked in a deep breath. Maya had left several hours ago, so any chance to catch her before she got far had long passed. Toni didn't have time to chase her or wallow in self-pity. "Terminate reminders." Terminate everything but the mission before her.

She dressed quickly and packed her duffel, tossing the offending d-tablet in last. She'd need it to track their route and keep in touch with their forward group. She deliberately avoided one last look at the bed where she'd made love to Maya and cursed her weakness when she added her shirt that Maya had worn the night before. She shouldered her duffel and walked out, slamming the door behind her. Time to prove she deserved the commander insignia newly sealed on her shirtsleeve.

❖

Ten freight transports, the paint still drying on insignia that disguised them as food-distribution vehicles, waited in a long line. Sunfire strutted before the lead vehicle, flashing her wings in a show of bravado and impatience. The vehicle's driver smiled and shook his head at the filly's antics. Toni didn't smile. She grimly checked and rechecked her d-tablet to ensure everything had been properly loaded.

Raven, Michael, and Diego, spaced at intervals along the caravan, stood ready to join other drivers. They'd catch naps along the way but be on hand to help Sunfire resist any daytime attackers. Their dragon horses would catch up to them after dusk so they could provide air patrol while Kyle and Sunfire rested.

When Kyle emerged from headquarters ten minutes before zero-eight hundred, Sunfire screamed an exuberant greeting. "Are your troops ready to mobilize, Commander?"

Toni saluted. She might have been mistaken about her abilities as a lover, but she was confident in her skills as an organizer and soldier. "Awaiting your command, Second Warrior."

"Good." Kyle returned Toni's salute, but her gaze wandered down the line of transports. "Where's Maya riding?" Her gaze returned to Toni. "Don't tell me that you managed to convince her to stay here."

Toni forced herself to meet Kyle's gaze, hoping to the stars that her expression gave away nothing of the anger and hurt swirling in her gut. "Maya elected to return to her…to your aunt's home. She said all of this was stirring too many visions."

Kyle's surprised expression assured Toni that she'd known nothing about her sister's decision. "That doesn't sound like Maya." She narrowed her eyes. "Did something happen between you two?"

"No." Toni glared at Kyle. "She was gone when I woke. The message she left on my d-tablet simply said where she was going."

Maybe Maya had done something like this in the past, because Kyle relented. She grasped Toni's shoulder. "Just because we're women doesn't mean we always understand them. I can't tell you what might be going on in her head, but I do know that Maya really cares for you."

Toni's brain, her heart stuttered. "She told you that?"

"Yeah. I'm her big sister." She smiled and squeezed Toni's shoulder before letting go. "Tan and I started out rocky, too, until we trusted each other." She paused and shook her head. "No. That's not right. Until we trusted ourselves and what we felt."

Toni's anger faded as hope blossomed. "How did you do that?"

Kyle chuckled. "I was persistent. Very persistent. So don't give up on my sister yet."

Nodding, Toni straightened her shoulders. She wouldn't give up. She had to trust her heart's insistence that they were destined for each other. "Then let's wrap up this war so I can go find her."

Toni took the earpiece Kyle held out to her and inserted it in her ear as she'd seen the warriors do before battle. She flinched when three tiny fibers snaked out from it and embedded in her skull.

"The piece reads your brain's intentions and automatically switches from voice amplifier to single or multiple closed messaging," Kyle said. She stepped back and saluted Toni again. "Give your caravan the order to move out, Commander."

Toni returned her salute, then strode off to the right so all of the drivers could see her from their transports. "Caravan, prepare to depart." She almost jumped as her order rang out through the earpiece's amplifier, then waited until the low hum of engines engaging built to a chorus. Kyle sprang onto Sunfire's back, and with a war cry and dragon call, they launched into the air. Toni raised her hand overhead and made a circling motion. "Move out." She ran around the lead vehicle and swung up into the cab as it began rolling forward.

Chapter Twenty-five

"So, everything is going okay at camp?"

Alyssa smiled at the casual tone of Tan's question as they walked down the hallway of the town's hospital. She was sure the concern radiating from Tan had more to do with her separation from Kyle than the risky surgery she was about to perform. "Kyle has everything in hand. She's an amazing Second Warrior. Danielle would be so proud of her."

Tan stopped at the closed door of a patient's room. "She's a natural leader."

Alyssa raised an eyebrow at Tan's uncharacteristic smile. "And…?"

Tan chuckled. "And I miss her like crazy."

Alyssa wrapped Tan in a quick hug. Their friendship had been initially tentative because of Tan's history with Jael. But Alyssa had come to respect and genuinely care for the tough-talking warrior who was a talented and caring physician. Even more, now that Kyle had softened Tan's hard edge. "The caravan should arrive some time near dawn, though I wouldn't be surprised if Kyle shows up sooner, after the others take over her escort duty."

"Then let's get this show on the road so I'll be free when she arrives."

"Tell me about our patient."

"Keung is a young warrior, bonded to Huǒ. A laser shot sheared off Huǒ's right wing and nearly severed Keung's thigh. The dragon horse dropped like a stone to the street below and incinerated in his own flame, but another warrior was able to swoop in and grab Keung before he hit the pavement, too."

"Will you have to amputate his leg?"

Tan sighed and stared at the closed door. "I can save his leg but not sure I can save his life."

"Meaning?"

"He curses the warrior who saved his life and has no will to live." Tan dropped her gaze to the floor, the muscle in her jaw working. "We had to restrain and glove him, or he would have already incinerated himself, like Huǒ did."

"Oh, Tan, no." Alyssa knew what gloving meant to a pyro. Kyle had explained when she'd come to Alyssa seeking help the day before. She was afraid her fury over Xavier gloving Tan would cloud her judgment in the upcoming battle. Kyle's father had gloved her when she went undercover to infiltrate The Natural Order. Gloving a pyro was suffocating, like chaining someone underwater and giving them a tiny cocktail straw to breathe through. So she understood Tan's conflicted feelings at taking this measure with her patient. She took Tan's hand in hers. "I'm so sorry."

"I'm afraid if we anesthetize him for surgery, he just won't wake up." The unspoken "like Danielle" hung in the air between them.

Alyssa projected a confidence she didn't really feel. "Let me see what I can do to help."

Tan opened the door of Keung's room and gestured for Alyssa to enter first. She hadn't needed to go inside, however, to feel the young man's total desolation. He was awake, but he didn't acknowledge their presence.

"Give me the key to his gloves." Alyssa held out her hand. "You can stay, but stand here. I want to approach him alone."

Tan hesitated, her body language tense. "Are you sure? If anything happens to you, Jael will roast my gonads."

Alyssa cocked her head and looked Tan over from head to toe. "Jael never mentioned that you had such appendages."

"Oh. A funny Advocate. Who knew?" Tan propped against the wall just inside the door. "Go ahead, but be careful."

"No worries. I'll sense if his mood turns dangerous way before you'll see outward signs." Alyssa turned back to her patient. A tented sterile sheet covered his injured leg, and the medical discs adhered to his bared chest wirelessly transmitted constant data to the monitor on the wall behind his head.

Keung was a beautiful man. Because the gene allowing a warrior to bond with a dragon horse was passed from generation to generation, a potential warrior had to be descended from a nearly undiluted bloodline. This meant they all displayed the physical traits of their most ancient ancestors. Keung's straight dark hair, smooth features, and almond-shaped eyes were evidence that his ancestors were originally from the First Continent, more specifically an area once known as East Asia. She absorbed his despair and projected back a soothing sense of calm. His hard stare still focused on the ceiling above his bed, but his eyes softened, and his tense shoulders relaxed slightly.

"Hello, Keung. I'm Alyssa. I'm an Advocate. Do you feel like talking?"

He didn't answer, but Alyssa felt his emotions shift to something tentative. He was receptive.

"Okay. Since you apparently don't, I hope you don't mind if I do."

Silence, but his emotions began to tumble together. Emptiness, but at the same time gutting pain. Most important, a desperate need to escape his misery and a tiny sliver of hope that he would. That hope was her door inside. "I'm going to unlock and remove your gloves, but only if you promise not to harm yourself or me. I'm an empath, so I'll know if you are lying or change your mind." She held up the key to the gloves that imprisoned his hands.

He glanced quickly at the key, then stared again at the ceiling. He blinked rapidly several times, and she could feel his indecision. At last, he sighed and nodded once without meeting Alyssa's gaze. She unlocked the first glove and removed it, then released the soft cuffs that bound him to the bed frame. He still refused to look at her but flexed his fingers. She could feel his relief and rounded the bed to free his other hand.

Again he flexed his fingers, then gave in to the urge to rub his hands together. He finally glanced at Alyssa.

"It's okay. Go ahead. It will make you feel better." Alyssa raised her hand, palm out to belay any reaction from Tan as Keung held his hands up and spread his fingers. Small flames sprang briefly from his fingertips before he extinguished them. Then he laid his hands flat on his chest. She felt his mood shift. "Don't forget your deal, Keung."

Silent anger flared as he apparently realized that though she'd freed his hands, she'd bound his soul when she demanded his promise.

He closed his eyes for a long moment, and tears leaked from their corners. Then his chest convulsed and his face contorted. "I feel so empty." His plaintive cry was a hoarse rasp, and she poured a cup of water and held the straw to his lips.

"Only a sip," Tan said. "He's headed for surgery as soon as he signs the consent form."

Keung did take a small sip, but his shoulders continued to shake as he quietly wept. Unable to turn away because of the apparatus holding his leg, he covered his face with his hands. "Please let me go. You don't know what it's like."

Alyssa laid her hand in the middle of his chest. "I do know, Keung." Her whisper, or maybe the peace she projected through her hand, quieted his sobs, and he lowered his hands. "Do you know who I am?" she asked.

He finally turned his gaze to her. "Everyone does. You're the First Advocate."

She nodded. "That's right. You were probably with the rest of the warriors when I had to speak before the pyre of Uri, my close friend and fellow advocate."

Anger flared again, and he spoke through clenched teeth. "That's nothing like—"

She matched his anger with projected fury as she cut him off. "But you weren't with me when those missiles turned the First Warrior, my soul bond, into ash. We were miles apart, but the moment that laser burned into her chest and those missiles exploded, I felt like a hand reached into mine and tore out my heart. I didn't even have a body to cry over or a pyre to light for closure." Alyssa paused, the remembered moment tightening her throat. She bowed her head.

Alyssa?

I'm okay. But I need you.

Assured Jael was on her way, Alyssa dragged a chair next to the bed and sat, gathering the strength to finish. "Only Danielle, who'd been cloned from Jael, knew the depth of my wound. I couldn't eat or sleep. The pillows on our bed still smelled like her. Her muddy boots were still on the mat by the door. I wanted time to go backward so I could scold her for throwing her soiled clothes on top of the hamper instead of raising the lid to put them inside...so she could keep me warm when I slept curled in her arms at night. Since I couldn't, I wished for death so I could follow her." She felt Jael enter the building and seconds later stand in the room's doorway, silently waiting. What she was about to share with Keung, she hadn't shared with anyone. Not even Jael.

"I sat in the dark, in her chair for two days, never touching the trays of food Danielle brought and never crawling onto our bed to sleep. But when Danielle thought I'd had enough time to wallow, she knelt before me to share her story. She'd lost her soul mate some years before when Saran fell to her death on a mountain-climbing trip. She had lived my devastation. She told me that every second, every minute, every hour would be a struggle, but people still living needed me. With Jael's help, she'd begun by going through the motions until she realized she could still find purpose and some joy in this life, even though the ache of Saran's absence would never cease. Stop wallowing, she said, and move through the motions of living...one minute, one hour, one day at a time." She turned and held out her hand to beckon Jael.

The First Warrior made no effort to hide her tears, taking Alyssa's hand and leaning down to hold it against her wet cheek. "I'm so, so sorry for putting you through that."

"It's okay, love. I hope I never have to crawl out of that hole again, but the experience taught me that I'm stronger than I ever imagined. It showed me that our bond can survive anything, even death. So, let go of that boulder of guilt you're shouldering."

"I don't know if I ever will."

"Perhaps a little restitution will help."

"Restitution?"

Alyssa nodded at Keung, who was watching them intently. When Jael looked his way, he pressed his fist to his chest in silent salute. The warriors had always admired Jael, but her return from death had made her a legend. Keung's expression and his emotions were a bit starstruck, and Alyssa wanted to cheer. If he could forget his grief for a minute, he could eventually manage it for a lifetime.

Jael smiled and returned his salute. "I'll forgive you for not standing when I walked into the room."

Keung hesitated, then offered a small smile. "Thank you, First Warrior."

The two stared at each other. Stars, warriors could be so clueless sometimes. She'd have to prime this pump. Alyssa rose from her chair and entwined her arm with Jael's, already regretting the need to reopen a second wound for her unsuspecting mate. "I asked Jael to come because she's experienced exactly what you're feeling. Those missiles not only separated us, but they stole Specter from her."

Jael stiffened beside her.

Alyssa.

Please, Jael. I can calm his emotions so that he makes it through surgery, but he needs more. He needs to know a future is waiting for him. Tell him about Specter and about your bond with Dark Star now.

Jael searched Alyssa's eyes, then surrendered. *You're a tough general.* She sat in the chair Alyssa had vacated.

It'd been a gamble because Jael would let few people close. Alyssa kissed her check, then grabbed Tan's arm to guide her out. "Tan and I will wait outside." As they were leaving, she heard Jael begin.

"What was your dragon's name?"

"Huŏ," Keung said. "She was a beautiful blood bay with black leggings that matched her mane and tail."

Alyssa closed the door to give the two warriors privacy.

Tan frowned at her d-tablet. "If they take too long, I'm going to lose my spot in the OR schedule."

Alyssa chuckled. "I don't think a single doctor in this hospital will stand in your way." It was true. The feelings Alyssa was reading from the doctors and nurses was a combination of awe and relief that Xavier's crew had been run out of town and that the local peacekeepers were dealing with any of The Natural Order believers who had committed criminal acts in the name of their beliefs.

Jael emerged a half hour later and pointed at Tan. "He wants to talk to you."

Tan hopped down from the gurney she and Alyssa had been sitting on—the one still reserved to take Keung to the operating suite if he consented—and disappeared into the Keung's room. Jael sat in Tan's place and slumped against the wall at her back.

"Are you all right, love?" Alyssa took her hand and stroked Jael's callused palm. "I'm worried that I shouldn't have put you on the spot like that."

Jael gave her a sharp glance. "No. You shouldn't have." She sighed. "But it did help me to talk about Specter with another warrior who's suffered that broken bond. I'm just not sure I helped Keung."

Alyssa was confused. "What makes you doubt it? He seems very positive…and determined now."

Jael was about reply when Tan emerged again.

"Off," she said. "I need this gurney." She waved to a nurse standing at the floor's med station. "I need some help taking this patient to the OR." The nurse waved another to join him, and they hurried to take charge of the gurney and transfer Keung onto it. Tan turned back to Jael and Alyssa.

"He consented to surgery?" Alyssa asked, just to be sure.

"Not the surgery I intended." She gave Jael a pointed look. "I don't try to run The Guard for you, so I'd appreciate it if you'd leave the distribution of medical advice to me."

Jael looked a bit guilty but met Tan's glare. "Would you have answered his questions any differently?"

Tan frowned but shook her head. "You know I couldn't."

"Then it was his decision."

"What decision?" Alyssa read defiance from Jael and resignation from Tan. "What are you two talking about?"

"Keung opted for amputation rather than repair," Tan said.

Alyssa gaped at her. "Why would he do that?"

"He'll recover faster and function better with a bionic prosthesis," Jael said. "I chose the same option in my life previous to this one."

They followed as the nurses emerged from the room and wheeled Keung down the hall, then waited for the lift doors to open.

"Are you sure this is what you want, Keung?" Her question was needless. Alyssa already felt his certainty.

"I need to get back on my feet." He looked to Jael. "As soon as I'm ready, the First Warrior has promised to take me back to the wild herd for another shot at bonding."

Alyssa patted his shoulder and smiled at Jael. "Well, I can personally vouch that the First Warrior always keeps her promises."

When the lift arrived, Keung offered his hand to Jael. "Thank you...for everything. What we talked about...it's just between us, right?"

Jael clasped his forearm in a warrior's handshake. "Absolutely. Warrior to warrior. Good luck, Keung. I'll expect to hear from you in a few months about that trip for a new bonding."

The nurse pushed his gurney into the lift, and Keung waved one last time as the doors closed.

Alyssa wrapped her arms around Jael, absorbing her warmth and strength. "Is being a warrior hard?"

"I suspect it's easier than being an empath," Jael said, returning her mate's embrace. "I'd feel like I had perpetual PMS if I had to absorb the emotions you do."

Chapter Twenty-six

Toni gaped when they rounded a curve and the transport's headlamps raked across the first pickup point. At least fifty people stood waiting in the field next to a large travel center. When Sunfire emerged from the night sky like a falling star and landed before them, they all clapped and cheered. Kyle dismounted, but Sunfire continued to strut before the crowd, glowing as if illuminated by an inner light and rattling her wings in a showy display.

Reassured that the crowd was friendly, Toni turned to her driver. "Looks like we might be here for a while, so let me out and then lead the other transports over to the center so they can plug in and top off their batteries. Tell the rest of the personnel to take advantage of the center's restaurant and facilities."

"Yes, Commander."

She inwardly flinched at being addressed by her new rank. She still felt like Toni the Pony, who'd so often been the brunt of teasing and jokes. She hoped she could live up to Jael's confidence and put together a competent platoon of shields. She shouldered the laser rifle and climbed down from the rig. They couldn't take everybody, so she'd have to determine which were the strongest. Kyle had said twelve warriors and six Guard were still fit enough for duty. Considering that she and Haley would shield Jael and Kyle, she needed sixteen more. Hmm. She also should also have replacements in the event of casualties, and a couple assigned to Alyssa and Nicole. Nine more should be sufficient. She nodded to herself. Twenty-seven was a good number. As the rest of the caravan continued to the travel center, several slowed for Raven, Diego, and Michael to hop to the ground and join Toni.

"Sun! How can there be so many?" Diego scratched at his goatee, a gesture Toni recognized as his tell that he was digesting and analyzing information. "Until you came along, we didn't know about these shields."

"I don't think they're all shields," Michael said. "I'm betting a lot are friends or family who came with the candidates."

"What's the plan, Commander?" Raven asked.

Technically, any member of The Guard outranked other officers, but Toni recognized that Raven was confirming this was Toni's show to run. "We see how many can pass my test," Toni said.

As they started across the field, Sunfire folded her wings and briefly touched her forehead to Kyle's before Kyle turned to the waiting crowd.

"I am Kyle, Second Warrior of The Guard, seven of twenty-one dragon-horse warriors who have been the invisible protectors of The Collective around the world for hundreds of years." She paused. "Actually, we are six until the First Warrior names a replacement for our most recent loss."

Toni touched her hand to her heart, then her forehead and lifted it to the sky in the customary tribute and wish for Furcho's released soul to have a safe journey to his next life.

"You honor us now by answering our call for shields." Kyle scanned the expectant crowd to be sure she had everyone's attention. "Before you step forward to have your gift evaluated, you should know the danger that awaits if you're selected. When the Calling was issued for candidates who could bond with dragon horses, we raised an army of fifty-seven, plus the seven members of The Guard." A titter of applause started at the edge of the crowd but died quickly when Kyle solemnly stared. "Our casualties have been many. Two of The Guard have fallen. Only a dozen of our new warriors have survived our clashes with the Natural Order, and a third of them will fight our next battle while still recovering from injuries."

The crowd began to shift and murmur among themselves.

"Some are uncertain now."

Toni whipped around at Nicole's whisper. "Nic. I thought you were staying at the camp."

"I couldn't. I need to be busy."

Toni gripped her friend's hand. "I'm glad you're here. You can help me select a few from these volunteers."

"I'll help any way I can."

Kyle waited for the crowd to settle. "This cult has progressed from using projectile weapons to missiles to lasers. Our warriors could easily melt their bullets, and we were victorious even when the missiles took their toll. But The Natural Order brought laser rifles to our last battle, and we had no defense against their slicing rays." Kyle pointed to Toni. "None, except Commander Antonia. We discovered in battle that she could deflect the lasers with her gift of shield."

Smiles and nods easily identified the potential candidates.

"Oh, Toni. They like that," Nicole said, keeping her voice low.

"She'll command the shield unit, so I'll turn you over to her." Kyle stepped back and beckoned to Toni to take her place while she conferred with the other Guard members.

Toni ran her eyes over the expectant faces. Some met her gaze, and others stared at the ground or glanced nervously at the people around them. Okay. She could do this. They were just like boxed supplies that had to be inventoried to see if they were actually what was advertised on the outside. She cleared her throat.

"I want to reinforce that Commander Kyle has not exaggerated the danger of this mission. In a moment, I will ask those who still want to volunteer to step forward. We will test and rank your shielding ability because we'll be taking only a handful of you. First, I want to describe the specifics of the assignment and ask you to consider carefully before you get in the line for testing. Maybe your family is dependent on the work you do or the care you give them. Maybe you already bear the responsibilities of being a parent. Maybe you're not confident your gift is strong enough to deflect a laser. No one will think less of you for deciding against joining us now that you have more information."

Many glanced at the people beside them. A few hands sought out the hand of a loved one standing with them.

"We will pair sixteen shields with dragon-horse warriors. They will fly into battle with the warrior to deflect oncoming laser fire," Toni said. "Those chosen must be able to raise and drop shields of specific dimensions in only a fraction of a second. We'll also select nine alternate shields to step up if the front line becomes too exhausted… or in the event of casualties. Until they are called up, those nine will protect key support staff." Toni paused.

Their faces told everything—who would step forward, who would choose to go home, and who were terrified for a loved one almost bouncing on their feet to be tested. She pointed to Nicole, then a spot at the edge of the forest on her right. "Those still determined to volunteer, go line up next to Advocate Nicole over there."

Nicole trotted to the designated area and raised her hand high to mark the location. Potawatomi, Bero, and Apollo landed next to their warriors, while fourteen potential shields joined Nicole. The volunteers were mixed—petite, husky, male, female, confident, hesitant, and one pair of twins.

"What can we do to help?" Kyle asked.

"If you could stay and help me test their shields, I'd like Raven, Michael, and Diego to take each one airborne. I need to eliminate any who become airsick or freeze with fear when they get up."

Kyle clapped Toni on the shoulder. "Good idea. I hadn't considered that idea." She walked with Toni to where the group stood and looked them over. She pointed to a husky young man, a nervous petite teen, and a tall, middle-aged woman. "You three come with me to be flight-tested." The lad jumped forward right at Kyle's heels, the woman calmly followed, and the teen joined them after a brief hesitation.

Toni addressed the rest of them. "All right. I want the rest of you to line up, your back to the woods, and spread out." They lined up facing her. "Now count off." Toni activated her d-tablet and opened the spreadsheet she'd prepared. She had to add a few columns since they hadn't anticipated this many. "Kyle will throw fireballs between you, and I will call out the number of the person I want to block each one."

Kyle had returned and began walking down the line flinging fireballs while Toni shouted out numbers. When Diego, Raven, and Michael returned, all three of their passengers slid to the ground, grinning as they thanked their pilots. The teen's face was flushed with excitement, her previous hesitancy gone. Check, great in the air. Kyle chose three more while Toni explained the ground test. Kyle went up and down the line several more times, increasing the intensity of her flame and aiming closer until she was firing flame so fast Toni barely had time to call out numbers. When the next three returned from their flights, one of them fell to his knees and vomited. *Strike, he's out.*

They continued, eliminating those whose shields failed under Kyle's onslaught. When all but six had flown, Nicole placed her hand on Toni's shoulder as she was about to name the next-to-fly group. "Split up the twins. I'm not sure which, but I think one is helping the other."

Toni nodded and pointed to the twin on the left for the next flight group. The young woman hesitated and looked to her sister, who paled but waved her away. "How can she be helping?" Toni asked, still watching the sister left behind. "I haven't seen either raise a hand yet, like the others do to throw a shield."

"I'm not sure how, but I am sure they're both upset now at being separated."

Toni made a note on her spreadsheet and continued to call out numbers as Kyle resumed her onslaught. When Toni called the twin's number, she ducked away from Kyle's fireball rather than blocking it. Toni crossed her off the list and gestured for her to step away from the group. More were eliminated by the time the dragon horses landed again. The other twin dismounted, her eyes wide when she realized her sister was no longer in the firing line. She slowly took her place again, while the last three went airborne. When Kyle resumed, the second twin ducked rather than blocked. Toni scratched her from the list, too.

Eight candidates remained after others were eliminated because of vertigo, fear of flying, or weak shields. Nicole was talking to the dejected twins. Toni shook her head. Nicole had such a tender heart.

"You'll be tested one at a time in this phase," she told the remaining candidates. "Number Ten, stand over there, facing me. The rest move off to the left." They shuffled to their appointed places. Ten was a slight, dark-skinned young man. Toni set her d-tablet on the ground and held up the laser rifle that'd been slung over her shoulder. "This is a laser rifle, The Natural Order's current weapon of choice. You can't just block it. You need to deflect the beam in a safe direction. Tonight, I want you to try to redirect it skyward." She waved over Haley, who'd been watching the process. "I need you to block any dangerous errant deflections."

"No problem," Haley said.

She began shooting on either side of Ten. His shield was strong, and after a few awkward tries that Haley intercepted, he expertly sent each laser beam skyward. The middle-aged woman from the first flight group also passed the test, but the laser proved too much for the shields of the next three.

The last five also passed the final test, where Kyle stood behind to see if they could limit the dimensions of their shields so they didn't also block the warrior's fire, then in front to test whether they could block Toni's laser without stopping Kyle's outgoing fire.

Before confirming them, Toni consulted with the others. Michael and Raven readily approved three of them.

"Two flew with me," Diego said. "The girl was shaky until we launched. She's a natural at flying. Bero liked her, too, and he doesn't like anybody. Sometimes, I think he barely tolerates me." He shrugged. "But that husky young man. He was heavy, even for a stallion like Bero. His shield is strong enough, but I'm afraid his weight disqualifies him."

"Thanks," Toni said. "I'm sorry this is taking so long. I never figured on this many coming forward." She started toward the five who'd passed all the tests.

"Toni, wait." Nicole was trotting toward her.

"Is there a problem with any of these five?"

"No, no. They all feel solid. Even the teen who was uncertain at first. She's full of confidence now. But I want to ask a favor."

"Anything." Toni was so happy to see Nicole so involved that the sadness in her eyes had temporarily abated.

"Test the twins with the laser."

"Once we separated them, neither could block a fireball. Why do you think they could deflect a laser beam?"

"Because together, they're probably the strongest shield out here."

"A dragon horse can't carry both of them and a warrior, Nic."

"They're also medics. They could work in the clinic with me instead of you assigning someone who'll stand around bored on the off chance that I need protection."

Toni considered this suggestion, then nodded.

Nicole placed a chaste kiss on Toni's cheek. "Thank you. I really like them."

Toni didn't want Nicole to be disappointed. "They have to pass the laser test."

"They will," said Nicole, waving to the twins, then pointing at the test spot.

They hugged each other, then ran to the indicated area, where they positioned themselves shoulder to shoulder with their outside feet slightly behind to form a V. Toni began firing. They didn't even raise their hands, but the laser deflected skyward time after time. Kyle joined in, and they bombarded the twins from both sides, but the young women only smiled as their shields absorbed Kyle's fire and deflected Toni's laser. One last test. Toni swung to the left and aimed close to Nicole, who stood about nine meters from the twins. They raised their left hands in unison, and the beam shot harmlessly skyward. Nicole was right. They were exceptional together. She lowered the rifle and nodded to Nicole, who waved for the twins to join her. They all hugged, and the twins chattered excitedly.

Toni shook her head, then walked over to her top five. "What's your name, buddy?" she asked the husky young man.

"Fifth, ma'am. When I was born, my mama told my daddy, 'He's the fifth and last.' So they named me Fifth." He was blond, handsome, and spoke with a deep, quiet drawl.

"What type of work have you been doing?"

"I've worked on my dad's farm all my life, so I learned to do lots of things. I can grow stuff, fix things, and tend livestock. I also have training as a veterinary assistant."

"Aren't you leaving something out, Fifth?" The middle-aged woman apparently knew him. She turned to Toni. "He's mildly empathic and a whiz at math and organization. His father would have lost the family farm years ago if Fifth hadn't taken over the farm's books and management."

Toni thought this information over. "Who would run the farm if we take you with us?"

His face flushed red. "Mama passed away last year, and Dad followed her a few months back. The farm was left to me and my brothers, but they all hate farm work and outvoted me to sell it. I got nothing tying me."

Bastards. Toni liked him, but she had to be honest. "I'm going to give it to you straight, Fifth."

"I'm too big, aren't I?" His eyes begged her to refute this fact.

She nodded. "You're a strong shield, but I'm afraid you're too heavy to fly with a warrior. In battle, they wheel and dip and dive like seagulls feasting on a school of fish."

Disappointment filled his features. "I understand."

"But...I think you'd be a perfect personal shield for the First Advocate, who is the First Warrior's mate. She's also an empath and director of the clinic at our home base. You'd have to be with her every minute she isn't with the First Warrior."

He brightened. "I'd be honored."

She extended her hand, and he took it in his. "No," she said. Still clasping his hand, she turned to the others. "Warriors greet each other like this." She grasped his forearm, and he instinctively grasped hers as she guided him to execute a quick, single pump up and down. "But as recruits, you will salute officers in this manner." She demonstrated the salute, and they mimicked it in unison. "All right. Grab your duffels. You have five minutes to say good-bye to anyone who came with you and five minutes to hit the personal facility in the travel center. Then report to the transports parked over there."

She turned to find Nicole and her new shields waiting. She pointed to the twins. "Same for you two. Ten minutes, then look for Nicole at the transports." They scurried off.

Toni rubbed her forehead. "At this rate, we won't reach our rendezvous point until tomorrow night."

"That's okay," Kyle said, joining Toni and Nicole. Raven, Michael, and Diego were already in the air, patrolling overhead. "We can take all the time you need. The lives of our warriors and the future of The Collective are at stake."

Chapter Twenty-seven

Maya roused and nearly panicked when she realized her small transport had stopped. How long had it been idling here? Had it taken her to the correct destination? She never trusted these self-driving things and was surprised that she'd managed to doze off. Her motion inside the transport triggered its computer.

"You have arrived at your destination," its pleasant female voice told her.

She rubbed her eyes. "Time?"

"The time is ten thirty. Do you require a forecast?"

"No." She peered at the roadside marker. City of Light. The transport *had* found the correct location. Blinding sunlight glinted off the windscreen. She'd walk from here. She didn't want to chance someone hacking the transport's computer and finding its home, the permanent base of the dragon-horse army.

"Computer, return home in two minutes."

"Returning home in two minutes."

She climbed out and secured the door. She looked up the mountain to its peak and shaded her eyes. The sun was still low in the sky, giving the impression it was balanced on the sharp steeple of a building that was an impressive display of glittering gold and glass. She waited another few seconds for the transport to rotate and turn onto the highway, then set her shoulders and began the march uphill.

❖

"It's time to be rid of Cyrus." Xavier's pain was making him edgy.

"If we off him now, he'll look like a martyr, and before you know it, he'll be remembered as a saint," Simon said. "We'll keep the nutcase around a bit longer."

Xavier sat back in his chair and rested his ankle on his opposite knee. He drew an injector from his pocket, pressed it to the vein throbbing above his soft leather loafer, and relaxed as the hypo-spray flowed into his body.

Simon licked his dry lips, his gaze fixed on the injector Xavier held. "That better be your own stuff. I don't have much left."

Xavier regarded Simon. He was beginning to hate the cruel little man's whining for a fix, even though he purposely encouraged Simon's habit. "I own many fields of poppies and coca plants. My supply is endless. This, in fact, is a new shipment, very high quality." He drew another injector from his pocket and held it out to Simon. "I'm happy to share."

Simon's bionic prosthetic arm whirred as he grabbed the injector and pressed it to the vein in his real arm. He closed his eyes and slumped back in his chair. "Good stuff. You get the best...so good." His words were slurred, and the last one ended in a whisper as Simon drifted off.

Xavier smiled. The dose he'd prepared for Simon was much stronger than the one he used to take the edge off his pain. Addiction would never rule him. He knew how to stop before he crossed the line, just like he knew how to push someone else over it. Addicts were the bread-and-butter customers of the drug trade, and Simon had been easy prey. In only a few weeks, he already looked like a skeleton, with sunken eyes and pallid skin.

Martyr or not, Xavier would get rid of Cyrus. Then he'd supply the overdose that would snuff Simon, too. He smiled to himself. None would be left to stand in his way when he claimed Simon's capitalist empire as his own. After all, didn't Simon say that only the strong should survive?

❖

"You're telling us that Dark Star can fly in daylight now just because Sunfire told him how?" Diego, ever the skeptic, was incredulous.

"I think it was more like convincing him that he can transform any time he wants. The sun doesn't ground them." Jael reconsidered. "At least that's what I think he was showing me." She shrugged. "I don't know if it's my hard skull or his late bonding, but I don't understand him as clearly as I did Specter." She tugged the shoulder packs from

Dark Star's withers and sent him a mental picture of him grazing while she talked with Raven, Diego, and Michael. She held up the packs. "I brought fire rock for your mounts."

"I figured it wouldn't take that long to reach the town, so we'd just feed them when we arrived tonight." His frown relaxed and curled into a smirk. "Needed an excuse for some flying time, or was the missus too busy to keep you entertained?"

She had been getting restless with Alyssa seeing patients at the clinic. So she'd flown out that morning after Kyle had reported their delay and told her where the others were resting until their mounts got their wings again at dusk. Before she sought them out, she made a side trip to check on the convoy. Dark Star, strangely enough, flew fast and direct, rather than lazily riding the shifting airstream in the meandering style most dragon horses preferred. Jael smiled at his showy posturing when they caught up with Kyle and Sunfire, who were escorting the convoy as they neared the town. He definitely had his eye on the filly. Kyle had given her a thumbs-up at Dark Star's daytime wings and reported that all was well, so Jael had redirected her reluctant stallion to the high meadow not far away.

Jael laughed and slapped Diego on the back. "Both. I was getting restless because Alyssa is busy helping Tan get our wounded warriors battle-ready again. And sometimes you need to feel the wind in your face."

Diego nodded and stared up at the sky, his expression wistful. All dragon-horse warriors understood the itch to be aloft. "What's it like to fly with the sunlight warming your back?"

Jael slipped her arm around his shoulders and guided him to where Raven and Michael were watching Dark Star with amazed expressions. They both saluted as she approached, and she lazily tapped her fist against her shoulder in return. She'd felt a lot more open and laid-back since her return. Maybe a few of Danielle's brain cells were refusing to alter to her more serious personality. Maybe Alyssa was changing her. Or maybe dying, then resurrecting had brought home to her that life could be short and she should live every moment to the fullest. "I'm hoping all of you can find out yourself." She reached into one of the packs and pulled out what looked like a salt lick for cattle. "I have four, one for each, including Dark Star."

Raven looked puzzled. "Salt blocks?"

Michael took one for Apollo and sniffed it, then stuck his tongue tentatively to it and made a face. "It tastes like fire rock." He turned it in his hand. "Pulverized fire rock? What'd you mix with it to make it into a block?"

Jael held up Dark Star's portion. "I think Danielle's need to always cook something up is lingering in my...our brain." She hefted the rectangular block. "One of the biggest impediments is the need to haul fire rocks everywhere we travel so that our mounts keep the hottest flame. These are half the weight of an equal-size fire rock. I talked to a geologist and an agriculture expert, told them what we needed, and they put this together in a few hours. The fire rock is concentrated to twice the potency of raw rock, so half the usual weight."

"You *have* been bored, but these will be handy," Michael said. "I bet Will could've done this sort of thing, but I never thought to ask."

"I don't know how to explain this, but I feel more whole now... like Danielle and I were two parts of the same person, and now I'm whole." Jael absently pressed her fingers to her chest. She'd always hold a part of Danielle in her heart. She searched Michael's eyes when he looked up at her. He nodded, almost imperceptibly. He understood.

"So, how do we teach our dragon horses to fly in the daylight?" Diego obviously wasn't interested in fire rocks.

Jael led them over to their mounts, who, after a few sniffs, licked then began to bite off bits of the blocks. They didn't need dragon teeth to munch this softer version of fire rock. "When they're done, I'll ask Dark Star to tell the others. Sunfire expressed to Kyle that all dragon horses could change at will, day or night. They forgot they could because the herd has spent generations transforming only at night so humans wouldn't spot them."

"That could explain why ancient writings speak of dragon sightings up until a certain time, and then as years passed, they were just considered fanciful tales." Raven cocked her head, sorting it all out as she talked.

"Let's try it," Jael said. She pressed her forehead to Dark Star's while he chewed the last of his block. When she withdrew, he bobbed his head and folded his wings but raised his muzzle to the sun and gave a dragon scream that got the attention of the other three. His shriek turned to a whinny as his dragon features disappeared in a blur. Bero and Apollo swished their tails in annoyance at the racket and began to search for some succulent grass now that the fire-rock blocks were gone. But Potawatomi eyed Dark Star with interest, her ears working back and forth. Then Dark Star reared high on his powerful haunches. His stallion call became a dragon scream again as he transformed back and launched into the sky. In a blink, Potawatomi reared and transformed to follow him. Upset at being left behind, Bero and Apollo trotted in circles and bucked in frustration. Then Apollo sprinted across the meadow, found his dragon, and lifted off in pursuit. A second later, Bero was close on his heels.

"Yes!" Raven said as Diego whooped.

"Starstruck," Michael shouted and slapped his hands together. "Look at them go."

Jael smiled. Her warriors had become more relaxed around her as she became more open with them. And she kind of liked it. She touched her heart again in a silent thanks to Danielle. "Guard, call your dragons down and let's rejoin the convoy."

Maya trudged along most of the day, ducking into the woods at the sound of an occasional transport, before the forest opened and she found herself at a service entrance in the city's high wall. She tried to appear casual as she circled to the main gates. Transport and pedestrian traffic was brisk on the wide, paved road that emptied into a large, busy parking lot in front of a huge cathedral of crystal and gold. Sun and stars, who could have imagined such a structure? She joined the line of people filing in, then realized each person was running their wrist over a security scanner to enter. Her heart sank. She had to get inside, or she couldn't alter what she'd seen in her vision. She didn't see a guard, so she'd try to melt into the crowd quickly if she set off alarms. She straightened her shoulders and inched forward with the rest.

CHAPTER TWENTY-EIGHT

D id she have to wear that war paint?" Toni kept her voice low so only Kyle could hear. Phyrrhos and Tan were the last to join the dragon horses and their warriors waiting to be paired with a shield. The warriors and the shields lined up about twenty meters apart like opposing armies on a battlefield, awaiting the call to charge. Phyrrhos, showboat that she was, lifted her wings high and pranced down the length of the two groups while Tan, fierce slashes of red and yellow marking her forehead, chin, and cheeks, glared at the shields.

Kyle shook her head, her lips curling into a small smile and her eyes gleaming as she watched her lover's antics. "She said she didn't want to pick a shield, then have them freak out when they saw her actually prepared for battle."

"I guess that makes sense." Toni watched Phyrrhos fold her wings, then back into the line of warriors at its center, forcing the other dragon horses to make room for her.

"Tan just loves the drama of intimidating people." The amused tone of Jael's comment didn't match her sharp, calculating gaze that swept over the shields, then the warriors. Kyle and Toni shifted for Jael to stand between them. "Brief me on our new recruits, Commander Toni."

"With the exception of the twins assigned to Nicole and the young man assigned to protect Alyssa, the sixteen shields on the front line tested strongest. The group gathered behind them are alternates in the event of casualties. They're nearly as good but are less practiced or have slightly slower reflexes."

"Commander Kyle, what's your recommendation to proceed?"

Kyle's gaze flicked over individuals in each of the opposing lines.

"Even though the shields don't bond with the dragon horses, Sunfire advises me they are particular about who they carry other than their warriors."

Dark Star touched down behind them and snuffled Toni's hair. Toni ducked away from him, but not before he left a sooty smudge on her cheek. "Dude, your breath is atrocious."

Jael smiled. "He likes you, and that makes a good match for you to be our shield."

Toni scratched his forehead between the V of horny spikes that ran the length of his long face. "I watched the two groups line up, and I'm betting some shields already have their eye on certain warriors."

"I concur." She clapped both Kyle and Toni on their shoulder. "We'll give the dragons first choice." She stepped back and leapt onto Dark Star's back. "Thank you, Commanders. I'll take it from here."

Kyle's eyes returned to her warriors, but Toni watched Jael. She was the ultimate leader, inspiring fierce loyalty from all she commanded. All eyes were glued to her now as she sat her mount easily, back and shoulders straight but relaxed. The warriors were dressed in silvery battleskin emblazoned with the black dragon-horse insignia. The red dragon horse of the First Warrior glittered on Jael's chest. Usually braided back for battle, her blond mane was loose, and a slight breeze played with the shoulder-length strands as Dark Star folded his wings and pranced down the length of the line of shields. Jael looked into the eyes of each shield she passed, power and authority permeating the air around her. When she reached the end, she turned Dark Star back and trotted to the center to pace a shorter circuit back and forth while she spoke.

"I am Jael, First Warrior of The Collective. I salute each of you for answering our call for shields to protect our warriors and secure the future of The Collective. Commander Toni reports you've passed extensive testing to be here. You still have one hurdle to leap before your final test in battle." She gestured to indicate the line of warriors. "The first pass at pairing with a warrior will be up to their dragon horses. They are particular beasts. If a dragon horse finds more than one of you acceptable, then it will be up to both warrior and shield to indicate their preference."

Dark Star halted and Toni tensed. This was it. Had she chosen the right shields? Would the dragon horses or their warriors balk at her choices? What if some found no match?

"Guard, forward." Bero, Apollo, Potawatomi, and Phyrrhos took several steps forward at Jael's command. "Choose your shields."

Bero didn't hesitate, going directly to the young woman who'd been tentative before her test flight on him. Toni wasn't surprised. She'd seen the teen purposely align herself directly across from him. Diego also appeared happy with Bero's choice.

Apollo walked down the entire line, then turned back and returned to the middle-aged woman who had joined them at the first stop. Michael seemed surprised, then leaned down to offer his forearm in a warrior's greeting. Match made.

Potawatomi took her turn but had passed only a few in the line when a man farther down stepped out and faced them. He was lean, with bronze skin a bare shade darker than Raven's. The ebony hair that draped to his shoulders shone like a crow's wing. "I am for you," he said. Raven cocked her head at his declaration, and Potawatomi raised her nose to gather his scent. In a display unusual for the normally quiet dragon horse, she raised her wings, rattling them and snorting small flames as she sauntered toward the man. He laughed.

"Your fierce display does not intimidate me." His eyes went from dragon horse to rider to dragon horse. "But the beauty of your power awes me." Potawatomi sniffed his shirt, then butted his chest, nearly knocking him off his feet. When he recovered his balance, Raven bent down and offered her arm for a warrior greeting. "She finds you acceptable. I am Raven."

"Wolf," he said, grasping her forearm and taking advantage of the greeting as leverage to swing up behind her. His war cry joined Raven's as Potawatomi leapt skyward.

Toni relaxed a little. So far, so good. But now the real test.

Phyrrhos blew out a cloud of soot, like a big dragon sigh of resignation, then walked directly to a tow-headed, boyish girl of about thirteen, took the girl's shirt collar in her teeth, and dragged her from the line.

"Hey. That's my favorite shirt you're slobbering on," the girl said, slapping Phyrrhos's long nose, then pulling back to run her palm against her jeans. "Ow. Those spikes hurt."

The complaint didn't move Phyrrhos, who swiped her tongue along the girl's cheek.

"Yuk. Your breath smells like rotten eggs."

The remark earned her another swipe of the tongue, and Tan

leaned over Phyrrhos's neck to glare at the girl. "How old are you? Do your parents know you're here?"

"Old enough, and I ain't got no parents." The girl peered up at Tan. "What's the deal with that stuff painted on your face?"

"Scares you, does it?"

Dung. Toni hurried toward the pair before the dubious pairing could escalate into an argument.

"I'm not scared of you or your fancy dragon horse."

"You should be. You look too small to be much of a shield."

"Actually, Vaughn tested very high." Toni smiled at the scowling girl. "Nearly as good as me."

Tan made a show of looking the girl over from head to toe. "Are you sure?"

Toni relaxed. Tan was messing with the girl.

Vaughn crossed her arms over her chest and stood as tall as she could. "I can block anything you can throw."

"We'll see about that." Tan scratched her jaw. "But since Commander Toni and Phyrrhos seem to think you'll do, I'll give you a try."

Vaughn eyed Tan's extended arm but didn't move to take it. "Maybe I'll give you a try," she said. "But only if you paint my face like yours. It looks kind of cool."

Tan shrugged. "Deal."

"Starstruck," Vaughn said, her scowl vanishing as she grasped Tan's forearm and scrambled up behind her.

The new pairing had barely lifted off when Jael issued orders for the remaining ranks. "The rest of you mingle until everybody is paired. If any dragon horse doesn't respond to the first line of shields, let them choose from the alternates grouped over there."

Toni let out a big breath and dropped her chin to her chest as she walked back to the sideline where Kyle waited.

Kyle grinned. "Tan was hooked the moment that girl confessed to being an orphan. She's a sucker for kids. I'll bet we'll be 'plus one' when this is all over, and looking for a spot to build a family cabin."

Toni's thoughts instantly went to Maya, and her elation at the successful pairing of warriors to shields dissolved. Was Maya even thinking about her? She hoped so, because Maya was always in Toni's thoughts, every moment of every hour.

❖

Maya held her breath and swiped her wrist over the scanner. The indicator flashed red, but rather than loud clanging, soft but persistent chimes sounded throughout the wide foyer when she stepped inside. All eyes turned to her, but none of the believers made a move to intercept or point her out. She made a show of staring at her wrist and thumping it as if something was wrong with her chip that should have scanned, then turned to march purposefully down the hallway to the right as if she knew where she was going. Before she completed her first step, she met a human wall, and a big hand clamped down on her shoulder.

"You have entered the City of Light without proper clearance. You must come with me." The voice was gruff but familiar.

Maya slowly raised her eyes up the huge body inches from her face, and then relief flowed through her when she saw her captor's frowning face. "Emile?" She spoke softly, uncertain of his stern expression and the badge on his chest that said SECURITY.

"You can't just enter anytime you want. The crowds would be too great. If you pass the screening, you'll receive an appointed day and time to worship for a maximum of two hours." He recited the instructions as he steered her down the hallway to left. They made several turns in the maze of hallways and stairs, and then her hopes rose when he opened the door to a large maintenance closet filled with cleaning supplies.

"Emile, I'm so glad to see you," Maya said. "Have you seen my mom? Do you know where I can find her?"

He put his finger to his lips and glanced both ways before closing the closet's door behind them. "You shouldn't be here."

She grabbed his loose shirt in her fists. "I have to find my mother. Where is she?"

He shook his head adamantly. "Everything is messed up."

"How do you mean?"

"This guy Simon, Xavier's boss, is meaner than Xavier. He's using your father and his followers to take over everything."

Maya frowned. "Mom said she could control my father's illness as long as she's with him."

"Xavier figured that out pretty quick and had me lock her in a room on the other side of the temple."

Maya brightened. "You do know where she is."

"There's a guard at her door. Your father's, too."

Something niggled at Maya. Why was Simon keeping her mother

around? Had he discovered her potential? That seemed impossible. "Are you sure Mom's okay? That Simon guy hasn't hurt her, has he?"

Emile shook his head. "He uses her to keep Cyrus calm, then separates them when he needs Cyrus to be crazy. It's like turning on a light switch. He's crazy, then he's not, then he is. Simon told your father that they have control of the world d-net now, so he can broadcast his sermons all over the world."

"How is that even possible?"

"One of those guys they call a spider set it up because Xavier's holding his family hostage and said he'd kill them if the guy didn't do what they want. They plan to flood the web with a d-vid of your father, and while everyone's watching Cyrus rant about The Natural Order, they'll be draining the World Bank and taking control of everything."

"We've got to stop them." This was bigger than getting her mom to safety. Bigger than saving Toni. Maya closed her eyes against the longing that came with every thought of their night together. But if Simon took control of the World Bank, this battle to save The Collective might be lost.

Emile shook his head. "It's too late. The d-vid will air tomorrow. They're just waiting for the spider to get the bank part of it ready." He opened the door a crack and peeked out. "You have to go. You're not safe here without Lieutenant Toni to protect you."

"I can't. I've seen something that's going to happen, Emile." She clutched his sleeve and pleaded with him. "I have to stop it."

He clasped her shoulders and shook her gently, his words a fierce whisper. "If they find you here, they will kill you." He released her and rubbed his hands over his face. "I'd be afraid they'd kill me, too, if you hadn't told me I would grow old with grandchildren."

Maya sank down to sit on an overturned bucket. "Emile, I don't want you hurt because you helped me." She couldn't bring herself to explain that the future she saw could always be altered.

He patted her shoulder. "I'll be fine. You'll be safe here. They just cleaned the floors and won't need these supplies for a few more days. I'll come back for you when it's safe to sneak you out." He shook his finger at her. "You go back to Lieutenant Toni. Your parents will take care of themselves. If they don't—" He shrugged his big shoulders. "Some things are meant to be."

Before she could protest, he stepped out and closed the door behind him. She dropped her head back against the shelf behind her. She was so tired, weary of thinking and exhausted from walking uphill all day. And her heart was sore from missing Toni. She moved her bucket into the shadows in a back corner of the room. She could relax against the adjacent walls and see anyone who might open the door. She slumped against them and closed her eyes, welcoming just a few minutes of rest while she waited for Emile to return.

Chapter Twenty-nine

I don't like it." Jael stood on the porch of the headquarters building and stared up at the stars. "But it's good strategy." She turned and pulled Alyssa to her, wrapping her in a tight embrace and burying her nose in her mate's short, soft hair. Alyssa's natural wave made her hair dip and peak like red flames without gel to stiffen it. Tonight, she smelled like strawberries warmed in the sun. "I don't want anything to happen to you."

"Then you know how I feel every time you fly off to battle." Alyssa's hands were so soft as they cupped Jael's face. "Together, love. We'll do this together. Besides, I'll have my shield with me."

Jael brushed her lips against Alyssa's. She never thought she'd experience such unfathomable love. It was deeper than her bond had been with Specter, stronger than her new bond to Dark Star. All the things that she thought completed her life as a warrior—honor, loyalty, command—paled against what they shared. Alyssa's heart beat in perfect rhythm with hers. Jael brushed the back of her hand along Alyssa's cheek. "Let's go tell them."

The Guard—Kyle, Diego, Raven, Michael, and Tan—rose from their seats around the conference table as Jael and Alyssa entered.

Jael returned their salutes. "Please remain standing." She tilted her head at the sound of footsteps on the porch, then looked around the table. "I've selected a worthy candidate to bring The Guard back to seven." The number, and its multiples, was sacred among The Collective.

Surprise and curiosity flickered over the faces of her team. They all turned at the light knock before Toni stepped into the room.

Toni hesitated when she realized everyone was focused on her. "I'm sorry. I thought you had requested me to come right away." She started to back out of the room. "I must have misunderstood. I'll wait until you're finished."

"You didn't misunderstand, Commander. Please join us." Jael took a few seconds before she began to speak. "Throughout the history of The Guard, we've all been pyros and dragon-bonded. We stand now on the cusp of something greater than our past, and I want you to welcome a new warrior into our ranks."

All eyes swung back to Toni, whose face reddened and jaw sagged.

"Guard." All came to attention at Jael's command. "Discovered by the First Advocate and mentored by the former Second Warrior, Commander Antonia has proven her worth many times in camp and in battle. She's taken efficient command of the quartermaster unit and now also leads the new shield unit so crucial to our next victory. Welcome her now as Primary Shield and Seventh Warrior of The Guard."

All, including Jael, saluted Toni, while Alyssa beamed at the misfit she'd plucked from a manure-shoveling assignment to become a jewel among Jael's command. Toni wordlessly returned their salute, then—after a nudge from Diego—went to the seat Michael held out for her.

"Let's sit." Jael activated the holo-map at the center of the table, and a part of the Rocky Mountain range appeared before them. "We've pinpointed The Natural Order's stronghold, and satellite surveillance confirms a new structure at that location." The map magnified to display the impressive cathedral. "We've also discovered a small transport was, uh, borrowed from the camp and returned a short while ago. Its data bank indicates it carried a passenger to the City of Light, then was sent back empty. If a spy among us took it, they were either stupid or hope to lure us to the location."

Kyle cleared her throat. "I might know who, ah, borrowed the transport."

"No." Toni's hand slapped down on the table. "Maya's message said she was going to her aunt's home, where she'd be safe."

Kyle shook her head. "I just checked with our aunt. Maya isn't there."

Everyone began to talk at once. Then Jael raised her hand for silence.

"We'll assume then that Maya has followed her parents to the City of Light," Jael said. "If she is there, however, she hasn't contacted Laine."

"You've been in touch with my mother?" Kyle asked.

"Yes. We'll get to that in a moment." Jael tapped commands

into the holo master board imbedded in the table. "Michael, you have control."

Michael's fingers flew over the auxiliary controls, and a holo-image of the world appeared before them. "Zack and Sam are tracking the work of The Natural Order's spider. He's set the framework to take control of the web of the d-net." A green web covered the map. "He's also hacked into the World Bank."

Jael picked up Michael's thread. "Cyrus has recorded a d-vid expected to flood the d-net and stop nearly all other digital traffic."

Kyle frowned. "Mother said she could keep father lucid until he's back on his medication."

"She can if she's with him. But Xavier separated them as soon as they reached their destination. Laine said Simon bragged that, as the world watches the d-vid, he will be draining the World Bank of credits," Jael said. "Michael?"

"The pipes to make this happen are nearly complete." Michael tapped a few more commands as he talked. "However, Sam and Zack are going behind their spider and setting traps to disrupt his code when it initiates." Tiny red pinpoints appeared along the green lines of the web.

Jael looked at their new member. "Toni, are our shields ready?"

Toni jerked as if awakened. She'd been quiet since the news of Maya. "We managed a few hours of practice, and after a handful of missteps, all appear well matched and in sync with their warriors."

"Excellent."

"How much time do we have?" Diego asked.

"I've been able to contact Laine several times telepathically, and she's developed a friend there who says Simon's plan launches tomorrow." Jael nodded to Michael, who tapped more commands, and the holo-image of the City of Light temple returned. "Assuming her information is accurate, here's our battle plan."

Twenty minutes later, she finished explaining their strategy and discussing the logistics. Jael sat back in her chair. "It's getting late, and I want everyone to catch at least three hours of sleep before we depart at zero-seven hundred. Any last questions?"

"How's your head?"

Jael smiled at her warrior physician and long-time friend. "Good, Tan. I've learned how Danielle lowered her shields without causing a headache. Even better, I'm enjoying the effortless quiet when I let them up again. I didn't realize until now how taxing it was to constantly shield from the millions of thoughts that bombarded every second of my awareness." Jael started to rise and dismiss her team, but Raven's soft voice stopped her.

"Can you tell us why you let Cyrus and Xavier go? We had both on that rooftop while Furcho was breathing his last."

Jael sank back into her chair. She'd expected this challenge from either Tan or Diego, but not the introspective Raven. The dynamics of The Guard were indeed changing. Tan was less prickly, Diego less gruff, and Michael had found the confidence to contribute more. All met her gaze. Except Kyle. "Kyle? Your team should know. They'll be risking their lives and the lives of their shields."

Kyle nodded and slowly raised her eyes. "She's my mother, but you probably understand better than I do."

Jael felt a swell of reassurance wash over the room, and she smiled inwardly. Alyssa was always softening the hard parts. She'd told Jael earlier that Kyle was struggling with the fact that not one, but both of her parents were somehow at the center of this upheaval. Maybe Maya, too. Jael wouldn't have understood their involvement either, had she not experienced that short joining with The Collective Council before she won her argument to return to the physical world.

"It's complicated and difficult to explain, but I'll do my best." She drummed her fingers on the table to collect her thoughts, then reached for Alyssa's hand. She hadn't shared parts of this with her mate yet. "I've lived many lives before this one. So, during the brief time that I was…absent from the physical world…my ethereal being joined the Council of Elders because I'd completed the apex of my journey."

Alyssa's startled eyes filled with tears. Jael lifted the hand that tightened around hers and kissed it, unmindful of the other warriors in the room. "It's okay. The price I'm paying for my unusual return is actually the very gift I begged for…a reset so that every time you reincarnate, so will I." She turned back to The Guard. "That joining with the Elders briefly opened a new dimension of understanding."

Brows knitted around the table.

Can you be more specific, love? Dumb it down to our dimension of understanding?

Jael smiled at Alyssa. *Let me try again.* She cleared her throat.

"Kyle has always felt her mother was more than just a healer, but my ethereal experience revealed to me what Kyle only suspected. Laine is born from the oldest, purest bloodline still existing and has been suppressing a powerful and unique gift because she longed to be only a wife and mother. She feels that her reluctance caused this threat to The Collective. Regardless of whether that's true or if the sequence of events was always meant to unfold this way, she is ready to fulfill her destiny. She feels that going with Cyrus and Xavier to the City of Light will open the door for what must happen. She shared that belief telepathically with Kyle and me on that rooftop." Jael gave Kyle a rueful smile.

"But you are First Warrior. Shouldn't it have been your decision?" Raven obviously wasn't satisfied. "You command all in this physical world."

"I did. But Laine's gift, her knowledge, and now her authority exceed mine. She is The Listener. She hears and understands every voice. She's more than a healer. She can absorb and magnify the gifts of anyone in her presence. She will lead The Collective to a new, higher understanding."

Realization dawned in Michael's eyes. "When you spoke in Furcho's voice—"

"Laine tapped into my telepathic connection with Furcho and turned me into a conduit so he could speak directly to Nicole." Jael stood. "There's nothing more I can explain, except that our objective has changed. Cyrus is not the deadly threat we first thought. Simon and Xavier are now our primary targets."

The others rose, too, and saluted their First Warrior.

"Zero-seven hundred is launch." Jael's return salute dismissed them until then.

The loud ringing of old-fashioned church bells woke Maya with a start. Stars. How long had she been sleeping? It was impossible to tell in a room with no windows. She wished she had the wrist IC her father had confiscated when he'd taken her from her aunt's house at the beginning of this nightmare. It couldn't have been long because Emile hadn't returned for her. She shifted uncomfortably on her bucket. She really needed to pee. She groaned as she stood and straightened from her hunched position. She was thirsty, too. How could she both be thirsty and need to pee at the same time? She shook the random thoughts from her head and grabbed the bucket and a mop for a cover story, then opened the door. A man hurried past without a glance her way, but she nearly collided with a woman when she stepped out.

"Oh, I'm sorry, dear," the woman said. "I was rushing to get a good seat."

"I should apologize for stepping in front of you," Maya said, returning the woman's friendly smile. She held up the mop and bucket. "They sent me to mop up a toilet overflow. I'm sure I'm in the right area, but this maze of hallways is so confusing that I can't find the personal facility."

"You're almost there." The woman pointed back the way she came. "Go left at that first hallway, and it's the first door on your left. If you hurry your mop-up, you can still find a seat open for the morning service in the top balcony. The balcony stairs are the first door on the right, if you turn right instead of left. You don't want to miss the sight when the morning sun gets high enough to shine through those crystal walls. The rainbow of colors is a glorious tribute to The One."

"Thank you so much," Maya said over her shoulder as she hurried away.

Seconds later, Maya closed her eyes to savor the relief as her bladder emptied. Almost immediately, she opened them again. Morning service? Sun rising? Had she slept all night? Where was Emile? How would she find her mother without him? Think, think. Maybe her mother would be in the morning service. If so, the balcony would be perfect for spotting her.

❖

Alyssa pulled the hood of her cape to cover her ears from the morning chill and rubbed her wrist. The security chip Sam had embedded there itched. She thrust her hands back into the pockets of the cape and fingered the soft swatch of T-shirt Toni had provided. Yes, she could feel Maya inside—anxious, but determined. What was she up to? Alyssa's empathic gift had grown tremendously, but she wished now that she was also telepathic. Reading emotions revealed only so much.

"The mountain air does have a bite," Fifth said.

Alyssa turned to her shield, who was behind her in the long line of believers. "I should have brought my gloves."

"You'll warm up once we're inside," he said.

"We'll miss services if they don't hurry this line," the woman in front of Alyssa complained. "There's not usually a security guard. You just swipe your wrist and enter."

This was both good and bad news to Alyssa. The increased security was a good indication they were right about Simon making his move today. But the guard was wearing IC glasses and likely using a face-recognition program.

Jael?

Sam's on it. The guard's IC will tell him you're a seamstress from a small town and Fifth is your brother.

When her turn came, she pushed back her hood and smiled as she looked directly into the guard's eyes and filled him with indifference.

"Next," he said.

The warrior in Jael rose with the warm Southern airstream the dragon-horse army was riding high above the mountains. War was a beast with sharp, cruel teeth, but Jael was born for battle. She savored the adrenaline rush of pitting mind and body against an adversary. It had always heated her blood and pumped her heart like nothing else. Until now. Until Alyssa. This battle was different, likely her last and definitely a stepping stone rather than her goal. That knowledge filled her with something else. Anticipation. Joy. A new life with her mate and, hopefully, children. Her senses sharpened as her warrior took control. Today, she'd cut down the last hurdles—Simon and Xavier—standing between her and that new beginning.

Maya pushed open the balcony's door and stepped directly into her horrible vision. Sunlight glowed through the crystal walls to reflect off the soft gold of the podium at the center of a broad platform of glass cubes at the front. The dais was still empty, but believers were filling the pews below. *For the love of stars, no. It's too soon.* Maya wasn't ready. She pushed past those pouring into the balcony and crowding the stairway to claim the last seats. But when she emerged in the hallway below, she froze. Which way? She closed her eyes and took a deep breath. In her vision, her mother had been brought in from the left. She opened her eyes and ran.

❖

Sun glinted off the crystal cathedral at the apex of the City of Light, bathing the buildings that ringed it one tier below and the rest of the mountain in a rainbow of refracted light. Jael took quick inventory her warriors. Sunfire, with Haley seated in front of Kyle, glided smoothly a wingspan from Dark Star's right flank. She was shadowed by a warrior assigned to watch her back when they split up and descended. Toni rode behind Jael, and their backdoor warrior trailed on their left.

Flying slightly behind and below them, teams two and three flew in V-formation. Tan, with Michael as her second should she fall, led one group of five warriors. Diego commanded another five, with Raven as his second.

Each pyro warrior, Guard included, wore a wide leather belt with quick-release couplings positioned on the left and right that connected them to similar belts worn by their shield warriors. Some shields rode in front of their pyro and others behind, depending on each team's preference.

Jael looked to Kyle, who had the only long-distance communicator in her ear. Kyle held her thumb up to confirm all were ready. Jael nodded and broadcast to The Guard.

Alyssa says security is tight, but they won't be watching skyward in the daylight. Remind your warriors their mission is to destroy weapons and only incinerate those soldiers taking aggressive action toward us or innocents. I want loss of life held to a minimum.

She listened as each of them confirmed her orders. Tan and Diego repeated them to their groups via their short-range communicators, then awaited Jael's command. One more check, a private communication to the remaining member of Jael's first team.

Ready, First Advocate?

No sign of our targets yet. The holo-vid Cyrus recorded just started, but everything else is quiet here.

Keep your head down. When we strike their armaments, expect that to change fast.

A pause. *Be safe. I love you, my warrior.*

And I, you, my heart. First team will await your signal.

It was time.

Teams two and three, engage.

CHAPTER THIRTY

Maya ran blindly down one corridor, then the next, only to find herself at a dead end with a locked door. This hadn't been in her vision. She must have passed the cathedral entrance she sought. Time was short. She tried to mentally retrace the turns she'd taken. She must stop the next sequence of events. If she couldn't locate her mother for help, the unimaginable would happen—Toni would die. Maya's heart nearly burst at the thought. She had recognized their soul bond, as she was sure Toni had. It was new in this life, but a bond forged over previous lifetimes. Maya turned and ran back the way she came. She rounded left at the first corner and smacked into her father.

"Father. Thank the stars I found you."

The man who glared at her, however, wasn't the benevolent father of her childhood. "Seize her."

Four black metal bunkers, confirmed by Zack to house generators large enough to power laser cannons, hunkered just outside the city's north, south, east, and west walls. Flying in perfect formation, the two teams led by Tan and Diego arrowed downward, then split into four to simultaneously attack the bunkers. Tan, Diego, Raven, and Michael— each accompanied by their next-best pyros—hovered beside the bunkers, while the remaining warriors dealt with laser rifle fire as The Natural Order soldiers scrambled a frantic defense. When the top panels of the bunkers began to slide back, both warriors and dragons drowned the exposed machinery in metal-melting flame. They destroyed the cannons before they cleared their covers.

Jael's group circled and watched. Everything was going as planned with the exception of one disturbing detail. Laine wasn't responding to Jael's mental queries.

❖

"Despite the heresy taught us as children and The Collective forces that seek to extinguish our light, we remain strong," Cyrus's holo-image declared. "And with the power of The One among us, we will rid our world of these heretics and throw open our doors to spread the word of The One to every person deserving his salvation." The holo-image seemed to assess the pews of believers. "Our journey has been difficult and our sacrifices great. Now, The One's chosen people will be sheltered, fed, and protected from those who do not honor him and live according to The Natural Order."

Two armed guards, not holo-images, entered from a door to the right of the dais. They each shouldered an arm of the limp figure they dragged between them.

Jael, I found Laine. She appears to be drugged.

Alyssa could feel the uncertainty of the believers who shifted in the pews, but she sensed righteous judgment from many more.

Laine's head lolled from side to side, her eyes open but unfocused as the guards propped her tall frame against a huge white X erected against the back wall of the dais. They secured her with a rope across her chest and more restraining her extended arms and legs.

Laine's dulled emotions were faint when Alyssa probed, but then something strong and sudden grabbed hold. Alyssa gasped. She fought the invasion, then remembered what Jael had said about Laine's gift. She opened to a peaceful warmth and let it flow through her and out. It was searching for something…someone. Cyrus. Alyssa clutched the cloth remnant in her pocket. Yes. Maya was with him.

The holo-image continued. "An early disciple of The One long ago stated that a prophet is not accepted in his own hometown. This week, I've learned that I have not been accepted in my own home, by the family of my past. My wife and the children she bore me all have betrayed The One to take the wide road filled by The Collective sinners." The eyes of the holo-image grew hard. "The One teaches that if your right hand offends you, cut it off and cast it away. As difficult as this is, I have cut ties with my wife and given her over to our board of disciples for judgment. If she cannot see His light after thirty days of fasting, the elders will attempt to flog the demon from her. If that fails, she'll be cut from our numbers." The image paused for effect.

"What does that mean," Fifth whispered. "He would let them beat and maybe kill his own wife?"

"You can't starve a demon. Flog her now or she'll be lost," one man shouted. A mixed chorus followed the declaration—gasps of surprise amid nods of agreement. More began to call for Laine's flogging but quieted when the holo-image of Cyrus stuttered and froze. A bent, near-skeleton of a man in an expensive business suit stepped onto the platform.

Simon. Is. Here.

The city seemed to vomit armed soldiers and a steady stream of fleeing believers onto the mountainside. The scene was both horrible carnage and a beautiful dance.

The shield warriors were fierce and exacting. Few blue beams escaped them, and those only singed a tail or grazed and barely penetrated a battleskin. Emboldened by this new armor, the dragon horses swooped and darted like giant, deadly hummingbirds. Their fire turned groups of soldiers into ash while the pyro warriors picked off individuals who brazenly fired from among groups of women and children. When the flow of innocents thinned, the shields began to ricochet the laser beams back at the soldiers rather than skyward, eliminating nearly as many as the pyro warriors. Some threw down their weapons to flee with the women and children.

Simon. Is. Here.

Alyssa? Jael's heart jumped at the strain in her beloved's announcement.

Busy. Come now.

Dark Star was already diving toward the cathedral.

"First team, engage." Kyle's order was unnecessary because it came seconds after she and their backdoors arrowed downward in pursuit of the First Warrior. "Shades," she shouted into her com. "Don't forget your shades."

"Prophet, listen to her. She will tell you the same that I have."

Maya's dying hope bloomed again. She'd been so focused on Cyrus, she'd failed to see that Emile was the only guard with her father.

"Tell him," Emile said. "Tell him everything."

"A demon controls her, just like her mother and sister. I can trust nothing she says," Cyrus said.

Maya would not be dissuaded. "Simon is not a disciple of The Natural Order. He and Xavier are driven by greed, not faith. They're conspiring to take control of everything."

Cyrus's hands went to his temples as though a sudden pain had struck him. "No. Simon is difficult but not a traitor."

A group of armed soldiers ran past them. Sun and stars. It had begun.

"Listen to me. They've hired a spider to drain all credits from the World Bank while your d-vid is broadcasting. When Simon has possession of the economy, The Natural Order and the rest of the world will be at his mercy."

Emile grabbed one of the soldiers who, along with a swarm of believers, had begun to fill the hall. "What's happening?"

The young soldier's eyes were wild and his face pale. "We're under siege, man. Grab your rifle. Those winged demons are flying in broad daylight."

Emile released him and put out a hand to steady Cyrus when he swayed. Cyrus dropped his hands, his expression soft now, but his eyes filled with confusion. "Maya? Where's Laine? Where's your mother?"

Maya shared a look of relief with Emile. "She's in the cathedral, and that evil bastard Simon is going to hurt her if we don't get there fast."

Cyrus shook his head and frowned at her. "You shouldn't use that kind of language."

His admonishment was familiar from her childhood. This man was her father, not The Prophet. "I'll wash my mouth out later, Dad. We have to hurry." She grasped one elbow and Emile the other to hurry Cyrus along. She could only hope they weren't too late.

❖

Alyssa had barely recognized Simon when he stepped onto the platform. Dark, sunken eyes stared balefully at the believers. They whispered to each other, and those sitting near the exits were slipping out in increasing numbers.

His gleeful cackle rang out. "Run if you want, but you can't escape. Every second that ticks by, I own more of you—your job, your home, your food, and your very existence. All the credits held in the World Bank are flowing into my personal accounts right now. There's no man in the sky. Your own fears and greed have duped you. I am Simon, not a god but human, and I control your fate."

Alyssa winced at the dark emotions flowing from him, but the panic growing among the believers alarmed her more. She gathered her reserves, then felt her own gift buoyed by Laine. *Calm, everything will be okay. You're safe here.* The crowd quieted as she radiated reassurances, until Cyrus burst in from a door on her left with Maya following.

"Laine, no." Cyrus stopped and pointed to Simon. "Guards, arrest that man." He turned to the believers. "That was not me on the d-vid. Don't listen to it."

"Shoot him," Simon said to the guards.

They both raised their rifles, but Emile sprang from the doorway behind them, tackling both to the floor. He grabbed one of their rifles and used it to knock both unconscious, then twisted to untie the bindings around Laine's legs. Another guard appeared and slammed the butt of his rifle against Emile's head. The big man went down, and the guard shoved his body off the platform. Cyrus surged forward, his eyes fixed on Laine, as pandemonium erupted.

Armed soldiers appeared to block each exit, and Alyssa struggled to quell the terror of the believers, but she was one against thousands. Laine's support had waned when her focus shifted to her husband.

A little help, Jael.

A quick movement drew Maya's eyes from her father. Another soldier was taking aim at Cyrus. "Dad!"

Cyrus ducked the blast, but an arm wrapped around Maya's throat and tightened.

"Did you think you could escape before I got my taste of you?" Xavier's breath was hot, his oily voice close to her ear.

Maya kicked at his knees, stomped his feet, and tried to elbow him without success. She couldn't breathe. She clawed at his arm and gulped air when he loosened his hold and tossed her to one of his guards to restrain.

"Don't pass out on me yet, green eyes. I want you to watch this."

"No. Please."

The guard's arm tightened around her neck this time, choking off her plea as Xavier raised his weapon. Just as Cyrus leapt onto the dais, the blue beam found its mark between his shoulders. Unable to draw sufficient breath, Maya could hear her scream only in her head, reverberating in her heart. The man who staggered a few more steps and fell at Laine's feet was not The Prophet. He was the gentle father who'd held her on his knee when she was a child and wiped her tears when her first visions frightened her. She'd failed. The air was too hot and the arm around her neck too tight. Her vision filled with a rainbow of colors, then faded to black.

❖

"Fireballs." Alyssa admonished herself and dug into her pocket. "Shades," she said, prompting Fifth.

Even with the protection, they both turned away from the wall that was a brilliant prism of Sunfire's projected light. Large sections of the crystal walls at opposite sides of the cathedral were melting, dripping into growing puddles of hot, liquid glass. Xavier and his guards backed away, one dragging an unconscious Maya by her hair. Frantic believers crawled over pews and each other to reach exits, only to have the soldiers pouring in push them aside. After impatient soldiers cut down a few, the rest fell to the floor or hid between the pews. Mothers tried to cover children, and fathers tried to shield entire families.

"Sorry, sorry. Keep your head down," Alyssa said as she crawled between and over them. A teen with terror-filled eyes crouched between two pews with four crying toddlers clinging to her. Alyssa whipped off her cloak and threw it over them. "Stay down and close your eyes. The dragon warriors are the good guys. They won't hurt you, but there will be a very bright light that might hurt your eyes."

She worked her way toward the melting wall on the left, Fifth right behind her. The guard dragging Maya turned her way and stared. Dung. Too late, she realized he was looking at their shades. He lifted his rifle and fired, but Fifth expertly deflected the blast to pick off the guard on the other side of Xavier. A blinding white light flashed through the room from behind them, and then a huge hole opened in the wall before them. Dark Star, wings tucked, sprang through the opening.

❖

Even with the shades, Toni had to blink away the spots before her eyes. In that half second that passed before she could see again, she felt for and thumbed the quick releases that tied her to Jael. Click, click, and she was sliding down Dark Star's broad flank, her feet in motion before she touched the floor. Soldiers and believers who hadn't been protected by pews stumbled about, temporarily blinded. Maya lay sprawled on the hard marble floor, limp and unresponsive even though she was being dragged by her long hair still clutched in the hand of the stunned guard as he staggered backward.

Jael's flame shot past Toni to swallow the guard, and she threw out her shield as she ran to protect Maya from it. Then she fell to her knees and tried to untangle the guard's burning fingers from Maya's hair. With one hand up to hold her shield, her attempt was futile.

"Toni, oh stars." Alyssa knelt next to her. "Is she okay?"

Toni shook her head. "Don't know." She blinked rapidly to clear the tears impeding her vision.

"I've got it." Fifth knelt, a long razor in his hand, and cut Maya free in one quick slash. "Just don't tell her I'm responsible for her new look," he said, kicking the guard's carcass away, then standing to replace Toni's shield with his.

Victorious outside, the warriors and their shields had joined the melee. Some battled the soldiers who fired wildly as their sight began to return. Others herded the trapped believers to safety. Still more soldiers replaced the departing believers.

Jael joined them, hurling fireballs around Fifth's shield. "Need some help?"

Toni shook her head stubbornly and gathered Maya in her arms.

"Toni?" Maya was coming around.

"I'm here, babe."

Just as they reached Dark Star, five soldiers emerged from the door next to the dais where Laine was still restrained. Jael whirled, her flame joining Dark Star's, and the soldiers were instantly lumps of smoking flesh and bone. Jael cursed. "Son of a dung-eater. They're like gnats. They just keep coming,"

Toni was only half listening as she fastened her belt around Maya's waist.

"What are you doing?" Maya was sounding stronger as the seconds ticked by.

"Got to get you some place safe."

"We have to help Mom."

"Leave that to us," Jael said, as she lifted Alyssa onto Dark Star.

Toni looked up. It was a tight fit, but Fifth was fastening Jael's belt around his waist.

"Is she alert enough to ride behind Fifth?" Jael asked. *I need you with me. Fifth goes where Alyssa goes. He'll keep Maya safe, too.*

"She'll be fine with them clipped together," Toni said.

Fifth eyed Dark Star. "You sure he can carry three of us? I'm pretty heavy."

Dark Star snorted.

"Don't insult him," Jael said.

Fifth shrugged and leapt up behind Alyssa, but Maya clung to Toni. "No. You have to come with me to change my vision."

Toni took Maya's face in her hands and kissed her. "Only two things can never change, Maya. I will always love you, and I will never shirk my duty."

Fifth offered his arm to pull Maya up as Toni lifted her. They clipped her belt to his, but Maya, tears streaming down her cheeks, reached for Toni one last time. "I love you, too."

"Shield."

Toni whirled at Kyle's shouted command and thrust forward a full shield. But this was no laser rifle. The blast came from a husky soldier with a mobile laser cannon on his shoulder. The wide beam slammed Toni against the wall at her back. Her last conscious seconds were filled with Maya's scream, the realization Laine was directly in the path of the deflected beam, and Jael's shout. "Dark Star, aloft."

CHAPTER THIRTY-ONE

Kyle was powerless to stop the cannon beam that hit her mother, but she wouldn't watch her burn. She turned, her fury extending flames from each hand like blue-white swords, and cut down soldier after soldier until she realized those remaining had thrown down their weapons and fallen to their knees, their heads bowed.

Kyle's chest heaved from anger and exertion. She retracted her flame. She wouldn't incinerate unarmed men, no matter their crimes. The rest of The Guard had joined her to survey the carnage, when a whirring noise drew their attention to the balcony. Its back wall was retracting to expose a laser cannon as large as those in the bunkers outside. It whined as it powered up to fire.

"Ah. The gang's all here," Xavier crowed from behind the cannon. "I can finish this in one sweep." A light on the cannon turned green. It had reached full power.

"The time for war has passed. Take up your weapons again only to throw them upon a purifying pyre."

Kyle turned slowly toward the familiar voice. Had battle released in her the same mental delusions that plagued her father?

Laine, still glowing from the laser beam she'd absorbed, stepped down from the dais and walked past them to confront Xavier. Nicole appeared at a side entrance and joined Laine. The twins who followed Nicole took up position on either side of the two women. When Laine took Nicole's hand and pressed her lips to Nicole's forehead, her Advocate tattoo glowed blue, then duplicated on both sides of Laine's face before she withdrew.

Nicole's voice rang out, pure and strong. "Behold The Listener. She hears all who come to her. She accepts the mantle of Prime Advocate to lead this world into a new era of peace and better understanding."

Xavier laughed. "I'm not afraid of your simple magic."

Kyle stepped forward, but Jael's hand on her arm stopped her. Had the First Warrior gone mad? She hadn't lifted a finger or palmed a fireball to take Xavier out. In the second that Kyle hesitated, a blue beam as thick as a man's arm shot from the cannon. "Mom!"

The twins calmly raised their hands and reflected the beam back at its source. Transfixed, Kyle watched Xavier's jaw drop in disbelief a nanosecond before the balcony exploded into flame, and his scream died before it could fully form. All went quiet except for the crackle and pop of the fire.

We're still transmitting directly to the net. Kyle jerked at Zack's telepathed message, then realized from the others' reaction that he'd broadcast to all of them. Nicole and Jael knelt like the humbled soldiers, and then Kyle and the rest followed suit.

Laine lifted her hands, palms up, and addressed all who watched from around the world. "The Collective has long embraced diversity—all colors of skin, all genders, all orientations, and all customs of all regions. We congratulated ourselves when lines drawn between regions were erased and individual nations merged to form a world government that distributed food, health care, the arts, and education equally. But if we truly embrace our differences, we also must accept diversity of thought and faith. All should be free to live and to believe as they wish, as long as they bring no harm or judgment to others." She raised her arms higher, her Advocate marks glowing with her next declaration.

"Hear and know this one absolute truth. There is but one rule for all. Treat and respect others as you would have others treat and respect you."

CHAPTER THIRTY-TWO

*A*nd we're out. Wow. That's one transmission the world won't forget. Movie to come later.

Kyle growled at Zack's irreverent joke. Nicole was tugging Laine back to the dais, urging her to come help Emile, and their warriors began to organize the soldiers to remove their dead and wounded from the cathedral. But this war wasn't over yet. Simon's body was not among the carnage.

I last heard him in the office above us.

Jael, in a break from telepath protocol, was reading her thoughts, but Kyle didn't care. She followed Jael into a hall that dead-ended at a locked stairwell door.

Jael stepped back. "This needs your fine touch," she said.

Kyle formed a hot flame as thin as a laser to slice through the metal lock. Then she pulled the door open and held it for Jael to enter first. They climbed the stairs slowly but met no guards or traps they would have expected to protect the entrance to Simon's lair. Jael paused when they reached the top, tilted her head as though listening, then shook it and opened the unlocked door.

A man with a smoking laser wound in the middle of his forehead above vacant, unseeing eyes sat crumped in front of a huge desk. Simon's frail, lifeless body slumped forward in the padded-leather chair to sprawl, arms outstretched, across the desk. His bionic hand clutched an empty hypo-spray injector. Two large monitors displayed several bank accounts with zero balances.

Kyle cleared her throat. "I'm betting that this guy was his spider, and Simon executed him when their plan to drain the world bank failed." She was surprised as she studied the slack face of the man who'd used her father and tried at different times to kill her and her mother. She felt nothing. No satisfaction that he was dead. No regret that he'd robbed her of the chance to incinerate him for his crimes against humanity.

"You okay?" Jael asked quietly.

Kyle nodded. "For all he did wrong, he did one thing right. He opened our righteous eyes. Mom—" Kyle smiled. "The Prime Advocate is right. Diversity is the core of The Collective thought. But if we truly believe in its principles, we have to also respect and accept that others have the right to believe differently, as long as their beliefs don't hurt others."

Jael smiled and saluted Kyle. "Thank the stars. I was afraid I wouldn't be able to retire, but you'll be an even better First Warrior than me." She waved her hand at the bodies. "We'll send someone else to haul these out of here."

Kyle didn't follow as Jael headed for the door. "Wait. First Warrior? I've been Second Warrior less than two weeks. Doesn't someone else have to decide this? You don't get to appoint your own successor, do you? Besides, I never said I wanted to be First Warrior."

Jael's laughter echoed in the stairwell as Kyle sprinted to catch up.

❖

Toni slipped into the shower and smoothed her hands down Maya's soapy ribs to grasp her hips. Maya hummed when Toni's naked flesh and hard nipples pressed against her back.

"You're supposed to be resting in bed."

"I can't rest without you in bed with me."

"You won't rest if I'm in bed with you."

Toni brushed off the correction and nibbled the delicious curve of Maya's neck. "Semantics."

"Tan said you should limit activity until your head has time to heal. You suffered a major concussion."

"I'm fine."

Maya turned in her arms, her eyes pleading. "Please don't be casual about this." Her throat worked to choke out her next words. "I thought I'd lost you. I'd seen you slam against that wall in my vision, and I was sure the blow killed you."

Toni kissed away the tears on her lover's cheeks. "I am being serious, baby. I consulted with your mom, and she pronounced me healed. She cleared me for, um, all duty."

Maya laughed despite her tears. "You did not ask my mother for permission to bed her daughter."

Toni scoffed. "Of course not." She brushed her lips against Maya's, then tightened their embrace and deepened their kiss. She poured every ounce of her devotion into a slow, thorough tease of her tongue against Maya's. Then she withdrew to rest her forehead against Maya's. "I asked her for permission to bond with you."

Maya's breath hitched, and she leaned back to stare at Toni. If she was reading Maya right, her eyes reflected surprise, then joy. "You want to bond with me?"

Toni peppered little kisses across Maya's face, down her neck, and back up to her lips. "That shouldn't surprise you. We've probably done it a few times in previous lives." She stopped, holding Maya's gaze. "I want to go to bed with you every night and wake up every morning with you."

"And have children?"

Toni cleared her throat when it tightened. Children? She hadn't thought about it, and she knew nothing about raising a kid. "We can talk about it if you're willing do the pregnancy part," she said slowly, kissing along Maya's collarbone so she couldn't see the terror in Toni's eyes. Though parenthood scared her, she'd never be able to deny Maya any request, unless she wanted Toni to carry a child for them. Nope. No way. That one thing was absolutely nonnegotiable.

"Yes."

Toni looked up, surprised. "Yes?"

"Yes. I'll bond with you." Maya switched off the shower and pushed Toni toward the air dryer. "But we can talk about that later. Since Mom cleared you for action, I have other things on my mind first."

"Lucky me."

EPILOGUE

Jael slipped out onto the porch and joined her old friend on the steps. His eyes were closed as he soaked up the sun's warmth. They didn't speak for a while, just listened to the laughter coming from inside the house, the patter of running feet and squeals of a child being chased.

At last, Han spoke. "All is as it should be."

Jael smiled. "Yes. This warrior has at last found peace…in my heart and in the quiet of Danielle's thick skull." She chuckled and rapped her knuckles against her head.

The door creaked as it opened and closed behind them.

"And an Advocate has taken up her mantle," Alyssa said, settling between Jael's long legs so she could use her mate for a backrest. "Laine has agreed to indefinitely suspend my duties as First Advocate." Alyssa turned to Han, her hand going to the Advocate's tattoo that ran up the left side of her face from neck to temple. "I'll always be an Advocate and available if she needs me, but I'm going to be very busy with other things in about three months."

Jael smoothed her hand over her mate's bulging belly. "We're both going to be busy."

Han smiled. "Twins are actually triple the work. Are you ready, First Warrior?"

"Ah, First Warrior, retired. I'll still help train the new pyros, but I've passed the title to Kyle." She shrugged. "It's not much of a job now anyway. Toni and Michael keep the camp humming."

Kyle and Tan were leaving the next day for the Second Continent, where Tan would introduce doctors to new surgical techniques while Kyle worked with villagers to update their agriculture machinery and growing methods. Diego and Raven had returned to their home regions, where they settled back into patrolling as they did before the Calling.

The only difference was that their shield warriors went with them. Diego adopted his young shield as his daughter, and Alyssa insisted that more than a warrior bond existed between Raven and her shield.

Jael kissed the top of Alyssa's head. "I'm more than ready to spend the rest of my days bouncing babies, then grandchildren on my knees."

"You should talk with Toni," Alyssa said absently.

"About what?"

"Maya's ready for kids, but the thought of parenting terrifies Toni."

More squeals came from the house, followed by a crash.

"Perhaps her fear is not unfounded," Han said.

Alyssa twisted to peer around Jael. "Should we check to see if that's anything serious?"

Jael laughed. "Nah. It's probably just Skyler climbing the rafters again. Last week, Kyle caught her clinging to the tip of Sunfire's wing while she flapped it up and down."

Skyler burst through the door, surprisingly fast and coordinated for an eighteen-month-old, with Nicole in pursuit. Jael grabbed the tot in the air when she launched herself off the top stair. "Whoa, there. No flying without a dragon horse."

"Dragon pony," Skyler chortled.

Nicole plucked her wayward child from Jael's grasp. "Thank you. I swear, it takes a village to keep track of this one. If I didn't have the twins to help me, I don't know what I'd do."

"Need me to fly you down the mountain?" Jael asked.

"No. Emile is coming to...oh, there he is now." Nicole yelled into the house. "Come on, guys. Emile's here."

Ten minutes later, all were piled in Emile's transport and headed down to the Advocate-sponsored school for elementary grades, where they all were teachers and volunteers at the local medical facility.

The quiet was deafening in the wake of their clamor.

Han extended his hands, their smooth movement matching the sway of the wildflowers in the meadow before them. "Feel the earth's rhythm. She is at peace again." He stood and stretched. "Will you join me?" He walked into the meadow without waiting for a reply.

Jael and Alyssa followed and bowed to their long-time sensei when he faced them. Han accepted their respect, then turned away. The three of them stood motionless for a moment, finding the flow and ebb of the earth, its tides, pull of the moon, warmth of the sun, and the strength of The Collective. Then silently, in perfect sync, they began the eighty-eight flowing movements.

About the Author

D. Jackson Leigh grew up barefoot and happy, swimming in farm ponds and riding rude ponies in rural south Georgia. She is a career journalist but has found her real passion in writing sultry lesbian romances laced with her trademark Southern humor and affection for horses.

She has published ten novels and one collection of short stories with Bold Strokes Books, winning a 2010 Alice B. Lavender Award for Noteworthy Accomplishment, and three Golden Crown Literary Society awards in paranormal, romance, and fantasy categories. She also was a finalist for two more GCLS awards and a finalist in the romance category of the 2014 Lambda Literary Society Awards.

Friend her at facebook.com/d.jackson.leigh, on twitter @djacksonleigh, or learn more about her at www.djacksonleigh.com.

Books Available From Bold Strokes Books

Between Sand and Stardust by Tina Michele. Are the lifelong bonds of love strong enough to conquer time, distance, and heartache when Haven Thorne and Willa Bennette are given another chance at forever? (978-1-62639-940-2)

Charming the Vicar by Jenny Frame. When magician and atheist Finn Kane seeks refuge in an English village after a spiritual crisis, can local vicar Bridget Claremont restore her faith in life and love? (978-1-63555-029-0)

Data Capture by Jesse J. Thoma. Lola Walker is undercover on the hunt for cybercriminals while trying not to notice the woman who might be perfectly wrong for her for all the right reasons. (978-1-62639-985-3)

Epicurean Delights by Renee Roman. Ariana Marks had no idea a leisure swim would lead to being rescued, in more ways than one, by the charismatic Hudson Frost. (978-1-63555-100-6)

Heart of the Devil by Ali Vali. We know most of Cain and Emma Casey's story, but Heart of the Devil will take you back to where it began one fateful night with a tray loaded with beer. (978-1-63555-045-0)

Known Threat by Kara A. McLeod. When Special Agent Ryan O'Connor reluctantly questions who protects the Secret Service, she learns courage truly is found in unlikely places. Agent O'Connor Series #3 (978-1-63555-132-7)

Seer and the Shield by D. Jackson Leigh. Time is running out for the Dragon Horse Army while two unlikely heroines struggle to put aside their attraction and find a way to stop a deadly cult. Dragon Horse War, Book 3 (978-1-63555-170-9)

The Universe Between Us by Jane C. Esther. Ana Mitchell must make the hardest choice of her life: the promise of new love Jolie Dann on Earth, or a humanity-saving mission to colonize Mars. (978-1-63555-106-8)

Touch by Kris Bryant. Can one touch heal a heart? (978-1-63555-084-9)

A More Perfect Union by Carsen Taite. Major Zoey Granger and DC fixer Rook Daniels risk their reputations for a chance at true love while dealing with a scandal that threatens to rock the military. (978-1-62639-754-5)

Arrival by Gun Brooke. The spaceship *Pathfinder* reaches its passengers' new homeworld where danger lurks in the shadows while Pamas Seclan disembarks and finds unexpected love in young science genius Darmiya Do Voy. (978-1-62639-859-7)

Captain's Choice by VK Powell. Architect Kerstin Anthony's life is going to plan until Bennett Carlyle, the first girl she ever kissed, is assigned to her latest and most important project, a police district substation. (978-1-62639-997-6)

Falling Into Her by Erin Zak. Pam Phillips, widow at the age of forty, meets Kathryn Hawthorne, local Chicago celebrity, and it changes her life forever—in ways she hadn't even considered possible. (978-1-63555-092-4)

Hookin' Up by MJ Williamz. Will Leah get what she needs from casual hookups or will she see the love she desires right in front of her? (978-1-63555-051-1)

King of Thieves by Shea Godfrey. When art thief Casey Marinos meets bounty hunter Finnegan Starkweather, the crimes of the past just might set the stage for a payoff worth more than she ever dreamed possible. (978-1-63555-007-8)

Lucy's Chance by Jackie D. As a serial killer haunts the streets, Lucy tries to stitch up old wounds with her first love in the wake of a small town's rapid descent into chaos. (978-1-63555-027-6)

Right Here, Right Now by Georgia Beers. When Alicia Wright moves into the office next door to Lacey Chamberlain's accounting firm, Lacey is about to find out that sometimes the last person you want is exactly the person you need. (978-1-63555-154-9)

Strictly Need to Know by MB Austin. Covert operator Maji Rios will do whatever she must to complete her mission, but saving a gorgeous stranger from Russian mobsters was not in her plans. (978-1-63555-114-3)

Tailor-Made by Yolanda Wallace. Tailor Grace Henderson doesn't date clients, but when she meets gender-bending model Dakota Lane, she's tempted to throw all the rules out the window. (978-1-63555-081-8)

Time Will Tell by M. Ullrich. With the ability to time travel, Eva Caldwell will have to decide between having it all and erasing it all. (978-1-63555-088-7)

Change in Time by Robyn Nyx. Working in the past is hell on your future. The Extractor series: Book Two. (978-1-62639-880-1)

Love After Hours by Radclyffe. When Gina Antonelli agrees to renovate Carrie Longmire's new house, she doesn't welcome Carrie's overtures at friendship or her own unexpected attraction. A Rivers Community Novel. (978-1-63555-090-0)

Nantucket Rose by CF Frizzell. Maggie Jordan can't wait to convert a historic Nantucket home into a B&B, but doesn't expect to fall for mariner Ellis Chilton, who has more claim to the house than Maggie realizes. (978-1-63555-056-6)

Picture Perfect by Lisa Moreau. Falling in love wasn't supposed to be part of the stakes for Olive and Gabby, rival photographers in the competition of a lifetime. (978-1-62639-975-4)

Set the Stage by Karis Walsh. Actress Emilie Danvers takes the stage again in Ashland, Oregon, little realizing that landscaper Arden Philips is about to offer her a very personal romantic lead role. (978-1-63555-087-0)

Strike a Match by Fiona Riley. When their attempts at matchmaking fizzle out, firefighter Sasha and reluctant millionairess Abby find themselves turning to each other to strike a perfect match. (978-1-62639-999-0)

The Price of Cash by Ashley Bartlett. Cash Braddock is doing her best to keep her business afloat, stay out of jail, and avoid Detective Kallen. It's not working. (978-1-62639-708-8)

Captured Soul by Laydin Michaels. Can Kadence Munroe save the woman she loves from a twisted killer, or will she lose her to a collector of souls? (978-1-62639-915-0)